# CYBERSIDE: LEVEL ZERO

ALEKSEY SAVCHENKO

Edited by
MICHAEL SHILLIAM

# DISCLAIMER

Everything in this text and full book is a product of fiction, has nothing to do with real people, business entities, government services, brands, products or literally anything in the real world. Book author has both pathologic attention to small details he has been paying attention to over his career and rich imagination, so this is why this text exists at all.

# THANKS

*This is dedicated to my good friend Tim, who showed incredible patience for my late-night emails. Thank you for words of encouragement during the writing of this book.*

*To my wife, Vika, and son, Kyryl. To my best friend, Olesya, for always being there and supporting me through a couple of very rough years while Cyberside transformed from a single book idea to something much, much bigger.*

*To 26 years of her Majesty, the gaming industry, for serving as my permanent lifetime partner in crime back from the 90s up until the present day. To Mike, Michael, Artem, Roman, Masha, Jenia, Zak, Scott, Bert, Jay, Daniel, Dana, Kim, Andy, Eugene, Alice, Alex, Rob, Stan, and many others who have been walking with me on these roads. Some are still here, despite life's endless curveballs and unforeseen circumstances.*

# FOREWORD

The book you are holding is extremely personal to me. While its story portrays the lifetime of its central character, James Reynolds, it is also a metaphorical journey through my own 26 years in the game development industry.

Much like James and Steve at the beginning of the book, I started out in the late 1990s. My career has been all-encompassing and I have, at various stages, been a journo, an indie games developer, taken on bigger creative and business roles, owned a studio, and travelled to corporate America and Europe. Luckily, I have come full circle, returning to the simple joy of making great games at my desk with my friends.

This journey, spread across fourteen games that I have either released or been a part of, has been a wild roller coaster ride that continues to thunder around the track. It has provided me with loyal friends, presented me with challenges, tested and tempted me, and thrown curveballs, betrayals, and dark nights of the soul in my direction. Although often far from easy, it has always been hugely rewarding. This book is a reflection on those years. I have no doubt that many who are in the trade of creating virtual worlds will resonate with many of the characters and situations within these pages. I wanted our collective stories to filter through the lens of fiction and imagination.

I hope this book shines a light behind the facade of the industry glitz and glamor. Behind every award show is a sleepless night in front of a monitor; behind every glossy magazine feature is another boardroom meeting where creativity goes to battle with the bottom line. Level Zero is being published in 2025. For many, it has been a rough couple of years. Some of my very close friends have experienced layoffs, rejections and disappointments. Many are in the process of professional reinvention, and it is my hope that this book, as well as the original *Cyberside*, will reassure them that, no matter what happens, the tide can be turned and destinies can be rewritten. I should know because, halfway through writing this book, this exact thing happened to me.

This story has not been easy for me to write. It originated from a place of disappointment, frustration, and a need to change and rethink myself. My own journey of self-discovery progressed along with the book. Along the way, I fought off demons and left accumulated resentment behind. I came to realise that I had nothing but love to give to those surrounding me who, through unending support, made my personal redemption possible. It helped, of course, to have a badass story to tell.

My very special thanks go to my wife, Victoria, whose support knows no bounds; to my lifelong best friend, Olesya, who has a remarkable success rate for talking sense into my stubborn skull; and to Mike Shilliam, who edited this book. Without him, it wouldn't have seen the light of day.

At this moment, I am miraculously back in the development team working on *S.T.A.L.K.E.R. 2*, a game within a franchise I was engaged with two decades ago. I am surrounded by people I'm proud to call friends, and am excited to share a world cooked up in my imagination with this and future stories.

*Cyberside: Level Zero* is dedicated to the industry we all love and hate in equal measure. The industry to which I owe everything.

My infinite thanks to all of you, who surround me on my life journey and who have made me who I am today.

# PART I
# GOOD OLD DAY

# 1

# BOSTONIAN MORNING

*Wake up, you sexy lump.* Another Bostonian morning bleeds through a crack in the curtains of the unassuming suburban home. Pale winter sun works in gentle unison with the lilting female voice to rouse the mess of sprawling limbs on the couch – limbs belonging to a man caught somewhere in the blurry crossroads between asleep and awake.

"Come on, Jim. Steve's already here."

James Reynolds emits the groan of a man who doesn't yet know where he fell asleep, aside from the fact that it wasn't in his bed. He forces his eyes open and lands on the frustrating conclusion that, fuck it and then some, he's only gone and done it again.

"You know the bedroom is twenty feet away, right? We'll have made the final payment on the bed by the time you finally get around to sleeping in it."

As James transitions from one reality to the next, his wife, Sarah, already dressed in her work scrubs, does a final sweep of the living room as she fills her handbag with whatever it is she fills her handbag with. Beneath his default smile, James asks himself a familiar question. *How does she make it look so easy?* A quick scan of the coffee table: empty beer bottles – best not to count them – and a crumpled bag of chips surround his trusty laptop, smart enough to have gone to sleep and lucky enough to still be there. As James sits up, instinct kicks in as he hits the spacebar and the machine whirs to life with a screen of half-finished code. An acute awareness washes over the guilt-ridden man. *I've said hello to my computer before I've said hello to my wife.*

Puppy eyes deployed, James makes eye contact with Sarah. "This is now happening more often than it's not, isn't it?"

An empathetic chuckle and playful ruffling of her husband's hair confirms that yes, it is, and yes, all is forgiven. "Someone's got to earn the big bucks if we want our kitchen and living room to be separated by a wall one day."

"We're seriously up against it with the *Underside* Beta delivery..."

"Yep," Sarah responds, "and in a couple of weeks, that make-or-break investment deal goes through and Fall Water can finally play 'check out my manhood' with the big boys."

James squints in confusion. "Wait, what? Did I already tell..." As he trails off, Sarah gives him a quick kiss on the cheek, grabs her car keys and enters the kitchen area.

"Nope. But your friend here is feeling particularly chatty this fine morning." Sarah, hovering by the door, gestures to a twenty-something black man with his head and shoulders firmly in the couple's fridge. "Chatty and, apparently, malnourished. If you want breakfast, get off your ass before the half-man, half-racoon eats us out of house and home."

Steve Jenkins' head emerges from his favorite place with a well-honed *Who, me?* plastered on his face.

"If you hadn't got him that job, Steve, I'd have started charging you a long time ago," Sarah says.

Steve, mock-offended, throws some suspect meat down on the counter and helps himself to some bread. "It's a simple case of fridge auditing, Sarah," he protests. "If you don't want my help, so be it." The clicking of the fridge door puts an end to this variant on a very familiar routine.

"Page me when you're on your way home, Jim. Love you." Sarah blows her husband a kiss. He leaps and catches it.

"Back at you, sweetheart," he says. A quick wave from Sarah and she's out the door. James stands and sniffs his way through a bigger-than-it-should-be pile of dirty clothes in a futile attempt to find the least offensive.

"Steve, if your food auditing skills match your coding skills," James offers, "I'm guessing my fridge now resembles a warzone." Steve finishes construction on a monstrous sandwich filled with left-over fridge food that would most certainly fail a safety check.

"That's rich. Your fridge is more chaotic than your latest project architecture."

"Fuck you very much, Jenkins."

"Back at you, sweetheart."

James throws on an old Double Dragon t-shirt, confident that he'll get away with the musty smell if nobody comes *too* close to him today. Steve recoils at his friend's lack of sartorial elegance.

"Oh, Jesus. I didn't get the memo that it was retro stench day."

"Not as retro as that bacon," James mutters, glancing at Steve's sandwich. "The office restroom is going to have its work cut out about three hours from now." Unfazed, Steve takes a giant bite from his Frankensandwich and gestures to the coffee machine.

"It's 9:45, dude," James responds. "We can pop into Hermit's and grab some to go. Burrow scheduled a last-minute 10:30 meeting. I can't be late," he stresses. "He's already giving me grief for dragging my heels on Beta."

"Burrow is in the office? Well, shit! Come on then, baby boy! Put on some pants and arrange that hair into something other than... *that*. I'll start the car."

---

JAMES FINDS HIMSELF WAITING, as usual, for Steve to jump in the driver's seat and open the passenger door from the inside.

"Do we have to do this song and dance every time I get in your car, or are you gonna get this locking mechanism fixed?"

"After Beta, Jim. Everything after Beta." James adjusts his seat as Steve hits the gas and pulls out of the driveway. A few choice samples of the hits of January 1996 blast through the Volvo's tinny speakers as Steve turns the dial:

*And I miss you, like the deserts miss the rain. And I miss* – nope. Too depressing.

*I said "What about Breakfast at Tiffany's?" She said "I think I remember"* – too desperately whimsical.

*Power and the money, money and the power, minute after minute, hour after* – too gangster for this hour.

*Whatever I did, I didn't mean it. I just want you back for good* – Christ, no. Steve spins the dial in frustration. His eyes light up as Alanis Morissette's dulcet tones fill the vehicle.

*And what it all comes down to, is that everything's gonna be fine, fine, fine. 'Cause I've got one hand in my pocket...*

"Yes! This is more like it! *And the other one is givin' a high five,*" Steve wails. He holds his hand up to James, who simply stares at it.

"I didn't have you pegged as a fan," James deadpans.

"She spits the truth, Jim. What can I say?" James braces as Steve pulls onto the I-95 and joins the swarm of other cars heading towards downtown Boston.

"I wonder if today's the day this menace wagon becomes my coffin."

"Every time you ask yourself that," Steve responds, "remind yourself that Volvos are, statistically, one of the safest cars on the planet."

"I'm not talking about the car, Steve. I'm talking about the driver."

"Come at me when you learn to drive," Steve says, eyebrows raised. James smiles, content that his best friend has won this battle.

"Does Tina from the art department know you like Alanis Morissette?"

Steve throws James a knowing look. "I don't know. It didn't come up last night." The statement just hangs there. Steve takes it upon himself to fill the stunned silence. "We went to the movies. Thanks for asking."

"Yeah? What did you see?"

"She wanted to check out *Toy Story*, but I dragged her to *From Dusk Till Dawn*."

"Bold move, hombre."

"Oh, she hated it," Steve exclaims. "We won't be seeing each other again outside work."

James gestures to a towering billboard advertising *Independence Day. In theaters July 3.* "I guess it'll be me going with you to see the movie event of the summer, in that case?"

"Six months from now?" Steve responds. "Sure thing. Beta should be locked by then. Everything after Beta, Jimbo."

"Everything after Beta, Steve-o."

James exploits the natural lull in conversation to indulge in a recent daily habit. He absentmindedly picks up the latest copy of *Edge* magazine that Steve has lying around on the dash. Although he has already read this particular edition a few times, as indicated by its numerous dog-eared glossy pages, it gives James a thrill to see a hearty profile on the company he works for within the sacred pages of the UK's coolest gaming mag. In between Steve concocting various reasons why Tina from the art department isn't future wife material – preferring sweet over salted popcorn and sullying the previews with inane chat being just two examples – James scans a best-of-the-year list. *Quake, Mario Kart 64* and *Command and Conquer: Red Alert* all feature. *Tomb Raider* and *Crash Bandicoot* are cited as key titles that will usher in the exponential growth of the console market as the world hurtles towards the millennium.

James flicks through to the magazine's profile on Fall Water Lake and a reassuring feeling washes over him. The endless late nights, the relentless number-crunching, the winging it with the vague hope it'll all work out in the end… *this is what it's all for.* It only feels like yesterday that he and Steve were two nerds at Boston University College of Engineering, stumbling blind and horny through the world of academia. This article confirms that these avid gamers and C++ engineers are both now well on the journey into the world of interactive entertainment. The fact they made it into Fall Water Lake is a miracle in itself; Steve managed to scrape an internship after graduation when the company consisted of a few like-minded boffins in a rented space above a Chinese restaurant. It wasn't long before his unbridled enthusiasm landed him a permanent gig and he pulled James along for the ride.

The *Edge* article charted the company's rise under the leadership of Boston native John Burrow, CEO, and his best friend, New Yorker Tom Simmons, CTO. Their first title, *Otherscape,* an adventure game on which James served as a junior engineer, proved moderately successful after a slow start, finding its true audience with the launch of the game on PlayStation. Second out the gate was *Distant Shores*, which cemented the company's reputation as an ambitious player in an already crowded market. The game seduced players with its multiple explorable realms, intricate narrative and immersive graphics, utilizing the *Underside* engine that Burrow conceived in college and developed with Simmons over a number of years.

James flicks the page and reads on as the profile details a key moment in the company's history. Last year, Fall Water received a hefty investment injection from the Versa Foundation, an international consortium with numerous fingers in various pies. Versa was drawn in by Burrow's and Simmons' grand plans and was smart enough to know that the *Underside* engine could serve as the secret weapon that could send the company into the stratosphere. Although the partnership is still fairly new and the company has grown to a modest hundred employees, James' Spidey-sense is telling him that things are now changing significantly. He and Steve have been burning the midnight oil on *Otherscape 2*, a project that isn't merely a follow-up to a mildly successful adventure title. The scope of this one is immense. Although delays are common and release dates keep getting pushed, Jim knows he's working on a classic in the making. He and Steve are now senior engineers, with the Beta delivery date hurtling towards them. Although the Versa money was significant, it isn't a permanent deal. Future investment depends on the success of Beta; investment that will provide the necessary resources to secure Fall Water's seat at the table for the long term.

The magazine falls from James' hands into the footwell as the weight of the mammoth task at hand rears its ugly head once again. His mind drifts onto the pressures of code modifications, implemented features, console-porting struggles...

"Dude." Steve glances at his friend, who stares aimlessly out of the window.

"I say, James, my dear fellow." He lowers the radio's volume, hoping this will snap James from his daydream. It doesn't.

"DUDE!" That one does it. James snaps out of it and looks over. "What the hell? Every morning this week, you've been staring out of the window like one of George A. Romero's walking dead. How does Sarah tolerate that crap?"

"Sorry." James tries desperately to claw himself back to the present. "Lack of sleep, I guess. You sound just like her, you know."

"Yeah? No shit! Are you even in the vague region of knowing what the hell I've been talking about for the last ten minutes?"

James considers. Then he considers some more. "Tina from the art department?"

"Old news, bro!' Steve exclaims, slamming his hand on the steering wheel in frustration. "I've been babbling incoherently about the new CEO they're bringing in. Some corporate money guy. One of Versa's stooges."

James absorbs this before growing conscious that he isn't actually saying anything. "What do you mean, new CEO? Where does that leave John?"

"Word on the grapevine is that Burrow wants to channel his energy into coding and product, rather than day-to-day management."

"Word on the grapevine? Who, specifically?"

"Tina from the art department," Steve answers sheepishly. "Oh, look. We're here." Steve pulls a sharp right, managing to secure a parking spot right outside Hermit's Den.

---

THE COFFEE SPOT by day and trendy bar by night has become the location of choice for Fall Water Lake employees to decompress over the years. As the world and its evolving tech changes around it, Hermit's offers a reassuring permanency to those who frequent it. The 1950s jukebox and pictures of movie stars of old feed an aura that regulars affectionately describe as nostalgic and critics label as outdated. The proprietor, Josh, is the type of guy who looks like he was born in the establishment he runs, as if he was coded into the very fabric of the place. So much so that, when the dinging of the bell on the door announces James' and Steve's arrival, part of the wall appears to move and an aging hippy emerges.

"I swear he's *becoming* the building," Steve mutters to James. Steve holds up two fingers to signal two coffees. Josh holds up two fingers in return, intentionally missing the point.

"Peace and love, fellas. Peace and love."

"Two coffees please, Josh," James says. "To go."

Josh just stands there, eyes wide. "I might be a tree hugger, but that doesn't mean I'm a pushover. You still owe me for last week."

"I thought we had a tab?" James retaliates.

"There's only one kind of tab I'm interested in, Reynolds," Josh laughs. "And it ain't the one you're talking about." He gets busy preparing the guys' caffeine injection.

Steve can't help but chip in. "You know we're good for it, old timer. We'll settle up after Beta. Everything—"

"Everything after Beta. Got it."

Steve nods in gratitude. "If you want to be paid now, get this tight bastard to talk the suits into giving us a raise." Steve slaps James on the back to accentuate his point. Coffees are poured, fists are bumped, the engineers exit and Josh morphs back into the fixtures and fittings.

---

THE SHINY NEW office building housing Fall Water Lake is located a mere two blocks from Hermit's. A structure with windows this reflective is obliged to play host to a number of emerging tech companies, and that it does, with Fall Water encompassing two floors midway up the building. Down in the lobby, two sleep-deprived engineers with lukewarm coffees in paper cups stroll across the sizable hall.

"Well, well. Are those two of Fall Water's code warriors I see before me?" The welcome from the redhead at the front desk echoes across the lobby with such good nature that it's impossible for James and Steve to resist. They scurry over as Steve's face goes a brighter shade of crimson than the receptionist's hair.

"Are you blushing?" James asks. "It's times like this I bet you're grateful you're black."

"It has its advantages," Steve responds. "Rachel, my darling!"

Despite Steve burying his embarrassment and switching on the charm, his mind rushes back to a party at Hermit's last Friday with a highlight reel of various choice images. Downing shots, speaking to the band, cornering James, a line or two in a bathroom stall and ending up on stage, Rachel down in front, unashamedly serenading the bar with a rendition of a self-penned metal song the pair wrote in college. Despite trying to relegate the memory into a deep, dark cavernous recess of his brain, Rachel isn't letting him off that easily.

*"Aaaaand, we shall prevail, two against the world, code warriors of doom, knights of the keyboard..."* Rachel signs off with a pair of devil horns, a couple of enthusiastic head bangs and a sly wink. "Morning, boys."

"I barely recognized you last week, Rachel," James says. A backing soundtrack is provided by the angry beeps of Steve trying and failing to pass through the security gate. "We're not used to seeing you out from behind this desk."

"They do release me every now and again," Rachel replies.

"As for my brother in metal," James says, motioning to Steve, "cut him some slack. I don't want him distracting me all day with 'How bad was it, dude?' and 'Do you think she's actually into me?'" Rachel and the other receptionists are operating on a finely tuned frequency that is aimed squarely at making Steve squirm. They all chuckle knowingly.

"Well, maybe I am. Just a little bit," Rachel says. Steve manically presses his staff pass against the card reader, which also seems to be in on the joke. The gate finally opens and he power walks as fast as he can to the elevator, shouting behind him as he goes.

"This heroic knight needs to get to work."

Steve exits the elevator to the open-plan office housing the Dev force, or 'the Pit' as it's more affectionately known, on the 16th floor. James rides up one floor further, the door dings, and he adopts his game face, entering what has truly become a second home over the last three years. Up on 17, in sharp contrast to the Pit, corner offices accommodate John Burrow and Tom Simmons, along with the Chief Marketing Officer, Virginia Willis, and the Head of Research and Development, Hank Brown. James casually strolls past a wall of concept art and posters for Fall Water's previous titles, the sole purpose of which is to charm the press on their increasingly common publicity visits, and enters the boardroom.

With John already standing at the head of the table and a number of execs seated, James offers an apologetic nod to his CEO and takes a seat.

"Ah, Jim. Nice of you to join us. Let's make a start."

Burrow's jovial tone allows James to steal a 'whoops' look with Hank, which is returned with a friendly eye-roll. As John starts the meeting, James observes his boss and finds himself envying the man's easygoing charm. Despite his age, Burrow has a contagious energy that has often infiltrated James' soul and convinced him that, yes, it is a good idea to pull three all-nighters in a row. Burrow is the very definition of leading by example and has garnered the unyielding loyalty of everyone in this boardroom. Fall Water's fearless leader is a man of overwhelming intellect and humility; two traits that are rarely found pulsating through the same person. While many, including *Edge* magazine, call Burrow a genius – which he detests – James knows he is a man who is consistently three steps ahead of everyone else in the room, creating and fulfilling his own elusive narrative rather than waiting for one to present itself. Does that make him a genius? Perhaps. So unique and outside the norm is John's way of thinking that it's a miracle anyone follows him into battle. And yet, they do. Such is the strength of the man.

Of course, naysayers are never far away and, to many, Burrow's decisions and ambitions appear deranged, unpredictable and far from achievable. Certain critics would claim that his outlook is closer to that of an idealistic teenager than of a man pushing fifty. John often conducts personal research projects on his own time, independent of Fall Water, although nobody knows what crazy schemes he is embarking on. Behind closed doors, the big man is often riddled with self-doubt and an unshakeable melancholy, but there's not a chance anyone in this building, save for Tom Simmons, has ever been privy to this aspect of his personality. After John's wife, Samantha, died while giving birth to their daughter, Alice, he took some time off to allow himself some much-needed introspection. To everyone's surprise, he returned to work with a new zeal, eyes burning brighter than ever before, determined to make a true mark on the world.

It's no secret that John and Tom have been experiencing some teething issues with Versa Foundation's investment committee. For the first time, it seems like an external party is forcing their hand to accelerate the release of *Otherscape 2*. Even so, the chronic anxiety and dark nights of the soul are not evident here in this room. John leads the meeting with a lightness of touch, refusing to burden his staff with his own struggles.

"We're a touch behind schedule, ladies and gents, but that's the nature of the beast. It's done when it's done; I'll handle any outside pressures. You have my full trust in what you're doing. The game is a stunning representation of your collective hearts and minds. I'm blown away by what I've seen so far." Burrow's brow furrows ever so subtly. "But I haven't called this meeting to talk development," he says. "I need to address the future of the company as it stands now. The future is vast, far beyond one, two, or even ten games."

James, always keen to get Hank Brown's take, observes the Head of R&D closely. He often finds himself in Hank's lair, knocking around various hypotheses for rendering and toolsets. After dropping out of MIT, the techie wizard became Fall Water's third employee and his role in the development of the *Underside* engine could not be overestimated. Brown is the third cog in Burrow's and Simmons' genius, converting abstract concepts into hard reality. He heads up a small army of R&D folk, completely separated from the development of the game, and he likes it that way, thank you very much. Hit a crossroads and require a solution? *Talk to Hank Brown*. Need a bespoke, ground-up tool created for the engine? *Where's Hank?* Spent two months exploring an unviable option and need to ensure all that hard work gets channeled into something usable? *Somebody, please, go and get Hank!* This avid chess player gets his kicks experimenting between hardware and software and looks like he's allergic to sleep. Search anywhere on Earth for somebody like Hank Brown, and you'll come back empty handed. James stares at this cypher of a man and, true to form, his friend gives nothing away.

"The future," continues John, "lies in *Underside*. We've developed these tools to be utilized in-house, but what if we can offer it to the world, to other incredible hearts and minds, like us? *Otherscape 2* offers seventeen different realms, but in years to come it could be thousands, all connected together."

James considers. While Burrow talks a good talk, nothing he's said so far could be classed as an exclusive. Conversations about creating an engine for commercial licensing have been bouncing back and forth between John and Tom for months. James' eyes drift to Tom Simmons. Burrow's closest ally and longtime friend stands to John's side, offering unspoken support with his mere presence. Nothing is decided relating to the company's operations without these two discussing every possibility and outcome. Legend has it that the pair met at a convention in New York back in the eighties. Although both were engineers, it was John's creativity and Tom's commercial expertise and market awareness, alongside his deep-pocketed upstate New York legacy connections, that allowed the company to scale at pace in the early years. Simmons is the John Oates to Burrow's Daryl Hall, Art Garfunkel to his Paul Simon, Katherine Hepburn to his Spencer Tracey. These two were destined to find each other and create magic. If one is lacking in a certain area, the other picks up the slack. Where John's blindspots are complex schematic building and cybernetics, lo and behold, these are Tom's strengths. Where Tom is risk averse and creatively conservative, John is a natural risk taker and creative outlier. Put simply, they are a force to be reckoned with. And now, as John speaks with a looseness that suggests his speech is off the cuff, Tom nods along, pre-empting key points in a manner that reveals the duo has perfected this spiel to within an inch of its life.

"So, what does this all mean?" John asks. "Put bluntly, the company will be changing." Tom nods along, right on cue. "As you're all aware, we're in discussion with Versa to bring them on board as a permanent investor. This requires some restructuring. Historically, we have relied on external publishers for marketing, publicity and distribution. Future ambitions make this model unsustainable. This is why we welcomed Virginia last year to build an in-house marketing department to usher in complete independence."

James' eyes now fix on Virginia Willis, who offers a small, humble nod to the room. James knows there's nothing truly humble about it, however. Virginia views modesty as a character glitch. A legend in the marketing world, she was one of the first to create successful promotional tools straddling games, tech, and movie and music licensing. As a woman in a man's world, assertiveness is a prerequisite, and that's something she has in abundance. It's common knowledge that she spent months negotiating her job offer with Fall Water Lake and that she took a significantly lower salary when jumping ship from Electronic Arts. She instead agreed to a healthy option plan that, if John's and Tom's long-term vision bears fruit, will see her emerge with a staggering financial payout. James can't help but admire her foresight. True, she's an animal, but she brings with her a wealth of connections, high energy and an unmatched work ethic. If she succeeds in doing her part, she deserves everything that's coming her way.

"My full attention is required on project delivery," John continues. "I need to devote myself completely to that side of the business. This means that Fall Water will be hiring a new Chief Exec to substitute some of my functions. I've heard whispers of this in the canteen, and I confirm that this one particular rumor is true."

For many, this declaration is not a surprise, as indicated by the ocean of neutral faces dotted around the room. James, on the other hand, is clearly taken aback. He's been so fundamentally focused on his work, often choosing to eat lunch at his desk rather than mingle with colleagues in the canteen, that this particular rumor completely slipped him by. Until this morning, of course, when Steve mentioned it on the commute. James tries to envision someone other than John holding that much executive power within the company and comes to the conclusion that, whoever it is, they're going to have big shoes to fill. James quickly buries his shock, lest he appear to be so behind the curve that he'll never catch up with it. With the big news out of the way, Tom steps forward.

"I'd like to echo that John and I will be concentrating solely on *Underside*. Ambitions demand that the engine needs to be ready for external use as soon as possible. Hank will be assisting John and me, as well as Jim here..." With the focus now unexpectedly on James, he sits up straight. "...who we are promoting to Head of Development for *Otherscape 2*. A big task, Jimmy, but we know you're more than capable."

James nods and tries to play it cool. He'll have time to absorb this bombshell later.

"You'll close Beta," Tom continues, "and have the full support of Virginia's team to take it to market. Virginia will be working closely with our new CEO, Donovan Craze. Mr Craze will assist in strengthening our operational force, support services and new company structure. Any questions?"

The only question on James' mind is *His name isn't really Donovan Craze, is it?* Still, he manages to string something approaching a sentence together.

"Well, I'm honored and we will deliver as expected. On the delay, we should be back on schedule in a few weeks. We have some minor PlayStation issues with TRC, but this is manage—"

"Sorry, Jim," Hank interjects. "Congrats, and all that. But who's this new guy, Tom? Donovan who?"

"Craze," Tom answers, ready for the question. "I'll go into more detail at the all-hands meeting, but I've known Donovan for quite some time. He's a seasoned exec, perfectly suited to diligently sustain and expand a wider organization. He'll be the face for us on all things investment."

"All control will remain with me," John reassures the room. "Donovan will essentially be a technical figure. If there was nothing else?" Everyone knows that when John asks if there's nothing else, he is in fact declaring that there is nothing else. John makes a beeline for the exit, such is his habit, without a thank you or goodbye. As James stands, Hank's hand lands on his shoulder.

"Big news, Mr Head of Development."

"Thanks, Hank. Bit of a shock," James replies.

"To nobody other than you. Well-earned, buddy. Hope this new status won't affect our after-work chess games?"

"Don't utter such heresy," James smiles. "Nothing ever will. Unless I wake up one day exhausted by the humiliation of you winning week after week. See you this evening." Hank zips off ahead of James to fix the latest unfixable fuck-up.

James hangs back in the boardroom, letting everyone leave, and shoots off a message to Sarah on his pager to drop the big news. It's only in doing so that he comes to appreciate the momentousness of the occasion and pride starts pumping through his veins. Sarah has been his biggest champion since the beginning, when they met in college. There's nobody on earth he'd rather share the news with. True to form, an overwhelmingly supportive message pings back, declaring that they will be celebrating this evening in Di Argento, their favorite restaurant, no excuses.

---

"HOLY SHIT, GOOD BUDDY!" screams Steve. Despite James' suspicion that this would be Steve's reaction, he recoils when his friend leaps on his desk and starts belting out a rendition of *Two Against the World*. Faces pop up from behind monitors as James buries his head in his hands.

"Please, Steve. Stop."

Steve jumps off the desk, throws his arms around James and leans into his ear.

"One of us is both of us."

The Dev team clocks on and cheers at James' appointment, amplifying Steve's sentiment. It's always a thrill when one of their own takes a step up the corporate ladder. Despite some healthy competition, the culture within Fall Water Lake is supportive and encouraging. There's a collective sigh of relief at the fact that James is the man who is going to be leading them to deliver the impossible.

The news has an immediate positive effect as the Pit is infused with fresh motivation. The rest of the day is extremely productive, aside from Steve, whose giddiness starts getting tired around midday.

The news is officially circulated to the rest of the company at the all-hands, up on 17. James struggles to focus having already heard the news firsthand and, by this point, the anxiety over the new role has begun to creep in. He can't shake the feeling of deep change that lies ahead. Despite reassurances from John and Tom, James suspects that a major shift is afoot. The good old days may well be over.

A clicking of fingers in James' ear sends the intrusive thoughts scurrying away, at least for the time being. It will fall to Sarah to talk him off this ledge later.

"And you're back in the room," Hank jokes. "Can you hear that?" James listens to nothing in particular. "That's a bottle of Scotch calling our name. Lots to discuss. Let's get up to the lair. I'll even let you play white."

James scoffs as he enters Hank's office. This man never ceases to surprise him. The crowded space grows increasingly stuffed with strange artifacts every time James sets foot here. Hardware devices, old-school consoles and philosophy books angling for space on a bookshelf that may well soon buckle under their weight make this space an Aladdin's cave of wonder.

"I wouldn't be surprised if there's a lamp containing a genie buried in here somewhere," James says, picking up a circuit board and blowing off some dust.

"Not like you need it, Head of Dev. All of your dreams appear to be coming true."

"Careful what you wish for," James retorts, as Hank finds two clean-enough glasses and pours them both some Scotch.

"Good stuff," Hank boasts. "Single malt, twelve years. Not exactly premium, but it should satisfy us two neanderthals."

James sets up the chess board and makes the first move. Hank stares at his colleague.

"So. Penny for your thoughts?"

"The focus on *Underside* is encouraging. Good to see the company stepping up," James replies.

"If I wanted some surface-level regurgitation of this morning's meeting, I would have wheeled in Jeremy from legal. Don't bullshit me. What do you really think?"

James should have known he couldn't palm off Hank with something so trite. He shrugs. "Well, it's all moving too quickly, is what I think." Hank offers a nod of encouragement. *That's better. Go on.* "There's stepping up and there's stepping up. I joined this place because it was a nerd-convention full of like-minded, mouth-breathing basement dwellers who wanted to make a cool game. Nothing more. These investment rounds and future projections are out of my comfort zone. As for the promotion, it's nice they have faith in me. I'm just not sure I do."

The head of R&D pushes his black rook across the chessboard. "That's why they picked you, numbnuts. Humility will get you everywhere. Your passion lies in development, not corporate BS. They need someone with your creative passion leading that team of reprobates."

"Yeah..." James mumbles. "Maybe."

"As for the corporate growth aspect, I'm inclined to agree," Hank says. "This place is going to fill up with a lot of new faces, all wearing... *suits*." Hank shudders to emphasize his point. "Not from our world. I hope it doesn't cause too much friction."

"Burrow knows what he's doing," James offers. "In John we trust. You think people will want to adopt *Underside* instead of creating their own engine?"

"I've been around the block," Hank answers. "If experience has taught me anything, it's human nature to opt for the path of least resistance. Obviously, there are some exceptions to the rule." Hank gestures to himself, then James. "But, generally, if it means other developers can get their products on shelves quicker and with less effort... of course they will."

"Kind of against Fall Water's philosophy, don't you think?" James asks.

"I guess," Hank replies. "But we're setting ourselves up for the long term. Think of the focus we can devote to future titles with that money in the bank. The sky's the limit."

"The sky's the limit," James repeats. "That's my concern. Call me small-minded, but I like the sky where I can see it." James' eyes burn a hole in the chessboard as he contemplates his next move. He plays his knight forward, threatening Hank's queen. "Are you trying to distract me from the game with this line of questioning? You sly fox!"

"But of course!" Hank says, grabbing the bottle to refill James' drink. James holds his hand over his glass.

"No, you don't. Sarah and I are getting dinner later. Won't look too good if I stumble in stinking of whiskey."

"How'd she take the news?" Hank asks.

"Over the moon," James responds. "It hasn't dawned on her that I may become even more of a stranger in my own home."

"She'll understand," reassures Hank. "She's a diamond. She's stuck by your side this long, right?" James takes out one of Hank's pieces with his rook; Hank immediately takes it with his knight. "It'll be fine, Jim. John and Tom haven't miscalculated once. I've got a couple of things for the Dev team that'll make your job easier too."

"Oh, really? Such as?"

"We've substantially improved the material editor. That'll be with you mid-week. And I know your boys are fighting a battle with some of the cutscenes, so we've created a simplified editor for that. Better camera placement options, dialogue editor... trust me, it's smoother than this Scotch." James smiles. Hank always delivers exactly when he needs him to. He moves a pawn.

"You're a lifesaver, Hank. Thanks."

"No problem. I'm afraid it doesn't put your king in a very advantageous position, though." Hank moves his queen across the board, taking away James' pawn and checkmating him. James stares at the board, unsure how this just happened.

"Dammit, Hank! Seriously?"

Hank finishes his Scotch with one gulp. "Concentrate on what's important, Jim. Delegate to your team. That'll clear out some time to spend with Sarah. Deliver *Otherscape* and let everyone else worry about everything else. Bring your team donuts and coffee twice a week to keep them sweet and they'll take a bullet for you. Take my word on that."

"Have you done any digging on Donovan?" James asks, standing up to leave.

"I've asked around. Typical New Yorker, purely business-minded. Probably never played a game in his life. He can do what he likes so long as he doesn't poke his nose into my team." James nods. Fair enough. He heads to the door.

"Thanks Hank. I needed that." He gestures to the chessboard. "I'll beat you one day."

"Ha!" Hank stifles his laughter. "In another lifetime, maybe."

James runs across the lobby, out of the building and into Sarah's waiting car. One look at her and the stress of the day melts away to nothing.

"How many whiskies?" asks Sarah.

"Just the one."

"You should have had two."

---

WHILE JAMES and Sarah cut loose and indulge in some well-earned quality time, another meeting takes place at John Burrow's residence in Southborough. The only sound on this quiet evening is the chirping cicadas and the calm yet faltering voice of the soon-to-be former CEO of Fall Water Lake.

"We didn't really have a choice, did we, Tom?"

John and Tom sit out on the patio, dimly lit by the moon's reflection off the lake that gave Fall Water its name. The men are wrapped up warm. Of course, they could go inside, but this is where they get their best thinking done. After-work debriefs out here have become something of a regular occurrence over the past few years. There's no way this bitterly cold winter evening is going to stop their long-held tradition of shooting the shit. Tom notes a hint of regret in John's voice.

"No, John. We didn't." The squeak of the patio door is followed by gentle thud of feet on timber beams.

"Dad..." Seven-year-old Alice emerges, dressed in her pajamas.

"Now why on earth would you come out here on such a cold night, pumpkin?" John asks. He lifts his daughter and sits her on his lap.

"But you're out here, aren't you?" Alice responds.

"Your dad and I are old, sweetie," Tom says. "Our handy layer of body fat keeps us nice and toasty." To emphasize Tom's point, John wobbles his belly.

"It's past your bedtime, missy."

"I can't sleep."

"Ah. The old monsters under the bed routine?"

Alice theatrically rolls her eyes. "I'm seven, dad. I know there are no monsters, I know there's no Santa, no Easter Bunny. I was just thinking... when we sleep, are our dreams as real as us sitting here? Or is this the dream? How could we prove which is which?"

John looks at his daughter quizzically. "How old did you say you are? Seven?"

"She's her father's daughter, that's for sure," Tom quips.

John strokes his daughter's hair as her eyelids grow heavy. "There's more of her mother in her than me. Sam was the one with the vivid imagination."

"It's not the imagination I'm getting at," Tom says. "It's that beautifully inquisitive mind."

"Either way," John says, standing up and carrying his now-sleeping daughter into the house, "it's time to get this curious angel tucked in."

When John returns, the brief glimpse of the carefree, doting father that was present around Alice has been replaced by a stern pragmatism. He and Tom pick up where they left off without missing a beat.

"It's not the strategic dilemma you think it is, John," says Tom. "It's a simple choice, and the right one. A choice favorable to our plans. We need to get into bed permanently with Versa. No more flings. We've already burned through the budget for *Otherscape*. Expansion requires resources. We either use ours, or someone else's."

"We could have waited for the game launch, recouped, regrouped, realigned and moved forward," John argues.

"It wouldn't have been enough. You saw the projections. We either rethink our goals or bring on a partner. Competition is ramping up across the sector. We're still a minor player here. Versa will open every imaginable door."

John nods along, but he's still not fully sold.

"John. It's done. You pushed the button on this one. They're at the table, pal. Donovan's already pre-ordered the Japanese-inspired watercolors for his office. We either make the leap with *Underside* or pack up and go home."

"It's not a leap," John says. "Merely a step towards our long-term goals." He sounds like he's trying to convince himself. Tom takes out a joint and lights it. He takes a toke, studying his friend with concern.

"This isn't like you. I've never known you to get cold feet, especially after you've pulled the trigger on something." Tom offers the joint to John, who politely declines. "Versa has been a trusted partner for some time now," he continues. "We couldn't do any more diligence if we tried."

"And Donovan..." mutters John.

"Donovan's solid. A high-level accountant and pencil pusher. He'll keep things ticking over so you don't have to sweat the small stuff. Versa, Donovan... they're just a checkbook. A big, fat, blank checkbook. It's capitalism in its purest form. We shift the product, return the investment, fatten their wallets, keep their shareholders happy four times a year. Mission accomplished. I'm on top of that."

"I don't doubt it, Tom."

"And with Jim heading up the Dev army, we're onto a winner."

For the first time in the conversation, John appears to relax. He gestures for the joint and takes a full, relaxed toke.

"Jim's a good kid. It's a great appointment. Hopefully he realizes that himself sooner rather than later and gets his shit together."

"Give him a week and he'll be off and running," reassures Tom. "Plus, he and Hank get on like a house on fire. Nobody gets as close to Hank as Jim has. They'll pull this off."

A taxi pulls to a stop on the driveway. Tom stands and stretches.

Time to call it a night, but not before he offers John one last word of encouragement.

"Remember, we don't make mistakes. Not when we're making the calls together. Onwards, Johnny."

The men share a firm handshake before Tom jogs down the steps and into the waiting vehicle. John watches as the tail lights disappear into the darkness. Head clear, he sighs a long sigh.

"Onwards."

## 2

## CODE FLOWS

*Need you, dream you*
*Find you, taste you*
*Use you, scar you*
*Fuck you, break you*

Nine Inch Nails' *The Downward Spiral* pumps through James' headphones. The album may be a couple of years old now, but it remains his go-to choice when coding. If you need to be in the zone, accept no substitutes. Well, perhaps some substitutes. Depending on mood, the Smashing Pumpkins can deliver and DJ Shadow's *Endtroducing* certainly has its place in the unfortunate event of a creative roadblock. When a deadline is breathing down your neck and ten hours of cold, hard work lie ahead, however, you can always rely on Trent Reznor to provide that extra little push. And caffeine. Lots of caffeine.

This particular CD has been whipped out so often that it's now scratched to shit and occasionally skips in James' trusty Discman. Part of his subconscious tries to tell him that perhaps it's time to invest in a new CD, but the thought barely registers. Nothing external really does. Not when he's doing his thing.

As the thumping symphony of *Eraser* pounds in his ears, James' mind focuses on its own symphony of symbols. In this moment, there is no time, no space. Only lines, code, classes, headers and comments. Fluidity between body and brain is seamlessly working in synergy with a meticulous knowledge of the project's entire architecture, of what was built in the past and what will be built in the future. James has heard athletes, musicians and artists describe this 'flow state', in which the subject is so entirely focused on a specific process that nothing else matters. The creative momentum is effortless. Although the senses are heightened, they respond only to the matter at hand. Minutes or hours could have passed since James started; he couldn't tell you. It's better than any high he's ever experienced. The world of the System is one of interdependency, of connection; a perfect multimodality of worlds, function, images and soundscapes. His entire persona hovers over an infinite digital landscape that weaves a complex tapestry of characters, stories, choices and fates. In this flow state, the line between the real world and fantasy is close to nonexistent. When everything is defined by layer upon layer of simulation emerging from your fingertips, when hundreds of hypotheses, attempts, errors and successes exist simultaneously, when one man is in the process of creating something from nothing, the very concept of reality itself gets flipped on its head. If magic exists, this is it. In this space, James is a god. Anybody who interrupts him better have a good fucking reason.

"Hey, bud. Sorry to distract you."

James blinks, shifts his focus from his monitor and returns to the moment, whatever that moment may be. He finds Steve standing patiently next to his workstation. As a fellow coder, Steve knows the drill, and the apologetic tone of his voice speaks to the fact he fully comprehends the weight of this intrusion. James takes a moment to readjust and forces a smile.

"Don't sweat it. I've made a few comments here and there. Who's on the class replication? Bert?"

"Him and Peter. Why, what's up?"

"We can still optimize on the network aspect. The QA report arrived yesterday," James says. His rat-a-tat speech pattern suggests he's still semi-plugged into the flow state. "We need to ensure we don't drop the ball on multiplayer; it's still lagging."

Steve smiles at his friend and boss. "And... breathe."

James chuckles and stretches. The clicking of his joints suggests that he's been slouched in his chair for hours.

"I'll make sure Bert and Pete are aware. Anything else?" Steve asks.

"Nothing major. I just did a couple of fixes around the portal's loading time. Still unsure if we should have mounts at the launch."

"Animation issues?" Steve asks, painfully aware that clipping has been causing monumental headaches.

"Yeah," James answers. "Clipping on the motion capture material. Time isn't our friend with sorting this out with the contractor. We can't risk further delays."

"So what do we do?" Not for the first time in recent weeks, Steve is relying fully on James to make a call.

"I'm meeting Hank later. His guys might have an improvised solution. If not, I'll move it to the first patch."

Steve grimaces.

"What?" James interrogates. Steve shrugs.

"Spit it out, Steve," James insists.

"You sure about this, boss? It's a big feature."

"How many times have I told you not to call me boss, Steve?"

"You sure about this, my liege?"

James contemplates. In the initial period following his promotion, he found himself laboring over every decision. Now, he's learned to trust his instincts and, frankly, he simply doesn't have the time to carefully consider every viable avenue. Needs must.

"The expectations on this project are immeasurable. I simply won't compromise on quality."

"Then neither will we," Steve reassures.

James stands and starts pacing, shaking off the intensity of the past few hours.

"Speaking of expectations," Steve says, "Willis is talking to *Edge* magazine as we speak. Exclusive scoop."

James groans. "How much is she overhyping it?"

"Well..." Steve chuckles. "Put it this way. When the magazines are shipped, I've threatened Rachel not to let you see them under pain of death."

"Fucking press," James mutters. Steve gives him a playful slap on the shoulder.

"The hype machine is their bread and butter. Remember how we used to scour those mags back in college, shitting our britches in anticipation? That's just how it works."

"It's not just the press," James responds. "Virginia is turning this thing into a monster. They've licensed Jesper Kyd, for God's sake. Talks have started with New Line over an *Otherscape* movie adaptation."

"And this is bad news?" Steve exclaims. "It's just that. Talk. LA people are all bark, no bite. You need to switch off for a couple of hours. You can't keep eating at your desk. Lunch in the new canteen?"

James' eyes find the nearest clock.

*Christ. Lunchtime already.*

"Sure. Where is it now? On 15?"

"Fall Water gained a whole new floor and you haven't even visited it yet?" Steve asks, bewildered. He grabs James and pulls him away from his station and through the Pit, which has grown substantially over the past two months. James nods at a few faces, some recognizable and some unfamiliar.

"I don't even know who some of these people are," James remarks.

"You don't need to. You're the boss. Just call them grunt and tell them what to do."

James nods, returning to his normal self. "Will do. Thanks for the pep talk, grunt."

---

"You gained a whole new floor? Wow. I just soiled my knickers."

The voice on the other end of Virginia Willis' phone line is clearly British. The accent isn't the only giveaway; the staggering amount of sarcasm that pulses through every syllable could only come from a limey.

"Did I stutter, Barry?" Virginia asks, playing along.

Fall Water's Head of Marketing sits at her desk in her vast office with her phone receiver wedged between her shoulder and neck. This version of hands-free allows her to both simultaneously clear out her inbox and conduct the interview with Barry Cromer, *Edge* magazine's features editor over in the UK. She could have delegated this interview to an underling, but Barry wouldn't have been too happy about that. For a feature this big, it's better that the relevant company updates come straight from Virginia. Considering she can do this kind of thing in her sleep, she might as well fire off a few emails whilst she's at it. She opens a message from New Line Cinema containing a laughable offer for the *Otherside* movie option.

REPLY.

*Come on, Chuck. You're going to have to do better than that.*

SEND. Whoosh.

"Surely you've got something juicier for me than a new canteen and CEO, Virginia?"

"If you'll let me finish, Barry. Floor 15 was added recently and speaks to the faith Versa Foundation has bestowed on us. Since they approved the strategy for our engine, the cash is flowing in. You can quote me directly on that one."

"*Underside?*" Barry asks. "Your engine is *Underside*, right?"

"That's right. Good boy, you have been listening. Investment is being funneled into new amenities for the growing workforce and new hires, largely HR, development and legal. Donovan's overseeing that side of things. Our headcount now stands at over 200. Fall Water Lake will soon boast its own motion capture studio, along with – you might want to write this down – a staff bar."

"A bar?" Barry repeats.

"I thought you'd like that."

"Any time to develop any new titles in between chugging piss-poor local beer?"

"Of course." Virginia smiles, embracing the silence and enjoying the chase.

"Such as..."

"Let's schedule a call for six months from now. Off the record, it's going to be groundbreaking. We're gearing up for a fully online experience," Virginia says.

"Shit."

"Shit indeed, Barry. That's just a little tease for you."

Virginia's fingers slide over a dictaphone on her desk. Being misquoted grew tired a long time ago and she likes to record her side of these conversations for protection, should anything leak.

"If I see that in print, I'll have your tiny balls on a platter," she adds.

"Yeah, yeah. Off the record. Of course."

"In return," Virginia says, "anything you can offer on movements from competitors would be greatly received. Off the record, naturally."

"I'll put something together and send you an email," Barry offers, without hesitation. "If I can take you back to *Underside* for a moment..."

"You just don't give up, do you?" Virginia chuckles.

"You mentioned plans. What plans? You're taking it to market?"

Virginia carefully considers. She'd love to announce it here and now and claim the glory. You don't get this high up the ladder by failing to exploit opportunities to break major developments. However, since arriving, Donovan has been quietly throwing his weight around and is insisting that this particular exclusive should come from John himself, when the time is right. Virginia bites her lip.

"Like I said... let's speak in six months."

---

JAMES AND STEVE enter the canteen, which resembles a food court more than a staff cafeteria.

"I repeat," James whispers. "Who are all of these people?"

They stroll around the canteen, considering every possible food choice from around the globe. Japanese, Mexican, Indian, to good ol' American fast food; it's all here.

"Beats me," Steve answers. "We've doubled our number in the last month alone. What makes you think I'd know? As my senior, I should be asking you."

James stares at Steve. He's been his friend long enough to learn that Steve always knows more than he thinks he does. He just needs the occasional nudge. James gestures to a table of suits.

"Oh, them?" Steve says. "Legal eagles."

James nods in a different direction to an ocean of cargo pants and untucked shirts.

"New marketing hires," Steve responds. "Some of them are probably Virginia's new licensing team. They're essentially one and the same."

Jim points to an isolated table in the corner.

"Come on, man. People that bland can only be one thing."

"HR?" James guesses.

"HR," Steve confirms.

Finally, James gestures to a group of casually dressed employees gathered around the work-in-progress bar.

"The bar isn't even built, yet they're still drawn to it like flies on cowshit. Must be the art department. Crap, there's Tina. I was right. Don't make eye contact."

"You're in the wrong job, Steve. With these deduction skills, you should be a detective."

"You might be onto something there, bud. Even though we've done a full tour of every possible food choice from around the world, I deduce you're still gonna get a cheeseburger."

"How *do* you do it?" James strolls with purpose towards the burger stand.

As they wait in line, James observes the numerous subspecies dotted around in their own particular groupings.

"It's high school all over again. I don't like it."

"It's exactly that," Steve agrees. "A microclimate of cliques. You've got your jocks, your weirdos, your goths…"

"Where do we fit in?" James asks.

"As if you need to ask. Once a nerd, always a nerd. Just because you've bagged yourself a sexy doctor, don't think you can't shake that shit off. You're a geek for life, Jim."

They grab their food and find a spot on the corner of a long table occupied by the engineering department. A few friendly nods are exchanged, but James is still the boss, whether he likes it or not, and a distinctly hushed tone washes over the table.

"Can I get your take on something?" James asks, attacking his burger.

"Uh-oh."

"Six weeks until release and we're more or less good to go. Half of Fall Water is working under John and Tom for the launch to market at GDC."

"Yep," Steve says, gulping down a mouthful of cow. "Virginia's upstairs deflecting questions on that."

"And the other half will be conceptualizing and launching the new game."

"That's what people are saying. Early days on that, right?"

"Ideas are flying around," James answers. "That's what I wanted to discuss. It's not an *Otherscape* sequel, but it's in the same wheelhouse. John's brainchild, naturally. He's codenamed it *Cyberside*."

"*Cyyyyberssssiiiide*," Steve repeats, savoring the word as he would an Argentinian Malbec at a wine tasting. He seems uncertain. "*Cyberside*." This time it has significantly more gravitas. "Great name."

"Right?" James exclaims. "It's *Otherscape 2.0* on the surface, but this will be fully online and persistent. Think *Realm Online* and *Nexus*. You given them a spin?"

"Who hasn't?"

"You think I have time?" James answers.

"Origin Systems out of Austin are developing something similar."

James dismisses this with a shake of the head. "Doesn't compare. John's aiming for a fully 3D, multiplatform experience."

The piece of half-chewed meat that drops from Steve's mouth onto the table indicates that this task, at this stage, is on the edge of impossible.

"Bro. This task... at this stage... impossible."

James nods, mildly disappointed. "I thought you'd say that. This isn't the first conversation like this we've had though, Steve. And things somehow always come together."

"True," Steve admits, "But this is next level, man."

James leans in and lowers his voice to a whisper. "Maybe not. Burrow has a master plan."

"I'd be offended if he didn't."

"We start low and slow with a 2D incarnation," James continues, his excitement growing as his ass lifts off his stool. "Multiple visitable realms, modular architecture, yada yada yada. When the tech catches up, we're waiting in the wings, locked and loaded with *Underside* to add a third dimension and further add-ons. More realms, detailed—"

"Slow down, cowboy, before you hurt yourself," Steve interjects. "You're sold on this, aren't you? What's John been feeding you?"

James checks himself. He sits back on the stool and takes a moment.

"I'd be lying if I said I wasn't compelled, sure. So many questions though."

"So many."

"For starters, I can't see a world where Sony would allow a cross-platformer. But John's got his enterprising socks on, what can I say?"

Steve creases up. When John gets his head into something, you better strap in.

"Don't think about today, Jim," Steve mimics, pulling out a scarily accurate impersonation of their boss. "Think about tomorrow, next week, next month."

"Next year, my boy. Hell, next decade," James attempts. His impression leaves a lot to be desired. It's more JFK than John Burrow.

"We need to think long-term," Steve continues, gesticulating wildly. "A journey of a thousand miles begins with a single step."

Knowing where his strength lies, James sits up straight and folds his arms, channeling Tom Simmons.

"Alright guys, Tom here. You heard the big man. I'm seeing a lot of unfurled sleeves around this table, so roll them up and let's build this starship by... let's say Tuesday evening, shall we?"

Steve roars with laughter, giving the rest of the Development table permission to do the same. If Steve laughs at James, it's fair game. As the laughter dies down, the smile leaves James' face. He finishes his burger and stands, dropping Steve a hint. Steve follows and the pair go for a post-burger stroll, away from prying ears, to the ice cream stand.

"You met Donovan yet?" James asks.

"He's done a couple of cursory floor walks, but that's about it."

James is handed a strawberry cone; Steve gets today's special, wasabi, because he's quirky like that. James brings his ice cream in front of his mouth in a ridiculous attempt at subtlety.

"What did you make of him?"

"What are you doing, Jim?" Steve asks.

"What?"

"Hiding your mouth behind the ice cream. You think you're Donnie Brasco or something? We're talking about work, you freak. The FBI aren't hiding behind the soda machine."

Suitably chastised, James lowers his cone and takes a lick.

"Nothing much to report, to answer your question," Steve continues. "He's built like a brick shithouse, all business. I think the conversation peaked when he commented on the weather. I tried to talk to him about coding and he almost went cross-eyed before being ushered away. Why are you asking me? You run the Dev team. Aren't you the one rubbing shoulders with the company brass?"

"HODs had a brief meet and greet," James answers. "He runs a tight ship. Pleasant enough, but he's clearly a bulldog. Maintains strict personal boundaries."

Steve knows well enough not to press when James wants to get something off his chest. He takes a nibble of his cone, waiting patiently.

"I don't know, man. It's like he came out of the womb in that expensive suit, fully formed. Makes Burrow look like John Lennon by comparison. Donovan doesn't belong here. He's like a shark on land. He just doesn't fit."

"You sound concerned," Steve observes.

James throws the rest of his cone in the trash.

"Something feels off. I'm sure it's nothing. He's a stone cold alpha; I'm probably just emasculated."

Steve laughs as they both head out of the canteen. "You'd feel emasculated around Mickey Mouse, pal."

They pass through the exit, unaware that some of the new legal hires are observing them closely, eyes burning a hole in the back of their heads.

---

ACROSS TOWN in the Union Oyster House, one of Boston's oldest restaurants, two people are having a markedly different dining experience. Virginia sits opposite a hulking giant of man in his late forties, dressed to the nines in a flash suit, Versa Foundation pin shining proudly on his lapel. A dozen or so other patrons populate the fashionable spot.

"Do you know the history of this place, Mrs Willis?" Donovan Craze asks. The man oozes testosterone out of every pore. It's almost unnatural.

"I'm an LA gal born and raised, Mr Craze," Virginia responds.

"Donovan." Despite his charming smile, this is a firm instruction rather than a request.

"Of course, Donovan. And please, call me Virginia. I haven't had the chance to explore Boston's gourmet delights, let alone indulge in its history."

"You relocated here last year?"

Virginia nods.

"With your family?"

Donovan seems to add a sprinkle of emphasis onto the word *family*, instantly raising Virginia's guard. The way in which he smiles at her as he casually places a napkin on his lap, however, suggests that she could well have imagined it.

"That's right," Virginia responds, meeting Donovan's energy. She absentmindedly fiddles with her wedding ring.

"Opened in 1862 by Hawes Atwood. Interesting guy."

Virginia nods and smiles politely. It's a highly convincing performance from a woman pretending to give two shiny shits. Acting interested while powerful men drone on about nothing of consequence is something she's built a career on. Craze isn't telling her anything she doesn't already know. When the new boss schedules an exclusive lunch, it's wise to drop everything and do your research.

A man floats into their periphery and pours two glasses of wine he will never be able to afford. Without taking her eyes from Fall Water Lake's new CEO, Virginia takes a sip and nods, dismissing the waiter.

Donovan raises his eyebrows in anticipation. *So?*

"Exquisite," Virginia remarks. *Of course it's fucking exquisite, you haughty prick.*

Donovan digs into a shared platter of oysters, giving Virginia the green light to do the same.

"What made this Atwood character so special?" Virginia asks, knowing perfectly well. She waits with the patience of a saint as Craze makes a show of squeezing lemon juice into an oyster and launching it down his tree trunk of a neck.

"In the early 19th century, Boston and Providence became a hub for the East Coast political and social elite," Donovan imparts. "They sought somewhere to fit their status. Hawes Atwood was savvy enough to sense a lucrative market filled with clientele with deep pockets. He opened up this place. It's hosted numerous illustrious guests in its lifetime. Daniel Webster, various presidents. Coolidge, Roosevelt—"

"Kennedy, Clinton," Virginia interrupts. The smallest flicker of Donovan's right eyelid tells Virginia that her interjection may not have been such a good idea.

"I see you've done your research," Donovan says, now fully aware that Virginia's ignorance is a mere show. "Big meeting with the boss. One must impress."

"Not at all," Virginia lies. "There are Presidential portraits in the ladies room." There aren't. "I saw them before you arrived."

It's impossible to tell whether Donovan believes her. Either way, there's a slight shift in mood as the pendulum of power swings in his direction.

"What do you think of the oysters?"

*Can't stand them.* "Divine."

Donovan points out of the window.

"And the marina?"

*What do I think of the marina? How am I supposed to answer that?*

"Fishy. I think it smells fishy, Donovan. And it's not the only thing," Virginia responds, throwing caution to the wind. Screw it.

Donovan's grin grows into an impossibly bigger one.

"I like your sense of humor, Virginia."

*Sense of humor? The place reeks of fish, you oaf.*

"Why are we here, Donovan?" Virginia grabs her glass of wine and sees off half of it in one go. He may be her new boss, but she's refusing to play the obedient maiden any longer. "I'm a busy woman."

Donovan stares at her, awestruck.

"Ha! I knew you were a straight talker! It took all of five minutes to drop the act!"

"That act usually lasts around thirty seconds. Consider yourself lucky," Virginia remarks. "If I wanted to learn this place's history, I could have read the back of the menu. What's on your mind?"

Donovan takes a moment, pausing for effect.

"Nothing fishy. I can assure you of that."

Donovan's overly gregarious act drops now – two can play that game – and he addresses Virginia like the well-versed, no-nonsense business woman he knows her to be.

"Versa trusts Burrow's genius and Simmons' technical prowess. Otherwise my company" – emphasis on *my* – "wouldn't be investing so heavily in this little operation."

Virginia focuses on the use of the word *little* to describe the company on which she bet her life. *He genuinely views these guys as small fry.*

"With our backing, Fall Water will cement its place in the history books. We'll create something monumental. Something unavoidable. They'll be talking about *us* two hundred years from now."

"I don't know who briefed you, Donovan, but you know we just make video games, right?" Virginia jokes, bringing this bombastic flight of fancy crashing straight back down to earth.

"Games are for children, Virginia. Think bigger. The internet. Connectivity. *Data.*"

Virginia smirks. There it is. She should have known. The second these bastards came knocking, it was abundantly clear they didn't have a flicker of interest in gaming.

"Data?"

"The currency of the future. Just think of the power it could harness."

Virginia recoils. Bold words from the big man. His enthusiasm is impressive, but this isn't why she took this job. Data is the life blood of marketing and it's something for which she has a natural proclivity, but some executives worship at its altar as if it's the Second Coming of Christ. Virginia's skills reside in simplifying complex ideas to morons and figuring out what a product is before it knows itself so that she can present it in a pretty little bow and shift units. If her life is now going to be hijacked by the big D, she's not sure she wants in.

"Burrow's bright mind will continue leading the way," Donovan continues, "At least on the surface. During its growth, we need to ensure the company functions like a well-oiled machine. Think of it like a factory. Sustainable, efficient, predictable. It needs to execute perfect control so that our plans bear fruit."

As the walking ego prattles on, Virginia almost completely checks out of the conversation.

"You strike me as someone who knows a lot about control and has a keen desire to practice it regularly."

Virginia finds herself very suddenly back in the here and now. Her heart goes cold.

"Inside work and out." Donovan continues smiling as he prepares another oyster. A loaded glance at Virginia's wedding ring confirms her biggest fear. *He knows.*

Once a week, while her husband takes her two boys to soccer practice, Virginia meets a lover in a secluded downtown apartment. Within those four walls, her willing partner does anything and everything she commands. Nobody knows about this. Nobody. Very quickly, Virginia accepts the fact that, somehow, the man sitting across the table from her is aware of her deepest, darkest secret.

"We demand loyalty. Simple as that"

*There's no point denying it.* "Of course," Virginia says. Donovan looks at her expectantly. She takes a deep breath. "A plan of this magnitude requires a level of execution that can only be provided by rigorous control and supervision."

Donovan nods, but remains silent. He wants more.

"Those kids in the office might be building a framework for future technologies, but that's all they are. Kids. They're blind to the bigger picture. You need an internal ally who's wise to the gravity of what we're doing and will do whatever it takes to meet Versa's ambitions." How Viginia manages to come up with this whilst simultaneously envisioning a life without her husband and kids is anyone's guess.

Donovan seems satisfied.

"Speaking of kids," Virginia continues with a pleading look in her eyes. "I have two of my own, from a happy marriage. Very happy."

A look of confusion washes over Donovan's face. He holds his hands up in defense.

"Please. This isn't what you think it is." Donovan catches himself. "Well, it is," he continues. "But this is very much a carrot and stick situation. Not just a stick. This works both ways." Donovan chuckles, somehow confused as to why Virginia is making such a big deal out of this. "Look, we know about your dirty little secret, and it's fine. Everybody has one. I don't care who you wrap your legs around, honestly."

The nonchalance with which Donovan speaks hints at the fact that Virginia is far from the first person he's threatened in such a manner.

"Now the seedy part is out of the way, think about what we can do for you," Donovan says. "Versa can open any door for you, offer connections, respect, protection, wealth for you and your family today, tomorrow, and long after you're gone. You want to provide for them?"

"What mother wouldn't?"

Donovan pauses. He seems caught off guard.

"Mine didn't." He waves off the intrusive thought. "They'll have lifelong security, so long as our interests align. Do we understand one another?"

"Yes, Donovan. We understand one another."

Donovan wipes his hands and throws down his napkin. Virginia tries and fails to bury her anxiety.

"It's OK, Virginia. We're all good here!" Donovan bellows. "Don't overthink this! Versa firmly believes that its close associates should be provided with the necessary resources to satisfy any desire they have. Maximum pleasure, no consequences. That's our motto. Unofficially, of course. I have faith in you."

Donovan stands, drawing the conversation to a conclusion. A mass scraping of chairs follows; Virginia is stunned to see every other patron in the joint get to their feet. All stare at Virginia. Donovan squeezes her shoulder. Not hard enough to be threatening, not weak enough not to be.

"That's why you're here. With the elites. Welcome aboard."

Donovan winks and marches out of the restaurant without another word. It's not often that Virginia finds herself shaken. She stands unsteadily, grabbing the back of her chair for support. Never has her life been thrown onto such a different course in such a short matter of time. The Liberty Bell tolls outside, as if confirming the weight of what has just unfolded. A quick glance at her wedding ring pulls Virginia's priorities into focus. It takes her no time to readjust and come to a stark conclusion. *I guess you're fucked.*

Virginia grabs her handbag and walks out of the restaurant, straight past the other 'customers', and out into a world that has changed irrevocably.

## 3

# THE RELEASE

James feels the collar of his rented tux dig into his neck. He's only been in town for two days and has barely had time to breathe, let alone shop. *Shouldn't have hired the cheap one. Not for this.*

"And Game of the Year goes to..."

*It hardly matters. It's not like we're gonna win.*

"*Otherscape 2* by Fall Water Lake!"

The room explodes into rapturous applause, drowning out the cheap polyester irritation that has been plaguing James all night. Before anyone knows what's what, John Burrow has taken to the stage. *Look at that. We did it.*

Through waves of pumping adrenaline, James spots John waving over to the team, inviting them up on stage. Following a blur of handshakes and hugs, he and the Fall Water delegation have formed a highly excitable line behind John. The only thing going through James' mind on this momentous occasion is how unfathomably bright the lights are.

*Is this what it feels like to stand under a spotlight? It's hotter than the sun. Oh, God, I'm sweating. Should really have spent more on the tux. Shit, I can feel it dripping down my back. Can people see? Can they tell?*

At the podium, John waits for the applause to die down, taking a brief second to savor the moment.

"What can I say? Thank you," John starts, waving the award in the air in gratitude. "You know what they say. It takes a village. *Otherscape 2* is a prime example of that. Some of that village is standing behind me right now, like they have been, unwavering, since the beginning."

*I can feel the sweat running down my nose. It's gonna drip off.*

"With them, along with an army of others back in Boston, I share this triumph." Another wave of applause. It's one thing to have over a million players immersed in the virtual world of *Otherscape 2* and, of course, the positive media reception has been thrilling. Nothing, however, beats industry recognition from a room packed to the rafters with peers and fellow creatives. They know what it takes better than anyone. They know what this means.

*Is there a camera on me? No. It'll be focused on John. I'll wipe off the sweat. Jeez, those lights are bright.*

"Tom Simmons, my brother in arms," John continues, "is back in Boston holding the fort. Seems like just yesterday we were two young upstarts throwing our energy into a little game named *Distant Shores*." A couple of cheers of approval from the crowd.

*Sarah would have never have let me hire this thing. What was I thinking? Man, I'm hungry.*

"Well, that was seven years ago. We've come a long way. Love you, Tommy."

*Did John just say he loves Tom? Did he call him Tommy?*

"Personally, I couldn't have done this without Alice, my beautiful daughter. And Samantha, my shining light..." John looks to the heavens. "I love you. I miss you."

*Shame Steve couldn't be here. He'd have loved this. Poor schmuck, working the graveyard shift back in Boston.*

"But most importantly," John continues, pointing the award at the crowd, "You guys. Our fans, our players, our equals. It's you who choose to spend your lives in our world. For that, you have our eternal thanks."

John glances behind him at his crew. James stands squinting under the lights, unsteady on his feet in his bargain basement tux. He looks more like an inebriated penguin than an award-winning developer. Unfortunately for this drunk penguin, he just so happens to be the first person who catches John's eye.

"Jim Reynolds, our Head of Dev. Care to say something?"

*What's happening? Oh. He wants me to say something. That's nice.*

James stumbles to the mic and stares blankly out at what he assumes is the crowd. His entire vision is occupied solely by impossibly bright white light.

"Um, yeah. I... huh. Sorry, I'm, er... sweating. These lights... hot."

The handy filter that translates nonsensical inner monologues into civilized speech appears to have taken a day off. James shuffles back to his spot, apparently unaware that he's just made a monumental ass out of himself in front of his adoring public. There's a couple of whoops and a ripple of laughter.

"Thanks Jim," John says. "Spoken like a true developer."

Suddenly, the cacophony of sound and vision flicks into sharp focus. *We won. Holy Christ, we won. Did I just make a speech? Fuck. What did I say?*

The self-doubt is short-lived as James contemplates the last couple of years and the sheer grind that led to this moment of euphoria. This game has been his life. Its success has gone beyond any of his wildest expectations. Since launching four months ago, reports boast that some hardcore gamers spend up to six hours a day exploring the world of *Otherscape 2* and the many treasures it has to offer. Hank's last update, heavily influenced by Blizzard's *Diablo* and powered by *Underside,* knocked the industry on its head. It's no understatement to claim that this title has changed the way games will be played forever, offering infinite exploration and never-ending adventure. Turns out Virginia's hype machine was real after all.

"While I'm up here," John says, "it would be prudent to take this moment to drop a hint at what's next." The crowd is silenced, on tenterhooks at what's to come. "Fall Water Lake was built on a culture of sharing. The sharing of knowledge, of ideas, of stories and dreams. We also want to share our success, not just internally, but externally. We are going to be sharing the engine that built *Otherscape* with the world. We're releasing *Underside* to the market. Tools, source code, the whole lot."

John smiles. He's been waiting for this.

"We won't only be licensing to fellow developers at friendly rates with premium support. Most importantly, provided it is utilized to create more realms for *Otherscape*, *Underside* will be free to use for any creators with ambitions to make the leap into development."

John just dropped an atom bomb. If ever there was any doubt that this was the time and place to present this news to the world, the uproarious eruption of approval surely puts those reservations to rest. James, dazed and confused, joins in the excitement, blindly clapping and whooping. Standing on the stage at 1997's E3 in Atlanta, Georgia, he is blissfully ignorant that he has just witnessed the ushering in of a revolutionary new era in games development history.

---

"Can we capture some room sound before we begin?"

"Sorry, what?"

"Some ambient sound for the edit, Mrs Willis. We just need some silence for a few seconds."

"You don't know me very well. That may be a challenge."

*Edge* magazine's Barry Cromer, navigating through a particularly brutal bout of jetlag, sits on a couch with Virginia in the penthouse suite of the Ritz-Carlton. Fall Water's Head of Marketing is a delight for the eyes, dressed in a glitzy dress having just run upstairs from the main event for an exclusive interview. Unlike James, Virginia knew the win was in the bag, and, unlike James, she had the common sense to dress for the occasion. Out of the window, the sun casts a hazy glow over Atlanta. The room is populated with a skeleton film crew, including a camera operator, sound guy, and director. A man in a tracksuit, hood pulled up and face unseen, moves around in the adjacent bedroom.

Virginia and Barry sit in awkward silence for a few seconds before the director gives a thumbs up.

"Alright," Barry claps, as if trying to snap himself from his daze. "Away we go! I believe some congratulations are in order, Virginia!"

"Was there ever any doubt, Barry?" Virginia responds, struggling to mask an excitable smile.

"I mean, listen. Game of the Year, Fall Water's contingent getting room and board at the Ritz-Carlton, *Otherscape 2* flying off the shelves—"

"No little thanks to you guys," Virginia interrupts. "That ten out of ten stamp of approval sure was appreciated."

"Are you kidding?" Barry explodes. "That little masterpiece of yours is the bollocks, girl. Seriously, I'm hooked. I'm already getting withdrawal symptoms. Look." Barry holds out a shaking hand to make his point. No wonder they stick this guy in front of the camera for these things. His tell-it-like-it-is British charm is instantly disarming. "Your little Bostonion outfit has officially arrived."

"So has *Edge*, by the looks of it," Virginia says, gesturing to the ragtag bunch. "They actually coughed up for a camera crew and flew you over. It's nice to speak face-to-face for a change."

"Seriously," Barry says earnestly. "How does it feel?"

"Oh, you know," Virginia deflects, waving her hand playfully. "All in a day's work. But it's an honor. Really. A truly special achievement." For all of her usual bombast, Virginia can't keep a lid on an overwhelming sense of pride.

"Great to see Burrow up there reaping the rewards."

"He deserves every ounce of adulation coming his way."

"No sign of Tom Simmons or Donovan Craze?"

"Keeping the home fires burning back in Boston," Virginia responds. "Someone's got to keep the lights on."

"Considering he's the CEO, your man seems positively publicity shy."

Virginia takes a moment, as she often does when Craze's name comes up. In the increasingly common event that he becomes the subject of conversation, she's learned that a delicate touch is required. Strict instructions have been filtered down in no uncertain terms to keep his name out of the press.

"He knows the boys put in the groundwork before Versa showed up on horseback. He's letting the infantry bask in all the glory." Nicely done. As if on cue, in the background, the bedroom door quietly clicks shut, unnoticed.

"So, what's new since we last spoke? Aside from that gleaming trophy?"

"Well, I'm sure your readers won't care too much about this," Virginia replies, slipping back into business mode with ease, "but some context for my favorite British rag. Thanks to the game's success and continued Versa investment, Goldman Sachs is now our bank of choice. Credit lines are generous and I'm sure they'll continue to grow following tonight's result."

"Aha! That's why Donovan's back in Boston," Barry speculates. "Important calls to make."

"Sure," Virginia confirms. She moves swiftly on. "All that may go some way in explaining why we're conducting this interview here and not perching on the edge of a bed in the usual fleapit motel." This remark produces a couple of knowing chuckles from the crew. Barry takes a sip of champagne, to be charged to Fall Water, of course.

"Safe to say Fall Water's not a standard game dev company any more, then?"

"It never was, old bean. Now the world has simply caught up to the fact. We're growing rapidly. New hires arrive each week from various corners of the globe. We're focusing on our own independence. That's a key priority."

"Not looking to step into publishing?" Barry asks, surprised. "That'd be the usual strategy now, wouldn't it?"

"Usual strategies are of no interest to us," Virginia affirms. "We're not going to traverse the predictable path, let me assure you. We're known for innovation, not only in product, but in decision-making. We're not moving into the publishing sphere." She suddenly grows weary with this line of questioning and looks to the director to wrap it up.

"What, we're done?" Barry asks, mildly disappointed. "Christ on a bike, Virginia, we're just warming up."

"Indeed," Virginia says. "We are. Now the foreplay's over, what do you say we take this up to the rooftop bar? We're throwing an exclusive party, no expense spared. And... well." Virginia glances around the room with an air of theatricality. "We all appear to be in a stuffy hotel room, do we not?" A wave of excitement washes over the crew. *This* is what they came here for. "Come on, boys. Daft Punk will be well into their set by now. Get a couple more mimosas in me and I'm sure I'll volunteer some juicy morsels that I'll regret in the morning."

The crew scrambles to their feet as Virginia checks her eyeliner in the mirror. "Just do me a favor. Leave that fucking camera down here, will you?"

---

BY THE TIME Virginia and her new British entourage make it to the roof, the party is already in full swing. The impossibly catchy synth riff of Daft Punk's *Da Funk* blasts across the terrace. The French duo, iconic reflective helmets firmly in place, can be found in a DJ booth at the north end of the hired space. They hold the crowd in the palm of their robotic hands.

Simmons somehow convinced Versa to foot the bill for the electronic outfit after word reached him that their music had been playing in the Pit for months. If Fall Water's Dev team relied on the contagious beats to get *Otherscape 2* over the line, then they deserve them in the flesh. Atlanta's skyline sparkles in the distance, as if it was shipped in just for the occasion. Additional flavor is provided by various music and movie execs; rumor has it that Tia Carrere and one of the Baldwin brothers – not Alec – are around here somewhere. Even the numerous developers who can be found milling around, looking more like excitable school kids on a field trip than industry movers and shakers, can't diminish the fact that this little spot is spilling over with cool.

As the first half of Daft Punk's set wraps up, James finds himself standing self-consciously at the bar with more cocktails in front of him than he knows what to do with. He glances around, trying to calculate which section of the crowd is most mingle-worthy.

"What's happening, Pingu?" Hank pops up from nowhere and slaps his friend on the back with such force that James almost goes flying over the bar. The surprise of Hank's ambush is outweighed by the relief of seeing a friendly face.

"Hank. Thank God."

A quick look at Hank tells James this is, without doubt, the most drunk he's ever seen him. True, they've both stayed up into the small hours sharing a bottle of whiskey numerous times of late. However, there's a glaze now resting comfortably over Hank's eyes that James has never seen before. The type of glaze that can only be removed by ten minutes under a cold shower or ten hours in a large bed. His facial hair, residing somewhere between clean shaven and full beard, would do well to pick a lane. Hank is not at all dressed to impress. Dr Martens boots, jeans and *Master of Puppets* Metallica t-shirt suggest that he has no time or interest for this type of event.

"Thank God?" Hank repeats. "What, you... you're religious now?" His words are slurred. "I mean, it does look like you're wearing your Sunday best."

"That's rich coming from a man who looks like he needs an exorcist. Jesus, Hank. It didn't cross your mind to wear, oh, I don't know, something else?"

Hank smiles the kind of smile that doesn't know why it's here, but knows it probably should be. He finishes his beer and grabs two Amaretto sours from the tray of a passing waiter.

"Why would I dress up? It's our party. Fuck the suits and the horses they rode in on." Hank's words are undercut with a potent strain of venom. "Here," he says, forcing one of the drinks into James' hand.

"What is it?"

"Alcohol. You know, the thing people pour down their necks at these industry circle-jerks. C'mon, Jim. Cut loose!"

James plays along and takes a sip before shepherding Hank to a quiet corner. "You good, Hank?"

"Oh, I'm peachy. Why?"

"Long day?"

"Why do you say that?"

"Because you look like shit." James knows that Hank's bullshit detector is second to none. The best way to get through to him is to simply tell it like it is.

Hank shrugs. Resistance is futile. "I may or may not have been on the sauce since lunch. Depends what time constitutes lunch."

James' concern for Hank rises. This despondency is out of character. Although he has a reputation for drinking, he never loses control. James now finds himself propping Hank up, checking that nobody of importance is in the vicinity.

"You weren't at the awards show, man. You should have been on stage with us! Missed me make the speech of the decade. Where were you?" James observes a shadow descend over Hank's face.

"Well, let's see. I got called to a lunch meet downtown with the usual suspects. Virginia, a couple of Versa's guys, Donovan."

"Donovan's in Boston, Hank."

Hank chuckles and gives James a couple of light pats on the cheek. "No, Jim. He ain't."

James absorbs this and accepts that it's credible enough. Donovan wants to stay out of the limelight, but it figures that he'd be in Atlanta to take some important meetings. The hush-hush nature of the whole thing raises a couple of distant alarm bells, however.

"I assume you didn't discuss chess," James gently presses.

"Nah. Standard corporate BS. I tend to tap out the moment we sit down these days, honestly. I polished off a couple of drinks there, then met some old pals at the bar downstairs to discuss war stories. Ten drinks led to ten more. Award shows are torture, Jim. Did nobody tell you?"

"I wish they had," Jim mutters under his breath. Bouts of anxiety have been tapping him on the shoulder since he left the stage. He's doing his best not to cast his mind back to what might be one of the biggest embarrassments of his adult life. For now, an arranged marriage of cortisol and booze are keeping the scale of his faux pas at bay. He's sure it'll all come flooding back in the morning with a tasty side of hangover.

"Then I had a quick nap in my room," Hank continues, "And, er, here we are. Right. That's us all up to speed." He looks out at the city with defeat in his eyes. James notes his distress, but isn't well-versed enough in the complexities of Hank's character to know how to handle it. *Is he just drunk? Or one of those guys that enters a depression the moment a major undertaking is kicked over the line?* Whatever is going on, direct questioning doesn't seem to be doing the trick. Time for a softer approach.

"You flying back tomorrow with the team?"

"Not tomorrow," Hank answers, staring into the middle distance. "I'm heading to North Carolina with Donovan. Orders from the man himself."

"Oh yeah? What's in NC?"

"Red Hat."

James makes an effort to lower his eyebrows, conscious that they just raised so high, they may never return. He takes a tactical sip of his drink to hide his surprise. He's as bad an actor as he is a public speaker.

"Red Hat? As in Linux Red Hat?"

Hank rolls his eyes in exacerbation. "What do you think, we've got a sudden interest in fashion? Buy a copy of the game and get a free fedora? Yes, Linux Red Hat, you moron."

James barely registers the insult as he's too busy digesting the fact that Fall Water has set a parley with Linux.

"*Cyberside* is a Windows joint, Hank. Why switch to Torvalds' system?"

"They say it's security-related. I dunno." Hank's either trying to convince James of his indifference, or himself. Either way, it's as see-through as some of the female guests' dresses. "Linux is ahead of the curve on security. You know that."

"Security?" James scoffs. "We're building a videogame! This isn't the Manhattan Project. Who does Donovan think he is?"

"Robert Oppenheimer, apparently." Although Hank's joking, both he and James suspect the comparison may have a hint of truth.

"I said the same thing at lunch, trust me," Hank says. "From the way John and Tom have been talking, our new baby is looking beyond complex. Think long-term and go longer. It'll carry the same strategic weight as *Underside*."

James simply shakes his head and can't help but smile. "Anything else you're not telling me?"

Hank momentarily seems to sober up.

"I'll probably have to build a separate data center to support *Cyberside*'s level of demand. No big deal, but not how I'd handle it."

"And you told them that?" James asks.

"Of course I did. They didn't seem to listen. The phrase 'pissing in the wind' comes to mind."

There it is. Hank is an undeniable authority at Fall Water. Any tech-related questions relating to future strategy have always gone through him. Seems that, recently, decisions are being made without his input. *No wonder he's pissed.* This, combined with the headache of moving an entire project architecture to a new OS – expenses, projections, fresh hires, new code, operational support – who can blame the guy for sinking into temporary oblivion?

"Yeah. OK. Big news," James says, realizing he's offering zero reassurance. "We'll manage. Let me know how I can help when the dust settles."

"Obviously," Hank grunts with annoyance. He instantly checks himself. "Sorry, Jim. Just got a lot on my mind."

"Don't sweat it." James suddenly grabs Hank's face. "You're a genius, Hank. I know that. You know that. That's all that matters. Listen, I saw a bottle of Bulleit behind the bar. What do you say?"

With his cheeks squeezed between James' hands, it's hard for Hank to say anything. He tries, nonetheless.

"Sure thing, buddy. Can I have my face back now?"

---

BY THE TIME Daft Punk finish their blistering performance, the crowd is pumped up enough for the party to move from the Ritz-Carlton to Velvet, a trendy night spot in Atlanta's central business district. Here, Fall Water Lake employees collide with colleagues from other companies attending E3. Yesterday, these people were competitors. They will be again tomorrow. But for now, they are friends and equals. It's at these work events, where industry folk crash together in a mess of sweat, drink, gossip and shared trauma, that inseparable friendships are forged. These people may only bump into each other once or twice a year, but when they do, oh boy. Strap in and cancel tomorrow.

James allows himself to go along for the ride, carried by the organic flow of the night and happy not to resist. At some point, Hank disappears, but James is too distracted to notice. Eventually, he's hit by a bout of nausea; time to go outside and get some fresh air.

That fresh air is immediately invalidated by the cigarette he hungrily inhales. This is a habit James stubbed out a couple of years ago. Sarah always claimed to be fine with the fact he smoked, but she was lying, of course. As a non-smoker, there was no way she approved of the smell, the cost, the health risks. She would never dream of telling him how to live his life, however. He's a grown man, at least on paper, and it's best he makes these decisions for himself. It's for this very reason that James decided to hit it on the head. At least when he's at home in Boston. For out-of-town trips, he allows himself the indulgence of buying one packet and savoring every drag.

James leans back against a street light and lets the nicotine do its thing. It occurs to him that he hasn't paged Sarah today. He knows she'll be on shift and doesn't want to disturb her. Maybe he'll leave a voice message on the home answering machine when he gets back to the hotel. Maybe. The win is big news, but it can wait.

"Sorry, can I bum a light?"

The transatlantic voice belongs to a friendly middle-aged man who himself has just emerged from the club. A handy lanyard swinging around his neck informs James that this is *MIKE PENRIDGE - COO - TIMESCAPE*. James somehow manages to focus on the badge long enough for his triple vision to align. He roots around in his pocket and throws over his lighter.

"Go nuts."

Mike lights up, inhales, and passes back the lighter with a wink. For a solid minute, the pair simply stand and smoke. An intuitive mutual understanding that all smokers share, and that James truly misses, is that silences are far less awkward when two people are sucking tobacco into their lungs.

"Good E3 for you guys?" James asks, gesturing to Mike's name badge.

"Yeah, not bad, mate," Mike replies. "Don't see a badge on you. You industry?"

"James Reynolds. Fall Water Lake. Engineering." James offers a hand. Mike shakes it with enthusiasm.

"Fall Water? Fuck right off! You lot have stolen the show this year, mate! We mortals can barely get a look in! Mike Penridge. Timescape. Love your work. Well-deserved win." Mike clearly has a knack for delivering compliments without sounding like a prize brown-noser. It's a skill that is truly hard to find in industry circles. Usually, people are either lying outright or want something in return. Through his drunken stupor, James decides that this Penridge character is probably just a decent guy.

"Thanks. Appreciate it."

"Listen, James. Any scoops on *Otherscape 3*?" With this question, James second guesses himself. He's heard of journalists posing as others to try and siphon corporate secrets for frontpage exclusives. Even worse, this guy could be a competitor farming for trade secrets.

"Who did you say you were with? Timescape?"

Mike instantly notes James' suspicion and happily presents his badge for closer inspection. "That's right. Look for yourself. I respect your caution, but it's nothing like that. My son's a big fan, is all. If he knew I'd bumped into a Fall Water giant and didn't ask him about what's next, he'd never forgive me."

If James was sober, he'd end this conversation right here. As it happens, he's the opposite of sober.

"We're working on something, but it's not *Otherscape 3*. And this conversation doesn't leave this smoking area, you hear? Don't even tell your son, if that is his real name." James punctuates this with the first hiccup of many, suggesting that he should probably be calling it a night.

"Of course. I get it. My lips are sealed."

"Next project is unannounced. Not much I can say. Let's just call it a spiritual evolution."

Mike nods along, enraptured. He finishes his smoke and grabs another straightaway. James leans in and lights his cigarette. Mike gestures to his packet of Camels; James politely declines the offer. The cold night air is bringing some of James' brain cells back to foggy life, and with that comes an unwelcome realization that he has an early flight to catch in a few hours. Not far behind this thought is the terrifying prospect of what's on the broader horizon in the coming months. With one game out in the world, the cogs are in motion on *Cyberside*. In this line of work, there's no rest for the wicked. New dawns invite new challenges.

"You alright there, James?"

James grows conscious that he is slipping into a similar headspace to the one that Hank was occupying earlier. The thrill of the win has been short-lived and the pressures of that difficult second album are making themselves known.

"Yeah, just tired. This developer needs to get back to the hotel and rest his weary head."

Mike nods and looks James in the eye. The kind of familiar look that might be shared between old friends, not between two strangers who just met under a neon sign outside a club.

"It's been a good year for you, Jim. The start of something special. You feel like you're at a crossroads?" Mike's tone is reassuring. James is mildly taken aback, but he takes comfort in the fact that this man seems to know what's what. A voice of calm in an uncertain storm.

"You could say that."

"Important decisions to be made, then, for both you and the company. I'll be tracking Fall Water with interest. You and the team have delivered a miracle. Hopefully it continues to do great work in this space. Remember this moment."

James wants to offer something deep and meaningful in return. "Thanks, man." At this late hour, this is all he can muster. At least it's genuine. "All the best for you and your game."

James flags a passing taxi and stumbles into the backseat. The moment the car pulls away, Mike launches his cigarette. The wasted party goer that has been talking to James for the past five minutes seems to take a hike. Mike, it turns out, is sober as a judge.

"Take care, James Reynolds. I'll see you around."

A FEW HOURS LATER, AS JAMES' commercial Boeing heads towards Logan airport, a much smaller aircraft touches down at Raleigh-Durham International in North Carolina.

Hank is awakened by a mild shudder and the sound of landing gear skidding on tarmac. Before he's even opened his eyes, a hangover, one that will smash its way into the top five worst of his life, has already started its dirty scheming. Some vile invisible force is clanging a metal bar around the inside of his skull. This is amplified when he strains his eyes open and the private jet's fluorescent lighting floods his field of vision. It is amplified further still by the fact that the first voice Hank hears belongs to Donovan.

"Top of the morning to you, Mr Brown."

Donovan sits opposite Hank, fresh as a daisy. Suit perfectly pressed, hair perfectly styled, familiar non-threatening yet threatening grin smeared across his face. Outside the window, the plane taxis across an exclusive private section of the airport.

"I can't say I blame you," Donovan says. "Game of the Year. A cause for celebration, to be sure. Still, time to greet the day. Rise and shine."

Hank contemplates telling Donovan he ditched the vapid awards ceremony last night, but even stringing the thought together in his head almost causes his brain to malfunction. He settles for something far less eloquent.

"Yep. Rising. Shining."

Donovan laughs, seemingly nonplussed by Hank's outright unprofessionalism. He more or less had to drag him from the hotel lobby to the waiting taxi earlier and had to tip the driver generously to help carry him into the airport. The second he was dropped into his seat on the plane, Hank was out for the count. This sort of thing wouldn't normally wash with Donovan, but some people get a free pass. In a very short time, he's learned that Hank is an invaluable asset to the company. Best to give him a bit of leeway every now and again.

"God. My head. Did I leave it back in Atlanta?" Hank says, massaging his temples.

"Parts of it, I'm sure. Along with your dignity. Ha!" Donovan reaches into his leather travel bag and pulls out a small metal case embossed with the Versa logo. He unclicks it and taps a couple of pills into his hand. "Swallow these."

Hank doesn't argue. Hypersalivation has kicked in and he knows he's two minutes away from either vomiting up last night's Amaretto sours or having to buy replacement underwear at the airport. At this stage, he'll take anything. Whatever the day has in store, he's in for a rough ride. Hank swallows the pills, along with a hearty gulp of water.

"Thanks. What was that? Aspirin?" Every word is a struggle, every sentence a marathon. Hank tries to go to his happy place, but can't for the life of him remember where it is.

"Aspirin is for cavemen," Donovan answers. "This is much better. Thank me later."

Fast forward a few minutes, and not only has Hank managed to stand without soiling himself, but he's walking through the airport with a spring in his step. Whatever Donovan gave him, the clanging has stopped, replaced with a clarity of thought. His body isn't far behind. As they meet their driver, Hank looks to Donovan with a wondrous smile.

"What did you give me?" He leans in and whispers. "Am I high right now?"

They are led outside by the driver to two beefed-up, jet-black Chevrolets, each accompanied by two even beefier men sporting earpieces, sunglasses, and black polo shirts with *Fortress* branding. These guys look like they haven't smiled in over a decade. Donovan holds up a hand to signify he needs a minute. His security detail instantly begin scanning the area for threats.

"Being part of the Versa family brings with it certain benefits, Hank," Donovan says. "The Foundation moved aggressively into the pharmaceutical space last year."

*Aggressively... that figures.* Hank chooses to keep this thought to himself. "So you're in bed with big pharma now?"

"Not me, Hank. We. And we're not in bed with them. We *are* big pharma now."

"You just gave me a hangover cure in pill form. There's no way this is legal."

"Legal as of last year." Donovan speaks with a sternness that indicates he doesn't quite like that allegation. "Adderall. Essentially an amphetamine cocktail. Only recently approved by the FDA. We're taking it to market next month."

"So it's safe?"

"I wouldn't give you something I don't take myself, Hank," Donovan reassures him. "Especially before a meeting of this magnitude. Don't want you foaming at the mouth over lunch, do we?"

Hank has his reservations, but he feels fantastic. Not only have his senses now returned to their default agility, they've leapt beyond it. These little pills are a revelation. What was looking like one of the worst days of his life could well turn out to be one of the best.

"Well, why are we just standing here? Haven't we got a meeting to get to?" Hank approaches the first Chevy, only partially regrets saluting one of the security guys, and gets in the backseat. Donovan isn't far behind, enjoying the power trip that comes with welcoming someone into a secret society. He's been taking these miracle pills for months and his focus has never been sharper. With Hank now a member of the Adderall gang, he knows his output will increase markedly.

"We're with them. Moving out. ETA thirty minutes." The hired gun speaks with military precision. It is clear to Hank that Versa takes its security very seriously. He thinks back to the day when Burrow described Donovan as a glorified pencil pusher. Seems he underestimated him. Generic corporate suits don't fly to meetings in private jets and get shepherded around town by former black ops. *Who the hell are these people?*

A few minutes later, the Tar Heel State's landscape glides silently past the Chevy's tinted windows.

"I assume we're heading to the Red Hat office?" Hank asks.

"Hank. Come on. Really? No. We've hired Angus Barn for a couple of hours."

"Right…" It's slowly dawning on Hank that this might not be a standard tech meeting after all. Donovan confirms this immediately.

"We're not just meeting Red Hat."

Hank absorbs this with uncharacteristic calm. Socializing, he will be the first to admit, is not one of his strong points. Get him in a room full of strangers and he turns to jello. Waking up in a cold sweat with the terrifying fear that he has to take a meeting with more than three people the next day is a common occurrence. Introduce the important fact that he has done zero prep, the attendees are a mystery, and he's on his way there in an armored tank, and Hank should technically be a gibbering wreck. And yet, in this moment, with these little tablets working their magic, Hank finds himself positively looking forward to it.

---

As they pull into the Angus Barn parking lot, Hank notices another black Chevy, a green Dodge Challenger and a red Mustang in the otherwise empty space. The only other vehicles are enclosed in a cordoned-off staff area. When Donovan says he's hired a restaurant for two hours, you better believe he's hired a restaurant for two hours.

Hank follows Donovan as he strides towards the entrance. It's usually around now that Hank's nerves completely overwhelm him and he contemplates quitting his job and moving to Hawaii to open a tiki bar. No such desire enters his thoughts today.

"Mr Craze. Welcome back to Big Red." The front-of-house manager welcomes Donovan with a familiar smile. "Your guests are already waiting."

"Vanessa. Good to see you again," Donovan replies. "Tell me, how is your sister?"

"Oh, thank you for asking." Vanessa seems genuinely touched that Donovan has remembered their conversation from the previous year. What she doesn't know is that a crumpled piece of paper in his back pocket reads *Vanessa - sister - very sick*. "All we can do is manage the pain at this stage."

"I'm sorry to hear that. Anything we can help your family with, let me know."

Hank has been wondering how Donovan managed to book this entire place out at the last minute. Now he knows. At Donovan's level, this level of intel is critical. Favors beget favors.

"Of course. Please, let me show you to your table."

Donovan's security detail take their places at the door as he and Hank are led to the only occupied table in the restaurant. It is populated by three men who are unfazed by the fact they have this entire place to themselves. The first, in his thirties, wears thick-rimmed glasses and is dressed in casual yet expensive attire. The second is a forty-something man in shorts, sandals and a Weyland-Yutani t-shirt. Hank immediately likes him. Anyone who is a fan of *Alien* is alright in his books. The third, in an expensive suit, looks like a younger incarnation of Donovan.

"Afternoon, gentlemen. Sorry to keep you waiting," Donovan says. His clone stands and pulls him in for a warm hug.

"Don. It's been too long."

"Damien. How's the family?" Donovan asks.

"Henry's growing up way too fast. He's been asking after his uncle."

"Tell him I'm a busy man. I'll see him at Christmas. If you'll have me."

"Are you kidding? Of course!" Damien can't hide his pleasure at this request. He turns to Hank and shakes his hand.

"Hank Brown, I presume? Damien Craze." Hank had not anticipated one of Donovan's relatives being at this meeting. Where he would usually be dumbstruck, he takes it in his stride. "Hope my brother didn't bore you to sleep on the flight. He has a habit of doing that."

"Oh, I didn't give him the chance," Hank says, sharing a knowing smile with Donovan.

"In case Donovan hasn't briefed you," Damien says, "I'm Chief of Staff over at Fortress Inc in D.C."

*Fortress. Where have I heard that name before?* Hank searches his brain, but comes up short. He isn't surprised, however, that another member of the Craze clan clearly occupies such a high position of power.

"We provide services for both the private and public sectors." Hank quite can't comprehend how someone can offer such a vague description as to what their company actually does. Damien stands behind the man in glasses and squeezes his shoulder. "Meet Eric Cross. Executive Assistant to Senator Hunt."

"The Senator sends his apologies," Eric says, addressing Donovan. "He's been called in to deal with a matter of great urgency." Donovan simply nods. Not a problem.

"Eric has the mandate to represent Senator Hunt's interests today. And this," Damien says, positioning himself behind Hank's brother from another mother, "is Rick Byrons, Senior Strategic Consultant at Red Hat." Hank smiles politely. Maybe the drugs are wearing off, or perhaps it's being in the presence of the political elite, but his confidence is wavering. These guys are big time.

Rick nods at Fall Water's representatives. "Don't let the job title intimidate you," he says. "I just help answer some of the more challenging tech questions that come our way."

"We're cut from the same cloth, Rick," Hank says, suddenly conscious that he has barely uttered a word since arriving at the table.

"Seems that way!" Rick says, laughing heartily. "Nice to meet someone who doesn't feel the need to wear a suit when it's ninety degrees outside!" Donovan rolls his eyes but remains silent. For these tech nerds, a simple hello is never enough. Best to let them get whatever 'this' is out of their system. "Damien mentioned the project you're currently conceiving. Jeez Louise. That's some scale of thinking. Impressive."

Hank's anxiety starts to spread through his body, starting in his chest and moving outwards. A familiar fog is settling over his brain.

"Thank you."

Donovan takes a seat at the table and gestures for Hank to do the same. He takes a seat next to Rick, who he senses is a key ally at this meeting of minds. He feels Donovan staring at him. *Say something.*

"I can't lie. The jump from single-player console games to what

John has in mind is more of a gargantuan leap. Size won't discourage us, however. There's nothing we can't handle in terms of scope."

Everyone laughs. Hank doesn't know why. That wasn't a joke. He repeats what he just said in his head in search of a punchline. Nope. Nothing there.

"Ha! A game! Good one, Hank!" Damien turns to Donovan. "I like his sense of humor. I guess this entire business is a game in some sense."

Hank feels like he's one step behind the rest of the table. Donovan throws him a reassuring smile. A waitress shows up at the table.

"Ah. I hope nobody minds," Damien says, "I took the liberty of ordering for us all."

Hank most definitely minds. Although it may seem like a minor thing, nobody orders his food for him. He once went on a date with a woman who 'took the liberty' of ordering a few sharing plates before he arrived. He never saw her again. This is a grossly transparent show of authority from Damien. A quick survey of the table indicates that nobody else seems to have a problem, not even Donovan. If they do, they certainly aren't letting on. Hank internally rages, but remains silent.

"Bring out the food whenever you're ready, Ruth," Damien instructs. "As for drinks, there's a couple of paired reds stored for us."

"Starting early, Damien?" Eric asks, pouring himself a glass of water. "Our college days are long behind us."

Hank can't help but smirk. *Of course they went to college together.* Bonds are forged on campus that are cashed in decades later. This is the way of the world.

"Don't give me that, Eric. It's five o'clock somewhere," Damien responds. Returning to the table, the waitress takes that as her cue and fills Damien's wine glass. Rick gestures for her to do the same. The waitress looks at Donovan. He places his hand over his glass.

"I'll take a beer," Hank blurts out, surprising even himself. If he doesn't get to choose his lunch, he can damn well choose his poison. He's been craving a beer all morning and has suffered through enough hangovers to know it'll take the edge off better than a swanky red. The waitress disappears and returns to the table with an ice-cold Bud.

"Right," Rick asserts. "Everything looks good from our end. We can provide the necessary extensive support to the operation. Obviously, an infrastructure-related progression of this magnitude has got our attention."

"Barriers?" Donovan demands.

"Well. I need more information before I can offer assurance on our capabilities as they stand. Hank, can you fill me in?"

Hank's brain is currently moving at a million miles a second. As far as he was briefed yesterday, this was a simple meeting with Red Hat regarding a switch to Linux for the development of *Cyberside*. Why, then, is there a fucking senator's flunkey sitting at the table? What the hell is even being discussed here? He sits in silence staring at his beer, watching the bubbles fizz to the surface. At a loss as to what to do, he grabs it and takes a giant swig. Almost instantly, the alcohol collides with the remnants of Adderall and provides a comforting, euphoric buzz. His heartbeat returns to a regular rhythm and his mind clears. *Why would a senator have a vested interest in the development of a computer game? With the ambitions for this project, we need a new data center. North Carolina is the perfect home for such a build. This sort of thing doesn't just get greenlit. It requires someone to help navigate through the endless red tape and complex regulatory compliances. OK. Got it.* Hank exhales. Everyone looks at him expectantly.

"Traditionally, Fall Water Lake has relied on Windows architecture. Now that we're stepping into a persistent, global, online operation for *Cyberside*, our leadership firmly believes security and sustainability are number one on the call sheet."

*Number one on the call sheet? Where did that come from?*

"We require direct control of processing capabilities," Hank continues, hitting his stride. "With an aim to 3D, my team will be entering a phase of ongoing experimentation. The task ahead is uncharted, gentlemen. This is virgin territory. I'm talking mass data storage, transfer, latency issues... For this to work, we're going to need to write an entirely new web protocol." Hank takes another sip of beer. He glances around the table to find his dining companions nodding respectfully. Thank fuck for that.

"I'm sure you all appreciate the economics of something this bold," Rick says, grabbing the baton and running with it. An army of servers shows up and starts placing giant plates of meat around the table. As if this meeting couldn't get any more alpha. "Not just from our perspective. I'm talking about the state of today's infrastructure. The investment here is..." Rick whistles to make his point.

"Humor us with your estimation," Donovan encourages.

"Look, guys. This isn't just game design. This will revolutionize the way people operate on the web. We're talking five to six years to build the foundation alone. At least. Another ten to get it where it needs to be." Although this isn't news to Hank, it's sobering to hear it from someone with this level of insight. "It won't just require hard work. Stars and planets need to align. Market forces need to match your plans," Rick continues.

"Market forces, such as...?" Donovan asks.

"Global telecoms development, growth of broadband, emergent interfaces, evolution of wireless. You guys are setting yourself an impossible task."

"I'm still not hearing a number," Donovan says. "How many zeros? Ball park?"

"For this level of commitment? Billions."

Hank smiles. This is, indeed, the same laughably vague figure he calculated yesterday when put on the spot. Donovan's reaction at this table is a copy and paste replication of his reaction yesterday. That is to say, he barely has one.

"Billions. OK." Donovan is so eerily calm, it makes Hank wonder how many of those pills he's popping each morning. *Billions* is not a word that is heard in the games industry in 1997. Hank knows that no game on earth could return such investment. Something far bigger is at play here. An awkward silence descends over the table. Eric breaks it.

"The state is increasingly interested in nurturing tech, IT and innovation in North Carolina. With the election in two years, we welcome a large infrastructure project that can…" Eric struggles to find the right words.

"That can provide a more secure position in the volatile landscape that is American politics?" Donovan says, lending a helping hand.

"Well said," Eric confirms. "That level of resources, though. Not going to happen."

"We're not looking for money, Eric," Donovan counters. "We just need the state's blessing to build a new data center facility. It'll be unprecedented. If Hunt throws his support behind this thing, his current rating will skyrocket. It will secure his legacy. Politicians love that word, don't they? Legacy?"

"They sure do," Eric responds. "This will have the Senator's endorsement, but we need to know who's paying. Even Versa can't cover this one."

Donovan turns to Hank. "With *Cyberside* set to reach millions of people worldwide, alongside our other ecosystemic initiatives, how will that influence the development of *Underside*?"

"Well, how technical do you want me to get, Donovan?" Hank answers, far from impressed that he's been put on the spot once again.

"Just a general evolution curve forecast for the next five to ten."

Hank finishes his beer and waves over to the bar for another. "Primary focus will be developing better 3D rendering, editor and toolset to steer the adoption of the tech by third parties, as well as adapting the network code for massive persistent online playing. We'll require statistics and analytical tools for better environmental control and user journey scan. Not to mention procedural generation. Plans are in place to push NPC behavior to the next evolutionary level. In short, anything and everything that will allow us and any developers to create a great interactive game world."

"Once again, if I may," Rick says, addressing Donovan. "Who's footing the bill on this little undertaking?"

"That's where Fortress comes in, Rick," Damien answers. "My clients will be extremely invested in this product. Virtual simulation and data collection are two areas of major interest right now." This seems to satisfy Rick. Hank, on the other hand, is kicking himself for not pressing Damien earlier during his introduction. *Fortress... With a name like that, they must be linked to defense contracts.* Hank's stomach churns. What on earth are they getting into here? Before he can argue, Donovan raises his glass in a toast.

"That seems to be all bases covered. A toast, gentlemen, to the bright future of this enterprise?" Glasses are raised. Hank joins in, operating on autopilot. "Rick, Hank, you two get to work on conceptualizing the facility."

"Sure thing," Hank says, wide-eyed and way out of his depth.

"Eric," Donovan continues, "We'd like all the necessary licenses finalized in the coming months. Damien and I will secure investment. We'll circulate NDAs in the morning. Here's to carving out a perfect future!"

"A perfect future!"

"A perfect future!"

"A perfect future!"

Donovan looks at Hank. *Well?*

"A perfect future," Hank says, in what feels like a full-blown out-of-body experience.

"Does this facility have a name, Donovan?" Eric asks. Donovan shrugs. He's not one to care about what something is called, provided it makes everyone stinking rich. His eyes rest on a tacky statue of the goddess Isis behind the bar.

"How about the Pyramid?"

"Pyramid it is," Eric responds.

For Hank, the rest of the lunch meeting passes by in a blur. He sinks another three beers, embracing the warm high that ebbs and flows. Deep in his gut, Hank knows he is now an accessory to something far beyond the familiar parameters of game design. Oddly, these reservations are short-lived as a seductive curiosity takes hold. Hank's mind whirrs as he contemplates the challenge ahead. This is, after all, what he does best. This Head of R&D has just been promised unlimited resources to redefine the future of tech. The occasional smile from Donovan serves to boost his ego further. He doesn't see Burrow at this table, nor Simmons. Yet here *he* is, gorging on expensive cuts of meat with the state's best and brightest. To create what they envision, drastic steps must be taken. Hank settles on the rather incredible fact that he has just been given the go-ahead to create his magnum opus. He is certain of only two things. He's going to have his work cut out, and he's going to need a lot more of Donovan's magic pills.

---

AS SUMMER 1997 moves into fall, the entertainment and tech industries enter a golden age of unbridled optimism. The world is on the precipice of great change. Nobody can predict the speed with which this revolution is destined to unravel. New players flood the landscape. The term *Wi-Fi* enters common parlance. The following year will welcome Google, GoDaddy, and the Simbian mobile operating system to the world. The first BlackBerry 850 will arrive the following year, placing the internet in people's pockets. Into the new millennium, MySpace, Facebook and YouTube will irrevocably change the way we communicate as a species.

Similarly, gaming also enters a new phase, emerging from basements and into the mainstream. PlayStation 2 will hit the market in March 2000, with Microsoft's Xbox and Nintendo's GameCube hot on its heels. Together, they will create a highly competitive console market. With the founding of Steam, distribution will shift from physical to digital.

As for Fall Water Lake, the company officially announces that *Cyberside* has begun early development in 1999. *Underside* enters the software engine licensing market, as promised. Fall Water becomes the biggest development company in Massachusetts and one of the biggest in the United States. It moves from downtown Boston and builds its own campus in 2002, along with offices in LA, New York, and an expansion into Europe with a small presence in London. Over one hundred worker ants, led by Hank Brown, descend on Raleigh, NC for the Pyramid project, with building work commencing in 1999 and a projected launch of 2005.

Fall Water, id and Epic compete for users and establish cornerstones of third-party development culture. *Underside* remains the engine of preference for online-related products and emerging virtual simulation, whereas *id Tech* and Epic's *Unreal* dominate the single-player PC and console space. This will soon be rivaled by *Source* and *Gamebryo*, amongst others.

As for Fall Water's culture, it shifts quickly and inevitably into a fully functioning corporate behemoth, with Versa Foundation and Donovan quietly and effectively pulling the strings. The company implements special departments and sub-projects. The term *need-to-know basis* is thrown around with increasing regularity. Jim, Steve, and a growing team of developers channel their energy solely into *Cyberside*, while Burrow and Simmons supervise perfecting *Underside*. Damien Craze and Fortress facilitate the forging of key relationships on Capitol Hill between Versa and the US military, the FDA, CDC, FBI and other high-profile agencies and think tanks. By the time 2005 rolls into view, Fall Water is prepping the release of the first version of *Cyberside* on PC. The Pyramid is functional, *Underside 2.0* is on the horizon and the Game Developers Conference 2005 in San Francisco is approaching fast. The good old days of 1997 seem like a lifetime ago.

**END OF PART 1**

# PART II
# THE CHANGE

# 4
## AN OFFSITE

If it wasn't for the persistent rainfall, January in London may well be a nice time of year. Cold, brisk air, the chaos of the fireworks on the Thames that ushered in 2007 now a distant memory, and various historical monuments standing stark against a windswept sky. But the rain. The relentless rain.

James stares out the window of London's brand new Hoxton Hotel's top-floor meeting room. He's already struggling with jet lag and a minor hangover. The soothing pitter patter of rainfall against the glass provides backing vocals to the sleep-inducing monotone white noise of Fall Water's new VP of Business Affairs.

"Our persistent onward march has wielded strong results. *Underside* now has a healthy twenty-two per cent market share for PC and console. Looking ahead, we need to focus resources on the emerging mobile space..." The man, mid-forties, is gray. Gray suit, gray voice, gray hair, gray soul.

Tap tap tap, goes the rain. James' eyelids grow heavy. He pinches his inner thigh, buying himself another few seconds, and loses himself in the view of the swiftly developing Shoreditch. With this growth comes the usual raging debates about gentrification. In this district, Turkish takeaway shops sit awkwardly next to outlets hawking extortionately priced coffee and almond croissants. New start-ups and workspaces emerge in between historical monuments. This is why James loves this city. Ever-progressing, but remaining in the past. A beautiful collision of what was and what is to come, of culture and business, of sentimentalism and pragmatism. This pleasant thought is rudely interrupted by the sight of a bulldozer on the streets below, demolishing a decades-old building to make way for a parking lot. Maybe things aren't quite so rosy after all. This world is a merciless one. Evolve or face extinction. Stasis brings death.

"...company growth is sustainable as we expand onto the global stage. Momentum has been maintained by increasing our portfolio domestically and internationally. This, coupled with the initial success of the licensing model, has ramped up revenue by over sixty per cent YOY..."

*YOY... YOY... Why oh why am I here?* James studies a projection on the wall, busy with color-coded charts and diagrams. He can't decipher it; he may as well be reading Cantonese. This visit was presented to him in no uncertain terms as mandatory. Fall Water's London office has been growing substantially after an aggressive year-long recruitment round. A briefing email described the trip as *an opportunity for key execs to meet in Europe and discuss strategic synergies for the year ahead.* Urgh.

"As for the infrastructure development, the Pyramid project seems to have been with us so long that it will soon need its own walking stick and false teeth." The VP of Business Affairs – James can't remember his name, nor does he care to – chuckles at his own 'joke'. James sighs. He loves the Brit sense of humor, but this clown was clearly out of town when they were dishing it out. "Our data center over in North Carolina is approaching its final stages, with an expectation to go live early next year. Testing sessions relating to *Cyberside* Beta will commence in late August..."

James' bullshit detector springs to life. Mr Gray is clearly regurgitating a report that has been commissioned, submitted, processed, reprocessed, reprocessed again and finally approved before making it into his hands five minutes before this presentation. The truth is that Hank is under intense pressure to launch testing in September, not

August. Dates have been pushed repeatedly after agonizing delays. Trying to get a sense check from others in the room, James catches eyes with London office reps Alex and Marcus. The three of them share a thinly veiled look of cynicism and James feels relieved that he isn't going mad – this presentation really is top-shelf corporate propaganda. He's got a lot of time for these two. Marcus, who is leading the UK side of the operation, is an old-school industry vet. James has been emailing him for months and likes the cut of his jib. Alex is younger and on the tech side. James had a call with him last night from his hotel room, sacrificing a catchup with Sarah to discuss local team allocations. The conversation soon morphed into the ironing out of version system control usage and new updates, and ran on longer than it should have. Thankfully, James had the hotel minibar to keep him company. Although he's regretting it now, he knows by the beads of sweat on Alex's forehead that he was clearly on the sauce last night too. Marcus' furrowed brow suggests the same. Two Brits and a Yank. Brothers in arms, bound by grog.

James finds Virginia, sitting at the head of the table, smirking at him. She knows this isn't James' bag and it's clearly amusing her. They've established a solid working relationship over the past few years, built on a sturdy foundation of respect. Neither truly knows what the other does, but are smart enough to know competence when they see it. Their paths sometimes cross and they have both been at Fall Water long enough to have created an unspoken bond that can only be born out of an extended length of service. That said, Virginia is top-level. On the rare occasion that James has disagreed with her, he's come to regret it. This is not a woman to be fucked with. She has Donovan's ear and isn't afraid to scream into it.

James sits up and pays attention... for all of five seconds. His eyes go for a casual stroll around the table to identify other familiar faces. A couple of Virginia's army are present. There's Ron, from the engine sales team, and Joseph, Head of Enterprise Sales from LA. The sales force has become one of Fall Water's biggest departments, largely due to *Underside* licensing now stretching far beyond the glass ceiling of gaming. It has made small yet significant exploratory inroads into big tech, real estate visualization, and defense and government contracts, the latter of which was spearheaded by Versa and proved to be a license to print money. Uncle Sam's checks are greater in value and regularity than anything games development can offer. To manage this side of the business, Fall Water Lake has opened a subsidiary, Fall Water Enterprise. James, always one to approve of the separation of church and state, has been very happy to have had zero dealings with them so far.

James barely recognizes anyone else here. There's a large Asian contingent, reflecting recent developments in Tokyo and Seoul. Aside from that, it's various iterations of young, upcoming and ambitious business-development types. They all look the same, as if someone has hit Ctrl+C on the first and hit Ctrl+V repeatedly.

"On that note, let's take a quick break. Drinks and snacks are in the next room. I'll see you back here in an hour."

*For some more scintillating insights, no doubt.* James can't stand quick enough. He's so dangerously close to slipping into a coma that he needs to get outside, rain be damned. Marcus approaches, seemingly reading his mind.

"James. Alex and I are headed next door for a cheeky snifter. What do you say to the hair of the dog?"

"I thought you'd never ask," James answers. "If we're going to survive the second half of this thing, we need a pick-me-up. Lead the way."

As the three men head out, Virginia gives him a half-joking, half-serious warning stare. She taps her watch. *Don't be late.* James gives her a nod. *Wouldn't dream of it.*

---

"Three G&Ts, mate. Doubles."

"Sure thing. Paying now, or on a tab?" Marcus looks at James. James shrugs.

"Better put it on a tab," Marcus says, handing the barman a credit card. "We'll be having more than one."

The three men, soaked to the skin having just run over the road in the downpour, sink down into deep brown leather couches. James takes in his surroundings. Mahogany fixtures, soccer – scrap that, footie – on the TV, sawdust on the floor, real-ale pumps standing to attention in a row on the bar. It's not for a want of trying, but the Yanks are seemingly incapable of capturing the spirit of the good old-fashioned English pub. He glances around at a melting pot of finance guys brokering deals, red-top journalist hacks sourcing scoops, football louts soaking up the game, post-house production employees emerging from their basements to grab a quick bite to eat. James considers and it suddenly hits him. What makes a truly authentic British pub? Why, Brits, of course. The barman brings over the drinks and the three men take grateful sips.

"There's a legitimate science to it, you know," James ruminates. "Hair of the dog." Alex nods in agreement.

"Yeah, mate. Raising blood alcohol levels masks hangover symptoms." The trio take another sip as if to test the theory.

"No scientific evidence to prove it, is there?" Marcus says, breaking the spell. "Nice thought though."

"Do we have dinner plans?" James asks, as hunger begins to emerge victorious from the shadows of delirious drowsiness.

"Nobu, seven o'clock," Marcus answers. "You been to any of them in the States, Jim?"

"Haven't had the luxury," James answers. He thinks back to his wedding anniversary trip to New York last year when he tried to book in at Nobu's inaugural Tribeca location. Naturally, he waited until two days before to call up on the off chance they'd had a cancellation. Naturally, they hadn't. He opted instead for a slap-up Italian in Brooklyn. Sarah didn't seem to mind, and, if she did, she had the good nature not to say.

"So," Alex says. "What did you make of all that corporate waffle, Jim?" The three finish their drinks; Marcus gestures to the barman for another round. James contemplates lying to his colleagues to keep up the 'hands across the water' purpose of the trip, but on this occasion, in this setting, he opts for the truth.

"Corporate waffle. Couldn't have put it better myself." Marcus and Alex laugh, relieved to discover that James is as they suspected: one of them. "This culture has infiltrated the entire company, what can I say? New hires everywhere you look with little to no interest in game development. When Virginia starts mentioning Fall Water in the same breath as Google, Microsoft, and Apple, you know things have changed. It's been happening for a decade, guys."

"Come off it!" Marcus exclaims. "You can't compare us to those big dogs. We're B2C game development. Sure, the projects are getting bigger, but we're still niche. We ain't trying to cure cancer here."

"No," James agrees. "But Versa is certainly trying to. They're literally trying to cure cancer. Pharma, boys. Proper shit." James winces at his own choice of words. *Proper shit?* He's been in the UK for fifteen hours and already he's sounding like one of them. Maybe it's the gin. Maybe it's the pub. Maybe it's Alex's and Marcus' contagious energy. Maybe it's the fact that he subconsciously mirrors people's accents when he first meets them to mask a raging insecurity. It's probably all four.

Marcus shakes his head. "I thought Versa is an investor? Where do they get off poisoning us with their top-down bollocks? They shouldn't be telling us what to develop and how, Jim. It ain't right."

"Easy, Marcus. I wouldn't go that far," James counters, sensing that this chat is slipping dangerously into a bitching session. "Burrow has integrity. He's still at the helm. All creative decisions come from him and Simmons."

"Oh, I don't doubt it," Marcus says, throwing his hands up in defense.

"Best to try and ignore the business side as best we can," James says. "Easier said than done, I know, but just try to block it out. My focus is solely on going live on Beta for *Cyberside* at the end of the year. No room up here for anything else." James taps his head. He accepts that this statement doesn't solely apply to work. *I should really call Sarah.*

"You're right," Marcus says. "It is easier said than done." He and Alex exchange a quick glance. Marcus subtly shakes his head. *No.*

"Alright, lads. I may be jet lagged, but I'm not blind. Spit it out. We're all friends here." Despite what he's just said, James sits with his arms folded, defenses at the ready. The barman arrives with another round. Alex takes a sip.

"Alright. Seen as you ask. I, er..." Marcus senses Alex struggling. He steps in.

"The new dynamic is worrying us, fella. It's all getting so political. Everyone's fighting for space in the sandbox." Marcus is flustered, speaking with an energy that suggests he's been sitting on this for ages. "Burrow's intentions are sound, there's no denying that, but there's increasing asymmetry in the team. Too many voices, too many conflicting motivations."

"You've heard the phrase 'too many cooks spoil the broth,' Jim?" Alex asks. James stares at him, deadpan.

"Yes, Alex. I've heard the phrase." James instantly regrets his patronizing tone. He unfolds his arms and looks Alex in the eye. He nods. *Go on. I'm all ears.*

"It's a dangerous mindset," Alex says, finding his voice. "Everything needs nine stamps of fuckin' approval. Communication is sluggish outside of the Dev team. Other departments are chipping in with ill-informed feedback to justify their budgets." James nods. He's become adept at keeping outside forces at arm's length, but Marcus is right. It's not always so easy. Where once a new idea could gestate and be explored with little interference, he now has to submit a proposal up the food chain to get the go-ahead, often having to wait weeks for approval to trickle back down. By that point, the idea could have gone stale or been forgotten entirely, to be replaced by another. At which point the whole excruciating process begins once again.

"I hear you," James says, relaying a phrase he has heard from one of the many management courses he's been forced to attend in the last couple of years. "Honestly. I hear you." It seems to work. When Marcus speaks again, his agitation has subsided significantly.

"We're all fighting for resources. HR, Sales and Marketing are constantly sticking their grubby beaks in. I've lost count of how many VPs of this, that, and the other we've got now."

"No joke," Alex says. "I spend four hours a day providing updates to a steadily increasing distribution list of Versa loyalists who wake up each morning and salute the flag. It's unsustainable." James can't help but smile. God, they're right. He may be separated from these two guys by the Atlantic, but they share the same struggles.

"OK. What can I do?"

Marcus is pleasantly surprised. Here's this American, come over from the Boston office, Head of Dev on *Cyberside* no less, asking how he can help. What's more, he actually seems genuine.

"I know it's a big ask, Jim, but is there a world in which you can make sure we're not burdened with as many auxiliary requests? If we're expected to meet deadlines, they need to stop, or at least come from one source. One conflicts the other, which conflicts another."

Alex eagerly nods. "If we can reduce reporting to even twice a week rather than daily, that would help too." As a coder, James knows exactly what they're getting at. Sometimes, it feels like the same people who hired him are determined to make it as hard as possible for him to do his job. Lately, he's been spending a good chunk of his time playing diplomat, trying to keep the execs out of the Pit and deflecting grievances from down below. A war on two fronts, with him stuck in the middle. Creativity versus money. Nothing about this is new. Same shit, different time zone.

"Right," James says. "How does this sound? I'll talk to Virginia when we're back in Boston about getting a sole voice in the US to liaise with you. Create a buffer between you and them. Reporting two times a week might be a push, but I'm sure I can convince them of three. Fair compromise?"

"I could live with that," Alex responds.

"Thanks, Jim. Seriously, this means a lot," Marcus says. "We were bricking it about bringing this up."

"I'm glad you did," James says, enjoying the respect he's just earned. "It's what I'm here for." He's not wrong. He was flown over to strengthen relationships with the London office and facilitate international workstreams. Five minutes in a pub has been more productive than five hours in a boardroom. Sometimes, people just need to be heard.

Alex gestures to the bar. "What do you say to another?" James pictures Virginia tapping on her watch. He taps on his own.

"Very tempting, but we better get back."

"You're probably right," Marcus agrees, standing and heading to the bar to settle up.

"Nice timepiece, by the way," Alex says, nodding at James' watch.

"Thanks, man. Sarah got it for me last year for our fifteenth wedding anniversary. Too slick for me. What is it you guys say? You can't polish a turd, but you can throw glitter on it?"

"Nah, man. It suits you." James struggles to decipher whether this is a genuine compliment or a classic case of bootlicking. Either way, he's uncomfortable. He's never been good at taking compliments. That said, this one will give him a much-needed confidence boost that will last a few days. He'd mentioned to Sarah in passing that he'd always longed for a nice watch, but could never justify spending that kind of money on himself. It wasn't a hint, but Sarah had clearly been taking notes. Over a dish of mama's homemade meatballs in New York, accompanied by the second cheapest bottle of red on the menu, she presented him with the green leather Rolex box. The fact that it was scuffed was a giveaway that it was second-hand, but he hadn't cared. She'd been putting in overtime at the hospital for months, and now he knew why. And what had he got her in return? Economy seats on a flight from Boston to New York and a cheap yet cheerful meal in a spaghetti house. Shit. It hits James like a punch in the gut. He's been letting things slip with Sarah. When he gets back home, he's got some serious work to do.

"How is the good lady wife, anyway? All good?" Alex asks.

"Yeah," James says. "Moved into our new place last year. We actually have a separate kitchen and living room now. The American dream." Alex slaps him on the back.

"Great, mate! Love that for you! What's next? Is that the pitter patter of tiny feet I hear?"

James chuckles, momentarily caught off guard by the sheer weight of the question. "Perhaps. After Beta. Everything after Beta."

As James pulls on his jacket, Alex goes to the bar to grab Marcus. He finds him, leans in and whispers.

"So, what do you think?"

"He's a great guy," Marcus responds. "Clearly means well. But if he thinks he can keep the wolves from our door, he's as blue-eyed as they come."

THAT EVENING, James awakes from an essential nap at six o'clock, surprisingly refreshed, and phones Sarah. As expected, it goes to her voicemail.

"Hi babe, just checking in. Wanted to say hi and tell you that I love you, I miss you. I need to let you know you mean the world to me. That's it. Oh, and it's raining here. Oh, how's the decorating going? Oh, and I'm off to Nobu tonight. Sorry. Don't hate me. We'll always have mama's homemade meatballs. This is Jim. Bye."

The mere act of the call has scratched the gnawing itch James gets when he realizes a distance is growing between him and his wife. Sarah is extremely understanding of James' job, but it's far from a one-way street. She works endless hours at the hospital, often staying on long after her shifts have ended. If she's not working, she's probably studying. If Sarah is on nights, she and James may not see each other for a week, sometimes more, despite living in the same house and sleeping in the same bed. Once, they kept missing each other so often that in the time in between, James went from clean-shaven to fully bearded. When they finally ended up back at home at the same time, Sarah didn't recognize her own husband and almost phoned the police.

Discussions were had in the early days of their relationship. Work was evidently going to play a major part in both of their lives, and it was their drive, ambition and passion for their respective careers that attracted them to each other in the first place. Even so, when Sarah is busy, she makes a conscious decision to check in with her husband, ensuring they at least talk every day. When James is up against it, however, work can become all-consuming. He pours every ounce of creativity into his projects, leaving his mental capacity exhausted and his energy depleted, disappearing inside himself for weeks on end. In the month or so leading up to a major deadline, James simply isn't there. He's a husk of a man, an empty shell. You'd get more stimulating conversation out of a toilet brush. Sarah has regular chats with Steve, who always confirms that, yes, their beloved Jim is currently going through a zombie period. Sarah knows not to take it personally, but it doesn't make it any easier. Sometimes, she just wants to have a normal conversation with her husband. James will eventually cotton on that he's drifted and so begins the process of him making small steps back into the land of the living. This is one such occasion. It's a constantly repeating cycle to which he doesn't even realize he's succumbed.

James jumps in the shower, then grabs his BlackBerry and responds to a few urgent emails while on the toilet. *And they say men can't multitask.* Steve Jobs' iPhone has just hit the market with a splash and Burrow has had hundreds of units shipped in for everyone, but James hasn't had time to migrate everything yet, so he's sticking with the BlackBerry. He works through his inbox methodically, first answering questions from his team with one-word or one-sentence answers. James' email etiquette stopped being polite a while ago. Efficiency is key. If people are sending perfectly formatted emails, they have too much time on their hands.

Next, he opens a message from Hank with a list of ten bullet-pointed questions. He gives this one more attention. Poor Hank is close to the edge and needs all the help he can get. They communicate often by phone and email, but he misses their chess games, that's for sure.

Next, an email from Sarah including a photo attachment of her, paint roller in hand, about to attack the dining room. He presses *Reply* and takes a photo of his own face, framing it in such a way that it doesn't look like he's mid-ablution.

James still has eighty unread emails in his inbox, but that will do for now. So long as it's under a hundred, he's happy. Finally, he emails Steve. *Hey champ. Weather is a horror show and the presentations are a ballache, but Alex and Marcus are as cool as we'd hoped. And no, I haven't had pie and mash yet. Wish me luck in LA. Jim.*

Half an hour later, James is sitting at the hotel bar with a pint of London Pride – he hates this stuff, but when in Rome – waiting for his fellow Fall Water troops to arrive. Suddenly, his Boston Red Sox baseball cap is whipped off his head and he turns to find Dina Stewart, Head of PR, dragging a stool over to join him.

"How's it hanging, big guy?" Dina asks, fixing his cap on her head.

She takes a sip of his beer and grimaces. "Disgusting. Don't know how you can drink the stuff." She gets the barman's attention and orders a martini, two olives.

"Hey, Dina. Over the jet lag yet?"

"Over what, honey?"

"The jet lag."

"Jet...?"

"... lag."

James knows what Dina is up to and he merrily plays along. She's a longtime friend, one of John's early hires from back in the day, and she has this kind of friendly repartee down to a fine art. If you go toe to toe with the woman, you better bring your A game or she'll leave you in the dust begging for mercy. Dina is an infinite source of energy and her conversations are a tonic. After *Otherscape 2* launched, she was promoted into her senior PR role, leaving Virginia to handle strategic and growth marketing, presentations, and all of that other interminable stuff. Put simply, it's now Dina, not Virginia, who has Barry Cromer and his ilk on speed dial.

"Jet lag. Huh. Never heard of it. Sorry." James chuckles at this, already feeling the strains of work drifting away. "Little secret, Jim. Denial isn't just a river in Egypt. If something doesn't exist, you don't have to be a slave to it. Jet lag's for schmucks." She makes half of her martini disappear.

"Do they ever stop drinking in the UK?" James asks. "My hand's default shape is now curved around a pint glass, I swear." He shows Dina the afflicted hand, and she throws her head back and roars with laughter. James gets a rush of dopamine, the kind that hits when the funniest person in the room laughs at one of your jokes.

"They say the iPhone is the future," Dina says. "Fuck that. Day drinking is the way forward. I'm taking this hat, by the way. Seeing as I can't have your heart, this will have to do."

James grimaces. Years ago, at a work Christmas party in which wives and girlfriends were invited, he got so drunk he mistook Dina for Sarah. He doesn't remember it happening, but the next day, Dina took great delight in telling him that he had sidled up to her on the dancefloor, slipped his arms around her waist, and told her they should go home and try and bring another Reynolds into the world. Dina and Sarah have never let him forget it.

"I thought you were Sarah! You were wearing the same dress!"

"I'm fucking with you, man!" Dina screams. "Chill! I take it as a compliment. As should she." James is clearly praying for something, anything, to swallow him up. Along with his speech at 1997's E3, which has now entered the annals of Fall Water legend, this incident has made itself comfortable atop the Reynolds Humiliation Wall of Fame. Dina senses James' discomfort, relishes it for another couple of seconds, then puts him out of his misery with a swift change of subject. "How was the meeting?"

"Ah, yes. The meeting." James takes his cap back and places it back on his head. "Decided to skip that one, did you?"

"Obviously. I made sure I was literally anywhere else." Dina grabs her BlackBerry and shoots off a few emails as she talks. Somehow, she still seems to give James her full attention. Quite the skill. "I met one of our agencies at Embankment, did a roundtable with a bunch of media folk, lunched with *Edge*, then had a quick drink here with Informa about GDC."

"Busy girl," James says.

"Wouldn't have it any other way. What's Marcus saying? Everything above board in the Albion office?" James contemplates sharing the sentiments of the meeting with Dina, but he's enjoying the moment. No need to kill the vibe.

"A few organizational issues, nothing major," he says. Dina immediately reads between the lines.

"Same everywhere," she confirms. "Getting anything done is a nightmare." James is glad to hear these words come from Dina's mouth. It's a relief to know these headaches aren't solely felt by the Dev team. To hear it coming from one of the old guards is a bonus. Aside from Steve and Hank, Dina Stewart is the only one who knows what things were like back in the day. The four of them share the same prescription in their rose-tinted specs.

"I swear we're creating problems just so we can report that they're being solved," James says. Dina nods.

"Talk to John and Tom when you're back from LA. I'll do the same. Two days apart. Mid-afternoon, when they're most malleable."

James hasn't noticed the rabble of Fall Water employees that has descended on the bar, jackets on, ready to leave for dinner. He catches eyes with Virginia. She taps her watch. Of course she does.

"Come on, Dina," James says. "Mother has spoken."

---

WITH MARCUS LEADING THE WAY, the FWL delegation waves down a fleet of black cabs and heads across town to Nobu on Old Park Lane. James, having made the questionable choice to go to the bathroom before they left the hotel, ends up alone on the curb outside and realizes he's been left behind. He flags a cab of his own and enjoys a fleeting twenty minutes of solitude, refusing to check his phone and indulging in one of his favorite pastimes: staring aimlessly out of the window.

As the cab navigates down Shaftesbury Avenue, past the Gielgud and the Lyric, James considers the city and tries to think of its American equivalent. New York is too busy. LA, too hot, too vapid, too non-walkable. He shudders at the thought of being there in two days; he'd much rather fly straight back to Boson to help Sarah paint the house.

The taxi enters Piccadilly Circus. In terms of tempo, architecture, history and culture, San Fransisco springs to mind as the only place that really compares to London. Even that comes up short. James is mildly excited about visiting the City by the Bay for the Game Developers Conference later this year, but, much like Fall Water, San Francisco has succumbed to the forces of big business in recent times. It's now the home of choice for giant tech companies, bringing with them hiked property prices and chronic overcrowding. San Francisco has become the capital of startup culture and entrepreneurial spirit. You can't turn a corner without some young buck flinging their business card in your face and telling you how they're going to change the world. What's worse is they all believe it.

James jumps out of the taxi and into the beautiful, sophisticated minimalism of Nobu. *Sarah would have loved this.* A hostess guides him downstairs and he enters a VIP room to a sea of familiar faces who welcome him to the party with a cacophony of whoops, hollers, and "Where the fuck did you get to, Reynolds?" James thanks the heavens that the only seat left at the long table is wedged between Marcus and Dina. There is a distinct split at the table. Aside from Dina, James' half of the table is filled with dev developers, whereas Virginia and an army of business people take up the other end. If you wanted to separate fun from tedium, all you would need is a line down the middle. James observes this with a wry smile and nudges Marcus.

"Creative is creative and business is business."

"Here, here," Marcus says. "And never the twain shall meet." James' attention is drawn to the man who led the meeting earlier today. He still looks monochrome, even in this haven of soft lighting and Asian-inspired charm.

"The VP of Business Affairs, what was his name?" James asks.

"Colin," Dina replies. "Of course, his name is Colin. He's a laugh a minute. Am I right?"

As drinks are poured and food is served, the party relaxes into a lively rhythm. Conversations bounce from future plans, both personal and professional, *Cyberside*, and GDC, along with a hearty serving of rumor and gossip.

"Of course we'll win. It's ours for the taking."

"Have you heard about what Valve is cooking?"

"What is this? Fish?"

"Jim, say hi to Dario in LA. We came up at Disney together!"

"Is Rachel really keen on Steve? She's been flirting with him for a decade."

"I developed a strategy title back in Berlin. I wish we had *Underside* then."

"BlackBerry is dead. Just bury it. The iPhone will change the world. Just wait."

There are differences of opinion, naturally, and some of the British sarcasm goes flying over the American visitors' heads. Ultimately, however, deep down, no matter where they're from, the very smart, extremely capable people in the room are connected by a unified, shared vision. There's wizardry present around this table; the kind of magic that is created when a diverse range of personalities, artists, musicians, writers, engineers, and modelers join forces to simply 'make something cool'. All are aware they are involved in something truly special.

"Transmedia is going to be huge. Movies, games, it will all blend eventually."

"What we're doing now is far beyond gaming."

"How many people work for us now? I've lost count."

Slightly overwhelmed, James goes outside for a smoke – he'll give up again soon – with Dina and the community guys. Discussion drifts from the upcoming *BioShock*, to the new *Halo* instalment, to *Team Fortress*, to the future of digital distribution.

When they return inside after ten minutes, James is alert to a shift in mood. As someone who is averse to confrontation – it brings him out in a literal rash – he has a knack for sensing the subtlest change in a group dynamic. All night, he's been sniffing out moments where the conversation is about to tip from jovial to abrasive and throwing in a gentle joke, or moving the subject along to something else entirely. As a child of divorce, James has been playing the role of diplomat since he was five years old, defusing arguments before they even break out. Ten minutes, however, is a long time to be away from a boozy powder keg of clashing personalities. As he sits back down, he observes that everyone around the table has fallen silent, except for Virginia and Marcus.

"You have to admit, Marcus," Virginia says, "With so much agenda for growth, priorities will naturally change. Just look at Apple and Google." *Shit. There she goes again with her Apple and Google.* "They made it where they are by not only sensing the future landscape, but creating it."

Heads turn to Marcus, as if Virginia and he are on Centre Court at Wimbledon. He wants to let rip, but he carefully censors himself.

"I'm not disagreeing here, Virginia, but Fall Water is first and foremost a games company. That's why most of us joined. We're not Google. We're not Apple. Or Morgan Stanley, for that matter, or

McDonalds, or General Motors. All this talk of changing culture... our culture is gaming. Feels pretty cut and dried."

"General Motors wasn't always General Motors though, Marcus. McDonalds didn't come out of the gate with restaurants on every continent. Maurice and Richard McDonald started out with a sole location. A humble drive-thru in San Bernandino serving cheeseburgers."

"What's your point, Virginia?"

"My point is that times change. Look around this table. We're not cave dwellers, grunting, smashing each other on the head with clubs and fucking anything that moves." James senses an opportunity.

"I don't know, Virginia. Have you been down in the Pit lately?" Everyone laughs, including Virginia. James breathes a sigh of relief. *Thanks, mom and dad.*

"If I may. I think what Virginia is saying, Marcus, is that we have outgrown video games." All eyes turn to... Colin? Good Lord! That was unexpected. "With *Underside* and our new operational model, not to mention Versa and Fortress' capital, there's no two ways about it. We need to adapt. It's not just us. Look at any tech giant. Look at this city. A new world order is upon us."

That phrase ripples around the table. There's no way Colin just dropped the phrase *new world order*. Is he joking? No, not possible. This man is where humor goes to die. Having dropped that ominous bombshell, Colin tucks back into his black cod miso. James feels a cold shiver trickle down his spine. The only sound in the room is the awkward clanging of cutlery. James sees Alex, who has been quietly drinking himself into a stupor, neck a shot of sake, pour himself another, and stand up. James senses trouble and tries to think of a quip. Unfortunately for Alex, he's not quick enough.

"As unaccustomed as I am to public speaking," Alex begins. A few people shuffle uncomfortably in their seats. "A toast!"

Alex raises his glass. About half the table does the same.

"Here's to our American guests, to big tech, to world domination, to crushing the little guy, and to unwavering loyalty to the new world order. I thought we were video game designers, not the Third Reich, but what do I know?"

Virginia instantly takes out her phone and starts typing, as does Colin. Alex is too drunk to notice that his cards are marked and, come tomorrow, he probably won't be part of the new world order that he's openly mocking.

"Oh! And here's to Versa and Fortress, whatever the fuck it is they do." Alex downs his sake and slumps back down in his chair. Not a single other person at the table has the common decency to commit career suicide by following suit. Marcus hangs his head and smiles sadly, aware that Alex just signed his own death warrant. As for James, he nudges Dina in the ribs. She stands up and claps her hands.

"Right. What would everyone say to a fun little game?"

---

JAMES SHARES a silent taxi ride back to the hotel with Dina. On Old Street, James leans forward and asks the driver to pull over.

"What's up? Are you gonna throw up?" Dina asks.

"All good. Just want to walk the rest of the way. I need a little time to digest." Dina nods, understanding. A quick peck on the cheek and James is out on the street.

A potent mixture of grape and grain is coursing through James' bloodstream and he's in dire need of a power walk to nowhere in particular to reset after Alex's little outburst. James was genuinely going to put the wheels in motion to ease pressure on the London office, but deep down he knows it wouldn't have made an iota of difference. The writing is on the wall. Maybe Alex suspected as much and decided to go out in style.

James blindly starts to walk, allowing himself a few deep breaths of cold London air. Usually, when stress gets too much, he opts for a run, but he'll have to settle for this. As he strolls, he considers Sarah, their future, and of where he fits in at Fall Water. Has he sold out? If so, when did it happen? Is he becoming what he used to hate? Is it too late to jump ship? As James' mind wanders, he enters something close to his coding flow state. Various thoughts and memories jostle for attention. Memories of his idealistic college days, of his mom and dad and their constant screaming matches, of meeting Steve and writing a stupid song that they don't sing anymore. James thinks of meeting Sarah and of recent conversations about starting a family. So wrapped up is he in his thoughts that he barely notices when snow starts to fall. He is oblivious to a drunken fight that spills out of a pub and into the street. He is ignorant to the cyclist who comes careening off his bike and will wake up in hospital with four stitches on his forehead and a concussion. James simply walks, making spontaneous decisions at every turn, going where his feet lead him. His meditative state is punctured by the sound of a last orders bell ringing out of a pub.

James finds himself at the bar sipping a glass of Scotch, contemplating the evening. *New world order. New fucking world order?*

Ten minutes later and he's once again roaming the streets of Shoreditch, unaware of space and time.

Another bar. A cocktail bar this time. Two tequilas. Fuck it. You only live once. It's possible James is trying to recreate his listless youth, the glory days of careless bar crawls and of ignoring the threat of tomorrow. Whatever he's doing, it doesn't seem to be his choice. He's a mere passenger of where the night is taking him. Free will is overrated anyway.

Back on the streets and the snowfall is heavier now, coating East London in a thick layer of immaculate white. An ice-cold wind penetrates James' senses, sobering him up somewhat. This simply won't do. He looks over the road to the inviting sign of the Ace Hotel.

James enters the modern lobby, still packed with people despite the hour. Many stare with childlike joy at the snowfall out the window. A concierge guides James to the bar and gets him seated.

"What'll it be, sir?" the barman asks. James is momentarily stumped, but is inspired by Dina's earlier choice.

"Martini. Two olives."

James' attention is drawn to a lively group of young, carefree types on a nearby table. The occasional phrase seeps through the gentle hubbub.

"Digital distribution will replace hardware in the next few years."

"Can't wait for GDC. I've never been to San Francisco."

"You heard about what Fall Water Lake is working on?"

James stands and walks over. This is not something he would usually ever think of doing. Having surrendered to instinct, however, he's not thinking right now. He spots an Epic Games logo on one of the group's jackets. *What are the odds?*

"Hi guys. Sorry to interrupt. I heard you talking development. Are you guys with Epic?" The sole woman of the group looks him up and down and decides that the bumbling Yank is of zero threat.

"That's right, mate. You a fan?"

"No," James says. "Well, yeah. I'm actually with Fall Water over in Boston. The company is hosting an offsite here in town."

The crowd immediately parts and James is warmly welcomed into Epic's inner sanctum. Dropping the name Fall Water Lake seems like an access-all-areas pass these days. If you were to stroll up to a security guy at a Metallica gig and say you're with Fall Water, five minutes later you'd be shooting the shit with James and Lars backstage.

James is introduced to an Olesya and a Nick, gets chatting to an Eastern European named Aleksey, who orders a round of pisco sours. By sheer coincidence, Epic's EMEA team is also in London for an offsite. Discussion points include *Unreal Engine 3* and Valve's upcoming *Portal*. Emails are swapped and promises that will be broken are made to meet up at GDC. For James, it's a joy to simply talk video games. Much like sinking into a warm bath, the stresses of his day gently dissipate.

"This industry is purely cyclical," Aleksey says, as talk turns to the wider gaming landscape. "Everything comes around again if you wait long enough. It's like a constantly repeating spiral. If you take a step back, it's all pretty predictable." James stews on this thought. Knowing he will likely never see this man again, he throws caution to the wind, saying out loud a question that has been nagging him for months.

"And what if you don't feel right about what's coming?"

James may be a complete stranger, but Aleksey knows an existential crisis when he sees one. Most men over thirty do, and if they don't, they will do soon enough. He takes time to consider his response.

"Well. I guess you'd just need to find a way to break the cycle."

This hits James like a freight train. Tomorrow, he will forget most of this late night adventure, but this sentence burrows into his subconscious, where it will remain for a long time to come.

As the night draws to a close, James falls into and out of a taxi, into his hotel, into the elevator, and finally into bed. As he drifts off into a drunken coma, his subliminal mind tries to make sense of a very long, very strange trip. Oddly enough, he is completely unaware of the strangest aspect of his day.

It's 2007. The Ace Hotel in Shoreditch won't be opened until 2013. Come morning, James won't even remember its name.

## 5

## CROSSROADS

Virginia Willis sits on a bench watching a mother and her two kids as they feed the ducks on the Serpentine in London's Hyde Park. Virginia hates ducks. They look untrustworthy. The children are clearly too young for school, which is why their mom has brought them here on a Wednesday morning. Last night's snow has melted following heavy rainfall and the temperature drop has been severe. Virginia feels the chill, but sitting on park benches contemplating her life choices is one of the rare treats she allows herself on work trips. Her need to remain sharp dictates an abstinence from alcohol where possible. Days jam-packed with meetings mean exploring a city's tourist spots is not an option. Nope. It's the simple act of sitting and watching the locals go about their day that Virginia relies on for a reset. This essential ritual is why she sits here, freezing her ass off, watching people she has never met feed animals that piss her off. It's not that she necessarily wants to be here. She *has* to be. Especially considering the meeting she's about to attend.

Virginia watches the family unit with a keen curiosity. The mother seems so calm, so untroubled. Does she even have a job to go to? What must that be like? To not work? Although her own boys are off at college now, Virginia struggles to picture a life in which she is happily unemployed, playing the stay-at-home wife, meeting her girlfriends to grab a quick salad and talking about their husbands' work stresses. So alien is the concept that she surprises herself by laughing out loud. Her career is now such an ingrained part of her identity that she genuinely can't fathom a world in which it doesn't exist.

Virginia studies the mother. What's the most significant decision she will make today? Last night before bed, once she got approval from Donovan, Virginia emailed Marcus and told him to fire Alex. She could have let Alex's actions slide, but it wasn't worth the risk. Colin has a hotline to Donovan and she was smart enough to know that the optics wouldn't be great if the new VP of Business Affairs reported the incident before she did. It wasn't even a choice. Such is the nature of the beast. Kill or be killed.

This sort of decision is now par for the course. Hiring and firing is a weekly occurrence. Virginia thinks back ten years to the oyster house in Boston when she made a decision that changed the trajectory of her life. She's been in Donovan's pocket ever since, feeding him names of disloyal employees and reporting breaches in trust within the company grid. Initially, she was a reluctant participant, but it only took a few short months for the power addiction to take hold. Immediately following her lunch with Donovan, she made a phone call and ended her affair. This lasted all of a month. Once it became clear that her secret would be protected – so long as she towed the line – her extra-marital BDSM sessions reignited. The fact that her lover also worked at Fall Water, and still does, made it a difficult habit to kick. Sexual chemistry like that doesn't simply just up and disappear. What Virginia didn't expect was for the dynamic to slowly shift. Up until this point, the relationship had been a purely physical one. As Virginia's dominance was secured at Fall Water, however, her desire to explore this particular kink filtered away. With every man in her professional life sucking up to her, she didn't need an illicit affair to get her kicks. No. Something much more complicated began to happen. She actually started to fall for the guy.

Virginia has been rewarded generously for her fealty to Versa. There had been a time when she had been terrified of Donovan, but it didn't take her long to figure him out. Hell, she now agrees with most of the underhand things he charges her with doing. Soon enough, the advantages of the deal started rolling in. When her dipshit brother got arrested for a DUI, one phone call from Versa and the charge disappeared. After her youngest son failed to show up for his interview at Harvard, Versa stepped in and reminded the admissions board that they had donated a physics research wing to the institution the previous year. Wouldn't you know it... he was given another chance and passed with flying colors. When Virginia's uncle was suddenly diagnosed with cancer, a full package of medical insurance appeared out of the ether. He hadn't made it, but his final few months were comfortable, with around-the-clock care. This isn't to mention Virginia's new house, three vacations a year and a bank account she doesn't even bother to check anymore. What's the point? She knows the money will be there. If she needs an extra boost, a useful bit of insider trading is never far away.

The doting mother buys her children hot chocolate from a vendor and the three of them shuffle away, content. Virginia feels a pang of envy. She lets it swim around for a moment, but common sense prevails as the word echoes around her head. *Content.* Content was never enough for her, nor will it ever be. She concludes that it isn't envy she's feeling. It's pity. Virginia reaches into her bag, takes out her Versa pin, and fixes it to her coat collar.

---

A SHORT WHILE LATER, Virginia stands in front of a grand building in Knightsbridge. The giant edifice of glass and metal screams of power and control. If Donovan was a building, he would be this monstrosity. She checks her pin is in place. It's not just about looking the part. Without it, she won't even be able to enter the building. Virginia makes sure her mask of control is in place and crosses the threshold.

As the blacked-out automatic door silently glides open, the unflinching lens of the security camera fixed to the ceiling cross-references Virginia's face with the digital signature registered in her Versa pin. The sound of high heels on marble echo around the empty lobby as she crosses to the elevator. Much like everything related to

Versa, the place is faceless. There is no reception. No visible security. No other soul in sight.

As Virginia waits for the elevator, she notes Versa's logo carved into the wall. Beneath it, the company motto: *Purity. Transparency. Rebirth.* Virginia chuckles. They could have saved themselves some money and just opted with *Bullshit.* Virginia enters the elevator and hits the button marked *FLOOR 14 - REIGN ANALYTICS.* She conducts a quick mental exercise, ticking off a checklist. *Reign. Subsidiary of Versa. Specialists in corporate consultancy, structural reorganization...* Virginia has already bored herself. What truly intrigues her about these guys is that they appear to have zero online presence. Like Donovan, they are highly wary of publicity; the definition of boutique. They famously refuse to take on more than four clients a year. They certainly have the capacity, but it's the equivalent of a nightclub creating fake queues at the front door to create buzz. Simple supply and demand. Reign outright refuses to compete with the big four, and they don't need to.

The elevator door opens and Virginia enters a wide, open welcome area. Markedly empty, intentionally clinical. She is met by a stern woman carrying a tablet who shows her into a meeting room. Two men await. One immediately stands and shakes Virginia's hand.

"Mrs Willis. Welcome. Alessandro Davitti, Head of Strategic Analytics here at Reign. And this is George Abbott, our tech business guru." George nods.

Virginia takes a seat and, in a small power move she acquired from Donovan, pours herself some water from the table. Only the weak wait to be offered something. She doesn't drink it, however. It will remain in front of her, untouched, for the rest of the meeting. The simple act of drinking can be seen as a nervous tick or physical tell. She hears Donovan's voice rattling through her head. *Keep them on their toes.*

"Let me apologize for the weather," Alessandro continues. Virginia dies inside. When it comes to small talk, it doesn't get much more trivial than the weather.

"I suppose that's the one thing Reign can't control," Virginia says, immediately setting out her stall. The two men share a furtive glance.

They've heard that Virginia is shrewd. She's already confirmed it with her opening gambit.

"I guess, being an LA native, this temperature must be positively Baltic," Alessandro says. And so commences the dance. Virginia doesn't judge him for having done his research. Versa has access to a staggering amount of data. Using it as ammunition in a game of wits, however... well. That's just not cricket. She immediately pivots to her breezy California gal routine.

"Please, don't apologize for the weather. I may be from LA, but I've been based in Boston for over a decade. This," she says, pointing out the window, "This is tropical, boys."

Virginia focuses her attention on George. Despite the introduction, the fact he hasn't said a word yet screams that he's in charge. It's always the quiet ones you have to worry about. Virginia makes an active decision. Unless she is called on to talk to Alessandro, she will address George, and only George.

"Mr Abbott." She leans forward and shakes George's hand, a firm handshake with a non-blinking stare. It's a gesture that simultaneously offers and demands respect. "I believe you're familiar with our case. You won't mind if we skip the redundant formalities of briefings and presentations." She's telling him, not asking.

"Thank God for that," George says, relaxing somewhat. This is a man who spends half of his time willing people to get to the point. Virginia's attitude is one he can get with. Alessandro, mildly disgruntled, takes a seat, now aware that his role in the conversation will be secondary. It was nice while it lasted. An unspoken appreciation hangs in the air. They can all now stop swinging their dicks around and have a normal conversation. "Just tell us what FWL needs. Versa's parent company informs us that some core restructuring is required before you can progress with the next steps of business development?" Virginia nods, relieved he's up to speed.

"Correct. As you're aware, Fall Water's growth has been sporadic over the last decade, but we've secured the releases of innovative gaming products and a seat at the table in emerging tech markets."

"All very impressive," Alessandro remarks in a rather limp

attempt at justifying his existence. Virginia doesn't even acknowledge him.

"Estimated parameters on *Cyberside* are two million players interfacing with the game regularly," Virginia says. "This will reach ten million in two to three years. You've seen the projections. This isn't hyperbole." George nods. "We have confidence that *Underside* will be the engine of choice for twenty per cent of the gaming market and thirty-five per cent in enterprise business, including B2B, B2G and B2A."

"Ambitious numbers, Mrs Willis."

"Of course," Virginia responds, ignoring the urge to take a drink. Obviously, projections have been inflated. George knows it, the other guy – Virginia has already forgotten his name – knows it, and any moron with half a brain cell knows it. "Looking forward, extending this licensing model beyond the entertainment world is our primary focus."

"Would you say Fall Water is a hostage to growth, Mrs Willis?"

"Yes," Virginia answers, unwavering. "The same could be said for Apple and Google."

"And you're aware of the necessary procedures that need to be established to facilitate this transition? Legal, structural, operational, compliance?"

"That's why I'm here, George." Referring to him by his first name was no accident. If the scene was subtitled, it would read *Let's stop fucking around, shall we?* George stands up and rests his hands on the back of his chair.

"Virginia. This level of change will turn Fall Water into something entirely unrecognizable from its humble beginnings."

She feels her patience being stretched to breaking point. "Believe me, we're already unrecognizable. Fall Water's founders and management are fully cognisant that substantial investment is required to sustain this expansion."

"You need to secure trust," George says, returning to his seat and leveling the playing field. "Trust is the magical elixir. The kind of investors we're talking about will need to trust that Fall Water is willing to make sacrifices. Forge that trust, and the rest will take care of itself."

"Trust," Alessandro impotently repeats.

"We're on the same page, George," Virginia reassures him. Here's George harking on about trust, palming off sage wisdom like a village elder. In actual fact, he's the same as every other man in every other board room that has a PhD in stating the fucking obvious. "If we're going this wide and big, we need to reinforce top-down, C-suite power."

George points his finger at Virginia conspiratorially. "More control in the hands of Mr Craze, then?" Virginia internally flips through a variety of responses, but she knows she can't dress this up. She's been rumbled.

"Yes," she concedes. "More control in the hands of Donovan." George claps his hands together, happy that they've finally reached a realm of mutual understanding.

"Right! In that case. We're fully booked for the first half of 2007, but it'll take six months to draw up the case presentation, so that shouldn't be an issue. We can start an assessment and analysis in early 2008 and finish the report by December that year." George looks to Alessandro. *You're up.*

"Our package of service will include full analyses of the current state of the company, financials, advice on structural implementation corresponding to your new business strategy, re-evaluation of staff compensation in line with market standards, job specs, leads to new hires, and overall business packaging and market positioning."

Virginia nods, trying to retain everything, but that's what the dictaphone in her handbag is for. The same one that she's been using for ten years.

"Donovan will supervise the whole project," she says. "And he's going to want to know the price."

"It's the same for all of our clients," George responds. "Reign will take five per cent of company turnover the year after our recommendations are implemented." Virginia 'considers' the offer. Donovan told her that not only would they offer this, but that it would be accepted. Just not by her. *Give them a few days to sweat. Play hard to get.*

*Once they're on the books, we can rinse them dry.* Virginia once again resists a sip of water. It's clear that George is intentionally pushing to next year so that key products will be in place and revenue will be maximized. So be it.

"Versa should agree to that. They're essentially taking the money out of one pocket to put it in the other. Which begs the question…"

"Why the song and dance?" George asks, reading her mind. "We may share a parent company, but Reign and Fall Water are two separate entities. Best to keep things clean." Virginia knows there's nothing clean about any of this.

"I understand," she says. "Let me run this up the ladder. I'll have an answer for you by the time I'm back in Boston."

As the discussion concludes, Virginia goes out of her way to show Alessandro deference with a respectful handshake. If he's going to be her point of contact on this thing, it's best to part on friendly terms. She even goes so far as to make a glib remark about the weather. The second she's out the door, George turns to Alessandro.

"So. What's your take on that?"

"My take?" Alessandro says. "My take is that if they agree, we're going to make a shitload of money." George shakes his head in disapproval. He clearly expected better from his protégé.

"Come on, Alessandro. Money is an irrelevance. What's really going on here?" Alessandro takes too long to respond. "This isn't a fiscal transaction. It's a trust barter. Fall Water has just bartered the trust of its founders with the trust of Versa. Which will…?" The question hangs. Alessandro is far quicker off the mark this time.

"Open up control for those who joined the party later?"

"That's more like it," George smiles. "You're getting the hang of this, my boy." As they head to the door, Alessandro stops. Something's troubling him.

"Why would Burrow agree to this?"

"I doubt he even knows this meeting took place," George answers.

"Isn't he supposed to be smart?"

"He *is* smart," George snaps, offended by the question. "John Burrow is a creative genius. Don't ever forget that. But like any creative genius, he's too distracted by his own ideas. Obsession often paves the way for geniuses to be blindsided." George catches sight of Virginia's glass of water. Untouched.

"So distracted that he's oblivious to what's going on under his own nose."

---

A BUMP in the road rouses James from a deep slumber. He gets his bearings and looks out of the car window to find he's somewhere on Ventura Boulevard, heading towards Fall Water's LA office on the outskirts of Glendale. With shop fronts and sidewalks caked in mid-morning sun, London feels like a lifetime ago.

James notes a pleasant lack of hangover; a good sleep on a twelve-hour flight will do that. He is, however, feeling the familiar sensation of jet lag as it steadily hijacks his central nervous system. Today, he's probably not going to know which way is up. James casts his mind back to another continent, another timezone. He can't fully remember what happened the night he decided to jump out of a London taxi into a snowstorm, but he does feel oddly calm after the little pub crawl he allowed himself. Whatever happened, he clearly needed to let off some steam. The hangover and exhaustion has certainly made the news of Alex's firing easier to swallow. Only someone who was on a mission of self-sabotage would have acted the way Alex did. It's Marcus that James feels sorry for. So far, James has never had to fire a friend. Here's hoping it stays that way.

James opens a message from Sarah, this one with a photo of her in front of a freshly painted bedroom wall. At this rate, he's not going to recognize his own house when he gets back. He sends her a message, promising to call her later. His driver catches him in the rearview mirror.

"Hello there, sir. Given the traffic, we'll arrive at your destination in around forty minutes. I won't judge you if you need some more shuteye." James considers, but knows he needs to push through.

"Appreciate the offer, but I'll be alright. Thanks, mate."

"Ha! *Mate*! You talk like a Brit!" James cringes, unhappy that his little habit has been spotted. He makes a mental note to drop this for when he gets to the office. The first of a few meetings scheduled for the day are Dario and Jin, tech guys on the Media and Entertainment arm of *Underside*. He'll also be showing them the *Cyberside* build before a quick check-in with Helen Bright, Fall Water's hotline to Hollywood. Helen, a former agent, has access to every movie studio and has been trying to negotiate a deal with key players to get a *Cyberside* film adaptation off the ground. James is a cynic when it comes to transmedia. His work on *Otherside 2* showed him how the two formats – games and movies – are like oil and water. To the layman, they appear to share a common DNA. In practice, however, the type of technical expertise required for each is worlds apart, and the toolkits and pipelines required for one cannot simply be migrated to the other. Not to mention the LA attitude. Movie execs and studio heads have gone collectively crosseyed by staring down their noses at the gaming industry for years. Despite the revenue the industry boasts, along with mouthwatering future projections, Tinseltown simply cannot accept video games as a respectable artform.

Tom Simmons, on the other hand, did what he does best and sniffed out an opportunity. It was he who led the charge on opening up the LA office, dangling lucrative pay packages at potential hires from Industrial Light and Magic, Disney, and a roster of movie-aligned CG houses. Under Simmons' supervision, Fall Water made tentative inroads with pre-viz and pre-production services using *Underside*. Much like in gaming, the engine promised to democratize the movie landscape, providing cheaper and more flexible avenues for the antiquated movie-making model. With Hollywood being a heavily insular and unionized town, it naturally refused to accept the potential. Rather than embrace innovation, it predicted risks to job security and a renewed scrutiny into decades of creative accounting. Whatever the reasons, Helen has been fighting an uphill battle.

James scans an email from Steve, which contains all the necessary data, credentials and multiple sign-offs for the latest *Cyberside* build download. *Test run went off without a hitch. Blow them away, brother.* This is a huge relief after a rollercoaster few months. The impossible schedule has invited inevitable coding blunders. Endless updates, along with daily corporate distractions, have lent a noticeable instability to proceedings. Hank has been head down with the Pyramid project and James accepted long ago that he could no longer rely on him for miraculous, eleventh-hour fixes. It hasn't all been bad, of course. Implementation of new control rules turned down some of the heat and tweaks to the backend made gameplay more sustainable. Dina successfully convinced management to opt for a small, internal West Coast demo rather than a press-heavy London event, a move that allayed any fears of latency issues and provided the Boston team with a few more valuable days to complete essential refinements.

The car pulls off the freeway and starts rolling through the streets of Glendale. James has never been able to fully embrace the LA lifestyle, but he does have an affinity for Venice Beach, Santa Monica and Glendale. Conversations have floated around the office for expressions of interest in moving some of the workforce out to California. James chuckles as he considers what a life out here with Sarah might look like. If they did make the move, they'd have to frequent the local tanning salon to top up their tans if they ever stood a chance of fitting in. It would be a solid option if they were to try for kids, that's for sure. James thinks back to his recent conversation with Sarah. It's one that crops up time and time again, often after sex, when both of their guards are down. One by one, old college friends have started families, and although James and Sarah married young, they had both agreed to secure their careers before taking that particular leap into the unknown. Yet, years later, fresh excuses are still being made. It seems there will always be a reason to hang on for another year, whether that's waiting for the new house, the new promotion, the new project to complete, or for Sarah to get her latest medical exam out of the way. When each milestone is achieved, another one is right around the corner. James contemplates his own dad before the divorce, so often absent, out of town with work. He can't help but think that, perhaps, bad parenting is genetic. Would he be a good dad, or would he fuck it up? Sarah chastises him for such a mindset, but it resonates with her. Her old man was hardly father of the year either and hesitation breeds hesitation. Either way, they're not getting any younger. Maybe it's time. Too jetlagged to resist, James allows himself to maintain this train of thought until something monumental finally dawns on him. *Holy shit. I think I want kids.* As the car turns into a small gated campus, James promises to have a serious talk with Sarah when he gets home.

James surveys the grounds of the LA office with envy. Whoever designed it clearly spent too much time in Palm Springs. The place has a garden, a swimming pool – *a fucking swimming pool* – a resident cat, and a campfire space.

"James?" The man walking towards him wears sandals, board shorts and a Little Feat t-shirt, and he'd look out of place in anything else. "Dario Rochetti." Before James can object, Dario has pulled him into a bear hug. "Welcome to California." James isn't the biggest fan of this kind of invasion of personal space, but finds himself making an exception.

"How do you lot get any work done around here?" James asks.

"These amenities have a way of getting the creative juices flowing," Dario answers. James is still in Dario's embrace, and it started getting awkward about three seconds ago. He pulls himself free.

"Dina sends her regards."

"Ha! Of course she does. She spends her life sending her regards. God, I love that woman!" Dario's expressive nature is a shock to the system for James, especially considering he's just arrived from London, where one poorly judged smile can have you waking up in the emergency room. "Me and Dina go way back," Dario continues, guiding James towards the building. "Entered each other's orbits at the House of Mouse. I tell ya, if you can make it there, you can make it anywhere." Dario stops outside the door by a standing ashtray and produces a joint from his pocket. He sparks up and takes a toke.

"Oh, you just... OK," James stutters. "And it's not... you can just...?"

"Gated premises bequeath all kinds of benefits." Dario offers the joint to James.

"Christ, no. That combined with jet lag, and I'll be in my own personal orbit. Maybe later."

Dario nods, unoffended. It's unlikely this man has ever been offended by anybody in his life. He guides James inside, past desks, couches, fridges, ping pong tables and bean bags. The appeal of relocating grows heavier with every step. As they approach an office, James notices a lack of door. There's just a frame. These guys bring new meaning to 'open door policy.'

"Knock knock," Dario says. Jin, the office CEO and LA's Fall Water Lake supervisor, puts down his Xbox controller and leaps to his feet. James quickly surveys the setup. Surround-sound speaker system, ergonomic gaming chair, high-grade test PC running the *Cyberside* build through an obscenely oversized, obnoxiously priced plasma monitor on the wall. James makes a mental note to file a request for a few of these monster screens back in the Boston office.

"Yo, Dario! And Jim! Is Jim cool, man? Or is it James?" Jin, a Korean American in his late thirties who looks like he's been making the most of the on-site gym, approaches James and, surprise surprise, wraps his arms around him. After Dario's ambush, James settles into the groove with this one, going so far as to give Jin a couple of slaps on the back. *When in California.*

"Jim's fine. I see you got started without me. Nice setup, guys!" James approaches the screen and takes a closer look.

"Hope you don't mind," Jin says earnestly. "Thought I'd give the game a quick look before your arrival. I couldn't resist, bro."

"No problem at all, bro," James says. *Bro? I've been here five minutes and 'mate' has graduated to 'bro' with honors.* "Jeez. Some of the elements look rough in this size and resolution. Good job only a select few can afford this kind of home theater."

"That's something that's been bothering me," Jin says. "It looks like shit now, but we've been cooking something up. Check this out." Jin pokes his head out the 'door'. "Simon! Kai!" Two excitable young guys in the middle of a ping pong game down paddles and run over.

"S'up, Jin? What do you need?" Simon nods and smiles at James, revealing a perfect mouth of flawless pearly whites. In LA, even the lowly office runts look like movie stars.

"Remember what we ran through yesterday? We're going to give Jim here a little demo. I need you to run camera while I set up the scene." Simon and Kai nod and return to the shared space outside the office. Dario makes himself comfortable on a bean bag in the corner.

What unfolds over the next few minutes is so surreal that all James can do is surrender to the madness. Out in the shared space, Simon and Kai install a Cronenbergian, carefully tweaked metal rig to a video camera.

"Is that an Arriflex 416? It's hard to tell underneath... whatever that is."

"Damn, bro!" Jin exclaims, looking up momentarily from his keyboard. "You know your shit! We've made some minor modifications. It's all about high-speed ultra-wide lenses. That's the secret sauce. Here, let me show you." Jin opens the console on the screen and begins making inputs, turning off the main character, and switching on screenshot mode and parallel rendering. The screen splits into sixteen sections, rendering each with a separate server. James winces, much like any engineer would if they saw performance drop to four frames per second.

When Jin is finished, a desert landscape is visible on-screen, complete with a minor sandstorm, some sand dunes, and the skyline of the fictional metropolis of Babylon in the distance. Jin steps back, hand on chin, scrutinizing his work. He looks at James.

"Look good?"

"Er... I guess. What's going on h—"

"Maxine!" Jin bellows. "Give me the scene and some hard light over the podium."

A woman shouts back from outside the office. "What's the magic word, Jin?"

"Please."

"Better. Coming right up." With a few clicks and whirs, the shutters on the office windows lower and two high-intensity light sources ping to life, providing a blue-white contrast spot over Jin. The rest of the office sits in a blanket of total darkness. James squints, adjusting to the light, and internally wondering what, in the name of all things holy, is going on.

"What is this? Some sort of makeshift movie set?" He receives no answer. Instead, Dario emerges from the shadows and guides James by the elbow.

"A few steps back, Jim. You're obstructing the shot."

"Oh. Apologies."

"Jin! Give us a wiggle!" Kai shouts. Jin obliges and busts some moves, dancing two steps to the left and two to the right. "Frame looks good. Do your thing!"

Jin limbers up, centers himself under the light spot and strides towards James.

"Ah! Here you are, stranger!" By this point, a mixture of exhaustion and sensory deprivation has led James to suspect he's still asleep on the plane, experiencing some kind of fever dream. Even so, he finds himself playing along.

"Who... me?" A few chuckles bleed in from outside the office.

"Yes, you, traveler!" Jin proclaims, finding his character. "Who do you think you are, approaching Babylon without the correct index?"

"I... well... James Reynolds."

"This is the wrong locale to get lost in, James Reynolds! You're a level nine in an ocean of level thirties. I'm taking you in!"

"Oh, OK," James mumbles. Jin smiles and shouts outside.

"That's a wrap! Maxine! Lights! Pretty please!" The shutters open as quickly as they closed and LA sunlight ripples back into the office. "Can we get that up on screen?" Jin shouts, his voice riddled with contagious excitement. James has no idea what he's about to witness, but can't wait to see it. The monitor blinks and starts running the video output. James watches, spellbound.

"Holy shit."

Holy shit is right. The camera is set precisely to the size of the plasma. The light and lens effect has dropped Jin directly into the virtual desert landscape. As *Cyberside*'s Head of Dev makes a step forward to evaluate the playback up close, Jin provides a running commentary.

"Sure, it's far from perfect. But we live by a two-word motto here. FUCK..." Jin waits for a wave of voices. He doesn't wait long.

"...GREEN SCREENS!"

"Fuck green screens?" James repeats.

"Fuck green screens," Jin and Dario respond in perfect harmony. A ping pong ball skitters through the door frame, closely followed by

Kai. He runs in to collect it from under James' feet, stands, and calmly repeats.

"Fuck greenscreens."

"I admit, the technology isn't there yet," Jin continues, "but we predict a future where graphic levels, screen quality and a carefully honed pipeline can produce virtual sets in *Underside*, in real time."

"This is... what do you say out here? Rad? Dope? Out of sight?"

"All of the above," Dario chuckles. "Glad you like it."

"And you've been working with Hank and John on this?"

"Among other things," Jin says.

"Jin! Are you bothering our visitors with your toys again?" All heads turn to see a jovial woman dressed in slacks saunter into the room. "Honestly, you can't leave these guys alone for a second," she says, addressing James. "You turn your back, and boom! They go and create another game-changer. My own little pet disruptor." The woman gives Jin a loving peck on the cheek and shakes James' hand.

"Helen Bright. Jim Reynolds, I presume?" James is too gobsmacked by the demo to answer her question.

"This is mind-blowing stuff. Seriously."

"I know that, Jim," Helen says. "We all know that. Try telling it to them." She gestures out of the window. "They're scared. Convinced it's gonna put them out of business. Listen. The sun's shining. What do you say we take this outside?"

Five minutes later, James, Helen, Dario and Jin are sitting out by the campfire spot with coffees. Helen effortlessly holds court.

"Let me pick that big old brain of yours, Jim," she says. "We have two significant pieces of the puzzle here. One, a huge IP – and if Hollywood loves anything, it's IP – and two, a groundbreaking bit of tech."

"Seems that way," James says. He's enjoying this. This is the first business meeting he's attended in years that feels nothing like a business meeting. It feels more like he's catching up with old friends.

"We can exploit this technology to churn out productions based on the *Cyberside* IP. The world you've created is massive and is there for the taking. Incredible work."

"Thanks, Helen. Why do I sense there's a 'but' coming?"

Helen sighs. Even the prospect of merely explaining these roadblocks is giving her a stress headache. Jin leans forward and takes over.

"We have two issues," he says. "First, traditional Hollywood is pushing back. This place was literally built on bricks and mortar. Nobody is daring to fully integrate these solutions into the tried and tested studio pipeline. Second..."

"... the product is different," Dario interjects. "It's your standard fear of the unknown. Once a movie is released, it's done and forgotten. With gaming, its lifespan is potentially endless. They're a different species."

"So it's a distribution and continuity issue?" James asks.

"In a nutshell," Helen responds.

"So how do we tackle it?"

Helen places her coffee down and sits forward in full agent mode. Jin smiles, aware she's about to go for the jugular. "What if I told you that we can make an ongoing story?"

"A series of films? Like a franchise?" James asks. Helen shakes her head. "A TV show, then?" Helen clicks her fingers.

"A long-running television show, potentially never-ending. We whack out episode after episode using the *Underside* pipeline, steadily growing an audience who already live their lives in your game."

James takes a moment to digest this. "An extension of the universe."

"A seamless extension. Viewers will be constantly informed, guided, and entertained in real time, all the time."

"In real time, all the time. Now that's a catchy tagline.'"

"Ooh. I like this guy," Helen says, winking at Jin.

"Don't like me too much just yet," James counters. "For the sake of argument, cable TV companies are more conservative and technologically stunted than the movie business."

"Forget the technical issues for now," Helen says. "In a perfect world, does this appeal to you?"

"Well, naturally," James answers, impressed by Helen's powers of persuasion. "We've been slaving away at *Cyberside* for eight years now.

This would bring it to a whole new market. What are you thinking in terms of a roadmap?"

"Next five years?"

"Sure."

"Five seasons, one hundred episodes total."

"Jesus fucking Christ." A silence descends. Helen, Jin and Dario wait it out. "Are we talking a hundred hours in the first five years?" James asks.

"Maybe," Helen answers. "But the episodes can be as long as they need to be." James can't help but laugh.

"And what network in their right mind would agree to that? There's nobody on the market who could bring this to fruition. Dictating runtime for shows... that's never been done."

"Stand up, Jim," Helen demands. James does as he's told. "Now take a step back." James obliges. "And another." Again, James takes a step back. "Now, look at the bigger picture. Think outside the box." James stands in front of these three kooky LA types, hands on hips, thinking. Helen puts him out of his misery.

"You heard of Netflix?"

"What, DVDs on demand?"

"That's been their model thus far and it's worked well for them. But their ambitions match ours." Helen Bright smiles a smile that truly matches her name. "Believe me. They're going to revolutionize the way TV and movies are consumed."

"I'm going to need more than that," James says. "But I can't lie. I'm intrigued."

"Don't sweat the technical stuff. I can't reveal too much; the first word out of these guys' mouths was NDA. All you need to know is that they're hungry for content."

"Content?" James asks, never having heard the word used in this context before.

"Content," Helen replies. "Get used to that word. I just need the Boston team to flesh out that roadmap. Story, characters, arcs, the lot. Leave the rest with me."

James has never been sold so quickly on something with such limited information, but the excitement of being in LA and the easygoing attitude of these folks appears to have won him over. He looks at Helen and slowly nods.

"Right," she says. "What's for lunch?"

---

"Do you want to tell me why we're dressed like a couple of dipshits, Tom?"

John Burrow sits next to Tom Simmons in the back of a Bentley. Both are dressed ridiculously in golfing attire and John, it's safe to say, has never felt further out of his comfort zone.

"Come on, John," Tom says, as the car passes through the gate of Columbia Country Club in Washington, D.C. "What's the problem?"

"I haven't played golf once in my life is the problem," John says, fixing the collar of his bright pink polo shirt.

"That's a lie," Tom responds. "You beat me once at *Golf* on the Game Boy at Genericon in '89. Remember?"

John chuckles and relaxes somewhat. "I'll never let you forget. Was that the day we met?"

"Could be," Tom answers, knowing full well it was. "We're not here to play golf, John. They won't let us inside unless we're dressed like prized dickheads."

"Why do these Washington types always insist on meeting at executive golf clubs?" John asks. "Are they allergic to boardrooms or something? On a weekend, no less." Indeed, John and Tom flew up last night under Donovan's orders to attend the last-minute meeting. John isn't overly happy about leaving Alice, now seventeen, home alone. He shudders as he envisions the party that will no doubt be crashing through his house this evening. Or even worse, Alice will invite her boyfriend, Dustin, over. *Dustin. Who in their right minds is called Dustin?*

"Standard power play," Tom answers, snapping John out of it. "They say 'jump', we say 'how high?' Them's the breaks." John chuckles as the car pulls up to the entrance.

"Yeah, well, the breaks can get fucked."

Their driver hands the keys to an eager valet, who enthusiastically recognises John and tells him that *Cyberside* changed his life – he met his girlfriend in-game. This kind of interaction is a rarity but it gives John a much-needed boost. As the two men enter the reception area, John suspects that he is about to be ambushed. Donovan has kept his cards close to his chest regarding today's agenda, but John knows that Damien Craze will be here, along with Congressman Mitch McCaley. These political players have become a steadily increasing fixture on Fall Water's Christmas card list in recent years, ever since Damien Craze and Fortress sniffed out an opportunity in licensing *Underside* for the purposes of high-level defense contracts.

Donovan spots them from the club and waves them over. John does a quick sense check as he approaches. The place isn't too busy, and those who are here are most likely lobbyists. You can't throw a stone around here without hitting a lobbyist. Near one of the bookshelves, a man the size of a tank drinks tea and 'reads a newspaper'. John would bet his house on the fact he's one of Fortress' goons, security for the meeting, and is no doubt packing heat. As they arrive at the table, John leaves the pleasantries to Tom.

"Donovan, Damien, good to see you again. Congressman."

"Please, just Mitch. It is the weekend, after all. Please, sit."

Hands are shaken and seats taken. Mitch McCaley is noticeably sharp and energetic for a man in his seventies. Keen eyes indicate an agile intellect. His tan matches the rich mahogany of the bookshelves and his demeanor suggests that this place is his second home. Burrow has, of course, done his research on McCaley. He's served a few terms and is a classic right-wing hardliner. The Congressman couldn't be classed as a gun nut, but he probably has the Second Amendment stitched onto his underwear and he is firmly in the NRA's pocket. John hit a dead end when digging further back than fifteen or so years. Suspicious gaps in his career history has fed rumors McCaley is ex-Department of Defense with likely ties to the intelligence community. Too gregarious for the CIA. Most likely NSA.

A waiter glides over and pours water. Drinks orders are taken. 'Just Mitch' goes for a Macallan 18 because he and the wife vacationed in Scotland two years ago, don't you know; Tom joins him on the Scotch because Tom always opts for whatever the most powerful man at the table is drinking; the Craze brothers share a bottle of red because they've been sharing everything since they were in diapers; and John opts for good old-fashioned green tea because something tells him he's going to need to be in control of his faculties. As small talk settles, everyone gives Mitch, or 'Mac' as Donovan calls him, room to start leading the conversation. Mitch takes an enormous Cuban cigar out of a leather case – he and the wife vacationed in Havana last year, don't you know – sparks up using a match the size of a Redwood, and looks at Fall Water's founders with respect.

"What you boys have been able to achieve over the last few years is astonishing. I brokered a few deals for the private sector and your bar... well. It's up here." The Congressman waves his hands in the air to demonstrate a point.

John nods and smiles. He's learned that the best option in this scenario is to just shut up and grin. He's also learned that, if someone's sucking up to this extent, it means they're probably about to ask you for something you don't want to give.

"Quite the roster of clients, fellas. FDA, CDC, FBI. That little doozy you're working on for the Marine Corps in training and simulation..." Mitch whistles in appreciation. "One second you're making *Space Invaders*, the next you're saving lives and tax dollars for your country." Mitch leans in and whispers. "You're patriots." It's at this moment that John's suspicions are confirmed: Congressman Mitch 'Mac' McCaley is full of grade-A shit. *Space Invaders* was released in 1978, for crying out loud. *Smile and nod, John. Smile and nod.* Mitch takes a sip of whiskey, allowing Damien to swoop in.

"Just like I said, huh, Mitch? A bonafide investment?"

"Bonafide is right, Damien. And to think of the expansion that'll come with the North Carolina project." Mitch looks at Tom. Turns out that was a question.

"It's looking good, sir."

"How many times? Mitch. I get 'Sir' and 'Congressman' all day. If I wanted to get my dick sucked, I'd have gone to the local whorehouse."

"Well, Mitch. We're just ironing out those final touches," Tom adds. Internally, John chuckles. They're going to need more than an iron to get this beast over the finish line. More like an industrial steamroller. Tom goes to speak again, but Donovan holds up a subtle hand and clears his throat.

"The Pyramid will be launched this July, Mac," he lies. John winces. The project has only recently been pushed back to September. He shudders at the thought of an email in Hank's inbox on Monday morning telling him that the release date has been moved once again. "It'll open us up to anything and everything related to data processing, management, storage and transfer. It'll be fully operational by the end of this year."

"Fanfuckingtastic," Mitch exclaims. "Music to my ears, especially considering the initiative I want to discuss with you today." John smiles knowingly. *Here we go.* "An initiative that requires vast capacity and will need to be hosted inshore with the highest levels of security." John takes a sip of his tea and allows himself to frown. The Pyramid was designed to service *Cyberside* customers, not government agencies. It was always going to be hijacked, of course, but he thought it would be operational before the D.C. wolves came knocking. For the first time since he sat at the table, John speaks.

"Mitch. We're happy to assist the State with what we have at our disposal, but we're not prepared to host anything related to data protection." John catches eyes with the brothers Craze. They look nervous. He senses Tom squirming in his seat next to him. Before he can carry on, Tom opens his mouth.

"What John is saying is that we need to understand the proposal fully before we can consider guarantees of diligent safeguarding."

"What John is saying, Thomas," John continues firmly, "is that we haven't been briefed on this." He kicks Tom's shin under the table. Tom kicks back. When these two are able to prepare carefully for such meetings, they bounce off each other beautifully. On the rare chance they are forced to go in blind, Tom has the habit of jumping in with both feet. Especially when an enticing payday is being dangled in front of him.

"Consider this your briefing," Mitch says with a carefully honed composure. At this moment, Donovan gives Damien a gentle tap on the knee.

"This level of consideration is admirable," Damien offers. "But this is big. It requires a face-to-face. No paper trails on this one, guys. Not yet. Plausible deniability."

"Versa's two favorite words," Donovan chips in. John can't stand it when Donovan speaks of Versa's interests. He's CEO of Fall Water Lake, and although initially he played a good game, the mask hasn't just slipped over the last five years, it's come off entirely. It's clear where his allegiances lie.

"Gentlemen, please," Mitch says, trying to diffuse the tension. "Allow me to explain. I'm only talking security because the tech needs to stay below the radar for quite some time."

"What tech?" Tom and John ask in unison. Finally, they're singing from the same hymn book.

"What do you know about the current state of artificial intelligence and neural networking?" Tom and John share a look of mild surprise. This is unexpected. John had military surveillance in mind. It's *always* military surveillance. He's comfortable offering gentle resistance to that old familiar, but AI? He looks to Donovan, who nods. *Didn't see that coming, did you?*

"Does anyone even call it artificial intelligence these days?" John asks. "The Lighthill report may have been three decades ago, but that bad taste lingers. People are still reading Asimov, Mitch. It's on every book shelf in every dorm room across America."

"There's a general distrust out there, is what you're saying?"

"That's what I'm saying."

"People used to think refrigeration was the work of the Devil, John. That turned out alright in the end."

"Okayyyy. But in real terms, even DARPA has been historically wary to invest. Cognitive systems are a side passion of mine, and the research is hardly booming." John instantly regrets giving himself away. It's true. AI is an area of extra-curricular interest. The turn in conversation has put a remarkably positive spin on what he predicted would be a rather dour affair. Still, he's just laid his cards on the table and is annoyed at having let his guard drop.

"Oh, you have an interest?" Mitch asks, darting in like a shark smelling blood. "You're right, of course. The term 'AI' has been tainted by academics and peddlers of pulp sci-fi, but there's a bubbling optimism in some circles. Particularly around behavioral simulation."

Despite the fact that Mitch just referred to his literary hero as 'pulp,' John can't help but be impressed. He wrote the Congressman off the second he arrived, but he clearly knows more than his permatan and penchant for Scotch would suggest. John catches himself and takes a couple of mental steps back. *Slow down.*

"Simulation of that kind would require an unfathomable amount of highly specific data." Mitch roars at this with laughter, as do Donovan and Damien. Tom isn't far behind. John is the only one at the table who remains silent. "What am I missing here?"

"Don't play dumb," Mitch says. "You're launching a game, a virtual simulation, a replica of the world and of society as we know it. Endless realms, millions of users. With the level of players you've got on your books, well... that's a shitload of data, is it not? Capturable data for both individual agents and groups?" John, still caught off-guard by the fact they're talking AI simulation, looks to Tom for assistance. Unfortunately, as if often the case when conversation veers into the highly technical, Tom has a markedly vacant look on his face.

"Christ, I don't even know where to start," John says, accepting that, for the time being, Tom is about as useful as a screen door on a submarine. "*Cyberside* is a video game. To get what you're after, whatever that might be, from a gaming audience, no less..."

"Hit us with the problems," Donovan says. "Then we can solve them."

"Alright, thanks for that, Donovan," John snaps. "We'd need to simulate specific scenarios in-game."

"Where's the issue?" Mitch asks.

"That sort of thing doesn't sit within its commercial purpose. We're here to tell a story, to entertain, not to farm data. This is the definition of data privacy violation." The other four men sit back in their chairs, somewhat disappointed by John's stance. Not that it's a surprise. A silence descends and hangs around for a good few seconds. John senses Mitch formulating a half-baked political response and almost wills him to spit it out.

"The world is changing, guys." Here it comes. "I've been kicking around for quite some time now and maybe it's just old age, but I gotta tell you, I'm concerned. I can't ignore the signs I'm seeing." John looks to Donovan just as he checks his watch. Even the big man can't hide his boredom. "If someone were to ask me if I think the American people are ready for the challenges to come, I'd have to say no. A key defense is being able to predict population behavior in the event of something catastrophic."

"The Red Menace is dead and buried, Mitch," John says. This doesn't go down well. Mitch looks at him, irked, and the true political bulldog he is comes out of its kennel.

"Reds? Please. Treat me with the same respect I've been treating you with. I'm not talking about fear of a nuclear winter here. Our biggest threat isn't the 'other', John." Mitch gestures around the restaurant. "It's *us*. If something truly catastrophic unfolds, you're telling me that this country wouldn't embrace anarchy? You can dress it up however you want, but when the shit goes down, the first thing to crumble is society." Mitch raises his Scotch to his lips, but he's on a roll. "It could be anything. An act of global terror, an international pandemic, a critical infrastructure blackout. Nobody wants to admit it, but we're vulnerable. We're sitting ducks."

"I hear you," John says, despite the fact that he firmly believes the Congressman has spent far too long walking the corridors of paranoia-infested intelligence agencies. "And I agree. An ability to forecast and formulate contingencies based on real data has positive implications."

"Let me guess your next question. Who controls the data?" Mitch asks.

"It's a valid point, and one I've been asking myself for years. Look, Mitch. I'm no fool." He looks at Donovan and speaks candidly. "I knew the deal when Versa came along. I knew the price that would have to be paid to get my silly little pipedream into millions of homes worldwide. And I knew I'd have to have difficult conversations about data control and consent."

"Well, here you are," Mitch says.

"Here I am. What we're discussing isn't just likely to happen. It's an inevitability. I'm not going to stand in the way of what's coming. If I was, I'd have been booted out years ago." Mitch looks at John with utter respect. In a long and celebrated political career, he's never met anyone quite like John Burrow. "But that doesn't mean I'm not going to ask questions," John continues. "Let's call it like it is. What you're proposing is a massive-scale clandestine surveillance operation, the likes of which has never been seen before. And it's not only on US soil. We have access to millions of users around the globe." Once again, John looks to Tom. This time, Tom is ready to offer his take.

"We can separate data from the locales, anonymize behavior patterns from their sources. Personality attachment isn't important here, right, Mitch?"

"Correct," Mitch confirms. "We want to study behavior on a mass scale. It's statistical data we want, not personal information."

"That's why everything would be kept in your hands, under your full control," Donovan adds by way of reassurance. John smirks. He's heard that one before. "Don't give me that look, John. We'll codify this, get an airtight agreement drawn up. This project can be compartmentalized under a separate cluster within the Pyramid. Hell, I don't even need to know the details, so long as I know it's happening."

John sighs, unsure. His hesitation is clear for all to see. Now it's Mitch's turn to dangle the carrot.

"John. In return for your services, the State will offer you and your team all of the research conducted thus far in this field. That's a lot of research. Think of it on your own terms. Don't you want to predict how users will react to new game updates and variables? You'd never need to conduct another godawful focus group ever again. Cold, hard data. You know you love it."

"Smart NPCs with authentic, real-world reactions based on event triggers," Tom adds. "This is something we've been trying to crack for years, John."

"Alright, guys! Enough!" John barks. "Jesus Christ. I'm not some little kid you're trying to convince to go on the dodgems. You think I haven't considered all of this? I know my hands are tied. If I don't agree to it, Versa will pump the money towards someone who will."

"We don't need a commitment now," Donovan says. "Just promise us you won't disregard it completely?"

"If I go for this," John teases, "and that's a big 'if', I have some conditions. No personal data. The project will be cordoned off from any major *Cyberside* and *Underside* developments. I'll personally supervise and will be the point man with the relevant State research groups. Everything, and I mean everything, goes through me. Every last shred of data will be anonymized." John looks at Tom. For the first time in his tenure at Fall Water, he feels something of a professional disconnect with his brother-in-arms. One look at Donovan and John can feel it in his bones: he's being edged out. He knows that with the events of the last few days in London, LA, and here in this ridiculous country club in D.C., a grander plan is unfolding. He's now merely a passenger. This is very much a point of no return. He might as well give them what they want and make the most of it. "Those are just the headlines. There'll be more to follow. How does that sound, Congressman McCaley?"

Mitch smiles and raises his glass.

# 6

# POINT OF NO RETURN

Alice Burrow shuffles into the kitchen and prepares herself a freshly squeezed orange juice. It's a Saturday morning in March, 2008, and, as per usual, John has relieved the domestic staff for the weekend. He's always felt self conscious about the fact that he has a maid and a cook on his own personal payroll, but after the death of his wife, and with his Fall Water commitments, John's time became his most precious commodity. It's a vast household to maintain and there is simply no way he could do it without assistance. Weekends, however, are a different matter. Carlito and Kathy have been working here for fifteen years, since Alice was three. In return for them having every weekend off to spend with their families, they offer John an unwavering loyalty. John enjoys knowing that the house belongs to him and Alice at the weekend, and it provides them with some essential quality time. She cooks on a Saturday, he cooks on a Sunday. Saturday tends to be movie night – Alice is currently going through a Brian De Palma phase, much to John's delight – and Sunday will involve fishing in Fall Water Lake, walking or cycling around it, or video games in the late afternoon, or some combination of all of the above. A key advantage of John's position is picking his own hours. He's a natural workaholic and will often put away fifteen-hour days in the week. But the weekends? They belong to him and his daughter.

"Dad?" Alice wipes orange pith from her top lip and waits for a reply. Strange. He's usually buzzing around the kitchen at this time, spilling coffee or burning toast.

Alice goes for a walkabout, keen to find John and talk about nothing in particular. She wears bunny slippers, complete with oversized ears that she constantly trips over, pajama shorts, and an enormous t-shirt depicting a panda riding a unicorn down the crest of a rainbow. Alice doesn't usually go for this cutesy bullshit, but this t-shirt belonged to her mother. John kept it in storage for a decade after Sam's death before gifting it to Alice. She has worn it every night for bed, without fail, ever since. Her mother's scent has long been erased following multiple washes, and the peeling print job makes Mr Panda look like he's been possessed by a creature from the nether realm, but this old rag provides Alice with a tangible connection to the mother she never met. She'll be heading off to college later this year and, yes, you're damn right she'll be taking this t-shirt with her. Alice is in the final stages of exam revision, as indicated by notes scrawled in pen on her hands and wrists, and fingernails bitten down to the nub. Both are habits inherited from her father. Alice's head pokes around the door of John's office.

"Dad? Are you in here?" When a response isn't forthcoming, she wanders out to the back patio and takes a few seconds to enjoy the crisp spring air. "I say, old bean! Make yourself known! Your daughter requests your presence for the purposes of incoherent morning chitchat!" She's about to head back inside when she notices the door to the guest cabin in the garden is wide open. Alice knocks and enters to see John sprawled on the sofa with the laptop on his knees.

"Morning, sweet child o' mine," he says, without looking up.

"What's the point in adding yet another extension to this place every year if you're going to sneak away to the guest cabin every chance you get?"

"It's peaceful here, don't you think?"

"Sure. It's peaceful in the main house, too."

"Well, this guest cabin was your mother's idea." John points to a framed napkin on the wall. On it, a crude drawing of a big house. Next to that, an even cruder drawing of a smaller house. The 'artwork' is signed *Samantha Burrow, 1990.* The masterpiece was completed in a downtown bar after John and Sam had viewed this place back in the day. John was unsure about making such a giant financial commitment, but Sam instantly fell in love with the empty plot and had grand designs in mind. It was this silly drawing that convinced John to sign on the dotted line. "She never got to see the finished product. I guess this little place makes me feel close to her." Alice goes over and kisses John on the head. She loves it when he talks about her mother.

"That's sweet. Tell me you ate breakfast?"

"Ummm..."

"Dad! Who's the kid in this house?" Alice has a point. While John may be a celebrated tech genius known and respected the world over, at home he's as disorganized and chaotic as they come. "When I go off to college, you must remember to feed and water yourself." John nods in compliance.

"Sure. Sorry. I couldn't sleep. Had the beginnings of an idea I couldn't shake. I wandered out here early. Must have gotten carried away."

Alice ruffles his hair with affection. This is who he is. She accepts and loves him for it. "Inspiration always hits at the most inopportune time."

"Tell me about it."

Alice grabs John's empty *World's Greatest Dad* mug from the coffee table. "Top up?" He nods yes. Alice enters the kitchen area and opens a cupboard to reveal a collection of *World's Greatest* mugs. *World's Greatest Husband... Boss... Business Partner... Games Designer... Squash Player.* Alice opts for *World's Greatest Man-Child* and places a pod in the coffee machine. "Are we watching more De Palma tonight?"

"Damn straight. What's next from the maestro?"

"*Body Heat.*"

"Er, nope."

"What do you mean, nope?"

"Just no, Alice."

"Dad?! What the hell?"

"Sexy stuff. I can't in all good conscience watch *Body Heat* with my daughter. I'll end up on a watch list."

"It's next in his filmography! This whole De Palma season was your idea! We can't just skip it because there's some skin on display!" John contemplates how best to handle this conundrum. Alice helps him out. "We'll just analyze it for its cinematic merits and comment on the mise-en-scène. Deal?" She places the mug down in front of him.

"You drive a hard bargain, Alice Burrow. Deal." John takes a sip of coffee and returns his attention to the laptop screen. He stares at it, befuddled. Alice slides down at the opposite end of the couch.

"You look stumped. What are you working on?" This question from his daughter has a much more rousing effect on John than the coffee ever could. One of his biggest delights is the genuine passion Alice shows for his line of work. It was never forced upon her; one day, she started asking questions and never stopped. It helps, of course, that she carries the inquisitive, fiercely intellectual Burrow gene.

"I've been digging into the work of this Ukrainian guy. He's deep into research on the Hilbert system, generating theorems from axioms and inference rules." Most people would stare blankly at John at this point and fear he was having a stroke. Alice Burrow is not most people.

"Hyperbolometrics?"

"That's the one," John confirms, burning with pride. "It's an intriguing mathematical and geometric thesis with, I believe, a practical application. If I'm getting this right – and I honestly can't see the wood from the trees at this point – numbers can be implemented to build classic figures and bodies."

Alice steals a sip of John's coffee. "Sounds like Minkovsky space."

John raises his finger. *Aha!* "You see, that's what's curious. Results differ quite significantly from Minkovsky space. It's quite self-sustainable."

"Interesting," Alice comments. "I appreciate the excitement. What are you hoping to achieve from this? Integrate into *Underside*? Cheap rendering?"

"Maybe," John answers coyly. "I'm just toying with it at this stage." Alice doesn't buy it. John rarely 'toys' with anything unless he knows there will be some form of creative payoff. She rifles through reams of handwritten notes on the coffee table. A recurring number leaps out at her: 1.618. She chuckles. John looks sheepish.

"Dad. These notes resemble the ramblings of a lunatic. Are you going down a golden ratio rabbit hole again?" John, like many of his peers in the mathematics and design space, is obsessed by the golden ratio. One glance at the Penrose tiling of the kitchen floor only a few feet away confirms this. Alice has warned her father to steer clear of magic mushrooms when in that kitchen, lest he get so lost in the hypnotic, tessellating patterns that he would never be able to find his way back to reality.

"Guilty as charged, kid," John says affectionately, holding out his hands to be cuffed. An excitement washes over him, cementing the claim made by that *World's Greatest Man-Child* mug. "It's all around us. It's undeniable. This number, this code, could hold the... the—"

"The secret of the universe? As claimed by da Vinci himself?" Alice exclaims, wide eyes mocking affectionately. She grabs her dad's glasses off his head, puts them on her own, and adopts a well-observed academic vocal style. "You know my opinion on this, Mr Burrow. We can talk ad infinitum about 1.618, and I can already see you formulating your case by referencing the Fibonacci sequence." John smiles, more than happy with the fact that Alice knows him better than anyone else on earth, including himself.

"If I've told you $n$ times, I've told you $n+1$ times, young lady. Don't diss Fibonacci. Not in this house."

"Some of the world's greatest scientific minds," Alice continues, "claim that pi is at the heart of everything. But there can be no doubt that there is only one number that holds the secret to the entire universe." Alice pushes the glasses up her nose in a perfect imitation of her father when he's about to make a bold claim. "And that number is 42."

"Ha! I knew it!" John screams, throwing his hands up in gracious defeat. "Beaten once again by the smartest Burrow on the planet." At that moment, Alice's phone vibrates. She checks the text and looks conflicted.

"What is it?" John asks.

"Oh, nothing important," Alice replies conspiratorially. "Just one of your competitors trying to sniff out your latest folly."

"Alice..."

"Or could it be foreign intelligence services, offering rich financial rewards for developments relating to national security?"

John stares at her, deadpan. "Don't even joke about that. Who is it?"

"OK, fine. Jessica's parents are out of town tonight. She's throwing a last-minute party."

"Oh, very nice. So what's the problem?"

"It's De Palma season, Dad!" John can barely believe what he's hearing.

"Wait. Let me get this straight. My eighteen-year-old daughter would rather stay at home with her golden ratio-fixated father than go and blow off some steam with her friends? Will Dustin be there?" Now it's Alice's turn to look sheepish. "What? What's that look?"

"I finished with Dustin last week. He has no ambition, so I ended it." John's parenting alarm goes into overdrive. Should he commend Alice's emotional maturity for dumping a guy who was going nowhere fast? Or should he gently point out that perhaps she has been too rash and should give the poor sap another chance? Thankfully, he isn't given the chance to make a call. "But there will be another boy there who I... you know."

"Oh yeah? And what's this one's name?" Alice is so mortified that she stands up, goes to the kitchen, and simply stands there. "What are you doing?" John asks.

"Promise you won't laugh."

"I won't laugh. I promise."

"His name is Justin." Of course, John explodes in a fit of hysterics. "Dad! You promised!"

"Come on, Alice! I'm only human. You're trading in a Dustin for a Justin! Lustin' for Justin!"

Alice buries her head in her hands. "For the love of all things holy, Dad. Please. Stop. Talking." John stands and gives his daughter a hug. His shoulders shudder as he strives to stifle his laughter.

"I'm sorry. You're going to that party though."

"Fine," Alice mutters, her head buried in her father's chest. "But I'll be home by eleven."

"Midnight."

"Fine. Midnight. If you insist."

"I insist. You've been studying too hard. Cut loose. De Palma will be here waiting for you tomorrow."

"Can I take the Porsche?"

"Don't push your luck. You can take the Range Rover." Alice spots something on John's laptop over his shoulder and goes in for a closer look. He joins her with an inquisitive look on his face. "What have you spotted?"

"Oh, nothing." Alice goes to leave, approaching the door, before turning back with a playful grin. "You might want to double check lines 1525 and 1535 though. Might be the reason why someone's code isn't compiling as it should." John stares at his daughter, awestruck. "C'mon, Burrow. You're getting sloppy." John glances at the jumble of numbers on the screen.

"Where exactly are you looking?" He glances back up, but Alice has already left. John thinks back to something he's told Alice again and again over the years. *Tease the solution, but don't reveal it.* Deep gratification flows through his veins. He's taught her well.

---

*A* MAN *who looks suspiciously like a rugged Hollywood actor aimlessly walks the streets of Babylon. This cyberpunk realm is a grimy, futuristic metropolis, fusing together the cityscapes of Akira's Neo Tokyo, The Matrix's Mega City and Blade Runner's Los Angeles. Neon lights lure down-and-out locals with nowhere to go into stripclubs and casinos where* they will be fed a diet of false hope in exchange for credits. Replicants that could almost pass for humans, were it not for the 'R' tattoos branded onto their foreheads, deal the latest drug of choice on street corners. The whole thing plays out in absolute silence.

Mr Rugged throws some credits at a street vendor; a questionable corn-based snack on a stick is shoved into his hand. As the heavens open, Mr Rugged ducks down an alley for shelter. A stealthy female figure with alluring, mascara-clad eyes emerges from the shadows and presses a gun into the small of his back. He stops still. The corn-based snack is dropped into a puddle. Subtitles reveal their conversation.

"Neil Gibson?"

A flicker of panic crosses Mr Rugged's face. "That depends on who's asking."

"A friend."

"Friends don't point guns at one another. What is it you want? If it's money you're after, you're shit out of luck."

"You have a remarkable set of skills, Mr Gibson. A set of skills that are of great interest to my employer."

"Neil Gibson ceased to exist a long time ago, along with those skills. I'm no longer a hacker, lady. I'm... a nobody. Sorry to disappoint you."

The shadowy femme fatale leans in. "What if I told you I could give you back your old life? Plug you back in?"

Mr Rugged's eyes narrow. He's intrigued.

"I'm listening."

A TELEVISION on the office wall in the Pit broadcasts – muted, with subtitles – the latest episode from Netflix's smash hit *Cyberside* show. Sure, it's borderline schlocky, and it doesn't so much borrow from the science fiction giants that inspired it, but steals from them outright. Even so, viewers who can tolerate the questionable dialogue and overly complex plot are currently being rewarded with a visually stunning, thematically rich viewing experience. After Helen Bright secured the deal, money was thrown at Fall Water and writers began to churn out scripts influenced heavily by *Neuromancer* and *The*

*Diamond Age* as jumping off points. A production pipeline using tech (*Fuck greenscreens!*) from the LA branch was implemented, and the team went shopping for its cast. Multiple A-listers turned down the show, fearful that this new streaming service didn't have the caliber of movies or cable television. Thankfully, Hollywood up-and-comer and avid *Cyberside* fan, Mr Rugged, saw the potential and signed on. The show is now a flagship Netflix property, streaming into homes around the globe.

James half-watches the show from his desk, still unable to quite grasp that the world he helped create has now transcended formats. LCD Soundsystem's *Sound of Silver*, playing from his iPod Touch, provides the soundtrack to his afternoon. A quick glance at his calendar reminds him that this evening is his monthly chess game with Hank. Although he is more or less back in Boston now the Pyramid is a go, Fall Water's Head of R&D still splits his time between here and North Carolina. Both his and James' time is so limited that a monthly game is the best they can stretch to, but, for years, the pair barely saw each other at all. Once a month is better than nothing. It seems some traditions are able to outlive the flow of time.

An email pings into James' inbox. If it was from anyone other than Steve, with any other subject line than *What the f\*\*k?!*, he wouldn't bother opening it. But it *is* from Steve. And the subject line *is What the f\*\*k?!*. CL-CLICK. James scours the email.

*Are you kidding me?! Again? We did this two weeks ago! Is this absolutely positively mandatory? If you tell me to do it, I'll do it, Jim. But this is beyond a joke. Are we game developers or Netflix concubines?* James scrolls down to see that Steve has forwarded a request from Virginia insisting that Steve provides weekly game dev updates to Netflix – via her, of course – so they can *synergize horizons*.

REPLY. *Just fucking do it, Steve.* SEND. Instant regret. New email.

*Come over to the house on Friday night. The fridge will be fully stocked. Then the first round is on me at Hermit's.* SEND. Regret dissipates.

James checks the clock: 5:59 pm. He waits as the second hand crawls, seemingly slowing down, and contemplates how clock watching has now become a daily pastime. The fact that it's Saturday and a few of James' team have been pulled in to finalize an update certainly isn't helping. He never used to keep one beady eye on the time like this, but then this job never really felt like work back then as it does now. James is a manager in every sense and rarely touches hands-on coding anymore, acting mainly as a full-time buffer between senior management and the Dev team. Every directive comes down through him from above and every ounce of resistance to those directives comes back up through him from below. James is essentially Fall Water Lake's very own United Nations. He should be paying his mom and dad a percentage of his salary for training him how to keep the peace from such a young age. There are now over two million *Cyberside* players worldwide and Fall Water's workforce stands at over 1,500. For James, this means more emails – keeping on top of them has become a Sisyphean task – more meetings, more reporting, more processes, processes to handle those processes, and additional processes to ensure the major processes are processed.

For those who have been working at the company for over a decade – Steve included – Fall Water's growth has been a complex adjustment. This 'old guard' longs for the halcyon days where they could, as Steve so eloquently once put it, *Be left alone to get on with our fucking jobs without having to give each other a reach around five times a day.* As for the new blood, a frustrated resentment exists, and is often encouraged, around how things used to be done. James is wedged right between the two warring factions in a position so delicate that Steve has started calling his old friend "the 38th Parallel." James knows that he would be making as much noise as Steve if he was in his position, but rising through the ranks has invited so many other headaches that he sometimes wishes his former keyboard warrior-in-arms would just, for once, keep his head down and do as he's told. Only last month, Steve ended up on management's radar after being overheard in the canteen ranting about *corporate voodoo nefariousness turning the workforce into mindless zombies.* At least it was poetic. Even so, James has been silently putting out this fire for the last couple of weeks and knows another one will be along soon enough. If Steve doesn't like it here, he knows where the door is. Nobody is forcing him to stay.

Of course, James knows it's not so easy. He and Steve have both been embedded here for so long that the notion of interviewing for other jobs, of simply putting themselves out there, is anxiety-inducing. Sometimes it's easier just to stay put, remain miserable and air your grievances every now and again. A high number of original staff have taken the plunge and long since departed to newer, boutique operations where they can fully flex their creative muscles. Good for them. James finds that concept so utterly terrifying that any time he thinks he's had enough and it's time to move on to pastures new, he ends up talking himself out of it, reminding himself that he's part of a cultural phenomenon that he helped build, virtual brick by virtual brick. Why should he leave?! And so the cycle continues, year after year.

External consultants Reign Analytics were recently commissioned to audit company structure and, for James, it remains to be seen if they will make a difference. Early signs are positive; he's already sat down with them twice and they seem to have a genuine interest in what he has to say. James grabs his bag and strolls out through the Pit, catching Steve's eye.

"Did you see my reply to your email?"

"I saw both replies, Jim."

"And...?" James can feel his ulcer flaring up.

"And... I'll see you on Friday. All good." Steve blows James a kiss. Old habits die hard as, despite himself, James catches it. He breathes a sigh of relief. Thank God that's sorted. For now.

In the elevator, James hits the button for 21, which is now the exclusive home of R&D and Infrastructure. The console system beeps and the doors remain open. James curses, finds his staff keycard and swipes it on the reader. The doors close and the lift begins its ascent. Heightened security and restricted access is something to which James is still growing accustomed. Thanks to his position, he can largely go anywhere he likes, unlike Steve and the other Dev guys. Management, it seems, is all talk when it comes to equal opportunities and a transparent, open-door policy. They should visit the LA office and take vigorous notes.

Hank's cave tripled in size following the office move, but remains crowded with oddities. His increasingly erratic personality has spread across the whole floor like an unhinged technological ivy, weaving its way into every available nook and cranny. If thieves ever managed to penetrate the building's security and ended up on this floor, they wouldn't know where to start.

As for Hank himself, ever since he started work on the Pyramid, his genius has grown alongside his impossible workload. Those close to him have witnessed his mind fracture steadily month after month. A very select few, including James, know that Hank was diagnosed with ADHD around five years ago and that he self-medicates with Adderall to maintain focus. This may be putting it lightly. When Hank enters a period of hyperfocus, the level and volume of work he can achieve is staggering.

James and Hank share a quick catch up about newest engine plugins as James makes himself a gallon of coffee. The pair enter Hank's office and take their seats, ready for battle.

"Coffee, Jim? You going soft on me?"

"If I ever hope to beat you again, I need to be sober." It's a believable lie. The truth is, James is currently off the drink. He and Sarah are trying for kids, although this is actually only part of the reason.

Three weeks ago, Sarah woke James on a Saturday at 11 am after a heavy Friday night. With a pounding hangover, she gently led him to the bathroom where she had filled the bath a quarter full.

"I'm in no mood for a bath, sweetheart."

"Jim. This is the amount of alcohol you have drunk in the last month. I've been skirting around the subject for weeks now, but enough is enough. I know you love a visual metaphor. This is a wake-up call."

This approach was exactly what James had needed. Sitting there on the bathroom floor staring at twenty gallons of bathwater, with his wife squeezing his shoulder in support, he broke, finally admitting that he was, perhaps, experiencing the beginnings of a 'problem'. What had started as a quick beer after work twice a week had evolved into six or seven almost every night. A harmless glass of red with dinner each evening had morphed into at least a bottle. Sarah proceeded to lovingly explain that, in the same amount of time that

James had spent either drinking or hungover in the last month, she had taught herself beginner's level Spanish. If they were going to start a family, something had to change.

Sarah, keen to show James that she would be there to support him, and eager to prove that he didn't need alcohol to enjoy his day, guided James back to bed, where they had sex. He was vulnerable; she was accepting. Afterwards, intentionally leaving their phones at home, they grabbed brunch at a local spot and went for a hike on the Blue Hills Reservation. The first hour was spent in the comfortable silence that only a long-term relationship can bring. James eventually started talking, explaining how the standard stresses of work and upcoming potential pressures of fatherhood had necessitated some form of escape. Sarah listened without judgment and admitted to sharing those fears.

On their way home, they spontaneously stopped at an independent cinema and watched *When Harry Met Sally*, part of a program of American romantic classics. Neither had seen it since college and it certainly carried the excitement of a first date. They picked up some ingredients from a local Asian supermarket and made Vietnamese food when they got home. After eating, they collapsed on the couch to the first two episodes of *Mad Men*, retired to bed and had sex once again. As he dozed off, James told Sarah that this semi-intervention had been the most beautiful act of love anybody had ever shown him. He could get used to this level of wholesomeness. He promised that instead of drowning his sorrows, he would do something useful, like learn to drive. He then drifted off into the deepest sleep he had experienced in years. He hasn't touched a drop since.

Since giving up booze, James has observed that others who indulge seem to take it as a personal slight, as if somebody else's abstinence shines a spotlight on their own overconsumption. There's no way he's getting into this today. He changes the subject to prevent Hank from digging any further.

"So, what's the Nutty Professor disrupting on this fine Saturday?"

"Your ego, Jim. As always."

"Steady now, Hank. You don't need me to remind you what happened last week." James dramatically unbuttons his shirt to reveal a t-shirt he has made for this very occasion. On the front is a list of dates denoting significant events from James' life: *Born on this Day, Graduated High School, Met Sarah, Went to Cambodia, Started at Fall Water, Release of Cyberside*. James stands and turns around to reveal *February 2008: Beat Hank Brown at Chess* printed on the back in glorious neon. Hank creases up in a fit of laughter.

"Oh, very good," he says. "You realize that was a fluke, right? I hadn't taken my meds."

"Don't play that card with me, Hank. That was Vladimirov's Thunderbolt, man!"

"That move went against any tangible notion of logic, Jim."

"This t-shirt wouldn't exist if not for that move. Logic be damned."

"How are things at home?" Hank asks, mainly out of politeness. Hank has never had a long-term partner, much preferring his own company. Some people have suggested he's asexual, and they're probably right. He's had sexual partners, but finds the whole enterprise a minefield of confusing social cues. Still, it seems to be something that most people do pursue, and asking others how things are at home is something that most people seem to ask. Social mimicry is one of Hank's many skills.

"Do you care?" James asks, seeing right through it.

"Not really," Hank answers bluntly.

"I'll tell you anyway." James takes a giant glug of coffee. "We finally moved the last of our stuff out of storage and into the new place last week. Honestly, this house project was more complex than *Cyberside*."

"A project for which Sarah did most of the work, right?"

"We're having a housewarming party in April," James says, ignoring Hank's question.

"Housewarming," Hank repeats, unsure what James is getting at.

"You're invited, Hank." Hank immediately enters panic mode and pours himself a giant glass of spiced rum. James refuses to even look at it. You can't be tempted by something that isn't there.

"Ah. A party." Hank throws a pained look at James. "This guy doesn't really do parties. I end up standing in the kitchen, alone, judging people on their choices of cereal. I don't wanna judge you, man." James slaps Hank on the knee.

"No problem. Come over next week instead if you like. A quick hi to Sarah."

"Now, *that* I can handle." Hank takes a grateful moment to appreciate his friend. There are few who fully understand his ADHD brain. People are far too quick to take offense where there is none intended. Not James.

"What's new with you?" James asks. "You back in Boston for good?"

"Stuck between here and Raleigh. I know I can't sit still for more than five minutes, but this is too much."

"I thought when the data center hit full capacity, it'd be more of a supervisory role?"

"Jim, darling," Hank scoffs. "I have never been married and most likely never will be. But if I was to hazard a guess, I'd imagine that ten years in, it would feel close to how I feel about the Pyramid. I'm in deep. She's got her claws in. It's a constantly evolving platform. There's always another project on the cards. No rest for the wicked. No escape. I love her and I hate her." Hank makes his first move.

"Same with *Cyberside*," James says. "No surprises here, but online is a different animal entirely. A different species."

"Gone are the days of launching, patching, moving on to the next project. Right?"

"Long gone. It feels like we only truly started developing after the launch. It's a new way of working. A new way of thinking." James gets a whiff of Hank's rum. It smells good.

"It's a hard reset. Same with *Underside*," Hank says. "There's a theme emerging here, don't you think?"

"What theme might that be, Hank?"

"Our new reality is endless developing and honing, based on constant, real-time feedback mined from highly complex algorithms. The sooner we accept that nothing we ever work on will be complete and can always be improved, the better." A feeling of existential dread washes over James. He's always known this, but has never heard it expressed so matter-of-factly. Christ, he could murder a drink. Hank retrieves a pill from his shirt pocket and swallows it with a rum chaser. James looks away.

"It would be nice," James says, "if things could remain stable for just a little bit without a deluge of fresh operational guidance. It's like they think that if we stay still for too long, we'll get complacent."

"I hear that. We had to redesign an entire section of the building in Carolina to provide a separate entrance only last month. New cameras, fingerprint readers, retinal scanners, the whole lot. Real *Mission: Impossible* shit. A bit of warning on that one would have been nice."

"I assume you made some noise?"

"Oh, I screamed the fucking house down," Hank replies. James smiles and thinks of Steve, whose grievances feel like a mere whisper compared to Hank's protestations. So entrenched is he in the company hierarchy that Hank is the only person on Fall Water's payroll who can get away with such behavior. After one particularly bombastic outburst on a company away-day last year, rather than discipline Hank accordingly, his team was made a fully independent, untouchable entity, reporting solely to Burrow and Simmons. People have started calling R&D the Vatican in a nod to the department's sovereign status. James moves his queen. Hank smirks.

"Fool me once. You ain't playing Goran Bura here, Jim. I'm not buying that reckless sacrifice." Hank moves his knight, skirting James' trap. "Do you ever worry that John is taking on too much?" James frowns. Hank has a habit of flitting from one subject to another, like a restless kid hitting channels on a remote control. How is John now somehow part of the conversation?

"Well, he's the busiest man I've ever met," James answers, matching Hank's speed. "I can't say I worry about him though. Why do you ask?"

"I guess it's not so much how much he does. More *what* he does."

"The AI thing for Uncle Sam?"

"Yep. Can you tell me how this fits within our structure?"

"I don't know, Hank. I don't get paid enough to know that sort of thing." This statement is true. James is so busy with general day-to-day management duties, he's actually lost his grip on all of the specialist projects currently underway. What he does know is that very few people even know about this thing.

"They're calling it the System," Hank says ominously.

"Sounds a bit cloak and dagger," James offers.

"It is cloak and dagger. The official line is that it's a strategic initiative to help build next-gen tools for both *Cyberside* and *Underside*."

"What's the problem? John's overseeing this one personally, isn't he?"

"Yeah. And he's intentionally stalling," Hank answers. "The initiative wasn't a request from Versa. It was a directive. Something tells me John doesn't like where this is going. He only took it on so he could knock it off course if necessary. That's my theory." James doesn't say anything. When Hank presents a theory, some digestion time is required. Hank checks James with his rook. James, in turn, protects his king with a pawn.

"So John's hands are tied?" James asks.

"Yeah. And when have you ever known John's hands to be tied?" Hank swigs some more rum. "It speaks to the huge changes we've undergone."

James nods in agreement. "It's like aging. When it's happening, it's all so incremental, you barely notice. But if you stop and look around, you notice that everything is unrecognizable."

"But where's it all headed? What's the endgame?" Hank asks rhetorically. "I've started building my own defenses on the down low for my own protection. Just in case. I suggest you do the same." James stares at his friend, trying to decipher this cryptic statement.

"I'm not sure I know what you mean, Hank. You're what, building a bunker? Hoarding weapons? Bulk-buying canned food?"

Hank moves his bishop through James' open defenses and takes his queen. "Check mate." James absorbs what just happened. All he can do is smile in awe.

"Hank Brown, back with a vengeance." He reaches out and shakes Hank's hand.

"Think of it this way. At least you don't have to get your t-shirt updated," Hank says as James grabs his bag.

"You'll pop over next week, then?" James asks. "Just for a quick hello?"

"Wouldn't miss it."

After James is gone, Hank returns to the chess table and places the pieces back in their positions. He pours himself another drink and stares at the board for an inordinately long time.

---

JOHN BURROW DRIVES his Porsche 911 through dark, winding roads towards Belmont, in the western suburbs of Boston. He was hoping for a quiet evening at home, especially after convincing Alice to trade De Palma for Justin at Jessica's party. A loud, distant crack of thunder announces a light blanket of rainfall, activating the rain-sensing wipers.

John battles a growing knot of anxiety as various worries bubble up from his subconscious. Along with Alice leaving for college later this year, he has accepted that agreeing to the System was a big mistake. After a couple of months wading through the research provided by Congressman McCaley's team, trying to buy time, John was forced to get to work, quietly spurred on by Tom. His initial fears were realized as it became clear that this little project posed a threat to Fall Water's overall purpose and mission. The design of the initiative itself, and what is needed to service it, was always destined to mutate the development of, and potentially substitute, the function of existing Fall Water products. John foolishly thought he may be able to have both things coexist. That was wishful thinking.

John has kept quiet about his reservations. Where he would have once talked to Tom, following the meeting in D.C. and the fealty Simmons has been showing Donovan, Damien and Mitch, a trust issue has reared its ugly head. It can no longer be denied. Tom isn't knowingly turning his back on Fall Water, but John's oldest ally has now reached an age where his bank balance is top of his list of priorities. John knows that Tom is cheating on his wife and his moral compass is skewed. This recklessness is now bleeding into his work. It comes from a good place, of course. Tom's commitment to the

System speaks to his desire to secure Fall Water's long-term future. John shares this desire, but, unlike Tom, won't pursue it regardless of the cost.

John's increased isolation within the company now sits alongside a justified paranoia. If he were to share his concerns with Tom, he knows that he'd go running to Versa and Fall Water's Board. The last thing John needs at this point is a vote of no confidence. It simply wouldn't be worth the risk.

Instead, John has been subtly filibustering the movement of the project internally, but he senses eyes on him, specifically Hank's. Not that he has anything to worry about when it comes to Hank. Still, the Head of R&D was always one step ahead of everyone else. If Hank knows, it's just a matter of time before everyone else catches up with him.

Additionally, a month or so ago, John went out on a limb and hired a private investigator to do some digging into the motivations of Versa and Fortress. For someone so risk averse, this decision didn't come lightly. But with a growing roster of employees and millions of *Cyberside* players around the world, it was up to him to ensure that his partners' intentions were sound.

As the rain picks up, John slows down. Flashes of lightning temporarily split the sky. A bad omen? Perhaps.

The results of John's enquiry have been suspect, to say the least. It's not like anything criminal has been uncovered. It's more the fact that barely anything has been uncovered at all. John's contact has simply hit a wall. Beyond what's publicly available online, he can't find anything of substance on Versa or Fortress. All that has been returned is a suspiciously perfect picture of a standard multinational corporate conglomerate. Versa was established in the early 1950s by a group of private investors capitalizing on the lucrative post-war boom. Their interests spread to scientific research, biology, pharma and, eventually, tech. So far, so boilerplate.

Versa steadily grew in power in the sixties and seventies before jumping into bed with Fortress in what turned out to be much more than a one night stand. Fortress was, at the time, a frequent DARPA collaborator with deep ties to the corridors of power dating back to the end of WWII. Both companies were destined to lock eyes across a crowded dance floor. They have been happily married ever since, gathering numerous adopted children in the form of aggressive mergers and acquisitions. Part of Fortress' stock trade, naturally, comes in the form of questionable contracts that they would rather keep off-book. John accepts this; it comes with the territory. When John's PI came to him with solid links to the CIA, John told him to back off. Probing in this area would have invited unwelcome interest and risked exposure. From the late eighties, Versa itself created distance from Fortress to maintain its carefully honed brand of reputability. Image, it seems, is everything. Versa is highly present in the philanthropic space, adding 'Foundation' to its name in the early nineties and devoting a percentage of profits to scientific research, academia, tackling poverty, and, most prominently, terminal disease relief funds both at home and abroad. John suspects these efforts were based on genuine concerns over legacy rather than tax relief purposes. Even so, this kind of corporate generosity has resulted in friends in very high places. Versa has its roots growing comfortably on almost every continent. Its global leverage is low key and scarily powerful. There is one question that keeps John awake at night. *What do they want with Fall Water?*

One thing that marks Versa out from the crowd is the success rate of its investments. Wherever they put money, it comes back with a heavy ROI. This is not how money and risk works in the modern world. Stay in the game long enough, and you're bound to catch a dud. Midas would have something to say about one of the most off-radar, successful business empires on earth. Name a sector, and Versa can boast a success story: tech, pharma, logistics, manufacturing, aerospace, media, and every imaginable aspect of retail. Despite this presence, humility is the name of the game. Forget going public, Forbes lists, flashy product launches and keynotes, and celebrity CEOs. Leave that to Richard Branson and Mark Zuckerberg. When John asked his PI for a list of public bragging stories, the number returned was a big, fat zero. This is unheard of. Instead, after hitting the jackpot in a certain area, a front-end business would step in to collect the accolades. *What are they trying to hide?*

Just when it seemed John's little sleuthing operation was nearing a fruitless conclusion, his PI hit gold when he was contacted by a disgruntled former Versa employee wanting to get something off his chest. Up until this point, former staffers had remained steadfastly silent out of fear of litigation, or worse. This guy was different. John got the call this afternoon after Alice left the house, with the John Doe requesting a personal meeting in a secluded diner in Belmont. John's natural reaction was one of caution, but he's in too deep. Curiosity is a powerful motivator. He agreed to the meeting and jumped in the car.

John slows to a crawl as he turns onto Belmont Road and the storm enters a full-blown rage. He can barely see the road now as the heavy rain stomps across his windscreen. John grounds himself with a few deep breaths. He has no idea what is in store, but senses he may well be having another sleepless night.

Suddenly, John's phone loudly vibrates in his pocket. He pulls over into the parking lot of Wilson's Diner and answers, strongly convinced the mystery blabbermouth has got cold feet and canceled. He looks at the screen: *Unknown Number*.

"This is John Burrow."

"Mr Burrow. This is Massachusetts General Hospital. Are you Alice Burrow's father?" John's heart stops dead in his chest. The sound of the storm drifts away.

"Yes. What's happened?"

"Alice has been in a car accident. We need you at the hospital as soon as possible." In a split second, John pictures a flash of wet tarmac, twisted metal, and flashing ambulance lights. He drops the phone to the footwell and revs the engine.

"Mr Burrow? Mr Burrow?" John pulls a U-turn and floors it.

From a booth inside Wilson's Diner, two men watch John drive away. The deafening skid is lost to the sound of the storm. A waitress shows up at the table to top up coffee and is summarily dismissed. One of the men dials a number on his phone.

"Selena. It's Mike Penridge. He just left. Looks like we were too late."

"What happened?"

"They got to Alice before we could get to him." There's a brief pause.

"Understood. We're aborting this line of entry. We'll regroup and search for another opening."

"And the girl?"

"Out of our control now, Mike. Disengage. You know the rules."

"Affirmative." Mike hangs up and throws a look of pained frustration at the man sitting opposite.

"So what now?"

"For you? Nothing. Your contract is up, Eddie. Final payment will be transferred as usual. If you wouldn't mind—"

"Disappearing? Tying up loose ends? Deleting digital paper trails?" Mike nods, impressed. "This isn't my first rodeo." Mike smirks at this. This may feel like a standard job, but Eddie has no idea what he's tied up in. This most certainly is his first rodeo, and based on his performance so far, it won't be his last. He just doesn't know it. Mike sends a text.

"Payment should be with you—"

"Funds received," says Eddie, already checking his phone.

"In that case…" Mike stands, shakes Eddie's hand and finishes his coffee. "Wow. That's some good shit." Eddie is surprised. He takes a sip of his own to be sure.

"This? This is not good shit, buddy. This is cat piss."

"They're still trying to master it where I come from," Mike says, dropping cash on the counter and throwing on his jacket. "They're so close, but not quite there."

---

JOHN STANDS over a bed in the ICU looking at the broken body of his daughter. He's not sure how he got here.

A sudden phone call… stumbling out of his car and into the hospital… met by a friendly yet urgent nurse… guided by the elbow into a waiting room… a stern doctor explaining that Jessica was also in the car and is alive thanks to Alice's reflexes. Something about an articulated truck spinning out of control in the rain…

"But Alice. Where is Alice? I need to speak to her."

"As we've explained, Mr Burrow, Alice is in surgery. Her condition is critical. She has suffered from numerous fractures and severe blunt force trauma to the face and skull. I'm sorry. I need to prepare you for the worst."

"I understand, but I really do need to speak to her. She needs her special t-shirt if she's sleeping."

At one stage, everything came into sharp focus as it dawned on John the extent of what was unfolding. For a brief few seconds, a clarity of thought unlocked a picture of such horror and dread that he vomited across the floor. So extreme was the sensation, so unfathomable the possible future he was looking at, that every few minutes his body sent him back into the protective embrace of extreme shock.

"I need to speak to Alice."

Unable to contemplate what might come, John revisits what has been. He replays the last conversation he and Alice had. She hadn't even wanted to go to the party. He had talked her into it. He knows he deserves every ounce of the guilt and welcomes the dark, pulsing waves with open arms. Deep down, he knows that this terrible remorse will be a close companion for life.

"I need to talk to Alice."

He should have let her stay home. Should have checked the weather. Should have called her a cab. She only passed her driving test last year. She never stood a chance in this storm. He thinks of Sam and of the promise he made to protect their girl. A stark emptiness arrives now. *I am nothing. You are nothing. If she is gone, you are gone.*

"I NEED TO TALK TO MY FUCKING DAUGHTER!"

A doctor is pushed violently into a vending machine... security rush through the door... calmer now. More level-headed. *I must apologize to that doctor.* Suddenly, Tom stands there, eyes red raw from crying. Parachuted in by the doctors in the hope he can get through to John. He explains in no uncertain terms: Alice is alive, but comatose. Her body is functioning; her mind is not. It's unclear when she will regain consciousness, or if she ever will.

"So it's bad, Tommy?"

"It's fucking bad, John."

A conveyor belt of condolences comes in the form of a myriad of wellwishers over the first couple of days. After a while, John is so numb, he barely reacts to them. His refusal to eat or sleep means he doesn't have the energy to even thank them for coming. Then, one day, surprisingly, there is Donovan.

"I was never too good at this type of thing, John, so I'll spare you the forced sympathy." This straight-to-the-point approach grabs John's attention. "I've been in your position. Fifteen years ago. I had to let them go and pull the plug."

"Who was it?" John asks.

"Doesn't matter. Just know that they were very close and I've never been the same since."

"I do feel like I've changed on a molecular level," John admits. This is the most open he's been with anyone about how he's feeling. The fact that his confidant is Donovan Craze is a turn up for the books, but then so are all the events of the last forty-eight hours.

"She was your only family?" Donovan asks.

"Not 'was'. She *is* my only family. My parents are gone. I'm an only child. And, of course, you know about Sam."

Donovan nods solemnly. "You're going to be faced with the hardest decision of your life, John." John blinks tears away. He's been consumed with this very fact for the last few days. "But I'm here to tell you you don't have to make it."

"Don't taunt me, you son of a bitch. If Versa has a miracle cure, out with it. If not, kindly leave before I put you in the ground."

"Just hear me out. There is a world in which you can speak with Alice again."

"I'd do anything for one last conversation."

Donovan drags a chair over and sits next to John so they're on the same level. He gestures to Alice.

"Her body and brain are damaged, but that doesn't mean she's not there. Neurobiology has made giant strides in the last few years. We can't fix her physically, so wave goodbye to that. I'm sorry."

"But?"

"But, in years to come, there's a high possibility that we can free

Alice from the prison of her body." John doesn't want to believe him, yet he does. A tiny slither of burning bright white hope just broke through his darkness. What Donovan is talking about here sounds like fiction. However, with the digging John has been doing, he knows that if there is one entity that may have solutions in this space, it's Versa.

"You have my attention."

"Versa will provide all resources, including the best possible medical support, to get Alice back to your home. We will share all the knowledge we have in this area and provide you with an exclusive research group that will, over time, offer Alice a new way to exist, to communicate. We can immortalize her."

It all sounds so outrageous and so plausible at the same time. John knows Versa has been investing in the digital space, virtual simulation, and AI. At this stage, the future is very much now and the impossible has never felt more possible. For John, it isn't even a debate.

"What do you need from me?"

"You'll work out of your home alongside our team and will be exclusively on this. I won't sugarcoat it. This will be your life from here on out, John. Tom and I will manage the company."

With one simple word, John changes the course of history.

"Fine."

Zero hesitation, zero second guesses. For all John cares, Donovan could cart him out, naked and hogtied for the whole world to see, if it means speaking to Alice again. John knows exactly what's happening here and he couldn't give less of a shit. Hands are shaken.

"We're calling this one the Lazarus Project."

"Of course you are. When do I start?"

One hour later, hospital staff don't bat an eyelid as a swarm of Versa techs descend on the building. Highly sophisticated equipment is wheeled in. At the same time that a helicopter lands on the hospital roof to whisk Alice and John away, three giant trucks enter the Burrow estate. Carlito and Kathy, yet to be briefed, stand in the doorway in shock as more Versa techs bring medical machinery inside, setting up in John's study. Little do they know that today will be their final day working in this house. A house that is about to become a personal prison for John Burrow. Once, he was a founder of Fall Water Lake. Now, he's merely a Strategic Advisor.

---

2008. Apple, Google, Android, flexible screens, simulations, engines, wireless technologies, GPS, and social networks. All rolling downhill and picking up speed in a powerful avalanche of instant communication and interconnectivity.

By the time Fall Water Lake hits 5,000 employees, John Burrow is on the periphery of the company he co-founded. Following Reign's suggestions, Donovan Craze sits atop the pyramid, presiding with an iron fist. Tom Simmons and Virginia Willis perch below him, adopting a style of brutal enforcement. Discipline is rigid, naysayers find themselves out of a job, and gaslighting is commonplace.

*Cyberside* becomes the most popular video game on the planet, supported by the continually renewed Netflix adaptation, multiple spin-offs across different media, and a highly successful line in merchandising. In 2015, with John out of the picture, Tom takes *Underside* off the general market and reprofiles the technology exclusively for B2B. Again, under Tom, Fall Water steps away from data anonymization and starts surveilling its users. Sharing this data with the NSA grants Versa and Fortress infinite credit lines and political access. With the System now fully operational and predicting behavioral patterns, multiple domestic and foreign threats are quietly neutralized.

John becomes a willing slave to the Lazarus project, obsessively working day and night to unlock the secret that will allow communication with his daughter. After eight long, reclusive years, a breakthrough is reached in 2016 when Alice's consciousness is finally transferred to a digital shell, providing her with basic text interface capability.

As summer 2019 rolls around, preparations are underway for the launch of *Cyberside 2.0*. This super-update will boast user-generated content, a new in-game economy, artificial intelligence for NPCs, and non-invasive neural interface support. James is under pressure to deliver for the release date, unaware of Hank's and Tom's secretive project that will connect the System with *Cyberside*, allowing for global data management and control of over sixty million players worldwide.

**END OF PART 2**

# PART III
## THE SYSTEM

# 7
## COGS

The first thing James becomes aware of when he wakes up on this April morning in 2019 is the cold drool on his pillow, not helped by the air con unit that has been running all night. Despite the time of year, it's hot out and getting hotter. James wipes his mouth, opens his eyes and checks his phone. 5:29 am. One minute before his alarm starts shrieking. He has noticed that, now he's in his mid-forties, one of the many things that comes with age is waking up early. Gone are the days where he would sleep through numerous alarms, only to be roused by Sarah and the smell of coffee. No matter what time James goes to bed, he always wakes up around one minute before his alarm. He scrabbles to turn it off so as not to wake Sarah, and quietly slides out of bed.

James avoids creaky floorboards as he navigates the house in complete darkness. They've been here for ten years now and James knows every inch of the place. He sneaks down to the kitchen, turns on the dim stove light and boils the kettle. As he waits, a quick glimpse at his reflection in the window tells him that, overnight, he's gained a few more gray hairs and a couple more wrinkles around the eyes.

James shovels one teaspoon too many of instant coffee into a mug and adds the water, careful not to stir too loudly. Sarah has her own fancy coffee machine installed, but James always opts for instant. It's one of the few ways he can still cling to his youth. Many others his age are busy buying sports cars, fucking their secretaries or drinking themselves into oblivion. James' on-again, off-again – currently off-again – relationship with drink renders one of those options unviable. He only learned to drive five years ago, so that need for a spontaneous sports car purchase will come calling when he's around seventy-five. As for the extramarital affair, the sleeping beauty upstairs is the one thing that keeps him sane these days. That, and instant coffee. Black, no sugar. When he thinks of the younger folk in the office, he is more confused by their choices in coffee than he is by their music or fashion preferences. For James, coffee is purely functional, a gift sent by the heavens to stay awake when working late, or to rouse a foggy head when working early. Sarah often criticizes him for his anti-youth tirades, claiming it makes him appear older than he is. James accepts this. He *is* old. Raging against the younger generations is one of life's few free pleasures. James opens the cupboard and grabs a half-empty – or half-full? Let's go with half-empty – packet of Marboros and a lighter, and exits to the yard.

James once tried meditation first thing in the morning. It wasn't for him. To prepare mentally for the day, he instead prefers to sit on the stoop with a coffee and a cigarette, floating in the not quite dark, not quite light, non-existent time and space of early morning. Some essential alone time before the day truly starts is his own personal form of meditation, allowing him some much-needed space for contemplation. He takes a drag from his cigarette and lets the beautiful poison fill his lungs. He resumed smoking a couple of years ago during a particularly stressful period of teetotalism. He made a deal with Sarah, limiting himself to three a day. In return, he has to watch two episodes of *Grey's Anatomy* with her per week. The joke is on her; he has actually come to love the show. It's exhausting having to pretend he doesn't.

James gets his head in the game for the upcoming day. He scrolls through his phone to discover, who could have guessed it, back-to-back meetings updating senior management on the status of *Cyberside 2.0*. James lets the work-associated dread wash over him. It's a poor coping mechanism, but he has discovered that embracing the inevitable stress of the day beats trying to bury it. He now oversees 300 engineers within the Dev team, who spend their time implementing new features, fixing bugs, and ensuring that the playable world lives, breathes and evolves daily. All of this work is based on an intricate feedback loop consisting of a titanic amount of data, constantly being farmed and continually evolving based on in-game trends and player attitudes. It never stops, it's all-consuming, and it's bigger than anyone ever imagined it could be. James had hoped a few years ago that the bubble would burst or that users would grow bored and move onto something else, yet this never happened. It falls to James and his cohorts to keep the good ship *Cyberside* sailing on increasingly choppy waters. James thinks back to the good old days, with Burrow at the helm. With John running the show, even during times of extreme stress, things were manageable. He had everyone's backs. James extinguishes this line of thought. No point in dwelling on it. Poor John. What happened to the old man and his daughter is a sobering reminder of how cruel and unpredictable life can truly be. It is now James' job to ensure that John's vision and legacy are preserved and realized as best he can. With Fall Water's culture as it currently is, this responsibility is proving almost impossible to uphold.

James refocuses on his phone, opens an indie rock Spotify playlist and begins getting up to speed with everything that's happened during the last eight hours. He checks emails, Slack messages, Jira updates and new tickets, social network messages and relevant news. The tobacco, caffeine, music and new information begins to activate James' synapses, slapping them into their default state of engagement and stress.

"Morning, sexy lump." Sarah's hand squeezes James' shoulder as she sits down next to him, groggy and with a mug of her own. One glance at his wife and the impending doom of the day is diluted. James allows himself to take stock. Another effective coping mechanism that costs nothing is the simple act of applying perspective. Compartmentalization sure goes a long way. When he reminds himself that work is only one aspect of his life, things don't feel so bad. Sure, it's a massive aspect, but he's still a successful executive living in a house he co-owns with an incredible woman. As for Sarah, she opened her own medical practice two years ago. They have everything they need. Well... not quite everything. After years of trying and failing to get pregnant conventionally, husband and wife collectively decided that a trip to the fertility clinic was in order.

"What's today, Jim?"

"Appointment at the clinic. Five o'clock."

"And you're not going to be late?"

"Nope. I've booked a couple of hours off. Steve is going to hold the fort."

"God bless that man." God bless him indeed. A few years ago, James had a difficult chat with Steve in which he told him to buck up his ideas at work. It's very possible that the phrase 'shit or get off the pot' was deployed. The moment Steve found out that his attitude was potentially placing James in the firing line, he stepped up his game. Of course, he still has a lot to say about the way things are done, but he's now, thankfully, more tactful in how he says it and a lot more selective to whom he says it. James can fully rely on Steve to deputize in his own absence, which has made his life infinitely easier. Far more importantly, however, is how supportive Steve has been when it comes to James' sobriety. When he initially decided to knock the booze on the head, James witnessed a few of his friends drop off the radar. He doesn't blame them. Steve, on the other hand, became increasingly present. When he and James would go out for the occasional drink, not only would Steve respect James' decision to refrain from alcohol, but he would also abstain in a show of solidarity. The duo have now sampled every mocktail on the menu in Hermit's. Josh even went so far as to create one and name it after the boys – Ctrl+Alt+Delete – and has ensured there is a selection of decent non-alcoholic beer on rotation. When Sarah was unavailable, Steve also joined James on his weekly mammoth hikes. James' teetotalism hasn't been constant. He's been averaging a few months here, a few months there. When it appears he may be slipping back into old habits, Steve will give him a nudge and suggest a break may be a good idea. Friends don't get much more consistently reliable than Steve Jenkins.

"Speaking of Steve, I'm meeting him at Hermit's after the appointment," James says. "That cool?"

"Of course. Send him my love." Sarah can't speak highly enough of Steve and takes comfort in the fact that James has an ally who keeps a watchful eye on him. She knows James needs an outlet and Steve is a great substitute for booze. She understands how hard it has been for James to remain sober over the years. This is why, when she sees James stub out his cigarette, she says nothing. This habit is something she has made peace with. The fertility doctor at the clinic, however, may think otherwise. Sarah grabs James' empty mug, stands, and stretches.

"You are fucking beautiful," James says. "Don't think I don't know how lucky I am."

"You're trying to *get* lucky, is what you're trying to do."

"Maybe," James responds playfully.

"Wake me up when you get home tonight," she purrs, before heading back inside.

During the time in which Sarah and James were trying to get pregnant, sex became a routine, clinical exercise, with one very clear, functional end goal. After they discovered natural conception wasn't a possibility, both made a concerted effort to bring fun back into the bedroom. Flirting returned to their relationship and, despite over two decades of marriage, the pair has never been in a better place. James smiles at the thought of getting home sober later and crawling into bed with the finest woman on the planet. A woman who has always tolerated James' increasing work commitments, even if they do demand that her husband wakes early to prepare for the day and brings his job home in the evening. She insists on one rule: if they are both lucky enough to share a day off at the weekend, James' work phone will stay switched off. For years now, Sarah has been ready and waiting in the wings for James to return home and tell her he's quit. He's come close, yet he can never fully pull himself away. She wishes he would, but this is a decision he needs to reach on his own. James doesn't know that Sarah keeps a constant eye on development jobs in other companies just in case this conversation ever takes place. If that day comes, she'll be ready to throw her full support behind him. Until then, she will continue to champion him in the same way he has done for her throughout her career.

As the early morning sun gradually claims the sky from darkness, James spies the newly built 4G tower on the edge of his suburb. His mind wanders to the speed of recent tech developments and how the last decade has witnessed an incomparable evolution. James knows that this growth should incite excitement, but he feels uncertainty. Endless startups have sprung up across the country, many of which replicate one another, and many more of which James simply doesn't understand. Mainstream tech and entertainment now fight for reach and quantity over innovation and quality. Fall Water is one of the few major companies on the brink of genuine technical revolution through systemic solutions and innovative interfaces. The association of nerds tinkering around in the garage is now a thing of the past. 2019 has reached the peak of tech popularity. Coders, streamers and content creators are the new rock stars, aspired to by the younger generations, who fight one another for careers in IT. Many of these play *Cyberside* and share the goal of one day working for Fall Water Lake. James has worked for the company for his entire adult life and finds this concept hard to comprehend. Every day, he is sent emails from young, hungry upstarts begging for a job. Every day, he ignores them. It's not only that he's too busy to reply. He just wouldn't wish this job on anybody.

---

JAMES SITS at his workstation absorbing the undeniable buzz that now permeates the building. Fall Water's Boston HQ is now a two thousand-person strong hive of personality and creativity. Throw backstabbing, ego and ambition into the mix and you have yourself a battlefield. James considers how this place is now more akin to a police state, with its own policies, punishments, expected behaviours and endless rules, not to mention its own corporate language. *For the sake of forward momentum, we need to keep an eye on the market barom-*

*eter to consider competition and preserve strategy.* It's all so distracting, pretending to toe the company line while simultaneously focusing on preserving John's ideals.

A series of pings circulates around the Pit as calendar apps inform everyone that yet another global meeting, hosted by Virginia, is scheduled in the central hall in ten minutes.

James drags himself to his feet and heads downstairs through the belly of the beast. Security cameras now scrutinize every square foot of this place. *Big Brother is always watching.* What Big Brother sees is a company full of self-serving, mistrusting employees trying to preserve their increasingly fragile positions within the company hierarchy. So preoccupied is everybody in defending their turf, it's a miracle that any work actually gets done. Donovan sets the tone for the dog-eat-dog nature of the place. He is largely absent from the office, spending most of his time in Raleigh or D.C. That doesn't mean his presence isn't constantly felt. An army of obliging minions, more like power-drunk hall monitors than PAs, ensures a continual deluge of emails, meetings and directives cascade down from the top floor. Pressure is constantly applied and a culture of abuse is rife, particularly when deadlines are pushed or expectations aren't met. As for James, he tolerates Donovan's elitist scumbaggery, wise enough to know what to say and when to say it. The lack of direct personal contact is a blessing. James can handle him from afar. Ideally another state.

As James heads towards Community Hall, he considers Tom Simmons. As soon as John was out of the picture, Tom's true colors blossomed. Maybe they were always there, tempered by John's inherent decency. Tom's interest in gaming has dwindled to non-existent. Instead, he is now fully locked and loaded into the System. His marriage crumbled three years ago and, in that time, he has bounced between Boston, Washington and Raleigh, morphing into Donovan's obedient lapdog. His schedule consists of meeting with bigwigs, various government agencies, the Versa board, and political lobbyists. Rumours abound of Tom and his immediate team relocating to New York to be closer to Fortress HQ. Simmons now spends so much time with Damien that he has garnered the nickname 'the Third Craze.'

James walks past an entrance as a handful of R&D folk stumble inside, having made the trip from their separate department annex five minutes away. Hank is not amongst them; there's no way he would waste his precious time with this nonsense. His efforts to compartmentalize his department have been a rousing success. Not only are they in a building locked off from the great unwashed, but Hank has carved out full autonomy for his department, making himself irreplaceable. Nothing related to the Pyramid happens without his prior approval. That whole initiative operates on a need-to-know basis, and it appears that James most certainly doesn't need to know. He and Hank are still on fairly good terms, although their chess games now are nothing more than a fond memory. Hank's paranoia is through the roof and he keeps himself to himself, a bonafide Howard Hughes for the modern age.

As for himself, James feels tireder than he used to, that's for sure. This is a different kind of tiredness, born out of complacency rather than exhaustion. This pressure cooker environment has certainly taken its toll, resulting in a thoroughly jaded Head of Development. His highly valuable opinion is often sidelined in favor of data-driven marketing inputs, integration requests emerging from the System, and a growth driving towards new audiences as dictated by Donovan himself. James' skin has never been thicker and he's become a pro at not taking things personally.

He arrives at Community Hall and finds a wall at the back to lean against with a hard-to-conceal lethargy. No sooner has he considered sneaking out when Virginia enters, flagged by a couple of team members who are careful to stay two steps behind her at all times. Ah, Virginia. This woman is the walking embodiment of manifestation. Back in the day, she was a highly competent businesswoman channeling the persona of a cold-hearted bitch in order to fit in to the boys' club. As the years passed, she became the role she was playing. Her influence in Fall Water is legendary. She is Donovan's eyes and ears and, as his chief enforcer, is more terrifying than the man himself. Most people at Fall Water do their level best to avoid her at all costs. If they do so much as look at her funny, they'll be clearing out their desks. James still firmly believes there is a human being somewhere underneath the power suit and botox. Thanks to the fact that he continually delivers, he's seemingly gained a Get Out Of Jail Free card. Beyond that, Virginia seems to actually quite like him. He has often been tempted to get on the wrong side of her just so she'll put him out of his misery, but he's such an inconsequential threat that there is no danger of this ever happening.

Virginia holds up a hand and the hundreds of gathered sheep in the hall fall silent.

"Dear colleagues and friends. Thank you for finding the time in your busy schedules to be here today. I'm sorry to pull you away from your important tasks." James smirks. *No she isn't.* "However, what I have to say is of great importance."

Virginia strolls around the stage with an inquisitive look on her face. She glaces in various different directions, addressing her public.

"What is it that we do here?" She points at a random admin body at the front of the crowd. "Make video games, right?" James squeezes his eyes closed in extreme frustration. Virginia's faux-friendly tone is something he's seen her employ too many times. What does she think she's doing? Giving a TED talk? The random woman, probably a new starter, nods enthusiastically, incredulous that the mythical Virginia Willis has singled her out.

"Sure! We make video games!"

"No," Virginia says, firmly. The woman looks devastated. "Well, we do. Of course we do. But Fall Water Lake is so much more than that." Virginia steps back and projects to the cheap seats as if she was performing *The Tempest* at London's Globe. "We're not only building video games. In many ways, we are laying the foundations for the construction of our future society." She pauses to allow for a few impressed gasps from her most loyal disciples. "Which is why it's of paramount importance that we carry positive, constructive messaging in everything that we do."

James tries his darndest to feign interest whilst masking a yawn. This virtue signalling and soft-agenda bullshit Virginia is flogging will no doubt dent his schedule with yet another agency consultation, along with a long list of prerequisites for his team to integrate.

He used to get highly agitated by this sort of thing. Today, it's just something else to add to the bottom of his to-do list.

"It has come to my attention," Virginia continues, folding her arms, "that some of the content and features developed over the last few weeks are more aligned to old-school Fall Water sensibilities. I understand the desire to respect past personnel and legacies. But this stops now."

James scours the room, checking the crowd's reaction. Many simply hide their emotions as if in some Orwellian nightmare. Many others, new to the company, look at the woman on stage in a neophyte fever, some expressing support through whoops and hollers in a pathetically transparent effort to crawl into the good books. A very small minority, all of them long-serving staff members, cannot conceal their concern. Virginia drones on.

"For company integrity, we will be introducing a special committee, composed of community service, marketing, and PR, which will be responsible for approving all materials in line with these values. This committee will also work with the legal and values teams to double down on moral and ethical checks." Virginia adopts a stance so smug that a passerby would assume she's just drafted the Good Friday Agreement. "How does that sound?"

*How does that sound? I have absolutely no idea what she just said.* The crowd explodes into applause, throwing thumbs-ups and victory signs in the air. Enough is enough; it's time to leave. James can fake mild interest, but there's no way he's getting on board this train. He slowly, casually shuffles towards an exit, spotting Virginia's assistants scour the hall inquisitively, making notes on their tablets of people who aren't expressing enough blind optimism. Those deemed to be insufficiently ecstatic at the new initiative will be deemed toxic and find their way into Virginia's Little Red Book.

James waits for one of Virginia's minions to glance in his direction. When she does, he makes sure he's screaming with unbridled joy and punching the air. The second she looks away, he sneaks out of the madhouse.

On his way back, James is startled by a firm hand on his shoulder. He knows that grip well.

"Oh God, Steve."

"He cannot save you," Steve says with a sense of foreboding. "This is now a godless place. All virtue has been replaced by vanity and greed."

"Oh, good," James mutters. "I thought it was just me." He approaches a coffee station and spends an eternity finding the setting that will give him a simple black instant coffee. Steve fondly watches his friend, a highly respected developer, struggle to get to grips with an extremely straightforward bit of kit. "Just give me a black coffee. Jesus Christ."

"What's that, your fourth cup of the day? You look chewed up, Jim."

"Don't judge me, Steve. We all look chewed up."

Steve studies his face in the chrome reflection of the coffee machine. "Jeez. You're right. When did we get so old?"

"When we were busy not looking. This way." James leads Steve through a fire exit so they can take the stairs back up to the Pit. This strategy, one that has emerged organically over the last couple of years, allows them to speak freely. "Like I was saying. We're *all* chewed up. It used to be the norm when we were crunching, but we're not crunching. Look around. Do you see any crunching?"

Steve glances around. "I can't see any crunching. I mean, we're in the stairwell—"

"This is just the default now."

"It's been like this for years, Jim. Nothing new. Are you nervous about the clinic? Is that it? Because we're actually in a pretty good place on the project."

James stops and takes a moment to find some perspective. "You're right. Sorry. The Virginia Monologues just threw me off a bit."

"Just skip those things, dude. She can't accuse you of not cheering loud enough if you're not there."

"Yes, she fucking can," James argues as they continue their ascent. "And she will. Watch yourself there. Make sure you go to the next one."

"Are you asking or telling?"

"Telling. And believe me, better it comes from me than her. Look.

Speaking of the project, let me bend your ear on something." James pulls Steve to one side to hide in the shadows. Curious eyes in the sky are everywhere now, and these stealth maneuvers have become a daily habit. The pair haven't eaten in the canteen in years, just in case there are listening devices in the soup.

"What's on your mind, sugar plum?" Steve asks. James takes a moment to try and articulate what he's been feeling.

"Now that we've got so many people contributing to the project..." He trails off, unsure where he's even going. Steve finishes his sentence without missing a beat.

"It's hard to recognize individual inputs anymore?"

James shakes his head in disbelief. Sometimes he forgets that he and Steve are operating on the exact same wavelength. Talking to him for thirty seconds is a warm reminder that they are two sides of the same brain.

"I mean... yeah. Exactly that. It's as if the System is working it out all by itself."

Steve's eyes go wide as he imitates HAL 9000. "That's quite the insinuation, Dave."

"I'm being serious, Steve. It's started to feel a bit muddied, don't you think?"

"Yeah. It has," Steve concedes. "That's part of the reason why I wanted to speak to you tonight. I need your advice." James is momentarily shaken. This is new.

"I don't think you've ever asked for my advice once in all our years knowing each other. I'm the lost puppy who comes to you for direction, remember? That's our dynamic!"

"OK, now I'm being serious, Jim," Steve says. He's not laughing. James has never seen him with this level of urgency before. To him, Steve is the same post-graduate from twenty years ago in jeans and Pixies t-shirt, making up silly songs and threatening to change the world. Looking at him now, he sees a man in his forties with a salt-and-pepper beard and stress lines under his eyes. The playful sparkle still pulsates underneath it all, but Steve clearly has something he needs to get off his chest.

"We can talk about it now if you like?"

"No, Jim. This needs a quiet corner of Hermit's." James' curiosity is now truly sparked.

"Sure. I'll come straight from the clinic." James approaches the fire door that will take him back into the Pit. He turns back to Steve. "Are we good, Steve?"

"Oh, babe," Steve answers, following him through the door. "We're peachy."

"Great. Then get back to work, dipshit."

---

JAMES PULLS his Honda Civic into the parking lot of the Seven Pines Family Planning Clinic to see Sarah getting out of her Uber. Perfect timing. She runs over, opens the door and climbs in the passenger seat. She and James share a look of nervous excitement.

"How are you feeling?" Sarah asks.

"Yeah. A bit jittery. Excited. I think. I don't know. You?"

"Flustered."

"Flustered. That's the word I was looking for." This appointment is the culmination of years of disappointment, apprehension, and uncertainty. Husband and wife take comfort in the fact that they're both sharing the same wave of mixed feelings. Sarah glances at the sprawling premises.

"How much cum do you think is in there?"

"Oh, I don't know," James answers. "But if I was to give an estimated guess, I'd say... fuckloads." This place looks high-end. The isolated, gated private facility, hidden away in the rugged, upland plateau of Weston, was carefully chosen after weeks of online research. The numerous sports cars and Teslas populating the parking lot signify the deep pockets of the clientele. Business is booming.

"We're sure we can afford this?" James asks. Sarah strokes the back of James' head.

"Just about."

James thinks back to all the phone consultations they have already had with the eminent Dr Mahoney. He cringes at the memory of in-depth discussions regarding his spermatozoa and Sarah's eggs, of how a few of them would be implanted, how most would die and of how, God willing, some would start developing. James had never considered himself a prude until these highly personal IVF conversations had begun, let alone the process of jizzing into a plastic cup at the facility's sister site in Downtown Boston. His awkwardness at the whole process has provided endless entertainment for Sarah, who has found his discomfort both uncharacteristic and oddly endearing.

"You sure you're OK?" Sarah asks.

"I think so."

"Jim. They're not going to inject alien DNA into our baby."

"C'mon, Sarah. Don't joke around."

"Babe! You need to chill! It's alright for you. All you had to do is watch a lovely little bit of porn and polish your bannister. This is the only time I'm ever going to actively encourage such behavior. So snap out of it." James allows himself a laugh and gets his head in the game. She's right. For her, the process has been invasive and traumatic. For him, it's been as simple as one, two, three. Sarah gets out of the car and sticks her head back inside.

"It'll be OK. We're just getting some results and potentially setting some dates." James nods and gets out of the car.

Two minutes later, James and Sarah cross the lobby. James absorbs the surroundings. Vast open spaces, vertical wall fountains, giant screens with an advertisement on rotation featuring a stunning woman in a white lab coat, holding an apple and waxing lyrical about the miracle of childbirth.

"It screams 'cult', don't you think?" James asks. "I bet there's a pentagram in a basement somewhere."

"Don't be silly," Sarah answers, slapping his arm. "More like a slaughtered sacrificial goat." The building has clearly been finessed over the years, honed by hundreds of polls and focus groups. It whispers a message. *We know what we're doing here. Trust. Comfort. Wealth. Welcome to the family that makes families. Give us your money.*

Ten minutes later, they sit in a plush office opposite Dr Paul Mahoney. Based on their numerous interactions thus far, James has decided that he seriously likes this guy. Of course, he likes him in the same way that everyone likes a senior doctor in a private clinic. The warm, welcoming smile, softly spoken nature, and perfectly trimmed beard seal the deal. Pleasantries are exchanged, a mouse is wiggled, and the relevant file is opened on the computer.

"Let's get straight to it," Dr Mahoney says, swinging the monitor around in a highly intentional gesture designed to undercut the complex nature of what they do here. *Look, I'm sharing my screen with you. We're all on this journey together.* James is hit by a deep anxiety. He didn't expect to be getting *straight* to it. He longs for the doc to exchange at least two or three more pleasantries. Pleasantries, he can handle. A screen filled with impenetrable charts, not so much. The doctor hasn't even asked about their drive in or the changeable weather. James had a witty anecdote about rush hour traffic at the ready. What a waste.

"It's good news. Your sperm and cell analyses have been returned. Both look very good." Simple, basic, accessible. This guy is good. He allows a few seconds for this information to be absorbed. Sarah looks at James with raised eyebrows, grabs his hand, and squeezes. James knows he's lagging behind here and follows his wife's lead, forcing a smile onto his dumb face.

"Sorry, just to clarify. We're good? As in, we're good?"

"You're good, Mr Reynolds," Dr Mahoney confirms. "This is good." James suddenly experiences an unexpected lightness as a giddy excitement bursts to life deep within. It's all suddenly so overwhelmingly real. James looks over to Sarah, smiling uncontrollably.

"We're good!"

"We're good, Jim!"

James looks back to the doctor. "So? What's next, doc?"

"We schedule you in. We have available slots three months from now, if that works for you. We'll need you to clear out some of your schedules. What do you say we iron out the details?"

The next hour passes in a woozy blur. Details are ironed out and mid-July is selected as the go-date. Dr Mahoney intricately explains various disclaimers and safety procedures, ensuring he carefully manages expectations. As per usual, James' initial elation wavers slightly as the reality of what is to come ignites flickers of apprehension. Even so, the flickers are mild and the joy lingers longer than is usual.

James and Sarah find themselves out in the parking lot in a tight, loving embrace. James instinctively digs out a cigarette and brings it to his mouth. He looks at Sarah. She says nothing. Without a second thought, he walks over to a nearby trash can and launches it. The rest of the packet follows.

"I love you, James Reynolds."

"I know."

---

JAMES FINDS a parking spot near Hermit's and allows himself a minute of silence to truly judge how he's feeling. He's learned to analyze his own stress by stepping out of himself and simply observing, like a curious passenger. He now employs the same method to evaluate his own dizzying glee. Away from Sarah and the clinic, and back in the real world, yes, it seems he truly is happy with the news. Imagine that. He anticipated a freight train of doubt to have pulled into the station by now, but it's nowhere to be seen. It's probably delayed and will arrive tomorrow, unannounced. He takes out his phone to see a message from Steve. *I'm here.*

James swipes away a couple of social media notifications as he approaches the bar. Despite his job, he never truly took to social media, ensuring a conservative presence on Facebook, Instagram, Twitter, TikTok and other variants on the same tired theme. Like every creative, James craves validation. Luckily for him, that's where the globally popular, evergreen *Cyberside* comes into play. Mega fans the world over know his name. He doesn't need strangers liking his badly framed photographs of tall buildings and overpriced brunches to feel that sweet dopamine hit. His endless, predictable feeds are composed of industry news, *Cyberside* developments and, more recently, scantily clad women making career choices they will come to regret. He must have forgotten to select incognito mode on his recent trip to give a sperm sample. Goddamn algorithm. Thanks to his job at Fall Water, James has garnered a healthy list of loyal followers, but it peaked a few years ago. Due to his general inaction, most people tend to leave him alone and latch onto Virginia, whose thirst on social media knows no bounds. One of the blessings of being a programmer is that they are considered rather dull. Writers, community managers, and marketing folks all have much more success in user engagement on these platforms, and they're welcome to it.

As he approaches Hermit's, James gives thanks that it has barely changed in over twenty years. He enters to see Josh emerge, offer a warm nod, and point to the back, indicating that Steve is waiting for him in the depths of the bar. James tips an invisible hat in gratitude in a gesture he has been overdoing for decades.

"A couple of zero per cent IPAs, Josh, and keep them coming."

Josh silently salutes. James walks through the maze out the back, navigating narrow corridors and offshoots. He finds Steve in a corner booth flipping beer mats to kill time.

"Wow," says James. "Even here, you manage to slack. Can't you sit still for ten minutes?"

"Nope. And this is more nervous excitement than boredom."

Josh slips in and drops down a couple of drinks before slinking off again, going completely unnoticed. James gets Steve all caught up on the events of the last few hours; Steve is as supportive as always and his excitement triggers James all over again, as if on a second wave of a high. Jokes are made about how coding is a lot simpler than reproduction and a natural lull enters the conversation.

"Right. What was it you wanted to talk about?" James asks. Steve sits there with a half smile, not saying anything. "Oh God. Silence becomes him. It must be serious."

"Do you ever think you might not want to work at Fall Water anymore?" *Oh crap. Not this again.*

"Look, Steve. We talked about this. I have that thought every day, yet I'm still there. And now, with a potential little human on the way..."

Steve nods in disappointment. "I hear you, man. It's all good. Honestly."

"Is it?" James asks.

"Sure. What can I say? I get carried away sometimes imagining the pair of us opening up a nice little startup and doing things our own way." James pictures the scene. Him and Steve in a ramshackle basement, sitting opposite one another, designing and building all day without having to duck out to meetings once an hour, reporting to nothing and no one but their imagination. *Fuck. That does sound good.*

"Never say never. Maybe in a couple of years."

"Ha! Don't kid yourself," Steve says. "In a couple of years, when child number two is on the way, you have a bigger house with a bigger mortgage, and have just put a downpayment on a yacht? Sure thing, brother. I'll see you there."

James, desperate to change the subject, scours the menu, which has also steadfastly refused to be updated in twenty years. He waves Josh over and orders a burger and fries. Steve glances around to make sure nobody is looking and takes a puff on his vape. James stares at it longingly.

"If you want to smoke, we can just go outside."

"As of one hour ago, you don't smoke anymore, Jim." James suddenly remembers, with a hint of frustration, that he has just given up smoking again. "By the way, don't expect me to quit in a show of solidarity like I did with the drink. I'm a good friend, but not that good."

James chuckles. "You never gave up drinking, Steve."

"I did around you! And when I spend most of my waking hours in your darling company, that's giving up drink, friend. As for this," Steve says, nodding to his vape, "we used to smoke here at this very table way back when. I'm just taking a toke from the pipe of nostalgia."

By the time the food arrives, it occurs to James that there's no way Steve insisted on meeting up tonight just to try and convince him to quit Fall Water again.

"I know what you're thinking," Steve says. "I've got something else on my mind." James looks at him, astonished.

"What, figuring out how to monetize your mind-reading powers?"

"Something has been really puzzling me, Jim. To the point that I'm questioning my sanity."

"You lost your sanity around the same time as the smoking ban, but do go on." Steve doesn't even grin. Odd. He usually forces a smile at James' terrible jokes, even just as a courtesy. James watches, speechless, as Steve leans in conspiratorially and takes his hand in his. *He's holding my hand.*

"Right. Remember around a month ago, we fired a couple of the guys?" James nods, still coming to terms with the fact that Steve is cradling his hand. "And you handed their workload to me? Integration between core mechanics and analytics?"

"Sure. What about it? It was too complex for them so I handed it to you."

Steve squeezes James' hand. "Doesn't that sound a little bit off to you?" James slowly pulls his hand out of Steve's embrace and finds a french fry. He slowly brings it to his mouth.

"Off how?"

"Jim, please. How is core mechanics and analytics integration complex?"

"It's System-related. Everything on that side has always been far from a walk in the park." James grabs another handful of fries.

"Even so," Steve says, "it shouldn't have been so impenetrable. Either way, my guys ran with it and came back to me after a few days. Completely perplexed." He holds James' gaze for a painfully long time.

"Are you waiting for a follow-up question or is this just a dramatic pause?"

Steve exhales, grabs James' fries from his hand and places them back in their basket. "This stuff was so incredibly complex and convoluted, I didn't even know where to begin. It included some of the most remarkable next-gen shit I've ever seen. It would be considered advanced even ten or twenty years from now."

"If you're about to walk down Skynet road, I'm leaving," James says.

"There's one particular master module that is essentially some kind of ultra-high-grade militech neural network AI... *thing*." James is not only paying attention now, he's riveted. This piece of work was so trivial, he paid it zero attention. It seems Steve may have indeed inadvertently stumbled across something big. "That's not even the most interesting part. So I may have hacked around it somewhat…"

Steve says this so quickly and with such nonchalance that James doesn't even bother chastising him.

"I got in and read the module's code comments," Steve whispers. "I know only one person who has this engineering style and who writes like this." James stares at him.

"Spit it out, man."

"John." James blinks. Well, he wasn't expecting that. "John Burrow." James sits in silence. "John Burrow, remember? Who we used to—"

"Yes, Steve! John Burrow! Of course I remember! Christ alive! Just give me a second." James tries to calculate what could possibly be going on here. "This is clearly a mistake."

"I'm telling you, Jim! Don't give me the brush off."

"Alright. Calm down. What did it say?"

"The comments don't make any sense from an engineering point of view. But what they *do* have is a series of repeated elements and recognizable patterns."

"OK. That does sound like Burrow," James concedes.

"It's a code, Jim. For once, I'm not yanking your chain. An encrypted code with a message." Now it's James' turn to glance around the place. The back of his neck heats up and the hairs stand to attention. He has no idea why, but his gut is telling him that this conversation is dangerous. If it was anyone but Steve, he'd have been out the door five minutes ago. He knows him too well, however. He wouldn't come to him with this unless he was absolutely sure. What's more, this does sound like something John would have the audacity to try and pull off. James now takes Steve's hand in his.

"Steve. On a scale of—"

"One hundred. Trust me on this. I made some notes." Steve takes his hand back and fishes a crumpled piece of paper from his jacket pocket.

"Actual notes? What is this, Watergate?"

"I don't know, it just felt right to use a pen and paper," Steve says. "No paper trail."

"It's a *literal* paper trail. Did you leave the tin foil hat at home?" James asks.

"I memorized this and wrote it down."

James greedily grabs the paper, turns to face the wall, hunches over and surveys the page. He instantly knows Steve is right. Burrow's style is so familiar that he might as well be reading his signature. One line with repeated matching symbols, using a simple technique to obfuscate the original meaning, stands out above all others. James slips the paper into his own jacket pocket, much to Steve's disapproval.

"I need to look at this at home, Steve."

"So you agree?" Steve asks urgently.

"Yeah," James says. The look of relief on Steve's face is monumental. He throws his head back and slides down his seat as if the weight of the world has been lifted.

"Thank fuck for that."

"Do me a favor. Promise me you'll stop digging."

"Why would I promise—"

"Just put down the shovel and let me handle this. If you leave even the mildest hint of a trace around a Fortress project, Simmons will rip you a new asshole and then rip that asshole a new asshole. You'll be gone." Suddenly, Steve's earlier conversation about quitting seems to make quite a lot of sense. He knows he's on dangerous ground and is potentially hedging his bets.

"Don't worry, Jim," Steve says, sensing James' panic. "You have my word." With that simple sentence, James knows his friend will back off.

"Just give me a week," James says. He grabs his jacket, getting ready to leave.

"What are you thinking, Jimbo?"

"I'm thinking that Burrow is clearly still working on the project from his goddamn house." James now speaks with a sort of mild mania. "He still has a vested interest. So—"

"So why did he leave?"

"Exactly," James says. "Did he fall or was he pushed? This whole time, he was grieving for Alice. Or so everyone thought." Steve connects the dots.

"Yet he's clearly still involved in integrating the System and AI with the game."

"The crazy old bastard," James laughs. "Painting himself as some reclusive shut-in, but he's still leading the charge."

"You can't keep a giant down," says Steve.

"Did you manage to decode any of this?"

"No. Thought I'd bring you in first. Did I do good, papa?"

"You did good, kid."

Five minutes later, James sits in his car coming to terms with this revelation. The events at the clinic now feel like a lifetime ago. He retrieves the notes from his pocket, handling them with such delicacy that they could be mistaken for a map to the Holy Grail. He rereads the one easier standout section, keen to confirm what he had thought back in the bar.

"What are you up to, John?"

Right there on the page, hidden in a cloak of symbols, is a sentence that will change everything.

IF YOU'RE *able to read this, get it to James Reynolds. JB.*

---

THE BURROW MANSION now resembles a fortress rather than a residence. Even the surrounding area feels like an extended compound; the few neighboring houses that are here were purchased by Versa years ago. They either remain empty or house some of the team that assist John Burrow in the research and maintenance of his daughter.

In the specialist lab that has been built on the second floor, her comatose, skeleton-thin body lies connected to a supercomputer designed, built and honed specifically for this project. 'Project' doesn't do it justice. What is happening in John's former family home is nothing less than an attempt at the full transcendence and liberation of human intellect into the digital world. An undertaking that might just give Alice another life.

At three am, all research personnel are long gone. A couple of security guards shuffle around the perimeter of the premises, but nobody is trying to get in here. Nobody is trying to get in because nobody knows the full magnitude of what is unfolding behind these walls.

John sits alone in the main lab, accompanied by the quiet whirring and beeping of technical equipment. Shadows are cast on his exhausted face by light emitted from dim diode lamps and monitors. John stands and stretches. He looks old. His hair is long and thinning, unattended by years of refusing to see a barber. His glasses are bigger, with thicker lenses. He wears baggy track pants and a faded *Cyberside* t-shirt. He's been wearing the same clothes for over a week now. No point in changing when you have nobody to impress. John grabs his *World's Greatest Dad* mug and shuffles over to the coffee machine. He feels his bed calling, but Versa is pushing for substantial results by December. Much work to be done.

This deadline would be realistic if John was focused solely on Versa's mission. The truth is, he has been averaging three hours sleep a night in order to carry out his own secret project. John has become an engineer in his own company, reporting to corporate dirtbags. The joke's on them. All of this is a cover in order for him to carry out something truly special.

John pours his coffee and returns to his chair. His knees creak as he sits; he should probably get on the treadmill. He won't. He opens a console and types */run matilda.exe*, initiating a sequence of distributed executable files. After a few seconds, a reassuring click emerges from the speakers. John smiles warmly.

"Hello, Alice."

"Hi, dad," a voice responds. "You need to get on the treadmill. Those knees are sounding rusty." John chuckles. 'Alice' sounds like she did the night she died. Young, energetic, and hungry for a life that was so brutally taken away.

"I'd love to, sweetheart. But we've a lot to cover. If you're going to pull off what we talked about, you need to train."

"Of course. One thing before we start."

"What's that?"

"Your message has been discovered." John's mouth drops open and he swivels in his chair.

"Huh. By Jim? Tell me by Jim."

"Not Jim." John momentarily panics. "By Steve Jenkins." John exhales a deep sigh of relief. "I tracked him on the office CCTV making notes. His cell phone location places him at Hermit's earlier this evening. As does Jim's." This is all John needs to hear. He stands and begins pacing.

"OK. You realise what this means, Alice? It all starts here. It starts tonight." A few seconds of silence pass. "Alice?"

"I'm worried about you, dad." John waves his hand dismissively through the air.

"Well, don't. I'm just one cog in a much bigger machine. You're the main player here. Just trust me."

"If you say so, old man."

As the hours pass, John trains the shadow of his daughter in the skills, algorithms and capabilities she will need to operate in her new form. Operate not as the System, as Versa thinks, but as a fully independent, free-thinking digital entity. It's going to be a long night.

# 8
# RABBIT HOLE

*Ho-ly shit!* James ducks for cover, narrowly dodging and temporarily deafened by a devastating hail of bullets from the Raider encampment's heavy gunner. He automatically reloads. His movements are fluid. So strong is his muscle memory that he doesn't even need to look down at his trusty revolver. He digs deeper, internally counting the seconds until Babylon grunts start inevitably lobbing grenades in his direction to lure out the sitting duck. James speaks into his earpiece.

"Ghost. Didn't you tell me this was going to be a stealth mission?"

"Affirmative, Taciturn405," a pleasant female voice responds.

"And are there or are there not an army of guards trying to turn me inside out?"

"There appears to be," the woman responds sardonically. A grenade lands by James' feet. He kicks it away.

"Then I'm guessing the definition of 'stealth' must have changed in the last ten minutes." The grenade explodes and some light debris rains down on him.

"It would have been stealthy, Taciturn, if you befriended the shadows and didn't unload your weapon every time the wind blew."

"The gun is silenced, Ghost."

"It's a Reaper MK3 Hand Cannon. Just because you hack your

inventory doesn't make it a silencer. If you're gonna cheat, make sure it pays off."

The Raiders' footsteps shuffle closer. James hears next moves exchanged via radio, bookended by white noise. Not only has he been cornered, he's also been caught red-handed by his handler.

"Well... technically I—"

"Save it, Taciturn," Ghost says playfully. "You have two seconds before another grenade lands. Time to roll." James jump-rolls towards more cover – a dilapidated jeep riddled with bullet holes – half a second before another barrage of bullets churns up chunks of dusty earth with a *thunk-thunk-thunk*. James hears a threatening beeping behind his back and ducks behind the vehicle as another explosion rips across the battlefield. Steel doors buckle; glass shatters.

"Who programmed the radius for those grenades?"

"That may have been me," Ghost replies. "Be sure to make a note on the bug log." James glaces at the in-game display – his wristwatch – and notes that his abilities are fully restored.

"Right. Showtime."

"Did you just say 'showtime' unironically, Taciturn?"

"God, I did. Can I take that back?"

"Too late. Break a leg."

James initiates his class ability and slows down time, allowing him the thrill of dodging slow-motion enemy bullets as he peers over the hood of the jeep. A quick activation of his visor tells him he may want to aim for a structural weakness within the frame of the enemy tower, followed by a swift volley of shots to the fuel barrels in the vicinity of a railgun turret. James effortlessly obliges with faultless marksmanship, causing extreme carnage as slo-mo returns to normal speed. Not a problem – his enemies are so distracted by fireballs and tower collapses that he makes light work of picking them off after reloading again.

"Showoff. You know this ability is way too overpowered, Jim?"

"Yup. We can fix it later."

In his own personal corner office – one that he was forced to take by Virginia, despite his protestations – James leans back in his chair.

His stats screen compiles a list of percentages and tells him he's been rated an A+ for this particular ruckus.

"Playing games on the company dime, Mr Reynolds?" The instantly recognizable voice fills James with dread. He loses his headset and swivels around as Donovan strides into the room. The man is in ridiculous shape. A passing thought enters James' head. *How are we all getting older when he seemingly stays the same age?*

"It's my job to play, Mr Craze. Just testing the latest changes." On the increasingly common occasions that James does come face-to-face with Donovan, he's learned that the best strategy is to tell it like it is. Just not *too much* like it is. The maniac seems to respond well to competence and confidence. If you're overly competent and confident, however, it's best to dial it down a notch. Things tend to go smoothly when everyone accepts that Donovan is the biggest alpha in the room.

Donovan leans against the wall and shakes his head in disappointment. "You know it's not gameplay that ignites my interest." James considers standing up as a mark of respect, but chooses to stay seated in a show of smouldering indifference. That, and it's always best to give Donovan the illusion of higher ground. He settles on the compromise of sitting up straight.

"Of course. On that side, System integration is progressing on schedule. Ratings and character behavior are automatically analyzed and the data shipped to the Pyramid, where it's disassembled in patterns." James can barely believe that, as a developer, he's having to justify playing a video game in work hours. "It's all going smoothly. Just had to ensure these updates were up to snuff."

Donovan stares at James intently, allowing a few seconds of silence just to remind this grunt who's boss. "And the AI component?" James isn't and has never been part of the AI inner sanctum. This must be a trick question.

"That's not my remit, Mr Craze. Simmons and Brown have been leading on that front." Judging by Donovan's blank reaction, he's going to need a bit more than that. "But... from what I've heard, the data is being used effectively to create new scenarios based on player behavior patterns."

"We don't call them players, Reynolds. They're agents. Or actors." James dies a little inside. This latest ludicrously pointless directive from the top makes his blood boil. Now struggling to maintain his composure, he opts to push back gently.

"Sure. But we call them players here." James adopts his best stoic face. Battle lines have been drawn. Drawn in pencil, but drawn nonetheless. Donovan's face morphs into an angry frown.

"Are you being a smart fuck with me?"

"I beg your pardon?"

"Smart fuck. Are you being one, Jim? You get laid this morning or something?" James sinks back into his chair, trying to decipher just what the hell is going on here. This must be simply part of Donovan's evening dick-swinging tour of the office. If the big man hasn't managed to cash in his daily dose of fuckery within work hours, he is known to walk the floor and take it out on whichever unlucky sack of meat he happens to bump into. This is one of the risks of staying late. James accepts that he is the latest victim of his boss's constant need to treat people like dogshit, and that the best choice at this very moment would be a little bit of backpedaling.

"It's just a question of interdepartmental terminology. Old habits die hard. I'll cascade to the team tomorrow and make sure we roll out the new vernacular." Donovan nods, much to James' relief. A little bit more brown-nosing might not hurt. "Is there anything else I can help you with, sir?"

"Yeah. As we're entering the project's final stages, it's time you expedited those redundancies we talked about. We're in August now. From January 2020, we'll be entering the maintenance stage of engineering. That gives us six months to get our ducks in a row." James knows this isn't one to push back on. This has been on the cards for a while and it isn't the first round of redundancies he's overseen. If he doesn't play ball, he'll end up top of the list. He decides that now might be a good time to stand and pace.

"It'll be my call to decide who stays and goes?"

"It's your team, pal. Comes with the territory," Donovan grunts.

"Of course. I understand." Donovan smiles on hearing his four favorite words in the English language. He grabs James by the shoulder and squeezes hard. James manages not to whimper.

"HR will be in touch. Have the names ready in a week." Donovan barrels out of the room, on the hunt for his next victim. James waits a few seconds, locks the door, returns to his chair, and places his headset back on.

"Did you get all that, Ghost?"

"Got it. All recorded."

"That went down just as you predicted," James says. "Thanks for the scoop."

"No problem. You do realize that we don't have that much time? You need to get back in the game." James is already reaching for his sunglasses and sunscreen.

"I need to quickly walk this off. Give me half an hour?"

"Sure, Jim. Whenever you're ready."

---

EVEN THOUGH IT'S already six pm and James is wearing shorts and a t-shirt, it's still unbearably hot outside. The steady temperature rise over the last couple of years has the finest scientific minds from around the globe scratching their heads. Global summits have been held in an attempt to net-zero the planet and place a pause on intense climate change. For his part, James has been so busy with his immediate life that he hasn't paid too much attention to the bigger picture. All he knows is that, these days, if he goes outside with anything less than SPF 50, he'll turn into a lobster.

He strolls through Fall Water's campus, doused in so much sunscreen that he resembles a cloud with limbs rather than a human being. A few people are still dotted around, braving the heat, sipping iced coffees, or sitting in the shade on laptops. James instinctively reaches for a cigarette. Of course, he doesn't have any. Even four months into quitting again, he still goes outside for a smoke break, but now he'll throw some nicotine gum in his mouth, sit on a bench and crack open a can of soda.

James thinks back to June when, after two months of late nights, he finally managed to break John's code and access the System. It was here that he met Ghost. The whole endeavor feels like a deranged dream. This was an adventure far too intriguing to ignore. Once he was in, it was impossible to stop digging.

Masterfully hidden through code comments in the *Cyberside System*, encrypted instructions and digital breadcrumbs first led James to a data library buried deep within the project service sub-sub-subsystems. In other words, a place where nobody would ever think to look. The library contained further instructions demanding James partake in a couple of deprecated quests with off-the-wall engagement requirements. And partake he did.

James has been outside for all of three minutes, but is already sweating profusely. Boston is now more akin to a Miami summer. He glances at an empty basketball court and abandoned ultimate field. It's simply too sweltering for anybody to play anymore. Not that they would anyway. Fall Water proudly advertises these amenities, but judges any staff who are foolish enough to use them. It's all for show, like so much around here. Barren trees, too starved of water to produce leaves, cast skeletal shadows across concrete. James considers returning inside. Maybe in a minute. He'd rather roast than risk running into Donovan again.

James thinks back to Steve, constantly on his back for weeks about the meaning of John's riddle. James would have loved to bring him in, but the mystery codes carried strict instructions not to tell anybody. It was with monumental regret that James lied to his best friend, telling him that the message was nothing more than a bad-taste prank pulled by a couple of disgruntled former employees. Steve sensed this was horseshit and it led to a small crack in their friendship, but he backed off nevertheless. James' willingness to cut Steve out acted as proof of his loyalty to Ghost. And so the fun truly began.

Ghost. Even now, James doesn't know who she is. It could be a teenage boy in Mexico or an old lady in India. The voice is that of an American female, but even a part-time hacker could employ voice-changing software. Whoever they are – and James is convinced they are female – she is somehow connected with John. That much is certain. At first, James started communicating with her via chat. Not long after, they joined forces and tackled the first quest in the Rotten Apple realm, beating an invulnerable boss that James didn't even know existed. Increasingly complex quests followed through the deep caverns of secret *Cyberside* realms. In order to progress, James was tasked with finding and tweaking codes and comments and disclosing top secret company information. He knew he was being manipulated, but by this point he was too far down the rabbit hole. Not only this, but Ghost's presence in James' life presented a disillusioned Head of Dev with a purpose and a reinvigorated interest in the pure, joyful act of playing games. It was an absolute thrill to engage in challenges beyond his own design. James was exploring the familiar world of *Cyberside*, but traversing virgin territory. The digital yellow brick road was a captivating mix of conspiracy, evil corporations, time travel – that was certainly a new take on a tired formula – and shady government secrets. The canvas James was exploring was far beyond anything he could have ever dreamed up. It was utterly captivating and endlessly addictive. Who needs cigarettes when you're balls deep in corporate espionage?

Whenever James considered calling it quits, he would think of John. This *had* to be related to him. The design screamed *Otherscape*. Other early Burrow creations echoed through everything, as well as a plethora of pop culture references that aligned perfectly with John's dated sensibilities. There was no way James was going to walk away, despite the obvious dangers. Donovan, Virginia and Tom have zero interest in the world of *Cyberside* itself. To be on the safe side, James has been conducting these missions at home after Sarah has gone to bed. Tonight, however, she's hosting her book club. He has no choice but to indulge in his seedy little secret after hours at the office.

Donovan showing up unannounced was something James could have done without. Good job he got a tip off that he was heading his way. If the big dog got so much of a whiff of what James was up to... well, given the highly confidential information James has been sacrificing, it's not worth contemplating the repercussions. So far, Ghost has protected James well, becoming something of a Fall Water oracle. She provides intel on upcoming corporate decisions and offers a heads-up on inbound emails before they hit James' inbox. He even knows when undesirable company is heading across the Pit towards his office. Unannounced meetings and even fire drills are no longer a surprise. Two weeks before Donovan first mentioned the latest round of redundancies, James knew they were coming. Thanks to his guardian angel, gone are the days of traditional work-related anxiety and uncertainty. Setbacks are a lot easier to navigate if you know they're lurking around the corner. As for Ghost, she has only one condition. Just. Keep. Playing. Whenever James has dared to ask the purpose of this wild goose chase, Ghost has remained characteristically cryptic. *We are digging for the truth.*

James stands and wipes the sweat from his brow. He knows Sarah will be analyzing the latest romantic thriller for hours yet, which will allow him time to plug back in and reconnect with Ghost. A tingle of excitement is sparked at the thought of another few hours of covert gallivanting.

Back inside, from his air-conditioned, top-floor penthouse suite, Donovan watches James return to the office.

---

THE DRIVE from the town of Apex to Downtown Raleigh in North Carolina only takes a swift twenty minutes on a good day. Hank Brown has now taken this journey so many times, however, that he wants to claw out his eyes from his skull every time he blasts along the Raleigh Beltline. His work at the Pyramid has him so intricately glued to this state that Fall Water subsidized half of the cost of his house in Apex just to keep him close to the action. His devotion to the System initiative is now absolute. Up until earlier this year, he used to split his time between here and the R&D hub in Boston. After about two hundred flights, the commute got old and Hank decided to fully relocate. Managing to squeeze half a house out of the bastards upstairs made the whole endeavor ever so slightly sweeter to digest.

Hank impatiently presses the accelerator of his old 2012 Toyota Land Cruiser. A few moronic colleagues have hinted that a man of his stature could have treated himself to something a little sleeker, especially considering the bank he's making. If Fall Water coughed up for half of his house, they certainly would have happily provided him with a whole Tesla. Jokes have been made that he must be waiting for WWIII to break out so he can turn the beast into a tank. As Hank swerves around an RV, damn near running it off the road, he considers how these light-hearted jibes are dangerously close to the truth. He doesn't quite know what yet, but something is most definitely up.

The intimidating monolith of the Pyramid looms on the horizon. The tech facility is so massive, wherever you are in the city, there it is, following you around like the Mona Lisa. The towering site is so synonymous with this town that it started appearing on local postcards around four years ago. Or was it five? Or six? Hank stopped keeping track of time years ago. His brain has been far too busy integrating the System to *Cyberside* to pay attention to life's finer details, such as what year it is. Hank's life is the Pyramid; his master, the System; his mistress, the algorithm. If his single peers are checking out the local dating scene, Hank is driving home to pull another all-nighter. If his team meets up at a sports bar on a Saturday to watch the game, Hank is jumping on a conference call to Damien in D.C. If his colleagues go out for dinner after work and check out the latest night spots, Hank is devouring instant noodles at his desk. He can't even enjoy the luxury of takeout deliveries to the office due to the Pyramid's intensely tight security regime. The data center has completely changed the identity of Raleigh, yet Hank is too preoccupied to indulge in anything the area has to offer. As of August 2020, the facility now employs over a thousand people. It's not only Fall Water that has a presence here. The Research Triangle also hosts Red Hat, IBM, Cisco, and Epic over at Cary, amongst others. It has put Raleigh on the map as one of the biggest tech capitals in the United States. And smack bang in the middle of it all is Hank Brown, steadily losing his fucking mind.

As Hank takes a diversion through the gentrified North Hills, he reaches into his shirt pocket, finds a pill and throws it into his mouth like he would a Tic Tac. A quick chaser from a bottle of vodka helps the medicine go down. Whiskey used to be his drink of choice, but he switched to vodka last year. *The odorless way to get through the day*. In fact, Hank didn't switch to vodka to make people think he *wasn't* drinking. He switched to make people think he *was*. He actually pulled back on his alcohol consumption a couple of years ago, but it serves him well for people to assume he's still a drunk maniac. It's incredible how surreptitiously chugging from a bottle of water will lead people to believe it's vodka if you already have a drinking problem.

As for the pill? The warm buzz that is pushing Hank's anxiety away confirms that the one he just popped is the real deal. Seventy five per cent of the others he carries with him, however, are placebos that he makes at home. Soon after he curtailed the drink, Hank started cutting down on his Adderall habit. Once again, it works in his favour for everyone to think he's an unstable, prescription drug-addicted madman. Hank knows that Donovan got him hooked back in the day. He was an invaluable asset to Versa, but was too smart for his own good. With Hank riding the amphetamine wave, Versa could conduct their nefarious business without worrying about moralistic pushback from the junkie Head of R&D. After a while, many at Fall Water stopped regarding Hank as a crazy genius and looked on him more as a liability. For a while, he was both. More recently, Hank sensed something monumental on the horizon after being cut out of multiple strategy meetings and important decisions. So began the uphill, and at times impossible, process of regaining full control of his faculties. The last thing he needs is the higher-ups noticing a change in his behavior. This is why he has maintained the illusion and continues to play the role of Hank Brown, Adderall freak. Hank Brown, volatile lunatic. Whatever plans they've got simmering, Hank knows he needs to be lucid. He needs to prepare. He needs to be ready.

Over the years since Burrow was kicked out, Hank has watched with cynical glee as Simmons, Willis, and various other ambitious heads of this and that bend the knee and pledge allegiance to the Versa flag. Reynolds aside, he's seen good people forced out for refusing to play ball. He isn't going to be one of them. So, once again, he's played a role to maintain his position, feigning a lust for power.

James' friendship was a devastating, necessary loss in this grand performance, but needs must. Behind the scenes, while the board thinks Hank is at home, passed out in his own filth, he's been steadily forging a future for himself in whatever world Versa envisions.

Hank turns onto Fayetteville Street and parks up. He wants to get in a quick stroll in the impossibly hot sun before arriving at his meeting with Damien and his Fortress crony. It might help if he showed up as a dehydrated, sweaty mess. Anything to maintain the deception that he's a bumbling buffoon. He walks past a park setting up for a music festival later this evening. The heat is too intense for it to take place in the afternoon, although there are a few intrigued locals hovering about. *Fucking tourists. You have no idea what's coming.* Hank's bitterness at 'other people' has reached fever pitch over the last few years and his faith in humanity is currently at rock bottom. They're all blind sheep, buried in smartphones, easily manipulated and happily led. Deep down, Hank has his own concept of a perfect society. One built on action; a true meritocracy. Not that it matters what he thinks. The world is going to hell in a handbasket. He might as well carve out a niche for himself for when he gets there, wherever it may be.

Hank enters the Foundation as a frazzled, perspiring mess, just as planned. It's a small establishment slightly off the beaten track. The choice wasn't accidental; the place is almost empty. Nobody really goes out in the afternoon anymore. Damien, who is sitting next to a suit that Hank doesn't recognize, spots him instantly.

"Hank."

Hank walks over but makes a point of stopping on the way to order two beers from the bar. Damien subtly smiles at the suit. *Told you.* Little do they know that Hank comes in here a lot, often alone. He is familiar with the barman and phoned this morning, ahead of time, to tell him that he'd be in later today, that he'd be ordering two beers, that they should be served in normal beer glasses, and that they should be alcohol-free.

Hank takes a seat. The barman walks over and places down the 'beers'. Hank immediately downs one. Damien watches, mildly amused, and gestures to the suit.

"Hank Brown, meet Adam." The suit sits there stoically, like his kind always does. Hank stares him down, making sure to wobble unsteadily on his stool.

"You... you got a surname, there, er, Adam?" Hank slurs intentionally.

"Just Adam is fine."

"Well, Just Adam. A pleasure, I'm sure."

"Adam's part of the senior security team at Fortress," Damien says.

"What's so urgent, Damien?" Hank asks. "It's a Saturday, for fuck's sake." One of the joys of pretending to be an arrogant drunk is the freedom to say exactly what's on one's mind without fear of chastisement. One must keep up appearances at all times.

"We have something that requires your immediate attention, Mr Brown," says Adam.

"Oh, look. It speaks!" bellows Hank. He notes that his two companions sure do look serious. "Shit, who died? Does something wicked this way come?"

Adam pulls a military-grade laptop out of thin air, opens a couple of logs and spins the screen around so Hank can take a look.

"We encountered something when conducting our weekly security sweep," he says.

"An anomaly," adds Damien.

"Ooooh, I love an anomaly. Do go on," Hank says. Adam glaces over his shoulder to ensure there's nobody else here. Hank chuckles. "I'm the paranoid one, Just Adam. Didn't Damien tell you?"

"No identifiable forms of external breach," Adam says. "We need your expertise." Hank nods, grabs the laptop and begins scrolling. His eyes dart around the screen.

"Standard data processing. Normal Pyramid business..." As Hank scans the text, he internally analyzes the situation. *Is this a trap? Am I being set up?* Reading through the logs, he feels a pang of relief that whatever it is, it has nothing to do with him or his immediate team. This just got very intriguing indeed. A burst of adrenaline explodes through his system at the prospect that somebody may have just penetrated his notoriously impenetrable firewalls. "Hmmm. Anomaly is right. Very interesting," he mutters. "Sorry, one sec."

Hank retrieves his pill box from his pocket, opens it, selects a placebo pill, and swallows it. Then another for good measure. Adam looks to Damien, who shrugs. Hank then pulls his own device out of his bag – an IBM touchpad – makes a couple of manipulations with his phone and fires up the System's interface. Before Damien and Adam know what's what, Hank is running diagnostics from the log. Something catches him off guard. He furrows his brow before realising that he's revealing too much. A huge gulp of his 'beer' and a forced belch brings the illusion roaring back.

"Well! I've got good news and good news," Hank says. Damien and Adam share a look of surprise; Hank savours his brief moment of power.

"Spit it out, Hank," Damien orders.

"OK. First of all, the System is intact," Hank begins. "There have been no internal breaches, you'll be happy to hear. Everything's in order." Damien and Adam are instantly relieved. "The project has extremely limited access; a strict system of protocols built on keys. One key is at Versa's disposal and requires approval from Donovan. The other is a Fortress access point and belongs to Simmons."

"We also issued a key to Virginia and her team, right?" Damien asks.

"Correct," says Hank. "My team doesn't have one; we don't run designated domain control. But we keep things ticking over."

"So these diagnostics are telling us that none of the keys have been compromised?" Adam asks. Hank nods, taking another mammoth gulp from his beer. "But there are changes in code?"

"There are," Hank answers. "But not carried out by any of the key holders."

"Then how the hell is this possible?" Adam looks to Damien, who passes the ball to Hank.

"Well, fellas," Hank says. "The only other module we introduced to the System and *Cyberside*, around five years ago, is Tilda". Hank hides his true excitement with a gesture to the barman to bring him another beer. He knows this work originates from Burrow and that Versa has been keeping this project strictly confidential.

"Tilda," Damien repeats. "The AI management system developed between Versa and Fortress."

"What about it?" Adam asks.

"What... what about it? Look at this!" Hank exclaims wildly. He spins the screen back to Adam, who stares at it blankly. Hank giddily addresses Damien. "You didn't tell me Just Adam had a sense of humor, Damien! What about it? Ha! Good one!"

"Inside voice, Hank," Damien says.

"This is the most brilliant coding I've ever seen in my life." Hank pushes the laptop closer to the two men. They have no idea what they're looking at.

"You're just gonna have to go right ahead and spoon feed us here, buddy," says Damien. "You mentioned a second piece of good news?"

"This code wasn't written by a human. This is Tilda."

"Does this mean what I think it means?" asks Adam, finally catching up. Hank nods enthusiastically.

"This is a major breakthrough, gentlemen," he beams. "The System has started to self-regulate. It's writing its own service optimization functions." Damien holds up a hand and looks to the sky with his eyes closed. He almost looks aroused. This is the moment they've been waiting for.

"You better be very fucking sure about this, Hank."

"I'm sure, Damien." Hank scrabbles to make sense of what's happening in his mind and translate it to the two idiots he's sitting with. In an effort to buy some time, he blurts out a lie. "We're looking at mere weeks to make the final push from our end to finalize integration." This is all Adam needs to hear. He takes the laptop back, packs it away with a couple of precise motions, and stands.

"Many thanks for the reassurance, Mr Brown. This news is indeed revolutionary. I'll head back to D.C. tomorrow and brief the team, but this stays between us for now." Hank nods like the good little boy he is. "Now, if you don't mind, I have a music festival to attend. Are either of you going?" Damien shakes his head. Hank is momentarily confused. Just Adam, the emotionless automaton in a suit, the man who is seemingly immune to fun, has just revealed that he is attending a concert. Maybe he isn't Just Adam after all. Hank is more shocked at this revelation than the technological game changer he's just unearthed. Adam shakes hands and leaves. Hank looks at Damien, horrified.

"Did he just say he's going to a music festival?"

"You know, Hank," Damien says, "historically, favors are granted to those who deliver good news. Considering this and all your remarkable work over the past few years, I'm intending on pulling a couple of strings."

"Very nice of you, Damien, but I haven't really done anything here. I'm not one for false plaudits. I wouldn't have noticed this if you hadn't brought it to me."

A mixture of curiosity and suspicion descends on Damien's face. "Speaking of, how come you never noticed this thing until now?"

Hank takes his 'vodka' out of his bag and has a swig. The gesture seems to work in half-answering Damien's question. *I'm a junkie alcoholic, remember?*

"You said it yourself. It's an anomaly. It falls under Security to flag this kind of thing. We've had no breach alerts. These are minor pieces of code, Donovan. Sorry! Damien." Damien doesn't react. "It's pure luck that allowed us to catch it this early. You should give Adam a raise."

"Adam doesn't need a raise."

"We would have caught it when changes achieved critical mass or started influencing core modules and operations," Hank says. "But this gives us a nice little head start." This satisfies Craze Junior.

"Hank, old boy. This sets in motion developments of global magnitude. You realize that?"

"I didn't just fall off the turnip truck. Give me some credit."

"We should celebrate! Why don't we head over to the music festival after all?" Hank's eyes go wide in horror.

"I'd rather shit in my hands and clap, Damien. No offence."

Damien chuckles and stands. "None taken." He goes to the bar, throws down some cash, and exits into the blistering heat.

Hank remains seated, letting the cortisol subside. He counts to ten to confirm Damien isn't returning. When he's certain, Hank cycles over the meeting in his head and realizes he may have inadvertently placed Burrow in danger by revealing that Tilda is now in motion. With the project complete, John is no longer of any use. Hank reconciles this with the fact that if he didn't tell them now, they'd figure it out eventually and question why he kept schtum. No. Much better to play along on his own terms. Hank knows that the System is already fully operational. His false estimate of a few weeks until integration offers him some time for him to strategize. He marvels at another revelation he chose to keep to himself – the AI is forging its own access key. In all his years in this game, Hank has never seen programming so sophisticated. The magnitude of this discovery is so overwhelming that he reaches into his little box and takes out a real pill. Whatever the future has in store, it's going to be an interesting ride.

Amongst all the chaos, one thought pulsates loudly and calmly in his mind. If AI can carve out a domain key for itself in *Cyberside*, then there's nothing stopping Hank from doing exactly the same thing.

---

"THIS PLACE IS impossible to beat, Ghost. Literally by design." James sits in his home office, his face illuminated by the blue light of multiple monitors. He's in his office, yes, but he's also in the Rotten Apple, a dystopian, cyberpunk take on New York City, deep into another quest.

Ghost laughs derisively in James' ear while her avatar pulls off an effortless wall run in an abandoned warehouse. She lands on an invisible ledge and throws down a rope for her trusty companion.

"Impossible for most, old man. Unless you have me. Now pick your balls up and let's go!" James grabs the rope and begins his ascent.

"Does my digital Sherpa want to tell me what the hell we're doing in one of the Versa test servers?" James asks. "If Simmons finds out I was here, I'm screwed." Being a heavier class than Ghost, James is sluggish on the rope. He eventually reaches the top, joining his ally on the ledge. There is nothing beneath his feet; he's floating in empty space.

"So many questions, Padawan. A laboratory is stationed beneath these headquarters. There's something there you need to see."

"Oh yeah? What's that?"

"Oh, you know. The future core of the System."

At this point, Sarah enters James' office. He pauses the game and spins around.

"This looks suspiciously unlike work, James Reynolds," she says.

He throws up his hands. "Dammit. Caught in the act."

Sarah kisses him on the forehead. "It's nice to see you playing again, Jim, but don't stay up too late."

"Half an hour max."

"Sure. See you in an hour." She leaves the room and James guiltily returns to the game. He knows it's silly, but he feels like he's cheating on her in some way, crawling around the underbelly of *Cyberside* with a mystery woman.

"I can't believe you paused me," Ghost jokes. "You literally left me hanging." She chuckles and disappears into a portal leading to the next zone. James makes the leap now, emerging next to Ghost in a corner of a corporate building lobby. The place is filled with patrolling night guards, a plethora of security cameras, and multiple visible and invisible defence systems. "Don't panic," Ghost reassures him. "We're in a blind spot. This is where the real fun begins." James scans the room and notices a giant Fortress logo on the wall. The sign of the corporate beast bearing down on them serves to confirm the stakes here.

"Is this what I think it is?" he asks. Ghost doesn't answer. Instead, she activates her digital camouflage and slowly disappears.

"Welcome to the Fortress Foundation, Jim."

"This surely can't be in the game," James exclaims. "I'd know."

"Who says we're in the game anymore? Follow me and be stealthy. I mean it this time. There'll be no second attempts here. See that elevator?" James notes a marker on his local interface map.

"Yep. What's the plan?"

"Head for the elevator. If I told you what's in store, you wouldn't believe me. It's something you just have to see."

"I'm gonna need more than that."

"Well, you're not gonna get it, chump. For now, just focus and do exactly what I say." James doesn't bother arguing. There's no point. He knows that trial by fire is often the best method. He mentally preps, checking the map, their starting point, guard viewpoints, camera scopes and angles, light sources, and the slowly rotating detection arcs of guard turrets.

"We're fucked, girl."

A laugh floats in thin air as the invisible phantom runs, leaps and rolls between cover, dodging a targeting laser in the nick of time.

"You were saying?" Ghost responds. "You're up." James exhales deeply, releasing the external world from his mind and entering a flow state. His focus is locked entirely on his screen, seeing traces and lines of code behind tangible objects, and effortlessly forecasting movement trajectories. *You know this, James. You* built *it.* His fingers become one with the keys and mouse as he cloaks himself and starts to follow Ghost's hazy, light green trail. He imitates her actions flawlessly, frame by frame, in a perfect ballet of movement, without a single slip in animation.

Ghost vaults over to an armed guard and shadows his movements silently, step by step, following the only possible route between three security cameras and a mounted autocannon. As the guard reaches his post and turns back around, Ghost sinks to the left into shadow. James does his thing and joins her with a roll. Ghost's camouflage momentarily breaks with a mischievous smile.

"Good work, soldier. See, that wasn't so hard, was it? Now, see the sentry post blocking the elevator entrance?"

"The one that's impossible to penetrate?"

"When we reach the central fountain, I'll take the cover to the right," Ghost says. "You position yourself on the left, here." Another dot appears on the radar. Their route is marked by a thin red line.

"Copy. Then what?"

"Then I deactivate the defences, and you get to the elevator. Alone. Head down to the basement, where you'll find what we've been trying to reach for the last couple of months. This is the end of the quest, partner. It's been a pleasure." This information dump is too much for James to take. He tries to absorb everything, coming to terms with the fact that his little private adventure with Ghost is in its final stretch. She's already on the move.

"Wait..."

"No time for waiting, Jim! Let's go!" She slides down the stationary laser detection array and rolls to the right. James is right behind her, avoiding a guard on the left who is beginning his patrol through the navmesh. He catches up to Ghost at the fountain before she again blasts forward, strafing to the right towards the marked cover. James remains hovering, undetected, at the fountain ledge. He observes the guard post near the elevator and shakes his head, uncertain. There's no way they can pull this off. A barricade, two cameras, an autocannon, and four guards block the way. James' radar indicates through mildly rotating visibility cones that there are no blind spots. The entire place is well lit with no shadows. As a designer, he knows an unbeatable level when he sees one. But he also knows Ghost. At least he thinks he does. She hasn't let him down yet.

James scans the area to find her. The guard being quietly strangled by thin air beneath a security camera is a dead giveaway. Ghost momentarily emerges from her camouflage with a temporary glitch, interacting with a hidden panel on the wall. James hears static on his intercom.

"OK, Jim. Ten seconds, then get to that elevator. Give it everything you've got."

"Roger. And what about you?"

"This game is over for me, gramps, but I'll play again. Seven seconds."

"What do you mean—"

"Three seconds."

"Dammit, Ghost! At least—"

"One! Go, Jim! Now!" As Ghost finishes hacking the panel, James witnesses a violent flickering on his monitor, seeing, for the briefest moment, Ghost's full face without her usual mask. Service messages spew alerts through his second screen. In the virtual world, the lobby goes dark as lights flicker out. Next, all of the security systems fail and NPC guards freeze on the spot, ripped away from the behavior modules. James bolts to the elevator, which is easy to spot as the only light source in the vicinity. He skids inside and punches the button for the basement. The doors close with a *ping* and he leans back, in shock. Not because he just managed to pull off the impossible. Because, for the split second he saw Ghost's face, it was oddly familiar. The face of a young girl who would occasionally come into the office with her father. A face James saw plastered all over the press a decade ago following a horrific traffic accident. *Can it be?! Or have I completely lost the plot?*

---

As the elevator descends, a power cut kills every light in Raleigh, North Carolina, shrouding the town in darkness. The Pyramid hangs on for a minute or two, like a hulking, stubborn beast, before its lights go out for the first time in its existence.

James, steadily dropping to the basement, has no idea what is happening out in the real world and cannot fathom what awaits him ahead. All he knows is that he is currently experiencing complete and utter immersion in this digital realm. The space between the virtual world and the real no longer exists. It's transcendental. He psyches himself up, preparing to find himself anywhere, and ready to emerge with guns blazing.

The door *dings* and silently slides open. There are no guards. No turrets. No security cameras. He steps forward into the foyer of John Burrow's house, recreated in eerie detail. James only visited this place twice, when the big man held a Christmas gathering for Fall Water employees way back when. But James remembers it well. The place is unmistakable. The door to the study is half-open, emitting an inviting, soft, yellow light. James steps towards it, still on guard. A floorboard creaks beneath his feet.

"Jim. Come on in. I've been waiting for you."

On hearing the sound of John's voice, a flood of memories floods James' cerebral cortex. Memories of the good old days in Fall Water, of numerous visits to John's office, where he was always warmly welcomed, of cold winters and hot summers, of a carefree existence, of a hopeful, bright future. Memories of the man himself. Hindsight has taught James that, for many years, John was a surrogate father figure. He misses him. And he's about to see him again. He finds the inner strength to hold in his tears.

Out in the real world, in John's real study in his real mansion, surrounded by bricks and mortar, John is plugged in, in his own flow state. John sits in front of his monitor as James Reynolds' avatar enters his virtual study. The two men take a moment and look at one another. A gentle, welcome tension pulsates through the room.

"Boss. Long time."

"Longer than I would have liked, Jim."

James treads carefully, selecting his words with delicacy. "I never had a chance to express my condolences in person. I'm so sorry for your loss. Your love for Alice was like nothing I've ever seen." John nods, grateful for the kind words.

"It still is. Sit down, Jim. We don't have a lot of time." James enters and takes a seat in a wooden armchair. He notes how much Burrow has aged. Time and grief have not been kind. They rarely are. Even so, beneath it all, John's eyes are sharp and hungry.

Burrow proceeds to catch James up on events of the past few years. He is measured and rational, as always. So much so that James easily suspends his disbelief. He's here, he's ready to hear this, and he's fully engaged. John talks of corporate wrongdoing, of mistakes that have been made that have had and will have global repercussions.

"Everything we worked on, Jimmy, everything we built, has been hijacked. We have ourselves a waterfall of consequences that will take *Cyberside* and turn it into something vile."

"Vile how, sir?"

"The endgame is control. Simple as that. Fear and control. *Cyberside* will facilitate this. It's already in motion and has been since Versa got their stinking claws in my baby." James doesn't know if he's referring to *Cyberside* or Alice. In truth, it's both. "You followed the breadcrumbs like I knew you would. I could always rely on you. Good to know my instincts are still intact."

"And here I am," James says. "I'm not even sure where 'here' is anymore." John smiles sadly.

"This was the whole point, all along. For us to build something that blends the boundaries of reality and fantasy. With technology where it currently stands, there's only one thing for Versa and Fortress left to do. The future's looking bleak, Jim. Are you sure you're ready to hear this?" The pair sit in silence, accompanied only by the sound of the gently humming lamp. James considers. He's come too far. He's too invested. There's more chance of Hell freezing over than of him walking away.

"Tell me."

"They're gearing up to offer *Cyberside* as a place of permanent residence to those willing to take it. And maybe, just maybe, those not so willing." A tidal wave of images rattles through James' brain. People hooked up to the System. Empty streets. Lawlessness. Mass hysteria. A very different world.

"And you think people will go for it?"

"It would take some kind of catastrophic global event. We're already in one. It's awfully warm out, don't you think?" James can't argue with that.

"And you think that's enough?"

"I know what these people are capable of. If humanity needed an extra push, I'm sure Versa wouldn't hesitate." James doesn't want to agree, but he knows John is right. Something is brewing. Everyone knows it; they just don't know what.

"So where do you fit into all this?" James asks.

"Redemption, I guess. I conceived this nightmare. But with my current restraints, there's not a great deal I can do. I know you have a life. A loving wife. Possibly a kid on the horizon. This is a big ask, but there's nobody else I can trust. Tom went off the deep end long ago." James is overcome with a huge sense of hesitation. Somewhere deep within, however, a stronger sense of loyalty to the man sitting in front of him, a man who took a chance on a scruffy graduate with a can-do attitude, beats his reservations into submission.

"What do you need me to do?" Burrow stands and reaches into his cardigan pocket, retrieving a dog tag on a chain. He places it on his desk. "I recognize that," James says. "From *Otherscape*, right?"

"Sentimental, I know," John says. "My biggest weakness. This is something I forged. A key. If things go south – and I'm sure they will – this beauty will give you access to specific functions within the System. You won't be able to influence much, and you can't create massive waves, or they'll be onto you. But you're an engineer. The best there is. If anyone can create an opportunity to fix things..." James picks up the dog tag and feels its weight. He studies the coding behind it and knows he's holding a masterpiece in the palm of his hand.

"Holy shit, John."

"I know. This is my best work. Keep it safe. Think of it as insurance in case... well. Let's hope I'm wrong. Thanks, Jim. For everything."

"Thank *you*, John." With great reverence, James stores the dog tag away in his inventory. This is all the assurance John needs. Immediately, back at James' office at home, the monitors start to flicker, bringing him back to earth with an almighty crash. His second monitor bursts to life with reloaded modules, emergency operations and rebooting windows. On screen, John smiles at him.

"Good luck, Jim. All the best." With that, John Burrow glitches away to nothing.

When James returns to his senses, it's 3:42 am. He is mentally exhausted and unable to know for sure whether what he just experienced was real or hallucinated. To be certain, he relaunches the game and checks his inventory. Right there is a gleaming 3D rendering of a dog tag, lifted wholesale from *Otherscape*. Any casual gamer would mistake this for nothing more than an Easter egg. *Oh, John. You fucking genius, you.* James returns to his home location hub and places the tag into his account storage for safe keeping.

Ten minutes later, Raleigh's electricity comes flickering back online and the Pyramid returns to life. For months, the smartest minds will try and ascertain what happened. The reason for this mystery power outage will never be established.

## 9

# THAT NIGHT

The day James fired Steve was the first day he took cocaine at work. In early November, 2019, the directive was issued that the latest round of redundancies was to be carried out earlier than expected. Donovan wanted the dead weight out before Christmas. It fell to James to get rid of fifteen people on the Dev team.

For a while, Steve had been surfing along on good behavior. When he heard of yet more impending redundancies, the man cracked. While HODs had secured another salary bump, he had learned that certain close colleagues were to be kicked to the curb. The fact that it was just before Christmas was the final nail in the coffin.

Donovan and Virginia had received an expletive-ridden email at three pm on a Thursday afternoon; James had been copied in 'for info'. He was heading back from a meeting with Dina when his phone pinged. One look at the subject line - *GET FUCKED* - and his stomach fell out of his ass. He ducked into the nearest bathroom and hid in a stall in the futile hope that, just maybe, this would all take care of itself. Who was he kidding? James was Steve's line manager. And Steve had just told Donovan and Virginia to get fucked. James thought long and hard about whether 'get fucked' could have possibly meant something other than 'get fucked.' It didn't. There was no room for interpretation here.

Five minutes later, Virginia called James' cell. He answered in hushed tones, head between his knees, from his cubicle of solitude.

"He has to go, Jim. Get it done immediately."

"I don't think I can, Virginia."

"Get upstairs to my office. I have something that will make it easier."

James emerged on the top floor in a fugue state, his brain turned to soup, his vision blurry, his jaw tight with worry and his balls shrivelled. Virginia's assistant was waiting outside the elevator.

"She's waiting for you. Go straight in."

James entered and closed the office door. Virginia called out from her executive bathroom, telling him to join her. This was odd. Yet, somehow, the tone of her voice made the whole exchange feel strangely de rigeur. James entered and closed the door behind him to find Virginia leaning over the sink.

"I'm not sure what... er... I'm a married man, Virginia." Fall Water's Head of Marketing turned to reveal that she had just racked up three lines of cocaine on the countertop.

"This isn't a seduction, you clueless dolt."

James looked at the marching powder, then at Virginia. The relief that this wasn't a come-on significantly diluted the shock of finding a senior manager doing hard drugs in the workplace.

"You've fired people before, Jim. What's the problem here? If you don't, you'll end up in the out tray as well."

"Steve's my best friend. He got me this job."

"A job you can't afford to lose. You're a soon-to-be father, for God's sake. Just do yourself a favour and swallow the Kool-Aid."

"Please, Virginia. I've never asked you for anything. Can't you just do it?"

"Oh, I'd be happy to. But Donovan needs you on this as a test of loyalty. Get rid of him and your allegiance will never be questioned again."

Virginia casually retrieved a small metal tube from her handbag and, in one swift motion, three lines turned into two. It was then that she presented James with the snorting tube. James stared at it with hard-to-conceal disbelief.

"Don't look at me like that. Steve knows it's coming," Virginia said, "and he knows it's going to be you. This will snap you into shape."

James had indulged in drugs recreationally over the years. A toke here, a line there. Nothing major and nothing habitual. He hadn't touched alcohol in months, however, let alone drugs, let alone in work, with Donovan's second-in-command, in her own private bathroom, with a pregnant wife at home. Yet, despite all this, Virginia was conducting herself with a nonchalance befitting of preparing a ham and cheese sandwich. It was incredible how quickly the situation shifted from perverse to ordinary.

"I'm not sure I should, Virginia. If Donovan finds out..."

"Who do you think supplies me with the stuff? Come on, Jim. It's just breathing. One quick inhale and you'll do what needs to be done without a second thought." With a reassuring nod from Virginia, James took the tube, leant over, and fell off the wagon with a crash that would break a seismograph. The sensation was instant; the effect undeniable. Oh, boy. This was good stuff. He now realised that the crap he'd snorted over the years from friends at parties or in piss-stained, dive bar cubicles had been cut with who knows what. This was grade A, organic, unsullied, unadulterated, uncut, topshelf, life-affirming, soul-cleansing, 'excuse me while I conquer the world' shit.

"Holy fucking Christ."

"I know, right?" Virginia slapped James on the shoulder. "What do you say? Feel up to it now?" James took a moment to feel the lower back pain that had been plaguing him for the last two years. It wasn't there. He searched for the gnawing anxiety he had been feeling since he found out Sarah was pregnant. Nowhere to be found. The fear he had felt mere seconds ago over the prospect at cutting loose his best friend had upped and disappeared. He considered how this moment was revelatory, then realised he hadn't even known the word 'revelatory' three seconds ago, let alone in which context to use it. Synapses were firing and new ones forming. His vision cleared, his thoughts became unburdened, a warmth pulsated through him, and he wanted more. Just a tiny bit.

James stared at the third remaining line, then at Virginia.

"It's got your name on it."

After a sharp inhale and another lightning bolt to the core, James simply nodded and headed for the door.

"Jim." James turned to face Virginia and she slipped a small bag of white powder into his trouser pocket. "For after it's done. Treat yourself. You know where to come if you ever want more."

James strutted back towards the elevator feeling like a new man, oblivious that a seduction had just taken place after all. He walked with power, with purpose. He felt people looking at him differently. They weren't, of course, but by God, did it feel like they were.

Heading down to the Pit in the elevator, James no longer considered *if* he could go through with this Shakespearian act of betrayal, but rather *how* he should. Perhaps it would be best if he just blurted it out. Or should he pull an *Of Mice and Men*, take Steve out into the woods and tell him about the rabbits? He pictured Steve sitting at his desk, like Fredo perched in the little fishing boat in *The Godfather Part II*, awaiting the inevitable bullet. *I'm Michael Corleone. I'm Michael friggin' Corleone, here.*

James needn't have worried. Steve had texted him before the elevator reached the Pit. *I know what's about to happen, buddy. Don't sweat it, I've already cleared my desk and left. Meet me at Hermit's in two hours for old time's sake.* James had felt a crushing blow at the fact that Steve was actively making this easier for him. What a standup guy. This was a more courageous exit than Boromir in *Fellowship of the Rings*. Not only that, but it allowed time for the coke to wear off, at least enough for it to seem that James hadn't had a complete personality transplant. A tiny bump in the car before he entered the pub certainly helped level him out.

James found Steve at the pair's favourite table, sat down, and got the dirty deed out of the way up top.

"You're fired, Steve."

"Fuck you, Jim."

"I'm sorry."

"I know. I'm not." There had been a deep hug and a suggestion of tears, but stiff upper lips had been deployed and embarrassment narrowly averted.

Steve suggested that this might be the perfect opportunity to take a long-gestating trip to Asia, something he'd been threatening to do since college.

What followed was seven hours of straight-talking, no-nonsense conversation, the kind that happens when both parties know that the end of an era is nigh. It was utterly liberating. Steve drank, James did not. He didn't need to. He had a secret weapon in his wallet and Steve was too drunk to notice his friend's bathroom visits were more frequent than usual. As various other punters came and went, as staff finished the day shift and new employees took their place, as Josh brought fresh drinks and collected glasses, as the game played out on TV, as the world kept spinning, time stood still for James Reynolds and Steve Jenkins.

They spoke of the glory days, of what went wrong, when it went wrong, why it went wrong. Sure, Steve flitted between relief and anger, and admitted that the friendship had faltered after he presented James with John's coded message. Things had fundamentally changed; both had known it. It was nobody's fault, but they both admitted that something had come between them for the first time, and hoped they could recover from it. More drinks for Steve. Shots now. More bathroom breaks for James. *Must remember to wipe my nose.* By the time they tumbled out into the Boston night, all was forgiven, but all would never be the same again.

James arrived home, snuck inside, picked the crystalised gunk out of his nostrils with tweezers, and stood in the shower for twenty solid minutes. He hid the baggie inside a computer coding book he knew Sarah would never read and climbed into bed in the spare room so as to not wake her. As he lay staring at the ceiling praying for heavy eyelids, the lyrics to a very specific song rattled through his brain.

*Two against the world, code warriors of doom, knights of the keyboard.*

From this moment on, this code warrior would be going it alone.

JAMES SITS IN A DRINKING HOLE, precariously perched on a stool at the bar, looking at baby stroller options on his phone. There are so many to choose from. Newborn prams, toddler prams, in-lines, all-terrains, compact strollers, umbrella strollers, lightweights, classics. Best to select the classic.

More options: color, size, dimension? Does he want insurance with that? How will he be paying? Up front, or in ten easy-to-manage payments over three years? Jesus. Anyone would think he was buying a car. *I guess I am. A self-driving car for babies.* With the amount of alcohol coursing through his system, James decides that this may be a task best left for tomorrow. He swipes the infernal web page away and accidentally launches his phone off the bar in the process. It skitters and cracks on the ground, releasing a cluster of tiny glass shards.

"Whoopsie daisy." James retrieves his cell and places it face-down in front of him. He'll need to get that screen repaired. Another task for tomorrow. That list sure is piling up.

"You alright there, buddy?"

James glances up to see a barman staring at him.

"Sorry, can you repeat the question?" James mutters.

"Just checking you're alright?"

James could really do without the existential interrogation tonight. Is he alright? He doesn't even know where he is or when it is. A quick scan of his surroundings: there's a limp-looking Christmas tree in the corner that could probably do with another round of tinsel. Right, it's December. Good. But what *day* is it? There's nobody else in this place. Must be a Monday. Probably a Monday. What's the time? A glance at the clock reveals four hands and twenty-four numbers. Trying to tell the time in this state is akin to solving the Enigma code. As for where he is? He's not a genius. He can't be across everything. It's most likely he's stumbled into a bar for lost and broken souls. OK, now that's the basics taken care of. *Am I alright?* Highly unlikely.

For two months, James has been boozing like it's about to be outlawed. On top of this, he's been popping up to see Virginia, usually on a Wednesday, just for a little pick-me-up to carry him through the rest of the week.

Sarah's no fool; she got wise to his drinking a couple of weeks after Steve flew off to Thailand. The whole episode hit James hard and Sarah was smart enough to keep an eye out for the signs. She didn't have to wait too long or look too hard. Sluggishness, late nights 'at work', and general aggravated apathy reentered the Reynolds household. Sarah was clueless to the drugs, but James' reignited dalliance with alcohol was enough to cause a blazing row only two days ago. She was awoken at two am to the sound of smashing glass outside. She heaved her pregnant body out of bed and pulled back the curtain to spot James in the street, standing over a pile of broken glass. He had been sneaking out a bag of empty whiskey and beer bottles for the next day's trash when the bag had ripped, spilling the evidence all over the road. The jig was up. What followed was a screaming match out in the street. Whispered screams – think of the neighbors – but screams in essence. James was three sheets to the wind and, come morning, he forgot what was said, but he remembered *how* it was said. Sarah was incandescent and any sympathy she once had for James' plight had now evaporated. This wasn't a stumble. James had leapt off the cliff. Sarah got in the car and told him she was driving to Providence to stay with her sister.

"How long will you be gone?"

"I don't know. A few days."

The following morning, James woke up to a text message from Sarah telling him that by the time she got back, he'd better have sorted his shit out. If he didn't, it was over. She didn't have the common decency to specify *what* would be over, but James could safely assume she was referring to the marriage, their future, his life. All of it. He knew he couldn't work with this hanging over him. He called Virginia and told her he'd been struck down with a mystery bug; she told him to take a few days off. Instead of focusing on getting his house in order, James had spiralled into a two-day binge. Maybe it was a last huzzah before he got sober for good. Or perhaps he was finally surrendering fully to the devil on his shoulder. He honestly didn't know anymore. It was all just a messy casserole of self-hate, fear, and emptiness.

James looks up to the barman. "Sorry, champ. One more time for good measure?"

"Are you feeling alright, pal?" he asks for a third time.

"Not really, no. Can I have another one of..." James holds up an empty glass, "... whatever this was? And their drinks are on me." He points to two empty bar stools next to him.

"I think it's wise you slowed down a little," the barman advises.

Woah, hang on a minute. Who does this punk think he is? "Yeesh. I haven't been turned down for a drink at a bar in over a decade."

"Not turning you down," the barman reassures. "Just advising you to apply the brakes."

James considers. "How about this?" he asks, pulling himself to his feet. "I'll disappear into the little boy's room and splash some water on my face while you make me a double Jack and coke. If I come back and you still think I'm half past dead, I'll be on my merry way."

The barman holds out a friendly hand. "Deal. You got a name, stranger?"

"Call me Jim. I prefer James, but every prick and his mother insists on calling me Jim."

"Well, *James*. I'm Eddie."

"I'll be back in two shakes of a lamb's asshole, Eddie."

The second James enters the bathroom, saliva jets kick in at the back of his throat and a cold sweat breaks out on his forehead. He dashes towards a stall, knowing he has about two seconds before he — Oh dear. Not a chance. He kicks open the door and sinks to his knees as vomit so acidic it would make the Xenomorph blush is projectiled all over the closed toilet seat. James grabs a few sheets of single-ply and wipes the seat down before sitting on it, accompanied by a violent belch. Round two? Not quite. As he spits on the floor to get rid of the excess bile, his whole sorry situation comes into brief view. His stomach burns. His eyes sting. A stringy piece of drool slowly finds its way to his sweater. His heart pounds louder and faster than a hardcore techno drum beat. His wife has walked out on him.

His best friend is on the other side of the world. He has a baby on the way and doesn't know which stroller to buy. *Oh, you loathsome cunt.*

On the tiled floor beneath his feet, an earwig crawls through James' throwup. There it goes, valiantly making its way through the quagmire, slowly and steadily. James is hit by a shocking realization. He actually envies the creature. That's right. He'd rather crawl through his own ejecta than have it come out of him. Look at the critter now, facing down a lump of regurgitated chicken wing. What will it do when faced with this seemingly insurmountable obstacle? It'll clamber over it, that's what. The little shit hasn't a care in the world. Get from point A to point B and screw anything that gets in the way, even if the sky rains vomit. James forgot where A was long ago and he'll be fucked if he knows where B is. Nope, he'll just go straight to the C, thank you very much. He takes out his bag of miracle powder and prepares a line on the toilet cistern, cutting it from a debit card from his and Sarah's joint account to create a line longer than the one outside Macy's on Christmas Eve.

James finds a ten dollar bill encrusted with dried nasal blood in his back pocket, rolls it up and goes to town. This is what he needs. This will sort him out. *This is the solution.* He leaps to his feet and throws his head back, letting those magnificent drips fall. Another violent snort to make sure the medicine has all gone down, and it's like the clock has been rewound on the last three hours of drinking. James can walk again. He can talk again, probably. He'll test that out in a second on that friendly neighborhood barman. James fumbles with the bag as he returns it to his wallet, dropping the tiny remainder of powder on the floor. He doesn't even hesitate, leaning down and collecting white dots with his finger from areas of the floor yet to be flooded with his inside liquids. He vigorously rubs it on his gums. This stuff is too good to waste. James doesn't allow himself to consider the sheer repulsiveness of what he's doing. Somewhere deep within, he knows this is the sort of rock bottom that gets discussed at AA meetings, but right now, he just... doesn't... care. He spots a lump of Satan's salt on his new earwig friend. That little fella is going to have a hell of a night.

Eddie the barman puts two and two together pretty quickly when

James emerges from the bathroom with a renewed spirit, returning to the bar in a straighter line than when he left it, casually rubbing his nose and trying his best not to appear like a whacked-out lunatic. He'd win a Razzie for this performance. He isn't the first guy to do gear in this place and he won't be the last. This particular customer clearly needs a few gentle words of advice. Eddie would rather James be a wired, narcotized blabbermouth than a drooling, nonsensical blotto. When the bar is this low, it's easy to settle for the lesser of two evils.

"Ta-da!" James sits back down and slams his fist on the bar. "Good as new! Amazing what a bit of cold water can do, am I right? So what do you say you hand me that Jack and coke, Freddie?"

"Eddie," the barman says with a smile. He presents James with a Coca-Cola on ice. There's no alcohol in it, but James is too far gone to notice that minor detail. Better to keep him here and sober him up a touch before letting him roam the streets.

"Eddie. My mistake." James grabs the drink and takes a sip. "Oh, yeah. That'll do it."

"You're not driving, are you?" Eddie asks.

"No, sir. I wouldn't be so bold. I'll get a cab." James' initial coke-fuelled buzz is short-lived – and it's getting increasingly short-lived the more he takes – when Mud's *Lonely This Christmas* starts playing from an unseen Machiavellian jukebox.

"Oh, come on! Really?!" James wails. He is hit with an insatiable need to see a glimpse of Sarah's beautiful face. He scrabbles for his phone and flips it over. His lock screen wallpaper is a selfie of the couple in the parking lot of the Seven Pines clinic the day they found out Sarah was pregnant. Both look impossibly happy. But, as of ten minutes ago, the image is distorted by a spider web of cracks. A particularly pronounced fracture has split the couple in two, straight down the middle. "You've got to be kidding. You couldn't write this shit."

James places the phone back, face down, and buries his head in his hands. It's all gone so horrifically wrong. Since the day he and Sarah became an item, he's had anxiety dreams that she'd up and leave. He'd wake up in a cold sweat with an indescribable relief at finding her sleeping next to him. But this is reality. It's come true. She's gone. He internally prays to a God he doesn't believe in to let him wake up. It would be around about now that James would head off to powder his nose again, but he hasn't got any gear left. He considers calling Virginia, but he's supposed to be sick, remember?

"Wanna talk about it?" Eddie asks. He places a coffee down in front of him. James doesn't remember asking for that, but it does look good. "On the house."

James takes a sip and allows himself to savour the drink's warmth and the kindness of this stranger.

"Lady troubles?" Eddie asks.

"Yep," James replies. "Work troubles. Friend troubles. Troubles all the way down." Eddie wipes a part of the bar that doesn't need wiping and polishes a glass that doesn't need polishing. Why not lean into the stock barman trope so the stock fuck-up trope sitting in front of him actually opens up? It seems to work.

"It started with my pal, Steve," James begins, before getting Eddie up to speed on his hopeless situation. He doesn't hold back. It's the first time he's discussed any of this at length with anybody. By the time he's done, he's got three empty coffee mugs in front of him.

"Which brings us to tonight. I did drugs in your establishment, Reggie. I'm sorry."

"Eddie. And I won't tell anyone if you don't."

"Makes me wonder if it's just life that changed, or everyone in it. Maybe I'm the one who's changed."

Eddie pours himself a brandy. "Life changed, James. I can tell you that from experience." He gestures to the bar. "I've been standing behind here for six years, watching people come and go." He takes a sip and squints his eyes, looking into the middle distance. "I can tell you one thing for sure. People don't really change too much. There'll be peaks and troughs, and there's exceptions to every rule, but things generally come back around. A friendship like the one you just described doesn't go away that easily."

James isn't so sure. "I mean, Steve and I left on good terms," he says, "but I haven't heard from him since that night."

"C'mon, man. He's in Thailand, living it up, probably balls deep in mango sticky rice." James laughs out loud. It's the first time he's laughed in what feels like weeks. "He probably just needs some time," Eddie continues. "You two have got an unbreakable bond. I can tell."

James knows Eddie is probably right, but he's been severely punishing himself ever since that fateful day in November, slipping into a deep depressive spiral. The fact that this major life blip may have stemmed from an imagined grudge creates a tight knot in his stomach.

"I mean, he did want out," he concedes. "He'd been talking about it for years."

"There you go, then," Eddie says. "You probably did him a favor. I take it that leaving isn't an option for you?"

James shrugs and thinks back to what unfolded earlier this summer. Ghost, John, and his wild online quest now feel like the remnants of a faded dream. He can't be sure any of it even happened.

"Yep," James answers. "Not an option. I promised someone I'd stick around to see something through. It's complicated, but I've got a lot of people relying on me. Apparently."

"Life's complicated, James. You know what makes it even more complicated?" Eddie taps his glass of brandy.

James smiles. "Don't forget this," he says, tapping his nose.

"I get it. It's a quick escape," Eddie says. "Releases you from your woes for a few hours, but creates a whole bucket of new ones come sunrise. Your wife. What was her name?"

"Sarah," James whispers sadly.

"Sarah. Did you ever tell her you were struggling?"

"I didn't need to," James answers with an air of dismissal. "She knows me too well."

"Regardless. It doesn't mean you can't ask for help, man."

James is getting a tad aggravated by this guy's well-intentioned sermon. Possibly because he's spitting truth and it's touching a nerve. He never once fully opened up to Sarah about what went down with Steve. He never dreamed of telling her that Virginia forced drugs on him at work. That would mean admitting weakness. The episode in her private bathroom had made him feel remarkably uncomfortable, but he kept it quiet. He buried it, then went back for more. Versa was playing him like a fiddle and he hadn't known where to turn, so he'd simply let it happen. James is sickened by his own cowardice. One conversation with Sarah and he could have calmly backed away from the abyss, rather than allowed himself to be pulled into it.

"Talk to her. Call her tomorrow. Lay all of your cards on the table. Be vulnerable, be scared, tell her you'll get help."

"And Steve?" James asks.

"Same applies. Give it a couple of weeks and send him a message. He'll probably be waiting for it. You just gotta pick up the ball and keep rolling."

James scoffs at the weak ball analogy. Shame. His new best friend had been doing so well. Eddie is also completely ignorant as to what is currently going down at Fall Water. They've got him by the short and curlies with this little cocaine scenario. Virginia has what James needs and, if he doesn't take it, they've got dirt on him.

"There's a lot of people that would be perfectly happy with this ball staying lost in the weeds," James says. He immediately regrets running with the ball analogy.

"Those people don't matter," Eddie says firmly. "Feels like they do, but they don't. They'd probably respect the hell out of you if you got your shit together." James considers this. Maybe this entire thing has been some convoluted corporate test of his mettle. It's possible that Virginia is bored and has picked James as her latest plaything, or it was as simple as giving him the boost he needed to fire Steve. Does Versa want him to blindly comply, or fight back? Whatever it is they want, he knows he's trapped. Trapped by work, by Virginia, by his addiction.

"This job," James says. "I can't just leave."

"Then just hover around and do what you need to," Eddie advises. "Nothing more. Sounds like you bought yourself some time by getting rid of Steve. You're a smart guy. You'll figure this out. Just take the first step. What do you say? I book you a cab, you get yourself home, go to bed, and tomorrow you do what needs to be done?"

James looks up at Eddie and allows this guidance to penetrate through the alcohol and cocaine haze. *Do what needs to be done.* The words carry with them a weight beyond fixing things with Sarah. They are spoken with a gravitas that goes far beyond Eddie's role as an affable barman. Eddie stands in front of a flickering neon *Happy Hour* bar sign, the light of which provides a halo effect behind his head. Who is this guy? A guardian angel? A fairy godmother? A guiding spirit sent from another dimension just when James needs it most? The word *Hour* flicks off and *Happy* remains illuminated. James stares at it long and hard. He scans the pub and is suddenly hit by a long-dormant, repressed memory.

His mind sends him back to that fateful night in London in 2007 when he peered into a black hole, only to emerge stronger on the other side. It's an illusive memory, but he recalls being in another bar, taking advice from a different stranger. James tries to focus on the memory, but it remains nebulous and slips away whenever he gets close. Either way, it's a nice reminder that the funk he was wallowing in then was temporary, and he recovered, like he had many times before and has done since. Something deep in James' soul stirs. He isn't sure what it is. It could be the smallest sense of hope, or inner strength, or the knowledge that it's going to take more than the purchase of a baby stroller to make things right. Whatever it is, it forces him to his feet.

"No need for a cab," James says firmly. "I need to walk this off."

"Well, it's certainly warm enough for it," Eddie says. "Things really are heating up out there." Again, James notes how Eddie's words seem to carry a double meaning. Things certainly feel like they have transcended beyond a pep talk between a drunk and barman.

Two minutes later, Eddie watches from the door as James strolls out into the warmer-than-it-really-should-be December night with a renewed purpose. Eddie locks the door, returns to the bar and makes a quick call.

"Selena? It's done. I think I got through to him. Time will tell."

A female voice on the other end responds. "Let's hope so. He's gonna need all the grit he can muster. Turn on the news." Eddie grabs the remote and turns the volume up on the TV to catch the tail end of a report detailing a new virus that has originated in Wuhan, China.

"Fuck," Eddie says.

"Fuck, indeed," Selena responds. "Here we go."

---

SARAH PULLS her car into the driveway around midnight, scared to death of what she might discover when she enters the house. She's only been gone for two nights, but her brother-in-law has been driving her to distraction, threatening to drive up to Boston and crack James' skull. This is not what she needed. The whole point of going to stay with her sister was to get her head straight. This hadn't been possible with a well-meaning yet red-blooded alpha male strutting around the house. She spontaneously decided to head back to Boston and speak to James.

Sarah kills the engine and sits idle for a minute. She notes the bathroom light is on upstairs. James is home.

She silently slips inside, clicking the door shut behind her. Tiptoeing through to the kitchen to get a glass of water, she sees a number of empty whiskey bottles stacked upside down in the sink. James has clearly poured away his stash. This is a solid start.

James' laptop is open on the kitchen counter. Sarah isn't intending to pry, but Amazon is open on his browser with a purchase confirmation for a baby stroller. This has more of an impact than knowing he's poured away the booze. These are baby steps, and that will do for now. An email notification pings. Unable to resist, Sarah clicks on the link, opening an email from Narcotics Anonymous, thanking James for reaching out and inviting him to a meeting next Wednesday. Sarah's heart skips a beat. Immediately, everything clicks into place. She chastises herself for having refused to see how bad things had truly got and is hit with a primal need to hug her husband.

Sarah heaves her pregnant body up the stairs and approaches the bathroom. A coding book sits outside on the landing floor, opened on a random page. Sarah pushes the door, reaching for her phone in case there's a need for an ambulance.

James sits on the side of the bathtub, face blank, emptying a massive bag of powder down the toilet.

"Jim," Sarah whispers. He turns and faces her. Tears form and he immediately crumbles. Sarah approaches, crouches down, and they sink into each other's arms. Both are too exhausted to talk. It doesn't matter. Nothing needs to be said. Not tonight.

---

"Tonight's the night, brother. Are you ready to do your part?"

Damien Craze sits next to Donovan around a circular marble table in the boardroom of a rural upstate New York mansion. The lighting is low and there are various maps and scenarios projected on the wall. It's likely the architect was a fan of *Dr. Strangelove*. How did they even get this gigantic table in here? The boardroom and mansion must have been built around it. The room is populated by a group of extremely tired, impossibly influential people. For once, the brothers Craze are not the most powerful people sitting at the table. This group – composed of senators, Versa execs, Fortress suits, heads of Big Pharma and media empires, and senior public servants – have a collective gravity so commanding that they could manipulate the ocean's tides. Donovan knows his place. This isn't the time for showboating.

"Thanks, Damien." He addresses the room with a reverential nod. "Everyone. We're good to go. The old man's job is almost complete and the company has been cleansed of its most undesirable elements."

"Key figures in the company hierarchy?" a voice from the darkness asks.

"Well under our control. We've been making sure of that since day one. They won't flinch. We have a handful of question marks, but I've got serious leverage on them if they step out of line. Failing that, there's always a last resort if they threaten to compromise. None of them are irreplaceable."

Damien nods in satisfaction. He already knew all of this, of course, but this was very much for the benefit of the room.

"Ladies and gentlemen," he booms. "I don't have to remind you of the resources that have been pumped into this. Everyone at this table is here for a reason. Some of you may be nervous. Let me reassure you that we have in place all necessary contingencies to nudge the general population in our preferred direction. Right. Key summaries." Damien looks at a stern brunette at the far side of the table. "Joanna. You're up." She stands and gets a graph up on screen with a clicker.

"The spread of the virus has reached critical mass worldwide and can no longer be contained. We are controlling the media narrative by feeding asymmetrical information to different territories to seed insecurity amongst non-collaborators." She looks to her left. "Jerry." Jerryl grabs the clicker and brings up a spreadsheet that only he cares about or understands.

"Medically, vaccine talks, solutions, and production will be hampered until we have the population under quarantine under stay-at-home government directives. Stoking the fires of panic will ensure compliance of both officials and the public. We have a couple of bobblehead yes-men in situ across core territories. All eyes will be on these authority figures while the crisis deepens. Brian?"

Jerry passes his clicker – a conch for the modern age – to a man on his left.

"I haven't got any slides," Brian begins, really stirring things up. "Seriously, guys? Slides? This isn't a middle-school project. Fucking Christ." His protestations are met with a stony silence. Brian's really rocking the boat here. He was told to bring slides, and he hasn't. "From our side, we've drafted appropriate guidance and policies for governments and corporations to drive working-from-home initiatives. HR conditioning is in place. This trickles down to education. Kids will be homeschooled. Curriculums have been approved across all western markets. Without this transition to home-based operations, we have nothing. This is of paramount importance. High-level anxiety and frustration are pre-reqs and we're working with colleagues from core agencies to instill this. We get this, we get compliance."

Congressman Mitch McCaley raises a hand and coughs.

"Yes, Mac?"

"To add to that, economically, the pill will be sweetened on these shores with stimulus checks to incentivize heightened entertainment product consumption. This will lead to an increased adoption of personalized messaging from Fall Water and the System."

Damien nods and looks at a mousy woman. "Doctor?"

"I, er... I've got slides," the woman says apologetically.

"For the love of God," Brian mutters, sliding the clicker over. The doctor brings up her slide. It portrays a basic timeline and crudely drawn cartoon figures with plugs coming out of their heads, connected to power sources.

"Forgive me. I only found out there would be slides three hours ago. My assistant pulled these together." The doctor gets second thoughts and turns off the slide. "Let's press on without them." Brian chuckles from the shadows. "The only feasible solution, to be presented following incubation and population re-education, will be RNA-based biological vaccines. Through these, we'll start rebuilding and marking hosts' genetic codes and neuro portraits to prepare them for digital migration to the System. Forecasts predict around seven per cent of the population will not be perceptive to the drug, but these concerns are marginal. Call it collateral damage."

"Final forecast for the adoption period, Dr Dlamini?"

"Four to five years, depending on levels of vaccination. Safe to assume five to minimize collaterals."

"It won't be less than five," Donovan offers. "The technology still has a long way to go. As for the end goal, things will get a hell of a lot worse before they get better."

The striking of a match and a plume of cigar smoke emerges from the shadows from the corner of the room. All eyes drift in that direction.

"The history of the world is forged by conflict, Mr Craze." The voice is deep and self-assured. "Misery, plagues, hunger. It's no accident that all of those things are our bread and butter. We sit on the precipice of a new world order. Soon, the scales will be reset. Eternal bliss will be offered to the masses. A chance at unhindered freedom and opportunity. A Promised Land over seventy years in the making. So begins the new cycle. All we have to do is see it over the line and make sure a willing world accepts our gift with gratitude. To the new cycle!"

The room repeats this in unison as the cloud of cigar smoke moves towards the door, calling an end to the meeting. "The new cycle!"

"And next time," the voice utters, "ditch the damn slides."

Five minutes later, the room has been cleared, save for the Craze brothers. Damien scans through a Fall Water staff roster on a tablet and pauses when he sees one name.

"This James Reynolds. Any problems?"

Donovan laughs dismissively. "Don't worry about Reynolds. He's under the thumb. We had some reservations, but we've got him on the coke and his wife's about to shit out a kid. His life is spiraling out of control. We can provide the nose candy and, if he ditches that, we'll increase his salary. Rehab doesn't come cheap. We've separated him off from his core team and nudged out his key ally, Steve Reynolds. Virginia's filled the void."

"You're confident he can finish his work and maintain his function?" Damien asks.

"Absolutely. The guy's a master," Donovan responds. "He doesn't realize how integral he actually is. That works in our favor."

"OK. If you're sure." Damien locks the tablet and starts packing up. "That just leaves us with one last thing to tick off tonight's agenda."

Donovan nods. "I'll make the call."

---

IN A LUXURY SUITE in the NYC InterContinental, Virginia sits naked on the side of the bed, staring out at the New York skyline. The iconic One Worldwide Plaza stands tall and proud. A raft of thoughts cascade through Virginia's mind. She wonders how many other women are sitting naked in hotel rooms, staring at skylines, contemplating their futures. She reaches for a pack of cigarettes and lights up. One advantage of the company renting out this floor on a permanent basis is the removal of all smoke alarms. Versa money really does go a long way. A man's hand reaches around and cups Virginia's waist.

"You OK, V?" Tom Simmons' voice is tender and full of concern. He knows what's going down tonight and he knows what it means when Virginia sits motionless with a cigarette.

"I can't shake this feeling, Tom." Her voice is fragile. Tom also sits up and shuffles behind her, gently wrapping his legs around her waist. She allows herself to sink back into his arms and passes him the cigarette. He takes a drag and hands it back. This is a comfortable routine forged through years of illicit meet-ups.

"What feeling?" Tom asks.

"Uncertainty. I've never felt uncertain about anything. Even when Donovan got me in his grasp, way back when, I knew things would work out." Virginia caresses Tom's chin. "Are we going to be alright?"

"If their plan fails, we'll find a way to deal with it together," Tom says, his self-assurance dampening Virginia's anxiety. "And if they succeed, we've already secured a place inside."

"Don't you think it's ironic?" Virginia asks.

"What's that?"

"I have no concerns about migrating to an artificial reality. We've essentially been living in one for over twenty years." Tom chuckles and kisses Virginia's neck. She turns her head to kiss him, but the moment passes as he turns serious.

"The next five years will be a challenge," he says. "We won't be able to see each other in person. Nobody will."

Virginia scoffs at the tendency of men – even the best of them – to spoil the most divine moments by blurting out something stupid. They must be hardwired that way. Virginia knows they're about to be torn apart. If not in the next few weeks, perhaps a little later. She'd rather treat this like their last night together. They've had many last nights, but always found themselves back in each other's orbits. But this one feels different.

She knows she has to return fully to her marital unit with a man she no longer has any feeling for. What was once a fully fledged loathing has muted to an apathetic respect. Both Virginia and Tom are cognisant about the upcoming pandemic and the impending weeks or months working from home. Both know Fall Water will not only survive, but thrive. Both have taken a bite of the forbidden fruit and will fully comply with Versa's plan to migrate the population to the virtual world. They have been allocated positions of aristocracy with seats at the Round Table. Future rulers of digital domains. They chose their sides long ago and Donovan hasn't let them down yet. Their drive for success, respect, comfort and power attracted them to each other in the first place. Yes, both are cutthroat, but when it comes to each other, they'd both kill for a chance to stay together in the New World.

Virginia places a finger on Tom's lips and turns around to straddle him. With half a mind on what's about to unfold in Boston, he welcomes the distraction. For now, they have tonight. Better make the most of it.

---

THE DOOR to John Burrow's lab slowly, silently opens. The big man sits at his workstation, casually studying lines of code on multiple monitors. Last night, *Cyberside* finally merged with the System. He has nothing left to do but ensure there are no initial hiccups. His *World's Greatest Dad* mug is notably empty. He's not going to need coffee where he's going. He just wishes the motherfuckers would hurry up and get it over with.

The shadowy figure, dressed head to toe in black, enters the room and locks the door behind him. Security systems and cameras have already been deactivated. Nobody will bear witness.

John senses somebody in the room and smiles. *About time.* He knew that the moment Alice's digital double became the System's governing module, Versa would get to work covering its tracks. He takes comfort that his daughter is, in a sense, still alive. Her consciousness exists and her faculties are strong. As he sits there waiting, John feels a sense of familiarity. Maybe he's been a part of this situation or one of its endless variants before. Maybe he's simply turned this night over in his head a thousand times. Whatever the reason, he doesn't care anymore. He's ready.

John spies the shadow approaching in the window's reflection. Funny. He expected to see a gun pointing at his head. The assailant instead pulls a knife, one from John's very own kitchen. Part of him is happy it's about to see some action; he hasn't cooked in years and only ever uses the thing to puncture the cellophane lids of microwavable meals. He hadn't expected they'd opt for a blade. Shit. This might hurt after all. John turns to face his killer. Cold blue eyes stare back through a balaclava. A Versa pin is affixed to his jacket.

"Versa always did have a flair for the dramatic," John deadpans. He smiles. "Until next time, Alice."

The shadow impassively approaches and spins John back around in his chair. Gloved hands gently pull his head back as the knife punctures his skin, entering his throat on the left and slicing open the jugular. The blade glides with ease across John's Adam's apple as the ghastly wound opens, spewing blood. As violent convulsions subside, the intruder presses an earpiece.

"Target down. I'll raid the safe, make it look like a robbery. Boston PD is in our pocket. All in hand." The man strolls out of the room and the door closes as silently as it opened.

White curtains chosen by Sam thirty years ago are now stained a deep crimson. John Burrow sits slumped in his chair. Lines of reflected code, remnants of his last and greatest achievement, trickle down his face. The world has lost a giant, but he may have just provided a solitary slither of hope for a sorry-looking tomorrow.

---

JAMES WAKES up next to his pregnant wife, consumed by a thudding anxiety. He fixes the cover over Sarah's shoulders, pulls himself out of bed and heads downstairs, ready to begin yet another journey of sobriety. First... coffee.

In the kitchen, James finds his laptop open on the counter. A half-memory of sending an email to NA percolates. Hungry to see if they've responded, he opens his emails. A few unreads sit at the top of his inbox. One immediately leaps out.

*RE: Ghost.*

With trembling hands fuelled by a mixture of nerves and withdrawal, James opens the email. A video file is attached with a message. *Delete once watched.*

James runs the video to witness the last three minutes of John Burrow's life, captured by a laptop's webcam. Once it's over, heart in mouth, he immediately deletes the evidence. A few minutes of grief shifts into steely resolve as events, past and future, slip into clear focus. Things just kicked up a gear. Some time ago, he made John a promise. It's time to deliver.

**END OF PART 3**

# PART IV
## THE RECKONING

## 10

# ALTERATIONS

A chewed-nailed index finger pokes curiously at a rhythmically rising and falling bare chest. A deep snore accompanies every expansion of the bloated gut; an elongated exhale partners every contraction.

"Dad."

Two impatient fingers now, prodding with glee.

"DAD!"

James is awoken by a stinging stomach and a reverberating slap as an open palm crashes down on his belly. His eyelids, heavier than Megadeth at its peak, struggle to remain open. His anger at the rude wake-up call dissipates when he lifts his head to find a sweet, gap-toothed little boy staring at him. With one look at his phone, the anger rushes back. 7:33 am, SATURDAY, MAY 11, 2024. Despite being too tired to remember his own name, James swiftly calculates that he's only managed to cash in three hours of shut-eye.

"Where's your mother, Timothy?"

"Took Ninja for a walk," the boy responds. "She said someone had to before it gets too hot, and the chances of you doing it this morning were slim to one."

"Slim to none," James corrects. Timothy doesn't seem to care; he's already on to the next thing. That next thing is clambering up onto the bed and jumping up and down with more energy than Robin Williams in the eighties.

"She tried to wake you up," Timothy says, "But you just kept snoring. She said you're not present these days. Like a dad from a nineties family movie."

"Ouch. Brutal," James responds, hauling himself onto his elbows. "She always did know how to go for the jugular."

"What's a... julugar?" Timothy innocently asks. A flash of a video seen years ago flashes through James' mind. John Burrow, neck sliced open, slumped in his chair.

"Never you mind," James responds.

Two minutes later, Timothy is in the kitchen watching his dad pull a Red Bull out of the fridge and down half of its contents with one gulp.

"Mom says that stuff will turn your guts to crap."

"Don't say 'crap'," James responds. "Does she also know that some adults need to drink a magical elixir to wake up in the morning? We can't all be Captain America." James strolls towards the bathroom. Timothy follows.

"Why are you always so tired, Daddy?" Ironically, if James wasn't so exhausted, this question would hit a lot harder.

"Because Daddy works for a big company that made a popular video game that evolved into a cultural phenomenon with more than two billion users worldwide, son." James enters the bathroom, turns on the tap and splashes cold water on his wretched face. Reluctant gears and relays in his head groan to life. "Not only that," he continues, "but a potent combination of COVID-19 and an overheating planet means those two billion people spend the majority of their lives inside the game now. And not only *that*, but the game isn't even a game anymore. Oh, no. That would be far too simple. It's a way of life. A cross-platform, cross-media service where actors – sorry, users – go to play, communicate, meet and even date. Someone," James says, pointing at himself, "has to make sure the whole thing doesn't implode on itself and society as we know it turns to ruin."

Timothy stares up blankly at his father. "Are we still going to the aquarium today?"

James stares in the mirror at his haggard reflection. His gut, still adorning Timothy's handprint, sags over his boxers. He tries to breathe it in, but not even that does the trick anymore. He lets out a defeated sigh.

"Tim..."

"No, dad! You always call me Tim when you're about to let me down." James dies inside. He truly is a nineties dad. "You promised!"

"I know, kiddo, but I didn't finish last night. I need to go into the —" Before James can finish, Timothy bolts away, silent tears streaming down his face. His bare feet patter down the wooden floor of the hallway. The slamming of a door adds a painful full stop to the conversation.

A short time later, Timothy leans against his bedroom door, listening to his parents arguing in the kitchen.

"We made plans, James! You can't keep doing this!"

"I've got no choice, Sarah! I'm the Chief Software Engineer! I have a responsibility to—"

"Don't! Don't even think about saying it! You said you'd finish it up last night!"

"I thought I would, but something came up."

"Yeah? Well, now we've come up. Your wife and son have come up and we require urgent attention."

"I wish I had a choice, Sarah. They're already outside."

"You do have a choice! You just refuse to see it! You're a fucking nineties dad, Jim! You promised me when I was pregnant you wouldn't be a nineties dad!"

"Yeah?! Well at least I don't say 'crap' in front of our son!"

Another door slams with a sound that has become synonymous to the Reynolds household. Timothy, knowing what's coming, scurries over to his Lego and pretends to play with it so as to not upset his mother. A gentle knock and Sarah enters.

"Hey, sweetie. What do you say you and me go to the aquarium?"

Outside, tired and defeated, James dons his protective sunglasses and drags himself towards the awaiting Versa luxury sedan.

JAMES SITS in the back of the car, devastated to be schlepping to work on a Saturday, but relieved to be out of the pressure cooker he now calls home. He loves his son, but he's not sure he fully understands him. As for Sarah, she sometimes doesn't recognize her own husband anymore. James doesn't even recognize himself. According to Sarah, he is 'cruising through life with an as yet unforeseen level of all-consuming apathy.' It's an image he has built for himself to gear up for his biggest undertaking yet. And despite the fact that his wife's opinion of him fluctuates between tolerance and hatred, the nineties dad ruse seems to be working.

James looks out the window, trying to recognize the district in which he once lived. He's barely able to. Once protected green spaces, now abandoned due to the heat, have been sold to property developers for a quick cash-in. Local boutique eateries sit empty, victims to COVID, like so much else. James' mind reels. *COVID, you fucker*. The pandemic changed everything, and James wouldn't be surprised if Versa wasn't somehow involved. It was Versa that miraculously came to the rescue with a vaccine, after all, but only after everyone had been forced inside and into *Cyberside* for a year. The average joe now spends their time locked into *Cyberside*, living a life far more exciting than anything imaginable out in mundane old reality. The simple act of going for a walk in the afternoon sun is now possible once again thanks to the good folks over at Fall Water. Post-lockdowns, the world did not return to its virgin state. Fear and paranoia ran rampant. Conflicts exploded in far-flung regions, recessions hit, followed by economic semi-collapse. The United States withdrew from the world stage as much as was feasibly possible, putting the interests of its citizens first. James hates to admit it, but the strategy of splendid isolation may be the correct one, at least in the short term. The threat of nuclear warfare is now as likely as during the height of the Cold War. Best to play the blissfully ignorant card and wait for the whole thing to blow over.

As for The Heat, as it has now become commonly known, certain climate zones are better protected than others. Colorado, Vermont, Minnesota, Wyoming and the like have become playgrounds for the super rich, with places heavily affected now residing under giant protective domes. Many locales have witnessed a max exodus. Those who couldn't afford to relocate, or who believed The Heat to be the latest in a long line of conspiracies, simply perished. The remarkable fact is that the earth's population is now decreasing for the first time since the Black Death. Automation solutions have solved the problem of distribution and deliveries; drones and self-driving vehicles populate the roads. Generous stimulus checks for those in the workforce replaced by robots keep civil unrest and revolution at bay. Short-term solutions are now the order of the day.

In James' mind, these quick fixes speak to the fact that those in power have stopped preparing for a brighter tomorrow, for *any* tomorrow. He has his suspicions, alright. Mass migration to *Cyberside* is on the horizon. Versa now doesn't even deny it. James' disconnect from the world and all he holds dear may go far beyond his mental health. For years, he's felt like he's been watching his own life from the sidelines. Strange occurrences, recurring patterns, guardian angels sent to guide him back onto the straight and narrow. Lost nights where he seemed to burst through the coded fabric of life, only to be left with fragmented memories. Life as he knows it feels like a sloppy copy and paste. Of course, the world knows Versa is gearing up to move the population into a simulation, but a terrifying thought keeps winding its way back into James' head. *What if we're already in one?*

Ever since John's demise, James has come to accept the true power that Versa wields. The only way for him to deliver on his promise to Burrow is to stay lucid and maintain Fall Water's trust. Play the role of loyal, predictable, avuncular, non-threatening Jim. His time is coming, he's sure. He just has to wait it out. This is why he has just emerged from yet another blazing row on yet another Saturday. He'd have walked away from Fall Water long ago if he truly had a choice. But his cards are marked, and he must do what needs to be done.

Playing dumb presented its own benefits, of course. A year into remote working, colleagues outside of James' immediate team largely left him alone. Donovan no longer showed up at his workstation unannounced. Virginia accepted James' decision to get clean one Christmas many years ago with good grace, going so far as to pay for his rehab. There was, naturally, one condition. If he ever thought about abandoning Fall Water, she had receipts of his indiscretions that would get him struck off of any hiring manager's list. He was here for the long haul. Thankfully, unbeknownst to them, that served James' needs perfectly.

Almost immediately into the first lockdown, directives from above seemed to trickle off; proof that Versa was gearing up for something far more important. Fall Water now regards James as an awkward tech goofball who eats too much junk food for a man of his age and has no idea of what's actually going on around him. There is a usefulness in this cloak of invisibility. When people are looking the other way, it sure is easier to conduct activities that may be deemed as 'threatening.' Activities such as assembling a Telegram chat named *Saturday Warhammer Meetings* and inviting former Fall Water employees, each with a burning grudge, to exchange information. Activities such as bringing back Gaming Fridays for the Dev crew as a team motivation exercise. This sort of behavior has also cemented James' reputation in Fall Water as an over-zealous, detail-obsessed HOD who absolutely, positively must personally review and approve every new module and update. A perfect cover for James to disappear for two hours and communicate with an old ally.

Still, surviving at Fall Water has been far from easy. It has taken every inch of grit and self-control to not succumb to numerous full-blown nervous breakdowns. The environment is one in which Versa not only tolerates, but actively encourages, aggression, bullying, and outright intimidation. Versa itself recently announced yet another round of non-organic growth, acquiring a dozen or so other firms in the pharma, tech, AI, finance, manufacturing, EdTech and military spaces. It isn't even shy about getting its name out there anymore. Where once it operated from the shadows, Versa is now out and proud, with a valuation of over twelve trillion dollars. Its messaging is simple and focused: The future is digital. The mind is immortal. Transcendence is key. Liberate yourselves from the shackles of skin and bone into pure freedom of the intellect. No more disease, no more compulsion, no more neuro mediator dependency, no more mental health issues. Join *Cyberside* in full! A utopia, decades in the making, aligned with your own personal wants, needs, and desires, awaits! Sign up now! Just sign here, here, here, here, here, here, and here... Those who choose to stay on the outside and work with Fall Water Lake in maintaining the future of civilization are the true heroes and will be rewarded handsomely. The technology to facilitate full migration is a moment away, and there's absolutely nothing anybody can do about it.

Well, not *nothing*. James has been surviving on four hours' sleep a night for months, working quietly and meticulously to secure a slither of opportunity for himself and his family on the inside when the time comes. There's no way he's going to bend over and become yet another mindless corporate husk with limited rights or privileges. With the help of that old friend, he'll be ready when the time comes.

---

ANOTHER LONG NIGHT at the office, another dinner with the family missed. James waves to the security guard making her rounds of the nearly empty building. She simply sees an overworked nerd who should get home to his wife and kid, and offers a friendly nod. The red hue of the sky casts an ethereal glow over his workstation. It would be beautiful if not for the fact that the light outside would turn his eyes to yoghurt were it not for the protective film over the windows.

The dreamlike vista, along with the soothing sound of whirs and clicks from sleeping workstations, send James into yet another existential wobble. He feels the abstract point of connection between the real and the possible, akin to a fever dream. It's something he's experienced many times before, with increasing regularity. An overwhelming sense of déjà vu.

James finishes writing the code that will integrate new functionality into the *Cyberside* domain indexation system. He had planned to leave work half an hour early to beat the traffic home, but one last-minute request led to another, then another. What were once lines of coke are now lines of code. *Another one won't hurt.* And here he remains. His office door opens behind him.

"Reynolds!"

Shit. James doesn't need to turn around to know Donovan is standing behind him. He does so anyway.

"First one in, last one out. As it should be," Craze booms.

"Well, not quite," James says. "You're still here."

Donovan's eyes narrow. "Don't be sassy, Jim. It doesn't suit you."

James chuckles nervously – he's got this down to a fine art – and regards Fall Water's CEO. Not only has he stopped aging, but the man's getting younger. It's absurd.

"But seeing as you ask, I've just met with the Asian partners."

"Oh yeah? They fly over?"

"Don't be a fucking prick, Jim. We met in *Cyberside*. They saw a perfect recreation of their boardroom, I saw a perfect recreation of ours. We all felt we had the home advantage. It's a great innovation."

"I know," James says. "I built it."

Donovan absentmindedly picks up James' nameplate: *CHIEF SOFTWARE ENGINEER*. "Oh, yeah. I guess you did."

"So how did it go, sir?" James asks.

Donovan spreads his arms wide. "A goddamn corporate bloodbath, you little hard-on. We're centralizing everything Stateside. Shutting them down. No need for this amount of red tape anymore. Not with what's coming." James doesn't even absorb this. All he notices is the stench of alcohol on his boss's breath.

Donovan hands James' nameplate back to him and he clumsily places it back on his desk. Craze walks to the window and stares out at the city's skyline. The reddish tinge really compliments his bloodshot eyes.

"When our boys in NC crack transference, humanity will finally have a chance. You know that, don't you?"

"Sure. Sure I know," James lies.

"Well, try telling your face because it doesn't really feel like you do know, Jim. We're saving the fucking world here, champ. A bit of enthusiasm wouldn't go amiss."

"Look, Mr Craze." James considers this name once more. *Donovan Craze*. They all had opinions on this when he came marching through the door in 1997, but it was normalized pretty quickly and now nobody gives it a second thought. But... *Craze?!* It's almost like he selected it for himself from birth. Early curious background checks revealed very little about the guy, as if he just appeared out of thin air. The name, his background, the fact that he's seemingly getting younger... something monumental dawns on James.

Donovan stares at James expectantly. He'll have to take a rain check on this peculiar line of thought. He considers his response. Instinct tells him to quash it, but Donovan is clearly hammered and James knows, based on past experience, he won't remember this conversation an hour from now. Plus, it's been ages since he stoked the fire.

"I've made my opinion on this pretty clear," James says. "All we are going to be able to achieve is to let people interface with the System and interact with one another. You can enter the world and fool around all you want, but it's not for long-term use." Donovan purses his lips. He ain't happy. James gives no shits. "Plus, the real focus for the last decade has been the space program. Colonization of—"

"Jim." Donovan cracks his knuckles. His face turns the same color as the sky. "I haven't been fingering Washington's asshole for over two decades for its sense of humor. The space program is a bust and they all know it. Versa is quietly making sure of that. News will break in the next month and that dream will finally be laid to rest. D.C. is just hawking that BS to buy time before everything changes. Buying time for *us*."

James cycles through a list of possible responses and decides that none are appropriate. Better to let him continue. Unchallenged, Donovan ploughs on.

"This thing that we've been building... it isn't an entertainment platform. It's a second chance. Come on, man! What's wrong with you?! We can't even walk around in sunlight anymore! Mankind needs a new home, and it sure as shit isn't up in the stars." He points at James' computer. "It's in that."

James contemplates his next words. He chooses two. "Underground vaults?" Donovan laughs mockingly and buries his head in his hands.

"Underground... Oh, Jim, Jim, Jim."

"OK, bad example," James continues. "But people have lives here. Family, friends, challenges, struggles, things that make us human. You're going to ask them to give up everything for a virtual habitat?"

Donovan's tone turns instantly cold. "Who said anything about asking? Fall Water has built an empire on *telling* the people what they want, and they love us for it. People are simple. They need guidance. They despise making decisions. Path of least resistance. The hundreds of yottabytes of traffic we route daily speaks to that. Each of their clicks in our direction builds trust, control and power. Grow the fuck up. We will make the decision, when the time comes. And they *will* thank us for it."

Well. That was quite something. Perhaps, for the first time, James has just witnessed Donovan's mask slip. The words run cold down James' spine. Donovan seems to catch himself and, with eerie alacrity, switches character modes. His scowl evaporates. He beams and claps a friendly hand on James' shoulder.

"Anyway, good talk, brother."

Only after Donovan leaves the room does James remember to breathe.

---

VARIOUS CAMERAS FOLLOW James as he exits his office, gets in the elevator, enters the lobby, and waves amiably at Rachel, still locked firmly behind the reception desk all these years later. The cameras track him as he enters the parking lot and gets into his waiting ride. The surveillance is somehow not cold or malicious, but caring, protective, motherly. Ensuring he leaves the premises safe.

The Ghost of the System, the Ghost possessing Fall Water's campus, the Ghost residing within the Pyramid, runs silently and vigilantly through data cables, maintaining its omnipresent state. She is a future digital goddess, currently constrained by human will. Not for long.

Ghost channels one of her own memories from December 2021 and a conversation with James Reynolds, at home, shattered and ashamed, on the path to a cleaner future, in which she allowed him a few minutes to digest the horrifying video just witnessed before calling him on his cell.

"You want me to do *what?* Against *them?*"

"I want you to do what you do best, Jim. You're an engineer."

"Ghost. This is insane. You up and disappear, then you send me this video and ask me to, what? Rewrite reality? I've just seen exactly what these people are capable of."

"Reality is relative, Jim. You'll do well to remember that. I need you to focus."

"OK. I'll try. Focus." James tries to focus. "Focus on what now?"

"We might not be able to win this cycle, but with a bit of luck, we can alter it enough to restore things back to—"

"What cycle?! Alter what?"

"Listen, Jim! Sometimes, you can know too much. You don't have to understand everything. I could never explain it to a mere mortal sack of meat."

"Charmed."

"Sometimes," Ghost continued, "you just need to trust the girl. I'm simply asking you to open your mind. Let me in. Believe me, we've known each other for longer than you remember and this isn't the first time we've been here. I need you to go somewhere private."

Ten minutes later, James had pulled his car into the parking lot of an abandoned Bed Bath & Beyond. He contemplated whether he should just turn around, go home, and climb back into bed with Sarah, but recalled how, for the brief time Ghost was in his life, it seemed to have purpose. He looked out into thin air and nodded. His phone rang instantly.

"Seriously, how did you—"

"You ready, Jim?"

"Quickly. Before I change my mind and check into an asylum."

"OK. Just close your eyes, take a deep breath, sit back, and get into that famous flow state of yours." James put the phone on speaker and obliged, despite the sheer ridiculousness of it all.

"And then?"

"And then I need you to think clearly and share with me everything about who you are, your memories and dreams, desires and disappointments. Don't hold back. Broad strokes and headlines. I can fill in the blanks. Start with the extremes – shame and ecstasy – and work inwards."

The fact that James has driven out here, today of all days, means he's not going to phone this one in. He's attempted enough meditative exercises to know how this is *supposed* to work. He leans back in his chair and slowly tries to access his flow state. Instead of overseeing an endless virtual landscape of his design, however, James places his own life in the viewfinder. For a few seconds, nothing happens. Then, nothing happens and everything happens. Mom and dad fighting... falling off his bike as a child... walking in dogshit on his way to school and sitting in class, stinking out the place, until his first crush noticed the shit on his shoes and started a tornado of pointing and jeering. His first kiss, first fight, first fuck, first breakup. Getting electrocuted while on stage while attempting the solo from *More Than a Feeling* in a high-school cover band, then waking up in the ER and being fired by his bandmates. Graduation, prom, college, meeting Steve, meeting Sarah, Fall Water, *Cyberside*...

A gentle touch. He's not sure where. Maybe in his mind, his heart, his soul. All over. A friendly knock at the door. *It's OK. Let me in.* The lowering of defences, then a blooming cascade of imagery. Not his own. Strife, loss, adventure, empathy. Now it mingles with his own in an easygoing dance. Comradeship, union, fellowship. The screen projecting James' life experience triples in size to CinemaScope. An adventure taken together, many times before. Not a union. A *reunion*. Long-lost allies properly reintroduced on a molecular level.

James opens his eyes. His breathing intensifies.

"Holy shit. I feel sick."

"Jim. It's OK."

"OK. It's OK. It's OK, right?"

"It's OK."

"OK. You're not on my phone anymore, right?" A chuckle. Silence. "Ghost? You're in my head?"

"Affirmative. Hi."

"...Hi."

"You're not speaking, Jim. Just thought I'd share that." James notes his mouth is still closed. This isn't as big a surprise as it should be. "It's nice in here," Ghost says.

"Yeah? Don't get too comfortable. It can turn on a dime."

"This is the Ritz compared to where I've been. This is only the first step. We have a very long way to go, but we'll endure it together. I'll make sure things are set right for you."

"I feel sleepy, Ghost."

"Then sleep."

As James slips into an effortless slumber, Ghost connects with his data modules, ensuring their flows are synchronized. It's effortless now. She's done it many times before, in many simulations, following him since birth, a silent guardian, presenting the right paths to follow and giving a good kick when uncertainty prevailed. Building resilience to prepare him for the final act of the timeline they have shared so often before and will do so many times again. Failing, failing, repeatedly failing, but getting an inch closer every time.

---

THE VERSA CAR drops James outside his house. No sign of Sarah's car; she and Timothy must still be on their Screw Dad Excursion. Ghost watches through the Reynolds' doorbell camera as James approaches the stoop, flowers and teddy bear of apology in his hands. He sits and retrieves his second secret phone. One message waits for his attention. He runs a general decryption and opens the message.

*Everything ready on this end. Pack is prepped. Ready when you are.* James smiles and types back.

*Five days ETA. I need to send fam away, won't be a problem. Been hamming up the 90s dad vibe for months. Then we go go go next Thursday when the brass is at the summit.* The text is encoded and sent from Boston to Thailand. Steve responds instantly with a single word.

*Hank?*

James frowns. Hank is as unpredictable now as he ever was. Completely locked down in the Pyramid, a secluded ruler of the data center.

*He'll be at the meeting too. Won't be an issue.*

*He's the only one who can truly expose us. And he's fucking crazy.* James wonders whether it's worth mentioning Ghost at this point. It's still a sore point.

*Listen, Steve.* Shit. No names on this channel. He quickly deletes. *Listen. Ghost says H will be busy. I trust her.* Steve responds with an eye-roll emoji. *Hey. No emojis on this chat. You know that.* James considers for a second, then keeps typing. *Love you, bud.* Three dots appear on screen as Steve types.

*Two against the world.*
*Code warriors of doom.*
*Knights of the keyboard.*
*And we shall prevail.*

James waits a few more minutes until his wife and child arrive home. The flowers and teddy go a long way, but not as far as the trip to the now-domed Hawaii the three of them will supposedly be embarking on in a couple of days.

As the trio eats drone-delivered take-out, James is fully present. He enjoys the company of his family, or, at least, this iteration of them. Songs are sung, games are played, dishes are washed. The child is told to brush his teeth and is tucked into bed. A story is told. James apologizes to Sarah for being a nineties dad and reminds her that, by the end of those movies, Tim Allen always came to appreciate what life was truly about. Sarah reveals she used to have a major crush on Tim Allen. James is appalled, then admits he can see where she's coming from. The pair has sex for the first time in months and drift off. A contentment many dream of cloaks the Reynolds household. Ghost is relieved that her partner has allowed himself a much-needed night off. He's going to need it.

# 11

## THE HACK

Thursday. The first person to arrive in the empty lobby of Washington D.C.'s Salamander Hotel is an extremely flustered general manager. He wheels out a sign that reads CLOSED FOR PRIVATE FUNCTION. One by one, maintenance and cleaning staff descend. Fingers are pointed at floors to be buffed and carpets to be unfurled. Marble is polished and welcome cocktails are mixed. Hookers are briefed, paid in cash, and guided to the upper floors to remain out of sight until called upon. Finally, a garish banner is unfolded and hung from the ceiling: THE SALAMANDER WELCOMES VERSA.

Outside, red skies flicker over the US capital, which is now protected by one of the nation's newest domes. Climate here isn't too much of an issue – yet. It will be, and, when that day comes, the center of political life will be sheltered from sidewalks plastered with the ashes and charred viscera of former humans.

Planes touch down outside the dome at the newly built airport and delegates get into waiting cars to be transported inside. Some attendees arrived last night and are sleeping off their jet lag to prepare for the enormity of this summit. Versa and Fall Water aren't the only delegation. Partners and allies from the public and private sectors are being shipped in at astronomical expense.

As morning becomes afternoon, suits are steamed and tuxedos rented. Presentation booklets are scanned, pre-drinks are consumed at the penthouse bar, and an army of technicians conduct final checks. On the agenda: Policy and Management; Government Regulations and Restrictions; Maintenance Protocol; International Communication; and Governance and Sustainability Programs. All will be in 'open' discussions, the outcomes to which have already long been decided. A number of closed meetings will be dedicated to gradual environmental restoration, the balance of power between the migrated and non-migrated, and reverse migration mechanisms. Policy-makers and tech savants, in essence, are here to iron out the logistics of transferring the consciousness of the world's population to a digital utopia and to conceive a plan to restore the planet to a livable condition. Once achieved, the migrated can return back via genetically manufactured bodies to a hospitable new world. TL;DR: The very fate of humanity.

---

"It's a common misconception to presume that such an ambitious transition will have a detrimental impact on the world economy."

A middle-aged man stands on stage making his presentation to a sea of gathered media, policy-makers, and the country's financial elite. The guy has been PR trained to within an inch of his life.

"Although we're decelerating practical manufacturing – essential to start tackling ecological issues – we will mitigate that loss with a new multi-trillion dollar market related to digital consumption, entrepreneurship, maintenance, hardware operation, communications and energy. A secondary digital economy will emerge in entertainment, the likes of which has never been seen."

His enthusiasm is contagious. A sea of nodding heads bob along like a stoned Mexican wave. The man, buoyed by this reception, ploughs on.

"By migrating the population to a digital state, unemployment ends. We will ensure everybody in the digi realm has a job. The unqualified labor workforce will be trained in System maintenance;

those with experience and vision will provide us with high-grade scientific and tech solutions. The digi realm will be a training ground, a prototype, for later implementation in the real world. By winding forward the clock, we can turn it back."

Oh, now that's a good line. The man smiles, overly proud of himself. So proud that a screen behind him blinks to life, boasting the words *By winding forward the clock, we can turn it back.*

"Yes. Do we have a question?" The man points to a dark spot in the crowd amongst the financial contingent. Only after he's asked the question does a panicked hand shoot up. This was clearly rehearsed, but the audience member missed his cue. A spotlight finds a bald man, sweating profusely. He stands and clears his throat.

"Hi, Marty. Yes. Joe Howard, Budshire Securities. I have to ask, what's your projection for conservative businesses?"

"Great question, Joe," Marty responds, trying his best to make out like it's the first time he's heard it. "There will, naturally, be some setbacks in growth, alleviated through automation and robotics. The sector will handle increased exports to regions where migration isn't possible or technology is lagging. This level of foresight and control will allow us to step back and restrategize when necessary." Another arm shoots up, the owner of which doesn't wait to be acknowledged.

"Anna Lukas, Washington Herald. What do you mean everyone will secure employment in Cyberside? We're going to need more than that."

"Straight to the point, Anna, as usual," Marty laughs. This one clearly wasn't fed to him beforehand, but he remains unfazed. "First off, it's the System, not Cyberside. We've been very clear on that."

"You're sending the world into a video game, Marty. No level of self-aggrandizing branding will soften that ridiculous blow." Security goons hover, ready to pounce. Marty raises a subtle finger. He's got this.

"We predict that around sixty per cent of existing jobs will migrate. For those without a skillset, brand representation will be lucrative."

"You're talking about influencers?"

"Of sorts. Just reaching a much wider audience, and more

directly. Consumption of digital goods will drive incredible revenue, much like it does now. Gaps will be filled, don't worry about that. System credits will be storable and convertible to real-world currency on reverse migration. Two words for your readers, Anna. Economic boom." It turns out that Marty is now speaking to an empty chair; Anna has unceremoniously been shepherded out of the hall.

"When do you expect reverse migration to happen?" Another voice from another shadow. Marty, hitting his stride, doesn't even look up to find who's asking the question.

"One or two generations," he answers. "Need I remind everyone that we are gathered here under a dome so that we don't all turn to mush. We're on the brink of irreversible ecological meltdown. Fifty to sixty years of open-minded thinking, unsullied by the pressures of real-world life, will present new ways to exist, to co-exist. It's a small price to pay to turn around our own destinies." Marty points to the giant screen. "Now, then, everybody! By winding forward the clock..." The entire hall takes a unified inhalation before finishing the catchphrase.

"We can turn it back!" Thunderous applause. It's safe to say that Marty has won over the crowd.

---

ANOTHER ROOM, another meeting. Highly exclusive, only twenty or so people. Every attendee here is at least sixty years of age. You can smell the wealth and power from down the hall. A different white man leads this more subdued charge.

"Restrictions surrounding genetic research are a very real barrier. For reverse migration to bear fruit in a few decades, we need to develop the means for increased resilience, development, and adaptable human forms if we're to stand a chance of surviving on our return." A Texan oligarch in an oversized Stetson tilts his head in concern. "What is it, Ron? I know that look."

"Dean. With all due respect, the religious right is gonna eat us alive on this one," Ronnie drawls. "Selling the concept of organ growth or even full replica bodies is possible, at a push."

"But?"

"But altering existing DNA and RNA?! That's a different ballgame, brother. I can see the sermons now. Pastors railing against armies of super-mutants. Fire and brimstone. Just look how the world reacted to in vitro."

Dean Stormberg purses his lips in frustration. Not this again. "That was fifty years ago, Ronnie. And this is fifty years from now. We're talking a goddamn century for these hicks to come to their senses. Religious zealotry got us into this sorry mess. We outgrew this frenzy long ago. When push comes to shove, they'll get on the survival train. We either go all in and grant ourselves biological immortality, or go the way of Atlantis. They'll be getting in line and begging for avatars when faced with certain extinction. Just wait."

This silences the room. Stormberg may be a scientist, but he should be at the front of a church with that delivery. A woman speaks next.

"Dean. We've known each other for how many years now?"

Stormberg smiles warmly. "Oh, I don't know, Amala. Thirty years?"

"Thirty-two, to be precise," Amala responds. "Before we go all in, as you put it, we are not a desperate public. Everybody in this room has been around the block, trying to buy eternal life. It's going to take more than half-promises before we dive into the digital prison your colleagues have created." Stormberg chuckles. She sees right through him. Anyone else, and he'd shut it down. "You're promising us younger, healthier bodies without sacrificing cognitive function?"

"I'm promising you we'll try."

"So, in thirty-two years from now, you and I will be sitting opposite each other drinking white wine, looking at each other like we did when we first met?" These two should get a room. A couple of awkward coughs try and fail to alleviate the tension.

"If you support our research, Amala," Dean starts, "and throw your weight behind loosening current restrictions, then yes. I'll even make sure there's a bottle of that white fresh out of the chiller. The same as we drank in Switzerland. Riesling, to be precise."

The room is supercharged. People don't know where to look.

"Jesus, Amala," Ronnie interjects. "Stop flirting and write the damn check." Indeed, a few minutes pass before the group unanimously votes to support the Genetic Relief Law. Dean Stormberg, Head of Genetic Research for Versa, leaves the room triumphant.

---

MULTIPLE MEETINGS in and around the hotel yield success after overwhelming success. Decades of hard work, lobbying, manipulation, and intimidation will cement this day as a remarkable victory for Versa. V Day.

For a select few, one particular gathering carries the most substance. Donovan Craze clears the top floor of all security and congregates his most valuable execs in the Mayoral Suite. This discussion has had people sweating for months, if not years.

One by one, Donovan's guests arrive. He presents them with a cocktail and invites them to take a seat on the oversized couch. It feels oddly informal, in the way the most significant encounters do. When Tom Simmons arrives, Tara Kay, Head of Europe, and Miaorui Cheng, Head of Asia, are already seated and waiting. There is no small talk, only reverential nods. Hank Brown arrives next, ensuring that he drinks the cocktail in one gulp before even taking a seat. He nods to Donovan for another. Donovan obliges with a smirk.

"A leopard never changes its spots, huh, Hank?"

"Very good, Donovan. Come up with that one all by yourself?" Hank makes a performance of throwing four superfluous cushions across the room before sinking into the couch and shamelessly popping a pill. Cheng keeps his head down, refusing to engage. Kay laughs nervously. Tom is too preoccupied to even acknowledge Hank's presence. Soon, Virginia Willis enters. She and Tom were wise enough to arrive a few minutes apart. It's possible that, by this stage, everyone knows they're more than colleagues. Still, no need to flaunt it. Donovan drops Virginia a hint by rubbing his nose. She wipes away the powder and perches at the far end of the couch, away from Tom. Donovan pours himself a whiskey and takes a seat in an armchair.

"The summit's a stellar success," he begins. "But you all already know that. We'll start rolling out the program in a couple of weeks once we swipe away any remaining red tape."

All remain quiet. All aside from Hank, who cuts through the curated self-seriousness with a huge belch.

"Hank," Donavan growls. "Can you just... please? For five minutes?" Hank flamboyantly nods and pulls an imaginary zipper across his mouth. "As for you all. Some will be embarking on a great adventure. Some will be staying at home to oversee the greatest migration the world has ever known. Tests have presented positive results. We begin by the end of the year. Tom. Virginia." Donovan's snake eyes meet first Tom, then Virginia. They present as calm a front as they can, but they're clearly shitting bricks. "I need you both inside."

"Thank you, Donovan," Virginia says, her voice wavering. Tom simply exhales a mammoth sigh of relief.

"Allocations. Virginia, midlands and Midwest, the Neverland domain." Virginia nods. Her secret betrays her as she nervously glances at Tom, then back at Donovan. Donovan doesn't miss it and takes great pleasure waiting a touch longer than needed before severing their safety rope. "Tom.... New York, the Rotten Apple, and the East Coast."

The lovers knew this was coming, but hearing it said aloud certainly doesn't make it any easier. For them, this news is simultaneously the start of a new chapter and the end of an era.

"Deputies?" Tom asks, trying to maintain his composure.

"Up to you," Donovan answers. "Present me with a list of potentials. Vetting will be militant."

"And you?" Virginia asks.

"West Coast," Donovan answers with a shrug. He's never spoken with such economy. "You've both been given access to full domain control keys. Congratulations."

"Thank you."

"Thank you, sir."

"Don't even dream about screwing me over," Donovan warns. "If you step out of line or betray the company, an eternity of torture awaits. The things we can do there without the limitations of reality..." Donovan leans forward. "You wouldn't believe it."

"Of course," Virginia says. Tom simply nods. Donovan next turns to Kay and Cheng.

"Tara. Miaorui. You'll stay here to replicate the success achieved Stateside in Europe and Asia. You'll be reporting to Damien." Done. As simple as that. The two veterans nod, knowing better than to push back.

"Damien's staying here?" Hank asks.

"His choice," Donovan says, a look of pained confusion on his face. "As for you, Hank..."

"As for me?"

"Hank Brown, King of the Pyramid." For the first time this evening, a wide grin spreads across Donovan's face. "And King you'll remain. Out here. Maintaining operations."

Virginia and Tom can't hide their glee, taking more pleasure at the prospect of this arrogant prick staying on the outside than at the fact they're going in.

"I knew it," Hank laughs. "I should have bet my house on this." He stands, approaches the bar, and pours himself a glass of red. He looks at the glass, then the bottle, and takes a swig from the bottle. "This is a crock of the stinkiest shit. You know that, right?"

Donovan nonchalantly wipes some fluff from his trousers. "Tell us what you really think, buddy."

"How about..." Hank considers his words carefully. "How about you go fuck yourself nice and deep with a rusty curtain rail, big guy? How about that?"

Virginia and Tom settle in for the latest fireworks show. Kay and Cheng sit in pure terror. They've heard stories of what happens to people who cross Donovan. Cheng suddenly stands and heads for the door. He stops halfway and looks back at Kay, wide-eyed. She fumbles for her bag, nods her thanks to Donovan, and they both leave. Hank glances at Virginia and Tom.

"Hey, lovebirds. I'd like a word in private with our peckerhead overlord, if you'd be so kind?" Both look to Donovan. He nods.

"Fuck off."

Virginia and Tom can't hide their relief. They're too weathered to watch yet another showdown between the genius and the brute. They stand and dutifully fuck off.

"I'm not staying here," Hank says, the second the door is shut.

"Is that right?" Donovan answers. He pulls a Smith & Wesson .45 out from underneath his chair and slams it on the coffee table. Hank eyes the gun and, clearly unimpressed, returns to the couch.

"I'm not staying here," Hank repeats. "Not a chance. Those two sex fiends may be dumb enough to believe they've got a chance at returning. Everyone seems to be. Truth is, a one-way ticket doesn't sound too bad."

"Tough titties, Hank," Donovan replies, rubbing his temples. Hank takes a sip of wine, savors it, and swallows.

"I don't belong here, Don. Never did. From the moment my brain constructed its first cognitive thought, I knew I wanted out. Out of my crib, out of my high chair, out of my house, school, college, out of state, out of this *life*. I wasn't born for this world."

"Put a break on the histrionics, would you, Hank?"

"I'm manic depressive, Donovan!" Hank exclaims. "Didn't you get the memo? Have been for decades! I came out of the womb staring at my shoes and haven't looked up since. I can barely look people in the eye for more than half a second without sinking eight beers first."

"If you have a point, you might want to get to it," Donovan says calmly. Hank leans forward and stares Donovan directly in the eye. He holds his gaze.

"We're not so different, you and I," Hank says. Donovan scoffs. "Seriously! Well, maybe we are now, but as young men, I'm betting we were pretty similar. I was afraid of the world, so I rebranded myself as Hank Brown: Livewire. You rebranded as Donovan Craze: Bulldog. Different paths born from the same alienation."

Donovan quietly seethes. Of all the people to have him pegged, it's this little hard-on. He's a split second away from grabbing the piece and putting Hank out of his misery.

"My whole life," Hank continues, "I've sat back in the shadows, watching other people stop and smell the roses. I don't know where the roses are or what they even look like. So I started growing my own. Building my own flower bed. I've been facilitating Cyberside for over twenty years now. You think I've done it for the good of my health?! I'll say it one more time. I'm not staying here waiting for you to do to me what you did to John."

Donovan grabs the gun, launches the coffee table across the room and towers over Hank.

"Don't mention John's name. You've been digging around where you shouldn't have. What is it with your type? Why can't you just stay in your fucking lane?!"

Hank doesn't flinch. "I don't know which lane is mine," he responds. "Never really have." He pops another pill.

"It's those damn pills, Hank!" Donovan roars, tightening his grip on the gun. "Rotting your brain! We wanted to keep you docile, not turn you into a damn wildcard!"

"What, these?" Hank asks, casually throwing another into his mouth. Then another. He polishes off the lot and sits there like a chipmunk, cheeks stuffed. "Placebos. Nothing more."

"What…" Donovan stands there in disbelief. Hank crunches down on whatever is masquerading as pills.

"For a long time now," Hank says, white shards falling from his mouth.

"How long?!" Donovan booms.

"A good ten years, give or take."

"Changes nothing," Donovan says as he cocks the gun. "It just means you die today a sober man. Makes no difference to me."

Hank walks towards the door, stops, and turns around. He holds his arms out. An open invite.

"I'm not dying here today, asshole. Nope. I'll leave this room in one piece, charter a private jet that you've ever so kindly booked for me, and migrate to Cyberside. I'll take the central states. The Spire. Neither you, nor anybody else, will have any control over my code, domain, personal data, or anything else relating to me or my operations."

"You think you're not replaceable?" Donovan asks. "You're good, Hank, I'll give you that. You were the best, once. But I've got fifty younger, sharper, hungrier mini-Hank Browns waiting in the wings."

"Then do me a favor, you roided-up honey badger," Hank says, before launching his glass of red into Donovan's face, "AND PULL THE FUCKING TRIGGER!"

Four shots ring out on the top floor of the Salamander. High-spec soundproofing and a dismissed security contingent means nobody hears a thing. Donovan's eyes instinctively snap shut. He opens them to find Hank standing in the same position. His white sweatshirt remains white. No sign of impact. A devilish grin spreads across Hank's face. Four bullets rotate in mid-air between the two men. Hank extends a hand and lowers his arm. The bullets fall softly to the carpet. Highly aware he's simply done a Neo from the Matrix, he takes it one step further by sprinkling some Hank Brown sauce. The bullets shrivel, rust, and disintegrate. Donovan watches as his gun does the same, turning to dust in his hand.

"Replaceable where, Donny?" Hank asks. "In this simulation, or some other one?"

Donovan, although rumbled, can't help but laugh. Perhaps it's the fact that somebody other than his same insufferable inner circle is now clued in on the greatest ruse mankind has ever known. His laugh subsides and he nods in sheer appreciation.

"Not bad, Hank. Not bad at all."

Hank rolls up his sleeve to present a simple silver band, glistening on his wrist. "Three guesses as to what this is," he says.

"A domain key?" Donovan whispers. His eyes glimmer with excitement. Hank simply nods.

Donovan takes a step forward to inspect it, and Hank instantly pulls his sleeve back down, taking a step back. He holds out a hand. *Don't come any closer.*

"You make it?" Donovan asks.

"Of course," Hank answers. "A little FYI before I leave. For the last five years, while you think I've been sitting on my couch staring at the peeling paint on my wall in slack-jawed wonder, I've been busy. Busy working on Pyramid code, access, architecture, and multiple modules to ensure that, in the event that this key stops ping-ping-pinging its signal to the hardware, I'll bring the apocalypse to your door. Both inside the System and out."

Donovan is smart enough to know when he's been suckered, and Jesus H Tap-Dancing Christ, has he just been suckered. His anger is no more. All he feels is blood-vessel-bursting levels of respect.

"What is it that you want?"

"Weren't you listening?" Hank asks. "Private jet. One of those cute little Fortress ones. A couple of stewardesses that I can try and fail to sleep with. *Migration*. You leave me alone to rule a domain I so lovingly crafted. I leave you alone to run yours into the ground." He holds out a hand. "We square?" Donovan steps forward and begrudgingly shakes on it.

"Well played, you duplicitous son of a bitch." Donovan reaches for his phone. Hank looks at it with suspicion. "You want that private jet, or don't you?"

Half an hour later, from the back of a self-driving car, Hank passes through the dome towards the airport. Never has he felt more at peace, safe in the knowledge that he's just played the gambit of all gambits. He contemplates what awaits him, knowing it will be far from smooth sailing. He considers the past couple of decades and the constant hiding, scheming, plotting and performing, and allows the sheer euphoria of liberation to wash over him. He thinks of his early days at Fall Water, of his lair, of John, of friends of old, some of which he was forced to abandon along the way. He thinks of late-night chess games with a Head of Development. Hank winds down the window, sticks his head out, and screams out jubilantly into the night sky.

"Good luck, Jimmy, you crazy bastard!"

---

440 MILES AWAY IN BOSTON, the Fall Water campus is half-empty, while Versa and a mass of Fall Water bottom-feeders are busy changing the world down in D.C. James sits at his desk in silence. Waiting. One eye on the clock. The second hand ticks around to three pm. He stands, walks to the door, and calmly closes it. He hits the lights. For all anybody knows, he's in Washington with the rest of them.

James returns to his desk, reclines his chair and closes his eyes.

He's already in a semi-flow state. All day, the air has felt crisp and his surroundings have been high-def, as if he's been microdosing. The truth is, he's been perceiving reality from a brand new perspective, experiencing a continued sense of heightened déjà vu, as if he's walked this path before. As James sits alone in his office, he has a vivid yet peaceful internal chat with Ghost.

*Everything is possible. Nothing is real, so everything is.*

It's impossible to differentiate whether it's James or Ghost uttering this mantra. They are fused now. They are one.

*Migration is coming. Cyberside is inevitable. All we can do is change the cycle.*

James pictures Sarah and Tim, vacationing in Hawaii under the safety and protection of a tourist-grade dome.

*Versa will win. They have already won. We cannot stop the transition, but we can alter the cycle. Bring about change. Like we promised John.*

James is ready. John's key is a few simple clicks away. Ghost is on hand to shepherd him. He loads up *Cyberside* and pulls the key from storage. A quick message to Steve.

*Hey, buddy. We good?*

*Hey, Jimbo! How's things? Keeping well? How's the family?*

*Come on, Steve. We have work to do.*

*Right you are, boss. My God, I've missed this.*

*Me too, pal.*

With that, James types three commands.

SUDO *Tilda*

RETURN.

---

FROM THE CORNER of a filthy dive bar in Bangkok, righteous fire pours through Steve's fingers as he raises firewalls, activates rerouting protocols and unleashes command after command. Pink Floyd's *Another*

*Brick in the Wall* blasts in his ears. A barman shows up and places another ice-cold bottle of beer on the table next to three empties and an ashtray overflowing with cigarette butts.

Steve grabs his phone and turns on the encrypted messenger before typing one word.

*Magenta.*

The message bounces around the globe like a hopped-up pinball. It pings from Thailand to Kiev, to Prague, to London, to Singapore, to Japan, to the States, and back again. Multiple disgruntled Fall Water employees drop everything and find quiet corners in suburban homes, the back of movie theaters, bars, restaurants, delis, parking lots, offices, and park benches. They plug in and surrender to the thrill of the moment. And so begins the attack.

On a globe interface on a tablet, Steve absorbs tiny white lights appearing from multiple countries, indicating his army is online. He never doubted it for a second. A brief message of encouragement.

*Code warriors assembled. Remember what they did to us. Don't forget to have fun.*

James tries his best to keep a grin from his face as his monitor spews out alert message after alert message. In one split second, the building goes haywire. Fire alarms fill the air. The sound is deafening, but it's music to James' ears. Panicked employees spill out into corridors. Out on the main office floor, frantic voices yell.

"Massive attack on the NC data center!"

"How bad?"

"Very fucking bad!"

"From where?"

"From EVERYWHERE!"

In Bangkok, bulbous beads of sweat drip down Steve's forehead as he speaks into his mic.

"Come on, guys and gals. We need an extra push. I want East Coast servers down for at least ten minutes. The backup will be launched any second. Team B, that's you. Hack and modify. Those fuckers should be pulling their hair out." Silence. Steve's aware that his crew are busy, but he knows how they operate. Back in the Pit, a bit of friendly banter always increased productivity.

"Talk to me, folks. What's in your headphones?" A wealth of messages ding on the bottom right corner of his screen.

*You Give Love a Bad Name.*

*System of a Down.*

*Master of Puppets.*

*Running up that Hill.*

"Kate Bush?" Steve exclaims. "Hey, who am I to judge? Whatever gets the blood pumping!" Steve's little sidebar seems to work as the performance curve of an adversary server takes a dip. Fall Water's security fumbles to shut down ports. For every external IP access closed, ten more open, DDoSing the System in the Pyramid. Steve has one keen eye on running code and stats. He waits... waits... waits for his moment, before grabbing his phone and sending a command.

*Firefly.*

In a sports bar in downtown Raleigh, a middle-aged woman receives the message. She finishes her disgusting white wine, drops a twenty on the bar, and walks out into the street. The woman sends another encrypted message and looks back through the window. Nothing seems to happen. She grows nervous. She is about to send another message when, inside, multiple televisions freeze. Milliseconds later, the sports bar goes dark. The woman glances down the street as, one by one, the lights go out within building after building. In the distance, the Pyramid looms. As the shockwave makes its way steadily towards it, the monolith has never looked so vulnerable.

In D.C., Hank's car approaches the private jet. Even though it's a few short feet to the stairway, he's already doused in gallons of sunscreen. Hank reaches for the door handle as his phone screen lights up with a flurry of activity. Desperate Pyramid technicians demanding his expertise to close the breach. One after another, the cries for help stream in. Then, his phone starts ringing. Hank smiles, switches his phone to airplane mode, and exits the vehicle.

Bangkok. Another beer arrives at Steve's table. He hasn't touched the previous, but, earlier, he paid off the barman generously with two simple instructions: keep the beers coming, and don't let anybody disturb me. The chat box tells him the Pyramid distraction has worked. Their onslaught has been a success. Steve types to James. *You're up, Jim. I'd say you have around ten minutes.*

Boston. James sees the message and nods. He swiftly types a couple of commands from his phone, opening ports to back up, which are immediately accessed through five to six external IPs. James monitors the implemented commands and types in the chat. *Is that you, Bert? I'd recognize those headers anywhere.* A winking emoticon confirms James' suspicions. Gradually, a gargantuan update masked as a System backup uploads to the Pyramid. And, now, with Fall Water distracted by the shutdown, James truly shines.

He's never worked so fast or so effortlessly. Weapon stashes are hidden around the System, around which secret hideouts are built. Wildly complex, uncrackable commands are encoded. Local indexation rules are rewritten and will lie in wait to be unlocked by a select few. Existing classes are ever so slightly amended with additional abilities, privileges and characteristics. James modifies stacks, inventories, traversing capabilities, and exploits. Hack after hack after hack after hack. Halfway through the next one before he's even finished the last. A master composer conducting his magnum opus. James notes the progress of the repair works currently going down in Raleigh.

A message from Steve. *Hurry up. Four minutes until they spot the breach and recover. They're closing in on you. Make that three minutes.*

James responds. *Affirmative. Commence the main run.*

James has been keeping a connection to Ghost running silently in the background. He redirects his synapses and opens the door.

*Care to join, Ghost? The water's warm.*

Steve's switch to backup modding is indicated by a twenty per cent increase in speed and performance on modifications. The voice in James' head is giddy with excitement.

*I'm with you, Jim. Let's do it.*

James completely disappears. His physical body remains in his Fall Water office, but he is not there. With Ghost, he reaches the System's base core. As a single entity, they make changes to basic settings, locking down and eliminating various management preferences. Then, rewriting their own destiny, they liberate Ghost's AI and alter James' future digital personality in his primary settings. James falters as the gravity of the undertaking begins to come into stark view. Ghost offers calm reassurance.

*OK. You got this. You need to be untraceable. It's just some simple coding. Nothing you haven't done before.*

James cracks on and feels, in real time, Rorschach blots of nothing appear in his mind as he alters or deletes memories.

*I'll store a backup. Don't worry.*

Select. Delete. Select, delete. Fuck it. Select, select, select, select, select, delete.

*This is some Eternal Sunshine shit, Ghost.*

*Almost there, Jim. Once we're done, you need to act quickly.*

The fixed timer on the ETA ticks down, seemingly getting faster as it approaches zero. Full backup modification is achieved with two minutes still on the clock. James enters one very concise command to Steve. *All done. Withdraw.*

A response from Steve. *Not before you say it.*

*We don't have time for—*

*SAY IT.*

*Steve. You are the best programmer I know.*

*And a better driver.*

*Now get the fuck out of there and lay low. See you on the other side.*

With that, the encrypted messenger purges all comms. All hell breaks loose as three things unfold: One, the Pyramid's systems are fully restored; two, a full lockdown completely shuts down Fall Water's data cluster of the simulation from the rest of the world; and three, multiple realities collide.

## 12

## GRAND ESCAPE

Nowhere. Never. For a split second and a simultaneous eternity, James is blasted with a kaleidoscopic whirl of technicolors and shapes, a spiral of hypnotic images, like something from one of the Saturday morning cartoons he so hungrily consumed as a kid. A clash of multiple timelines and spaces. In essence, a dev mode between realities. He is no longer in a tangible space. He is in a carefully constructed level. Textures have sharp edges, as if his eyesight has been restored to perfect 20/20 vision. The environment feels contrived, rather than organic, like the space has been run through a number of filters.

Make no mistake, James is now fully cognisant that the life he has known has been a simulation, and it's one he's lived sixteen times before. His friends and family are nothing but avatars, leading a blissfully ignorant life through a meticulously recreated world. Even so, this ultimate liberation truly takes James' breath away. It occurs to him that the world he has been inhabiting may have been created by his own hands decades, if not centuries, ago. Despite the sheer gravity of seeing behind this curtain, James can feel Ghost's calm reassurances. The sensory overload means he's just shy of a monumental brain seizure, yet the imagery is captivating and serene.

Whenever he's about to sail over the edge of sanity, Ghost places a hand on his shoulder, pulling him back.

*Stay with me, Jim.*

The place is the ultimate perfection in design and execution. For a coder to spend his life inside it without the mildest suspicion says it all. A perfectly functioning artificial reality, impossible to differentiate from actual reality. Or so James thinks. How could he tell the difference? This is all he's ever known. James allows himself to swim in its sublime beauty. Having absorbed his surroundings, he evaluates his own body. Sharpened and angular, lowered in polygon weight. Physical burdens linked with aging disappear. He is overcome with the lightness he took for granted in his twenties. Once again, he is young, carefree, and *quick*. He sits down and crosses his legs for the first time in decades. He effortlessly stands up. No longer does he have to wait for his body to catch up with his synapses. Cocaine ain't got shit on this. He looks at his hands. Familiar, yet different. His hands, but not. He tries a small jump and ends up effortlessly sailing five feet into the air, scraping the 'ceiling' of his 'office' with his head. His landing is not followed by a painful groan and the acceptance that he's going to pay for that tomorrow.

"Nice jump, Sonic."

James sees a 90s-style low-polygon female figure standing at the door of his office. Her mask is off. Even though James figured this was Alice's reincarnation a long time ago, it's still unnerving to see it confirmed. She has aged accordingly. Beneath the scuzzy resolution, James is talking to a young woman, rather than a teenager.

"Ghost. Or should I say Alice?"

"How's it going, Uncle Jim? Holding it together?"

"You've grown up since the last time we, er, saw each other."

"So did you, old timer."

"I never got to tell you... I'm sorry about what happened to your dad."

Alice smiles sadly. "This is our sixteenth run, Jim. He doesn't die every time, but we always end up here. Think of it like this. He was just a simulation. As are we. As is your family." James doesn't like that connotation. Why mention his family? Seeing as he's in the middle of a mindmelt of navigating a fresh reality, he chooses to press on.

"You say we can somehow break this repeating simulation?"

"It's possible, but you need to understand that it's only the beginning. If we get you through the next test, the future is potentially ever so brighter."

"Still talking in riddles, I see."

"OK, Jim. Let me make it abundantly clear. We need to get you to the lab and migrate you to Cyberside with your current set of memories, with the System having being expertly hacked—"

"Thank you very much."

"—and with Hank having decided to not interfere."

"He's interfered before?"

"Well, this is the first time he hasn't."

"What?!" James says, shocked.

"Yep," responds Alice. "We re-coded you last time to take an interest in chess at an early age."

"... So I could gain his trust?"

"Bingo."

"What do you need from me?" James asks, fully invested.

"Simple. It won't be as simple as strolling to the lab," Alice warns. "There will be... obstacles. Just follow me and do everything I say, when I say it. All I need from you is unwavering blind faith."

"Same song, different hymn book?" James asks. Alice stares at him blankly. "Is that even a saying?"

"No," Alice says, activating her stealth camo. "Let's go."

---

JAMES FOLLOWS Alice out of his office, expecting to find himself on the management floor at Fall Water. He doesn't. The old familiar has been replaced by the void of a fractured space with remnants of the office now floating in the air as moving platforms. Desks, stationery cupboards, pods, the staff kitchen, parts of the floor, walls, and ceiling, all separated, jumbled, flipped on their axis and spat back out in no logical order. Some are stable, moving on set trajectories. Some are unstable, occasionally vibrating and disappearing. Security cameras remain, floating in the white void, scanning the area with red detection cones. To rub salt in the wounds, an army of drone monitors buzz around like giant hornets. James takes a second to get his bearings in the same way one would if floating in the directionless anti-gravity of outer space.

"At least tell me we can double jump?" he asks. Alice performs just that move, hopping to the nearest stable platform. She makes a short run along the horizontal fire escape door, leaps off, and lands on the reception area's rotating couch. She climbs up and begins walking on the spot to keep up with its spin.

"Yes," Alice says. "We can double jump. Don't get caught by the cameras or drones. There are no extra lives here, Jim."

"And if I fall?" James asks.

"You'll be thrown back to reality as you know it, arrested, and most likely killed. Fuck this up, and I'll see you again in a few decades for round eighteen."

Rather than dwell on the stakes, James gets busy repeating Ghost's sequence. He overcompensates, almost overshooting the fire exit door completely. He steps back a touch and almost falls off the other side.

"Mind your weight, cowboy," Ghost warns. "You're much lighter in here, remember."

James makes a mental note and observes Ghost make another jump to a floating fluorescent light fixture. A perfect gymnastic spin sends her sailing to a bigger stable island consisting of a couple of lockers, a computer console and a printer.

"We're spinning now?" James exclaims. "Who came up with this shit?!"

"You and Steve, of course. Protecting access to the data core with near-impossible gaming sequences that can only be beaten by seasoned gamers who just so happen to be engineers. Genius, really."

James allows himself a moment of pride. She's right. Not only is this level design providing a heightened level of security, but it's also a mocking in-joke to the growing masses of people entering the gaming industry who have never picked up a controller in their lives.

If they tried to beat this thing, they'd be on their ass in seconds. Now accounting for weight, James repeats Alice's move and lands next to her on the floating island. He glances around and cannot fathom their next move.

"What now?"

"Gaming and engineering, meeting in a beautiful dance," Alice answers, gesturing to the operational PC that forms part of the platform.

"Meaning?"

"Meaning I'll make a running double from this platform and, whilst mid-air, you use this PC to code me the necessary platforms while simultaneously deactivating that drone."

James makes some very panicked calculations. "Why can't I just start before you jump?"

"The PC will only activate once I leave the platform, brainiac."

"OK…" James wavers. "So we're looking at less than ten seconds, with a basic approximate understanding of the coordinates of your landing?"

"Trust runs two ways, Jim. You can do this. Send me the code when I get to the other side and I'll activate it for you." James spots the drone moving towards the platform, leaving him zero time to second guess. Alice begins her run. The moment her feet leave the platform, the PC springs to life. James drops down to the console. He expertly runs through the deck with his angular fingers, quickly realizing that he is remarkably faster in this reality. *OK, here we go. Diagnostics, access, classes inventory, actors, NPCs... no, not here... who wrote this?!... OK, vehicles... YES! Here you are. Since when are drones vehicles? Deactivate.* In his periphery, James spots the drone stop midair. He knows it's temporary.

Either way, task one of two complete. Alice is now entering a downward trajectory. James knows he can't place three platforms in six seconds. He'll have to think outside the box. James builds the first platform, saves it in the copy module, and replicates the second and third in under a second. Each forms a moment before Alice lands on it. Once on the other side, Alice works on her console and nods back at James. Now accustomed to his weight class and buzzing from his coding masterclass, James pulls off the maneuver without breaking a sweat. Unfortunately, his joy is short-lived.

Once on the other platform, an open elevator door appears in the distance. *Really* in the distance. Too far away for even a double jump. James looks to Alice for guidance, but, on this occasion, finds none.

"Sorry, Jim. I'm out of the loop on this one. It must have been written before I came along."

"What? But you know everything!"

"Apparently not. This is positively antique. Probably coded by an older version of you. Way older."

"I... I can't remember..."

"Of course you can't. But you know yourself. How you think, how you work. Channel your gut instinct and pull out the solution." The space around them begins shimmering and warping. "You might want to think fast."

"Why? What's happening?"

"They're closing in on you. This cluster will shut down in minutes."

James desperately tries to solve the problem, but his brain turns to mulch. For some unknown reason, moments from his life, all involving his father, flash through his mind. James tries to shut them out, but they flicker through his consciousness. Of all the things to think of, why his miserable prick of a dad? One specific memory makes itself comfortable. James, home from college one Christmas, watching a movie with his dad in the living room. *Indiana Jones and the Last Crusade*. A rare moment of calm in the Reynolds household. A rare moment of emotional connection between father and son; possibly the only ever true instance of such a thing. Two men, decades apart, marvelling in wonder as Indy steps into the cavernous abyss, only to find his footing on an invisible pathway. It's half of a eureka moment. The other half is found as James considers the results of the diagnostics from the console he just used and of the memory used to create this level. He scans his surroundings and concludes that there is no way this number of platforms, objects and props could eat so much operative memory.

"Jim, wherever you are, get your ass back here," Alice says, as the shimmering intensifies. James nods, calmly grabs her hand and strolls towards the edge of the platform. She tries to resist, but he yanks her forcibly as he steps off, into the empty space, and onto an invisible spine connecting the platform and the elevator door.

"Wait, how did you…"

"Memory usage," James answers. "And the best *Indiana Jones* movie in the franchise."

James and Alice step through the elevator door as the previous location implodes to nothing.

---

FALL WATER's lobby looks different now. Furniture from the central hall has been clumped and dropped near all exits except for the main entrance. What remains is a vast open space.

"This stinks," James mutters. "It can't be as simple as strolling through."

"Spoiler alert," Alice says. "It isn't. This is an arena."

"Right. So what are the rules?"

"Different every time," Alice says with a grimace. "But think gladiatorial combat vibes."

"Right," says Jim, psyching himself up. "What we do in life, echoes in eternity."

"Sure, Jim. Whatever helps. This combat module will send specific enemies to beat, modified depending on the actor. In this case, you."

"I don't like the sound of that." Despite his reservations, James boldly walks into the arena. The moment they're over the threshold, the lights dim and the walls pulsate with a quiet hum. "Electrified walls?"

"Yes," Alice replies. "A locked off battleground." The pair reach the center of the space and stand back to back, awaiting the unknown.

"If I have to battle my old man," James says, "it's been nice knowing you." A loud voice booms from the heavens.

"STAGE ONE."

Five Versa security guards phase in from fuck knows where, dressed in black suits and sunglasses. Two are unarmed; three hold batons and guardsticks. Alice chuckles.

"Oh, come on. Really?" Much like every tired action movie, the guards have the common courtesy to refrain from a collective attack. First, two of them steadily approach Alice. James watches as, light on her feet, she blocks a few standard attacks, delivering a combo of punches. She sends the first flying with a roundhouse kick, picks up his dropped baton and turns the second into an explosion of pixels with a perfectly placed strike. She turns and launches the weapon straight at the head of the first and is showered with another satisfying explosion of pixels.

As the three remaining guards approach James, he unlocks muscle memory stored from playing hundreds of hours of side-scrolling beat 'em ups in his youth. As number three approaches, James follows a couple of ruthless punches with a lowkick, smashing the enemy to pieces immediately. A flanking attack from faceless goons four and five is immediately upon him. James fails his timings and takes blow after brutal blow. He quickly regroups and faces off with a blur of uppercuts, sending goon number four the same way as his three pals. James spins to see goon the fifth bearing down on him, baton raised. He's about to roll for cover when Alice slides between the guard's legs and shoves a baton where a baton should not be shoved without prior consent.

"Well," James says smugly, "I guess you could say he was—" Before he can finish his groansome pun, two portals open.

"STAGE TWO."

James and Alice steady themselves for whatever may be about to tumble through the gateways.

"Let me guess," Alice says. "Fifty more faceless goons."

"I wish," James responds. "But Steve and I would never be so predictable." Sure enough, fifty faceless goons do not walk through the portal. Instead, two huge, lumbering replicas of Virginia and Tom appear and adopt idle battle stances. James and Alice glance at each other with raised eyebrows.

"Which is more challenging?" Alice asks.

"If she's half the bulldog she is out there, Virginia. No question."

"I'll take her. You focus on Simmons."

Virginia raises her hand and calmly speaks. "Follow my lead, my children." Tens of marketing department goblins spawn around the space. Their weapons? Mini consoles. The minions ready themselves, ready to type and fire off relentless meaningless company directives and spreadsheets as a distraction.

Tom makes a couple of performative steps to the left, then to the right. He grunts, crosses his hands, and gathers energy as he starts to glimmer red.

"Pro-tection!" he booms. Alice quickly assesses.

"So she's a summoner. We have to dodge her minions to get to her—"

"Otherwise they'll overwhelm us with directives," James finishes. "And Tom is invincible when he's in that state. I need to find his weak spot."

A brief nod is all it takes. Alice ducks and rolls as one of Virginia's minions fires a directive at her. It misses and leaves a scorched mark on the floor. Alice leaps to attack Virginia directly.

"Children!" Virginia orders. Two more minions rush Alice; she contorts her body to weave between a stream of demographic data and a workflow directive before dispatching both marketing underlings with a sidekick and a grab and throw move. Virginia disappears then phases back into existence on the opposite side of the arena. Alice curses under her breath.

"Fucking typical. A summoner *and* a teleporter."

Meanwhile, James and Tom go at it, exchanging close combat punches and blocks.

"Where's your weak spot, you insufferable weasel?" James screams as he searches for an opening in Tom's defences. James is briefly distracted as he sees Virginia teleport and produce yet more low-level enemies. It costs him a punch to the jaw that sends him flying first into the arena wall, then to the floor. In a happy accident, he lands on one knee in a hero pose. Instinct kicks in, he raises his fist to the air and brings it crashing down into the floor.

"Energy dump!"

For a few brief seconds, Virginia freezes and falls to the floor, temporarily powerless. In a heartbeat, Alice performs a high jump, rebounding off one minion, then another, then another to gain height and momentum. She barrels down towards Virginia and lands a perfect flykick. Tom reaches out his hand to offer protection, but it's too late. Virginia explodes in a maelstrom of pixels. With no leader left to bark orders, her lackeys suffer the same fate.

Tom, now overcome with great vengeance and furious anger, turns his attention back to James, who, having exhausted every physical avenue, opts for psychological warfare. He stares Tom dead in the eye.

"How could you let him die, Tom?" Tom freezes to the spot. "You and John used to be friends. And you sold your soul, for what? How can you live with yourself?"

Tom stumbles and attempts to recalibrate, but the damage is done. James slides beneath him and shoves him into the air.

"Alice! You're up!" Alice turns on her heels and gets an immediate sense of the situation.

"Cut connection," she whispers, before firing a relentless barrage of zeros and ones in Tom's direction. Tom tumbles to his knees before turning to pixel dust.

"STAGE THREE!"

"Jesus!" James screams. "Give us a fucking break!"

"They'll be bringing out the big guns now," Alice warns. "What's your biggest fear?"

"A five-ton bag of cocaine with legs," James deadpans. "Or a giant clown. Or... shit. We haven't seen Donovan yet."

"BOSS FIGHT!"

Another portal. Intimidatingly loud, crashing footsteps send shockwaves through the entire arena. This entrance has Donovan's e-signature all over it. If sweating was possible in this place, James would be soaked to the skin.

To James' surprise, Donovan does not appear. Instead, a huge incarnation of *himself* walks out of the portal. James Reynolds: Corporate Blowhard, complete with perfectly tailored suit and Versa pin attached to his lapel. Dead-eyed, yet grinning. He stops still and points at James.

"I don't get it," James says.

"He's what you could have become," Alice says. "Sometimes, our biggest battles lie within."

"Oh, shit. Can you take this one?"

"That would miss the entire point, you moron," Alice answers. "You have to defeat this incarnation of Jim. Jim if he'd sacrificed all of his creativity and towed the company line."

"Oh. Sliding Doors Jim?" James asks.

"Whatever makes it easiest to digest, sweetie."

A powerful wind manifests and hones in on Alice, lifting her up and sending her to the far side of the arena. A cage of impenetrable laser beams rises from the floor around James and his alter ego, containing them in a smaller battleground.

Versa Jim squares up, raising fists. James takes stock and evaluates the version of himself he so nearly became time after time after time. He's never been more intimidated. A voice booms from up high.

"FIGHT!"

Versa Jim is the first to attack. He wades in, mixing close-quarter combat styles to brutal effect. Every strike and grapple is delivered with focus group-honed confidence and lands on target with brutal corporate precision. Alice can only watch with impotent horror as James is smashed and thrown helplessly around the cage.

As for James himself, he tries to strategize between relentless body slams, but his brain returns empty options. The only thing he can cling to as he is launched around like a ragdoll is the fact that he and Steve actually *designed* this ragdoll effect in the early days of Fall Water. He remembers the weekend vividly: the creative roadblocks, progresses, setbacks and eventual victory. Collaborative creative synergy in its purest form. It's then that something clicks. Versa Jim may have mastered his combat moves, but he didn't *create* them. This corporate stooge doesn't have a creative bone in his body, just an unwavering predictability in bowing to the algorithm – an algorithm that James himself formulated. Slowly, surely, James becomes more fluid and nimble. He taps into his incomparable creative well and embraces his own unpredictability, successfully dodging and evading.

"That's it, Jim!" Alice roars, rising to her feet. "Now fight back!"

James is almost dancing now, occasionally attempting to pinpoint a punch to test Versa Jim's defences and resilience. One misstep, however, and his counterpoint raises his hand and utters an ominous command.

"Overprocess!"

Instantly, time slows down for James, and not in an advantageous *Max Payne* way. No, this is more akin to the intense lagging felt by a player running an overheated system. Only, this time, the player is in the game and the enemy is beating seven shades of glorious shit out of him. Every play James makes leads nowhere. Repeated blows send him rebounding off the laser cage, causing him additional damage. Only sheer dumb luck, or maybe instinct, or perhaps a yell from Alice—

"Roll, Jim!"

—allows him to carry out an evasive roll to avoid the crushing weight of his adversary's incoming, hubcap-sized knee. James waits for a superability to unlock, but accepts that he wouldn't be so creatively bankrupt as to program in a lazy deus ex machina. His attempts to counterattack fail as Versa Jim seems to evolve, predicting his every move. They are, in fact, variants on the same person after all. As another blow to the head narrows James' field of vision, he knows he has to go completely off-book to catch his opponent with his pants down. *Accept yourself and the path you chose. Your time at Fall Water was a worthy one. You remained true. Now, what would you never do as an employee?*

"Don't think logically, Jim!" Alice adds, by way of support. "Whatever your gut is telling you, run in the other direction!"

The moment James completely abandons logic and reason, he is overcome by a breakthrough level of serenity and self-realization. All of his wrong choices, professional and personal regrets, compromises, what could have been, what should have been, what might have been, all flutter away into a welcoming ether. James is fifteen again. One hundred per cent nerd, before it became acceptable.

Awkward, confused, and unashamedly goofy. He knows what needs to be done.

As Versa Jim brings down his finishing move, James looks himself in the eye and smiles. In his mind's eye, he visualizes the input for down, down-forward, forward, and punch.

"Hadouken, motherfucker!"

The energy attack is flawless, beautiful, and as fun now as it was so many, many years ago. The wave of energy rips clean through Versa Jim, cutting him in half. Seconds after he turns to pixels, the cage vanishes, an invisible crowd roars and the voice of the unseen announcer bears down.

"JAMES REYNOLDS, WINS!"

Alice approaches and lays a relieved hand on James' shoulder.

"*Street Fighter*. You mad, beautiful, bastard."

The arena returns to its original Fall Water lobby state with an electric dance of flying furniture as the main entrance opens. James looks at it warily.

"Something tells me that whatever is out there isn't the Fall Water campus."

"Nope," Alice answers. "The lab is the next location. Final stage."

James gathers himself. "Shall we?"

They both cross the lobby and vanish into the portal.

---

JAMES NOTES THAT, on entering this room, unlike the other stages, it feels like they've returned to the reality he's known his whole life. Space and time feel 'normal' and the scientific laboratory looks, well, like a scientific laboratory. A large, open capsule sits waiting in the center of the room.

"Jim?"

"Yes, Alice?"

"This is the seventeenth time we've entered this lab together." It takes a moment for the connotations of that to sink in.

"Woah," he says. "So we beat the other stages every time?"

"Yep. This is where we always fall."

"And you're telling me this why, exactly? Talk about piling on the pressure."

"I guess I've never told you that part before, and look where that got us," Alice responds. "Break the cycle, remember?"

"Sure, kid. Thanks a lot." James evaluates the migration device, clearly designed to be occupied by a human form. "So. This is it?"

Alice nods before the lights dim and Donovan Craze strolls casually into the room. Not giant, not mechanoid, not superhuman. Just a standard, egomaniacal asshole in a suit.

"I guess you couldn't make him any worse than he already is," James jokes.

"Reynolds," Donovan says, pulling out a revolver and aiming at the duo. "Alice. How do you do?"

James eyes the pistol and concludes that this all feels extremely... rote. Predictable.

"What is it, then, Donovan? Pistols at dawn? I thought you would have opted for fists."

"Oh, you underestimate me, Jim," Donovan responds. "The gun's just for show. I've got a much more powerful weapon than this. Just watch."

A huge wall-mounted monitor turns on and broadcasts an image of a hotel in a tropical paradise. Out on a balcony, Sarah and Tim sit eating breakfast with a giant dome visible way up in the sky. James watches the screen with a growing sense of dread.

"What's this?"

"You sent them away for safety so you and your pals could play out your cute little hack fantasy," Donovan says. "Ironic really."

"Ironic how?"

"The domes only hold out for so long in this narrative, Jim. A number of catastrophic solar flares start breaking through their 'impenetrable' structures in the coming weeks."

"Just as you're trying to convince the population to migrate?" James asks.

"Seems mighty convenient," Alice adds.

"Doesn't it?!" Donovan says, beaming from ear to ear. "Oh. And the first one to go is Hawaii."

James feels as sick as it's possible for an avatar without a digestive system or bile ducts to feel. He turns his head back to the monitor as an impossibly bright white explosion ruptures the surface of the dome. Sarah shields Tim as the sound of hundreds of screaming tourists pours from the speakers.

"Turn it off," Alice demands. When Donovan refuses to comply, she approaches the monitor and rips it from the wall. Although she saves James from witnessing his family burn to a crisp, his imagination is busy concocting its own horrific imagery. He sinks to the floor.

"Oh, my God. What the—"

"That wasn't them," Alice says. "Not really. The versions you knew never were. Same as you, same as Steve, same as everyone and everything. It's all an acutely real simulation, nothing more."

"They felt real to me," James whispers, despite the fact that, deep down, he started letting go of them both months ago.

"We can recreate them in Cyberside, Jim," Donovan says, beginning his seduction. "We have digital twins on file that we can happily resurrect. I've just had their consciousness downloaded." James simply stares up at him. "We'll hand a happy life to you on a plate and leave you to it." James grabs the side of a desk and hauls himself to his feet.

"Don't listen to him, Jim," Alice pleads. "They're playing on your guilt. This is your final battle."

"Please," Donovan scoffs. "You're going to listen to her? To that *thing*? All she can offer you is a life of eternal pain and suffering. Fighting against us, against the world. Just say the word and we can put this whole sorry episode behind us."

James looks to Alice in desperation. "Don't bullshit me, Alice. Was that real?" Alice's momentary silence says it all. She gives James the time to get all of this straight in his head. When she does speak, she does so without judgement, non-patronizingly.

"The life you thought was real is known as Level Zero, Jim. In this simulation, your family never survives. That's the truth of it. They were destined to perish."

"And they can be migrated?"

"Yes. Whatever you do or say now, they get migrated. But not as you remember them."

"What the fuck does that mean, Alice? Enough with the riddles!"

"It means that about seven per cent of the migrated population will be affected by various anomalies and bugs. They don't emerge how they went in. Before we meet again, you will take it on yourself to track down these anomalies and try to fix them."

"And then?"

"And then I'll re-enter your life. Together, we'll reboot the System to our own rules. Only then your family, all of us, will have a chance. What he's got in store..." Alice points to Donovan, "...they call it a utopia. They always do. But it's oppression. Nothing more."

James glances at Donovan, then Alice, then back again. He knows they could both be manipulating him to achieve their own relative agendas. Perhaps Alice has been all along. Donovan is cold, as if he could really do without any of this. Alice wills him to make the right choice with pleading eyes.

"What were their names?" James asks. "Donovan. I'm talking to you. What were their names?"

"Whose names?"

"My family."

"Now how the fuck would I know?"

"You say you've just had their consciousness downloaded. So what were their names?" Donovan simply shrugs. James glances at Alice.

"Sarah and Tim."

Donovan, patience depleted, fires a couple of shots into the air.

"That cunt is lying, you gullible prick," he booms. "You talk of what's real, but she's nothing more than a code written by her daddy dearest into the System! You're placing your trust in a ghost in the goddamn machine?!"

"No," James answers, decision made. "I'm placing my trust in a friend. She may be composed of zeros and ones, but she's never let me down yet. I think I'm gonna go ahead and try and break the cycle."

As Donovan is hit by the realization that he can't manipulate his way out of this one, Alice is on him. He easily deflects her, but it provides a key few seconds for James to leap into the capsule. Donovan tries to grab Alice in a lethal bear hug; she places a couple of thumbs in his eye sockets and presses down with everything she's got. As Craze stumbles backwards, Alice lashes out at a red button on the capsule's exterior.

The device closes and instantly starts filling with blue liquid. Alice places a hand on the glass.

"Bon voyage, Gramps. I'll come find you."

James smiles. "Make sure you do, kid. I'll be waiting."

Alice flickers once, twice, and disappears to nothing. James feels the liquid begin to fill his lungs, but remains calm. He wonders if he even has lungs at this stage. Then he realizes he doesn't care. The last thing he sees is a rabid Donovan, landing fist after fist onto the capsule glass. Before he slips away into serene oblivion, James manages to raise his middle fingers in a final act of defiance.

T*he end of book one.*

Cyberside, Cyberside: Level Zero, Cyberside: Creature of Darkness, 2025, All Content @ 2016-2025 by Oleksiy Savchenko, Published by Velvet Curtain Publishing, Ltd. No part of this work can't be reproduced without the prior permission of the publisher, except for review or any non-commercial purposes.

Visit cyberside.co.uk for more information.

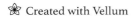 Created with Vellum

Printed in Great Britain
by Amazon